GRACE

GRACE

A Novel

Natashia Deón

COUNTERPOINT
BERKELEY

Portions of the novel appeared in B O D Y and The Rattling Wall.

Library of Congress Cataloging-in-Publication Data is Available

Cover design by Elena Giavaldi
Interior design by Megan Jones Design

ISBN 978-1-61902-720-6

COUNTERPOINT
2560 Ninth Street, Suite 318
Berkeley, CA 94710
www.counterpointpress.com

Printed in the United States of America
Distributed by Publishers Group West

10 9 8 7 6 5 4 3 2 1

For Ava
and Ash
and Lee
my sister, Katrina
Momma and Dad
and You.

The stars we are given. The constellations we make.

—REBECCA SOLNIT

Part I

I AM DEAD.

I died a nigga a long time ago.

Before you were born, before your mother was born, 'fore your grandmother.

I was seventeen.

Still am, I reckon. And everyone that was there that night is dead now, too, so it don't matter that I was a nigga.

Or a slave.

What matters is I had a daughter, who had daughters, and they had theirs. Family I could've saved a whole lot of trouble by tellin 'em the things that I know.

But there are some stories that mothers never tell their daughters—secret stories. Stories that would prove a mother was once young, done thangs with men she could never tell, in ways she could never tell, and places she should never. Private stories where love, any 'semblance of love, would lead a person like me to the place I was that night in 1848. When I died.

⁌⁍

FOR TWO DAYS and two nights we been running.

Me, and the child inside me.

Pain is trying to get me to stop, make me push away the pain but I won't push.

My pretty yellow dress is stained red and brown now. Not by the blood of the man I killed, like they think. It's mine.

The dark of night's been hiding my running for a while, muffling the sounds of my chest gushing in and out from my own hard breaths. Every few steps, the blue light of the moon sneaks past the treetops and strokes my face, urging me on—the only mercy I get in these hot Alabama woods. The devil's coming and I have to keep moving, for this baby, for me. But the pain's burning so bad now, I cain't hardly do nothing but fall against this old tree, hands slip-sliding down its trunk, stinging.

Barking from the hunting dogs is shooting across the air, bumping around inside me. I have to move faster, run like Sister once told me to.

I beg my belly, "Hold onto me. It ain't time."

But this baby got a plan. Its head's at my opening spot, burning hot, ripping my hips wide apart, carving a way out.

I hold in my screams and bow over hard in the dirt, knees first. A man's voice shouts, "This way! She's up this way."

I want to live.

Want this baby to live.

But she's betraying me. Every muscle in my body's slamming shut so I push. She's tearing through me. I push. I don't want to, but I push. Screaming mute deep inside myself, pushing so hard but hollering so low they cain't hear me.

A wave of warm pours out of me, carrying my joy and deep sorrow. Before God and this oak tree, she come. And she don't cry. I guess she want us to live, too. I move her into the triangle of moonlight that sets my arm aglow. She see me and I see in her the good part of love.

The weight of 'em push me over—these dogs, clawing and biting at my back. But the pain ain't gonna make me give her up to 'em. I got to protect her, get up, keep running.

I feel my legs, so I bend 'em. Feel 'em firm on the ground, so I push up. I hold her close with one arm and pull up with the other. I can make it. I tell myself again how to run, counting my steps—one two, one two, one two.

A spark of light. A loud pop.

Nothin.

My last thought is to not fall on my baby.

✛

RAY THROWS UP his skinny arms like he won something, stepping right through me, making me see what's left of me—a hazy mist of what was—arms and legs, a face, body shaped like mine.

Am I dead?

"Murderin' bitch sure as hell weren't gon' get me, too." He marches ahead with his smoking gun at his side.

Where's my baby?

"Bobby Lee!" he yell. "Where the hell you at?"

Growling dogs echo from all around us. He stops and squishes his eyes together, trying to see through the dark, wipes his meaty hands down the front of his stained shirt. A jagged piece of fingernail, packed black with food, catches on his clothes. He bite the nail and spit it.

He sets his gun on the ground, tilts it between his knees, cups his hands on the sides of his mouth, "Bobby Lee!"

Bobby Lee's voice races through the darkness, desperate. "Call off the dogs! Call off the damn dogs!"

"Where you at?" Ray say, snatching up his rifle.

I see them dogs tugging her from my body, trying to rip her from under my arm, but I helt her tight. Made sure of it before I went.

For the first time, she cry.

Her voice is so beautiful but so scared. It anchors inside me.

Bobby Lee dives on that dog, hammers his fists down on it, shaking my baby free.

"What the hell you doing, Bobby Lee! Set that nigger baby down and let the dogs get a go."

Bobby Lee pulls his knife, cuts my baby's cord and ties it up. "It's alive!"

"And we don't need it growing up like the momma," Ray say. "Murdering white peoples. Bounty's same, dead or alive." He calls out into the woods, "Hen-ray! Get your pasty-white ass out here and help me. Your cousin done lost his mind."

Henry comes falling through the tree line and stands next to me, fat and out of breath and smacking on a nasty pine needle. The slobber on it's dried sticky and white and his sick breath rises from it, turning clean pine to outhouse shit. He doubles over his lap with his hands on his knees, catching his breath. "Bitch must be part Indian or some shit," he say.

"No match for no pure-blooded Virginian!" Ray say, flinging his rifle hand above his head.

They so proud of what they done to me.

Henry say, "What her name was again?"

"Reba or some shit like that," Ray say. "Just another of Cynthia's whores."

Naomi. My name's Naomi.

"Bobby Lee, I thought you'd be happier than a two-peckered billy goat," Henry say.

"That's what I'm tryin to tell you, Cousin. He done lost his mind," Ray say. "Bobby Lee, let Henry wrap the body and give the dogs their reward."

But Bobby Lee don't listen. He carries her strides away to a nearby bush where the moonlight is.

He drags his shirt off and over his head one-handed, switching my baby back and forth from arm to arm as he do. He wraps his shirt around her, whispers, "You all better now. You gon' be all right." With his muddy hands, he wipes away the blood and white mess from her face, says to himself, *It's a girl.*

At the crunch of Ray's steps, Bobby Lee puts his hand beside his own gun. Laughter, bursting from Henry, sends Ray back to my body to go see what the fuss is. When he get to it, he see Henry hovering over them dogs eating the afterbirth from 'tween my legs.

"You like that, nigger?" Henry say. "I'm sure you used ta having dogs in yer privates."

I don't care he laugh at me, though. I only care that Bobby Lee don't leave my baby. He lay her on a bush, rewrap her in his shirt as Ray come back his way. Bobby Lee says over his shoulder, "She got blonde hair."

"Still a nigger," Ray say and fires his pistol at my baby. Almost hit her this time.

Bobby Lee yells at him. "What the hell you doin, Ray?"

"That ain't your baby, Bobby Lee," Ray say. "Yours is dead. Two years now. So let that nigra one go."

But Bobby Lee don't. His breaths are slow and long, and the air stutters out his nose. In a raspy voice, he say, "I know it ain't mine. I heard some slave traders down in Tallassee was looking for negro babies, is all. They just a quarter-mile up the road. Might be worth something. They buy and sell all time of night."

"How much you think they give us for it?" Ray say.

"Least fifty. You and Henry gon' wrap up that mother. Get our reward for her. I'll go see about this one."

"Ah, naw! I'm goin wit you," Henry say. "You trying to keep the money all to yourself. We posed to split everything. Bitch and baby."

"Take Henry," Ray say to Bobby Lee. "I don't like the way you been cuddling up to that thang."

"I don't need him slowing me down. He mess around and make it die before we get our money." When Bobby Lee march off, Ray grabs him, holds him still, but Bobby Lee say, "We family, Ray. You know I wouldn't cheat you."

Ray lets go. "Come on, Henry. Help me wrap up this whore. And Bobby Lee, you don't 'cept less than forty-five."

"I want forty-five, too," Henry say.

"We cain't all get forty-five," Ray say. "Math don't work that way."

++

BOBBY LEE DIDN'T get back 'til nearly four hours later.

Ray and Henry were already 'sleep, crouched on the side of the road next to my body. Ray wake up, yelling, "What the hell took you so long?"

"Couldn't find nowhere to sell that baby," Bobby Lee say. "So I tossed it in a field. Coons and critters will have her by morning."

"You throwed the baby out!" Ray say.

"I knew it!" Henry say. "You just trying to keep the money."

"Show me where you left the baby then," Ray say.

"I said it's dead and I ain't got the money. Check my pockets. Go'n check 'um. See, nothin."

"Aw, y'all," Henry say. "We shoulda let the dogs get a go."

It was the first time a man lied for me. It was the familiar ring of lifesaving untruth. A death rattle that has followed me all my life. And it was the sound that plunged me into the flashes.

1 / FLASH

Faunsdale, Alabama, 1838

THE KNOCKIN'S ALWAYS there behind the wall in Momma's room. I call it Momma's music. My sister Hazel calls it Momma's tired tune, a shrill note sucked and blown from a stiff reed.

Hazel's the closest thing I got to a good daddy so she never beat me for misbehaving, never leaves me long, and never tries to touch me the wrong way. She keeps me safe in this world, keeps me safe from the knockin.

We sit in the back of our dark two-room shack, huddled under a blanket together. She's trying to drown out Momma's song with her hand cupped over my ear, fogging it up with her whispering, telling me we gon' play a game called "Let's see who can fall asleep the fastest." But after ten minutes of trying, even the late of midnight cain't shake my eyelids free so now me and Hazel gon' play a new game. It's called "Who can be the quietest the longest."

We always quiet, though. We got to be so Massa don't remember we here. Hazel say Massa might forget about her, like he did me, since I was born early and he ain't sure I come at all. The whiskey keeps him guessing and asking every year. He come out to the yard in the falltime to hand out our yearly portions and he mumbles his question about me under his breath and to the air like he ain't really asking. Hazel say he scratch his head, squint his eyes, rub his belly, and mumble some words about a baby from a while back, too unsure to make his words clear but hoping somebody pick up on 'em anyway and cure his memory, tell on me.

But nobody do.

My Momma's worth protecting so everybody look at him walleyed 'til he leave the question alone.

Me and Hazel go out late at night or at dusk when Massa's gone to town, or ain't coming back for days. We was wrong twice. Had to run back fast. The fear made me faster than Hazel. Faster than Massa, too. It was dusk both times.

Dusk is where it's safe.

And dusk is where the magic is. Where you can hide things in the orange-pink shade of a losing day. Even the green waters of Moss Lake get blended gone from dusk. You can stand a running leap away from its wave and not see the water. Like it's just another part of the field.

Dusk blends me away, too.

It's why Hazel takes me out in it, hand-holding, running me through the short patch of the woods to the flatlands where gray shadows form four feet above the ground, mouth height, and buzz. Netted clouds of gnats, they are. And we race the light through 'em and they spread when we do, then close behind us, recaptured. I spit out the slow ones.

Hazel say I get my speed from my daddy. I hate that we ain't got the same one, though. Her daddy was the nigga before Boss. Mine was a tenant farmer that Massa tried to sell a bad piece of land to. "Before you know it," Massa woulda told him, "you'll have your own slaves"— the same way he promised every poor white fool renting land from him. Probably made the offer on one of his celebration nights when he would spend the money he didn't have and invite the whole town, make Momma dress up and smile.

I tell peoples my daddy was a Indian like the ones I seen around here. Hazel keep my hair braided long down my back to prove it. We lie 'cause family's more important than truth and ain't no point in remind-ing Momma.

The knockin's getting louder so Hazel say she gon' whisper my favorite story in my ear. "And when the prince came, he gave her a kiss to remember him by." Thas how she always try to finish my story.

"Ugh! Not a kiss, Hazel! Tell it right."

Hazel's gon' be full-grown soon. She turned eleven her last birth-day. I picked the same day for my birthday so I be just like Hazel even though she come four winters before me. Momma said when Hazel was born, she could hardly push her out on the account that Hazel was fat. But that ain't why Massa couldn't sell her like I first reckoned. He sell big fat babies all the time. Even the ones with big heads. Hazel say it's 'cause money come hard for white folk, too, like it did when Massa lost most everything he had. That was the year I was born. Hazel say he sold off most of the slaves that lived here with us and said he was gon' buy some new ones but they never come. So we got a two-room cabin on our own, separated by a wall and a door. Me and Hazel stay in this back room where cain't nobody see us.

We sleep together on the feather-stuffed mat inside a bed box and keep a wood barrel turn upside down next to us. We use it for a table most times but if Massa seem like he gon' come back this way, Hazel cover me with it and put our piss pot on top so he don't get tempted to wonder.

Hazel's smart. She know everything. Even thangs Momma don't know.

"A'right, a'right," Hazel say. "When the prince came . . . he give her a tickle like this!" She grab my foot and rumble her fingers around. I laugh so hard my mouth git stuck open and fill up with air so cain't no words, no sound, nothin come out and I cain't breathe.

"Pleeeasseee! Stop, Hazel, stop."

"Sssh!" she say and look over her shoulder toward the back wall lis-tening for Momma's music. It's still playing. A soft knock. A louder one.

She pinch my big toe, tug it out like she gon' crack it. *I hate that.* She whisper, "Say, 'I smell like stinky cheese.'"

"You smell like stinky cheese," I whisper, giggling.

"No, say, you—Naomi—smells like stinky cheese."

I catch the sound of my laugh in my hands.

HAZEL'S MAKING SHADOWS on the wall now. I ain't got a dog but Hazel make me one. She use both hands to put a shadow of me on the wall, too, and make the legs walk.

Hazel say she put everything she love on that wall cause it block out the bad. Thas why she mark on it for everyone thas gone. She up to five scratches now, all of 'em baby girls. Most of 'em came between us, all but one. That one come and go last summer but I don't miss her. There ain't enough room for a baby and ain't enough warm when cold winds blow through.

Massa tol' Momma that he give her a better life than the others on the row and say he can keep a good eye on us where we is. He's particular about everything—how they hang clothes on the line to dry and how Miss Dean spin the cotton and stitch the clothes. He make a rule that Hazel got to keep her candle burning on the nights he come so he won't mistake her for a rat or a coon and shoot her. She never forget. The candle she got burning now is brighter than ever.

Massa brung that black man with him tonight, too. The one who started the knockin. I can feel him thumping Momma through the wall. It sets a pace in my chest like a drummer 'bout to lead a marching band. When I close my eyes, I imagine I see 'em, black boys dressed in raggedy clothes, holding fourth-hand instruments, ready to please the crowd.

Knockin's stopped.

That means Momma's through.

Me and Hazel tiptoe fast to the split in the wall. Hazel always beat me to it cause she don't never want me to see Momma after the knockin. Say it's private. But I want the light from the other room to slide over my face, too, so I cheat and step back a little, just behind her.

I can see Momma sitting on the edge of the bed wit no clothes on. That black man that was on top of her don't have no clothes neither, just walking 'cross the room like he ain't got no care in the world even though he black like us.

He make the light disappear when he pass us.

Massa Hilden's in there, too, standing in the corner watching. He don't never wear the jacket to that brown suit. His whole body's swole up in the material, making it cinch tight around his waist like a blouse. A gap in his shirt spreads open where the button's gone. It mouths silent words when his gut moves from breathing. The hair on his belly is poking through the gap, thick and coarse and tangled like a pile of wadded thread, brown and white. It loops and crisscrosses over his shiny pink belly fat.

Cain't see his silly shoes, though.

Those make me laugh cause they long and skinny and ugly like the pillow bandages Hazel make for our monthly flow. He's walking in 'em.

On the back of his trousers, a lump sticks out above his butt where he keeps his pistol. Its off-white handle, the color of new teeth, is showing just above his waist and it keeps everybody in order, even white peoples. He always got it on him, can get downright dangerous when he's drinking. Killed a white man a few years back. He tells people it was an accident but Hazel say he meant to. He shoot at a lot of people. Even my real daddy. It's why Hazel knows my daddy was fast. Massa said my daddy wasted his time, wouldn't sign the papers to buy that land, coulda sold it to somebody else so he shot at 'im. He called the law on Massa. Didn't nothing happen, though.

"Naomi, get back! You gon' mess around and get us all killed," Hazel whisper.

"I just want to see his shoes, is all."

"Shhh . . ." she say, waving me away.

I ease back a little. "They leavin? Momma ready for us now?"

I hear Massa. "I need males. Nine months of waiting needs to pay off bigger for me. These girls ain't pulling in nothing. No more girls, you hear me? Else they gon' end up like you."

"Yes'sa, Massa Hilden," Momma say. "God gon' bless me wit a boy this time."

"And how's Hazel?" he say. Hazel slides away from the wall slow like she don't want to hear. She come toward me and I step aside, pretend I ain't interested in getting in front of her to see Massa's long baby feet.

"She should be of age now," he say.

"No suh, no suh," Momma say in a hurry. "She's just a baby."

"You just make sure it's a boy this time."

"Yes'sa, Massa Hilden. Yes'sa."

I tiptoe around Hazel fast so she cain't catch me before I get to the wall but she don't race me this time. I smash my face in front of the opening. Cain't see nothin. I get on my knees and look through the bottom hole. All I see is Momma sad and Massa gone.

Hazel's on the other side of the room now, sitting close to the candlelight, flipping through the pages of her Bible. Massa's mother gave the Bible to Hazel and two cousins. Said it would keep every one of us from being a heathen. But Hazel's the only one she taught to read it. Just the first page before she died. The rest Hazel figured out on her own.

"'In the beginning,'" Hazel say with tears seeping through her lashes, "'God created the heavens . . .'" Her voice cracks from the tears caught in her throat. The free ones roll down her face and drip on her page. She looks at me, whispers, "You see that poker near the fire where Momma is?"

I turn back 'round on my knees to see through the hole again. "The one you found?" I say.

"That's it. You see the end? It's sharp. I grind it myself. It's strong now. It's ready."

"Ready for what, Hazel?"

The door slams shut in the other room and I jump up. "Come on, Hazel! Momma's ready for us!"

Hazel reach out to stop me even though she ain't close enough to get me.

I stop anyway. "But I want to see her, Hazel."

"Not now."

"I want to see her."

"Not now, Naomi!"

I stomp my foot, twist up my arms.

"Momma needs more time," she say. "Not like before. She gotta try harder, make a baby. A boy baby for Massa Hilden. Get the most money."

"I know she wanna see us."

"Naomi, look . . . what Momma's doin . . . what he make her do. Changes women. Makes 'em different."

"Somethin's wrong wit Momma?"

Hazel sighs the way she do when we daydreaming on the porch at night, when she's telling me about her North. I go close to her, dress myself with her, slipping under her arm and resting there. "North," she say, "is a place where we could belong to ourselves and to the people we choose, in love and kindness, and in the sharing of God's good things."

"Let's go North," I tell Hazel to make her happy again. "Let's find that star. Take Momma and go that way."

"Ain't just a direction," she say. I hold her hand up to the end of my corded braid and she takes it between her fingertips, unbraids it, and combs her fingers through. "The North Star don't mean nothin to those who cain't read it. Could mean south or east or west, just the same."

"That's why I got you," I say. Hazel's my guide, my light in darkness, one of them stars that like a handful of little moons were shrunk to pebbles, then flung to the heavens where they sat.

"Then I'll teach you," she say. She wraps her arms around me and pulls me into her softness. "One day, we gon' go to Boston where it's safe. We gon' wear the pretty dresses Momma made us and drink sweet tea all day long."

2 / FLASH

Faunsdale, Alabama, 1846

SINCE ME AND Hazel had our birthday four months ago and I
turned fifteen, I started to notice thangs. Like how every spring
the musty smell of grass and dew warmed by the sun clogs my
nose and makes me sneeze. And how the cotton fields throw small balls
in the air and twirl 'em around in the wind. The boys trample 'em under
their feet and the girls make doll babies with 'em. Sometimes I imagine
the cotton pieces are alive 'cause of how they chase me.

I notice how Mama Dean always sits in the same place in the middle
of the quad next to that spinning wheel, talking to it. She look young
even though her gray hair say she old. Been white since she was fifteen,
she told me. Her skin is still smooth and it's charcoal black—a color
only God could paint and make look right.

I been sitting with her for hours today, studying how she move
with that machine, holding firm to that cotton, pacing it through its big
wooden wheel when it zip and creak around.

From far away, the wheel looks tacked in the sky on nothin. From
here, though, I can see its two wooden hands reaching up from the
bench, pinning the wheel between 'em, coaxing the cotton from Mama

Dean's man-sized hands. It slip through her fingers like webs sliding out of spiders. "Simply trial and error, Naomi. Would you like to try?"

Mama Dean speaks better than us. She spent three generations in the Hilden household, teaching and cleaning and caring for Massa's momma 'til she passed. His momma hired a doctor to come daily with vials of pain medication and had him stay to make sure she'd die of natural causes and not them.

Massa stayed bitter about how the doctor's visits subtracted from his inheritance.

Then she died.

That's when Massa told Mama Dean that he needed the spare room to "organize his affairs." She was slow, he said, and taking up space, he said, and he could use Violet in the house and the field, he said.

So she's with us now.

"No, Mama Dean . . . all I do is tangle it right up."

"Your mother started off tangling things like you. Then she became the best. She could spin the most beautiful textures for you and your sisters' dresses."

I look over at Momma sitting and rocking on the porch all blank-faced and quiet, the same place Hazel put her this morning. Hard to imagine her moving any other way. My mind ain't like Hazel's. She remember thangs from when she was two years old. I might have a pocketful of memories from before eight. That was about the time Momma stopped talking all together, the same time Hazel put the sixth and seventh marks on the wall—twin girls.

Hazel say pain's got a way of etching memories into people's minds, even a child's, and holds its place there for a lifetime. That's why she remembers. She say her memories keep her guilty, blame her for not doing the thangs that only grown folks woulda known to do. She say she's aged into her bad memories, helpless as the day she got 'em 'cause she still cain't go inside 'em and fix nothin.

"Naomi!" I hear from behind me. Hazel's flying out of the woods, calling me and grinning, and calling again. I get up and smile, too, 'cause I know she got something good to say. Trailing behind her is her skinny, big-eyed beau, James. They holding hands even though he ain't supposed to be here. They been sneaking through the woods together since last summer, going to secret meetings. I followed her one night and saw her meet eight negroes from the plantation down river where James come from. All of 'em was boys except the two piss yellow green-eyed girls and Hazel. All but Hazel was house negroes.

They sat around the fire, real close and quiet, talking private. Hazel started off the group praying, reading the Bible and that was all right, I guess. But after then, they got to talking crazy, talking 'bout running North. But I don't understand. What do house niggas got to run for? What they got to lose? They live in the big house, get treated good. Now they trying to trade an easy life and a kind master to starve. Worse, get kilt. "Freedom," they said. "North," they said. I keep my freedom in my mind.

The more I listened to Hazel, though, I could see her almost fooled by 'em. They probably want to leave her somewhere, make her the 'scape donkey. She nodded her head with 'em saying her *um hum*s and *thas right*s. I knew she didn't mean none of it, though. The only reason she go to them meetings is 'cause a James. He's sweet.

I've seen the way he is with her. When they're walking, he'll reach for her side to guide her this way or that, hardly touching her but she's moved. If not direction, inside herself. Her hardened brick body becomes something looser. Frail. Like crumbling rock. No . . . sand. Like she's made of drying wet sand and any brush could crumble her away. And that night I last followed 'em, he skipped his fingertips along the back of her hand, then around to her palm and through her fingers before settling into the spaces.

She didn't break apart, though.

Only her gritty edges tumbled away. Changed her. One day, I want to be changed, too.

When she get to me, I say, "Tell me, Hazel! Tell me!"

"We gettin married!"

We both scream and hug and Mama Dean claps her hands, then holds 'em to her mouth. I say, "You gon' have to practice me now, Mama Dean. We goin to a weddin'!"

I grab James and do a twirl and a jig wit him, do another dance on my own. Hazel puts her hands on my shoulders, trying to hold me in place. "Naomi?"

"I'm just warmin' up, Hazel!"

"Naomi?" she say, pressing down harder on me. "We goin North. We gon' run."

My stomach drops out of me.

My feet stop directly.

All I can think about is Berry and Francis who only made it as far as the creek, then didn't. "Run?" I say.

"They talkin 'bout war, Naomi. War to free us. The time to be a slave is over."

I don't want to die.

I unpin my hair and turn my back to Hazel so she see I want her to braid it, but she only runs her fingers through it once, then pats my head. "We all goin together," she say. "You and Momma comin, too."

I start fixing Hazel's hair real fast and put it how she like it so she forget about running.

"Me and James'll be like Abraham and Sarah in the Bible."

"You want your hair up or down?" I say. "It's pretty up."

"You hear what I said, Naomi?"

I want her to stop talking about war or leaving so I bend my arms in her face to get her hair good. It's an accident that I'm smashing my arm in her mouth so she cain't talk, but her mushed mouth keeps moving anyway.

"It's your wedding, Hazel. I'm gon' make you the prettiest bride ever was."

She untangles herself from behind my arms and yells to Momma on the porch. "Momma! Me and James gon' ask permission. We gettin married!"

Momma don't move.
She never do.

3 / FLASH

Faunsdale, Alabama, 1846

THE RAIN'S BEEN slapping the ground all day, soaking through the house, making our floors mud.

Hazel put a fire on to keep us warm. I like to watch it burn yellow and orange and see-through—a halo of colors birthing light through the ruins like the rainbow after the flood. It reminds me that God's still here.

I been getting better at my reading since it's been getting dark early. Hazel's been practicing me for hours today and my butt bone hurt, but ever since she said, "Use the only part of your backside wit some meat on it," I been tilted up on my thighs so this oak chair don't hurt so much. If I was big and healthy like Hazel, I could sit any ole kinda way, but as it is, I got to sit crooked.

The boys especially like her healthy. You'd think them boys could see right through her clothes the way they stare at her chest. She keeps her arms crossed when she outside so cain't nobody see 'em. Peoples think she got a bad attitude because of it. Truth is, the only thing she ever hated was her big tits. I wouldn't mind if I had 'em even though she say they sweat underneath. I'd be happy to wipe 'em dry all day long but I ain't even got a bump yet.

Hazel promised that my fat's gon' come after I get my period. I ain't told her it come last month cause I'm gon' surprise her. Just wake up one morning wit a big fat butt and big tits and Hazel gon' say, "Why you wearin' my britches?" And I'm gon' say, "My ass too big for mine." Then we both gon' laugh.

But today, I got just one fat leg.

Yesterday, a wasp stung me on it when I was popping berries from that ole mulberry bush next to the pigpen. It hurt so bad and I cried so loud 'til I seen my leg getting big. By the time I got home, it was swolled up like an air-blown pig gut. I ran back to that ole bush and spent the rest of the night swatting at it so that wasp come back and get the other one. He didn't come back, though. Now I got just one pretty leg. I been sitting wit it half off the chair, swinging it around so Hazel can see. But she ain't said nothin, yet.

Momma's been pacing the room since she got back from the church gathering this morning with Massa's nana and the other white folk. She allow Momma to go, stand outside the window and listen.

Momma's brushing the dust off the window shutters wit her fingernails. More like a scraping but we don't stop her. Thas how she keep busy sometimes. It let me and Hazel keep to our reading. We take turns. It's Hazel's turn now. "'Yay though I walk through the valley of the shadow of death, I will fear no evil for thou art with me; thy rod and thy staff, they comfort me.'"

"Hazel?" I say. "God like art?"

"What? No, *art* means are. You *are* with me."

"Well, why they talk like that? Thy and though?"

"That's just how God talk. Let me finish."

"A'right."

"'Thou preparest a table . . .'"

"Hazel?"

"What."

"You think God understands us then? We don't talk like that."

"He understands all different kind a talk."

"What about Momma? She don't talk. He understand her, too?"

"I imagine he do. Now let me finish, then you can read."

I be quiet.

She starts slow like she think I'm gon' say something but I'm just gon' listen this time. She say, "'Thou preparest a table before me in the presence of my enemies.'"

"Hazel? What 'preparest' mean?"

"God's expecting you. Always with you. Even when you don't think He is. When your enemies are all around you." She push the Bible to me. "Here, now you . . ."

A hush covers our room. The rain quit beating, the bugs quit chirping, and Momma stopped scratching, all at once. The kind of off-quiet that make you pay attention and expect. Like the moment after lightning, waiting on thunder.

Hazel turns 'round to the door, then back to me but not looking at me, listening for something. When it don't come she taps her Bible, say, "Now you read."

A loud knock at the door stops me, scares me. I don't know who that knock belongs to 'cause it's hard and slow and nobody's supposed to be out after dusk on a Sunday.

Hazel listens to the door, using her whole body to hear it, watches, but don't get up.

Momma starts brushing the shutters again.

"Hazel?" I whisper.

She puts her hand over my mouth. When the knock starts again, she gets up quickly but I don't want her to answer it.

She go to the shutters, peeks through the split, then dashes back to me, whispering, "It's Massa Hilden. Go in the other room with Momma."

She snatches the Bible and pitches it under the table. I run quiet across the floor, grab Momma's hand on the way, and we slide through my bedroom door. I turn over my hiding barrel to get it ready to cover me, but when I see Momma standing alone, I don't get under it like I should. I wait near the door with her. Want to listen. I leave it cracked open to see.

Massa walk in before Hazel get back to the door.

"Massa Hilden?" Hazel say. "We wasn't expectin' you. Momma came down wit a spell this mornin, been sick all over the place."

He strolls to the middle of the room carrying that silence with him. He stops next to the table, wipes down the arms of his brown suit jacket—first time I seen him in it—and straightens the cuffs while he looks around. He takes a cigar out of his pocket, lights it, and like a baby on a teet, he sucks on it in short spurts to get it going. His eyes draw to the floor when he do. He moseys over to the Bible there, picks it up, throws it on the table, flips through its pages.

Hazel stands watching him from next to the opened front door. I reckon she hope he blow out.

Massa closes the Bible, walks his fat fingers across the tabletop, then around to the backside of the table, next to the fire pit. He picks up the poker, stabs the wood, sizzling ash.

Hazel don't know what to say over his quiet. Finally she say, "I'm sorry we not so tidy this Sunday evenin. Momma's been fightin a bad sickness and I don't want you to catch it."

"Darlin. I'm not here to see your momma. I'm here to see you."

He pokes at the fire, then stabs a log with the sharp end of his poker, shakes it 'til the log falls off in a thud. "It's been quite a few years now. No boys from your momma, just the girls. Got a pretty penny for 'em but I still need my boys, they bring in the real money. You understand that don't you, Hazel? Finances." His eyes slide toward her.

I open my door a little more so I can see better.

He say, "I need someone to take your momma's place. A strong woman. Good hips." He raises his hand, waves at the opened front door. "You don't mind if my friend, Boss, come in, do you, Hazel?"

That black man come in. He ain't nobody's boss except that he the same one who lay on top of Momma.

Massa keeps poking at the fire and don't say nothing to Boss even though he came in like Massa asked. Massa buries the orange tip of his cigar into our table, finally say, "Now then, Hazel. Let's see what you can do."

Hazel creeps back to the wall, passing by our door. She look over her shoulder and into my eyes, then straight away. She hangs there in place. Ain't no crying from her—there never is no more—but her breathing is fast like a mouse caught in a jar. There ain't nowhere to go but fly. Boss grabs her arm, pulls her back into the middle of the room where Massa is. He snatches the back of her hair so her face shoots to the ceiling.

I want to be strong like her and don't cry neither.

I scoot back along the wall, squat down to my old peeking hole and frame my hands around it. I mash my cheek to the wood and air streams through the space, watering my eye. My tears are cold before they fall. I wipe 'em away, making the sight of Hazel across the room clear.

Boss presses his front against Hazel, smashing her back against the warm wall next to the fire. She shuts her eyes and turns her head. A soft wisp of hair falls and soaks into the sweat on her face. Boss brings a dark finger to the strands, sweeps it away to kiss her cheek. A kiss that musta sickened her cause she buck up, her legs rearing and sending a knee between Boss's legs.

But she don't get away.

Boss grabs her waist, lifts her up but her legs and arms keep moving like she running on the ground, then they go wild, swinging, sending her and Boss back against the wall. Her foot slides in the fire.

I wish I never looked through this hole.

Hot tears pour down my cheeks while the firelight flickers on Momma's face. She stands in the door's gap looking to Hazel.

She don't say nothin.

Her eyelids flutter.

I hear Massa in the other room. "Hold still, girl," and there's a shuffle. Their back and forth turns the shadow show on Momma's face into movement, the three shadow lines down her face, a dance. The shortest line in the middle is Hazel. The two shadow lines come together on her face making Momma's skin gray. She don't blink, though. She come alive.

At once, she burst through the door. "Choose me!" she yell to Massa. "What chu want me to do? I do it."

"It's too late, Letti," Massa say.

"I'll give you a boy this time! I'll be good. I could do it this time. God gon' bless me wit a boy. Please!" She throws herself down and wraps her arms around Massa's leg, hugging him like she loves him. He kicks her off.

"Momma!" I yell, stumbling in the room.

"No!" Hazel say.

"Hot damn!" Massa say, scared or surprised. I don't know which. He tilts his head from side to side trying to place me. Then finally, "I knew it! You look just like that bastard. I should've killed him when I had my chance, thieving from me."

Massa comes close to me, leans into me. His swollen nose is laced with thin red veins, like he walked into a bloodied cobweb.

"I'm ready," Hazel say. "Massa . . . I'm ready."

He touches my cheek with his damp yellow fingers. "Where have they had you hidin, darlin?"

"Leave 'er lone!" Hazel say.

"Don't worry," Massa say, grinning. "I won't bite."

I hold still, hear the buzz of that strange silence again. Broken now by footsteps trotting up our porch outside. A knock at our door follows. This time, quick and eager. *I know that knock.*

Nobody moves.

"Get it," Massa tell Hazel.

She don't go.

"Girl!" he say.

When she get to the door, she opens it slow. James is there with a handful of freshly picked wild flowers. His smile is like the sun on 'em, but when he sees her, his face dims. "You all right, Hazel?"

From where I stood behind her, I could see a tear fall from her chin to her chest. She shakes her head slowly trying to make it so Massa cain't see. James takes a step back down the porch.

"Don't leave the boy waitin," Massa say, pushing the door open all the way. He puts his arm around Hazel. "Take the flowers, girl."

Hazel's slow to. But she do.

"Where's my manners? Come on in, boy."

James obey. He's with us now.

His head's hung low as he walks through our door, searching the room with his eyes. He stops across from us, alone and small-looking.

"So what brings you my way on a beautiful evening like tonight?" Massa say. "Oh . . . the flowers. That's real nice."

James bows his head meekly and folds his hands in front of him so he ain't a threat. His Sunday shirt hangs past his knuckles. James say, "We was gon' ask permission, suh."

"You was gon' ask permission?"

"Yes'sa. Got permission from Massa Lewis and . . ."

"I look like Massa Lewis?"

"Naw, suh," James say. "If you just have a word wit Massa Lewis, suh."

Massa relights his cigar, puffs it slow, patting the top and bottom of it with both lips. He say, "Seems to me I got a fox in my henhouse, Boss. A fox messin 'round with what's mine. What I clothe, feed, and provide shelter. Screwin 'em before me. What you think about that, Boss?"

Boss shakes his head. "Very disrespectful, suh."

"How you punish somethin like that?"

Boss lifts his shoulders. "Don't know."

Massa pulls his cigar out of his lips slow but makes a quick jerk of his hand. Before I know where it went, the wall explodes a hole of blossoming splinters. Shards of wood fly in my face and prick the front of my neck and chest. The sound crashes in my ears. I cup 'em to stop the ringing but a smell like burnt hair and wood sweeps the air. Everything sits still now except for Massa's gun making its smoke dance.

Hazel and Momma throw themselves to the floor but James ain't moved.

His big brown eyes are wide open, with a hole in his forehead.

A line of blood slides down like sweat.

He falls to the floor.

Hazel's hands draw to her mouth and tears cover her eyes.

"Shit!" Massa say. "See what you made me do!" he say to Boss. "You short-poured the lead again. Made the bullet split. I told you to re-melt the whole damn thing together. You can't patch a bullet!" Massa slides his hands down the back of his head. "Fuck me!" he say. "You know what that's gon' cost me, Boss? Do ya? I was just gonna scare 'im."

Massa rams his pistol back down his pants and its pearly white handle flashes us from under his brown jacket. He follows the bullet's path to the wall, touching the impact. "See, Boss? It shoulda missed and gon' clean through here."

"Yes, suh, Massa, suh."

Massa blows out hard, washes his hands over his face. "You made me kill that fox."

Hazel won't move her sight from James. Tears drip steady from her chin while Momma cry, "Jesus, Jesus."

My hands stay on my ears. I'm afraid to move 'em, 'fraid to let out the ringing that's in 'em and make all this true. I imagine its church bells instead.

"Now, where were we?" Massa say over the ringing. "Yes, the girl . . ." He look at me.

Hazel wails.

Massa say, "Boss, get that fox outta here."

Boss picks up James, but cain't get a good hold on him. He folds James's limp arms across his chest to make 'em stay put, carries him to the door, leaking red.

I ain't letting go my ears.

Momma's knees creak back and forth on the floor.

"Where were we?" Massa say again.

He staggers toward me and I walk on my knees away from him, the invisible wall that keeps space between us pushes me back toward the fire. He forces me to the side of the table where I knock my head and my hands let go my ears to hold the table.

The pain of what Massa just done rush to me, red-blooded. My neck's getting hot, my hands is sweating. Hazel's cries is louder. She runs over to Boss, pulls his arms from James, beg to let him alone.

Massa say, "Gon' get 'im outside."

That ready-poker. I see it next to me, pressing me to take it.

Boss opens the door.

I spin around and grab it, launch it deep inside Massa's belly before my mind tell me no.

Massa's mouth falls open.

His eyes bulge.

He begs me to stop but I ain't gon' stop. I push it through him and my hands slide down the pole. His blood squeezes out warm around my fists. And he stops reaching for me. *I want this.*

Boss drops James when he see us.

He throws hisself at me trying to beat me loose, but I cling to that poker, shake it in.

Boss rams his fist to my hand. I still don't let go.

Rams my head. My face go numb.

I try to stand, but cain't. I don't wanna fight no more.

I push across the floor, crawling my way to Hazel, half-blind. She's hunched over James trying to fix him. Momma's on top of Boss. Got that poker in his back, the other end in her hand. She's digging it in. His blood rains on the floor.

A second blast races around the room and I throw myself to the ground. Don't know if I'm hit or dead or deaf, the sound exploding from everywhere—a long whistle in my ear. Don't feel myself hurt.

When I open my eyes, Hazel ain't moved from cuddling James. I squint toward Momma, find her staring at me like she just asked a question and she's waiting for an answer. But her calm expression turns painful. She don't let her eyes fall from mine when blood spreads from the middle of her dress. "Momma!" I yell. She hunches over and falls as Massa sits perched on his knees across the room holding that pistol. The weight of it flops his hand sideways and he fall with it.

"Momma!" I say, scooting across the floor to wake her, to make her well, but she ain't moving. Only the wind of her last breath do.

Behind us, Massa takes his last, too.

The wet of her dress makes my hand red. "Hazel! Momma's dead!"

But Hazel won't look away from James. She's holding his hand. I can hear her talking to him. Praying. I try to wait . . . wait long enough and say, "Hazel, what we gon' do?"

Hazel don't get up. She stay praying. Seem like a hour before she say, "Amen." Finally, she stands, strong as always except when she sees Momma, her knees buckle.

Calmly, she say, "I want you to go, Naomi. Far as you can. Go where cain't nobody find you."

"Where I'm gon' go, Hazel? I cain't leave you and Momma."

She nods and goes over to the fire pit, pulls her smoldering Bible out the fire. She presses it on her dress to stop it smoking. And I cain't stop shaking. "Momma's dead, Hazel!"

She comes to me, hugs me, but her comfort ain't enough to stop this pain or the tears that pain makes to carry itself out of me.

Hazel twists two bundles of my hair into one loose braid. It unravels.

"Naomi, listen. Listen! You gotta go outta here. You gotta go north, you hear me? Ain't nothin here for you." She presses her Bible against my chest. I hold it tight.

"I don't know where North is!"

"Follow the star like I showed you. Go only in the night." Boss starts moaning from the floor.

I cain't do this no more.

Hazel go over to him, stomps that poker further into Boss's back and he shuts up. She heaves it out and tears her clothes with it; slices into her own flesh, along her ribs 'til she bleed. She brings it to me and puts it in my hand, bloody. "You gon' need to protect y'self."

"Hazel?" I say.

"You gon' need food." She gets the stale rolls from next to the oven and shoves 'em down my blouse. "You water yourself in the stream."

"But Hazel . . ."

"People gon' come lookin, Naomi. Come lookin for all us. Ain't nobody certain you was ever here." She peels off Massa's dark-brown jacket, rolling his fat, doughy body from side to side when she do.

"Hazel, please!"

She puts his jacket around my shoulders. "We was all attacked," she say. "I got to be here to tell 'em."

"But I cain't make it without you."

She pulls open the front door. "Go, Naomi."

I creep to it, wiping my tears. "Hazel? Please."

"Go!" she yell.

She grabs the back of my head, kiss my cheek before she push me out the door. I hurry out, looking up to the starless, clouded sky, running through the dark, holding Massa's jacket high above my head.

"Don't look back, Naomi. You hear me! Don't you look back!"

I cain't breathe.

Maybe Hazel put a mark on the wall for me, too.

4 / FLASH

SOME SAY YOUR life flashes before your eyes when you're about to die.

It don't always.

Not for me.

I didn't have not one flash before I went.

Not everybody gets to see their first birthday again. Their father's face laughing. The day their sister got married. The friends they've loved.

Maybe you won't neither.

Not before you die.

It's only now that I see the flashes. They come and go, and choose what day of my life to show me and I ain't got a say in it. It happens to all of us dead. It's more than just seeing the moment, it's taking part in the memory as if it were happening again. And when you in the flash, you don't even know that what you're seeing is from a time already gone. You get lost in it. Feel like you got all the time in the world. A future. But it's just your old life repeating itself and repeating itself and repeating itself. Those shivers you felt on warm days were just you—in two places at once.

So powerful, these flashes. Ask the dead. Ask the people who survive near death. Ask 'em how the flashes change their whole life from then on.

Or for the empty, it changes nothing.

I guess the most important parts of life ain't measured by years or days or minutes but by moments. Moments that come in flashes here, only some of 'em good like seeing my sister, Hazel, again. I was seven years old in one of them flashes. Twelve in another. My favorite was the time when Hazel was teaching me how to tumble. And in another, I was six years old and she helped me lose my first tooth with a string and a slammed door.

The hell is the bad memories. Going back again and again and not being able to make a damn bit of difference. But God had mercy on me.

It's been said that justice is getting what you deserve. And mercy is not getting the bad you deserve. Grace is getting a good thing, even when you don't deserve it. So if I would've named my good thing, I'd have called her Grace. But someone else named her Josephine.

Part II

5 / 1850

Tallassee, Alabama

WHERE DO WE start when we tell the stories of our loved ones? On the day they were born or the day they mattered? Mattered to other people, I mean, did something worth talking about. I guess I could start with who begot who like the Bible do, but where somebody comes from only matters to people who come from something and as it was, she came from me.

Me, and the men who would become her fathers.

See, my baby's real father wasn't the man who loved me. But if wishing could make it so, I'd of traded him for the man I shoulda loved—Charles. I woulda made him the first daddy to her 'cause first means something.

Charles wasn't the man who got me pregnant.

He wasn't first to hold my baby with his hands, either, or feel her tiny bones wiggling 'round in a loose bag of see-through skin. It was somebody else who was first to listen to her soft breaths flutter.

Charles shoulda been all them.

But he wasn't.

When I first knew Charles, I never thought he'd be the kind of man who woulda made a good daddy. He never seemed like he needed nobody, especially a child. And his body never looked like it could care for one, neither. His hands too big to care for little baby thangs, his face too beastly to call a comfort, his arms too strong to hold something gentle. I'd reckon he'd crush her reaching for sugar. And he was alone when I first knew him. Alone is how he liked it. Safe. Never having to wonder what it would be to give hisself to somebody completely.

But I was wrong.

Wrong, 'cause he chose my baby, Josephine. Wrong, 'cause he once tried to choose me.

I wish he woulda smelled sweet to me like a man looking for love or seemed soft like a man who could love me silly and forgive me for the thangs he didn't know about me. I wish I woulda felt his sun on my cheeks, breathed in his cool air and noticed the difference, like stepping from the cool shade of the trees to the hot sun directly. I wish he woulda scorched goose bumps on my arms so I woulda thought of him regular.

But he was just Charles. Another man, not a miracle.

Momma used to say that when you meet the one God sent you, you'd recognize him at once 'cause we all got souls trapped in our bodies and our souls got memories of a better life before this one; memories that come to us in our dreams, even when we awake.

I didn't remember Charles that way. I mighta loved him if I did. The way Josey did.

She saw through the deep folds and scars on his bald head from when he was set on fire. She saw through the wash of skin on his burned face—healed slick. His nose was flattened to a valley. And still, she managed to love the man I shoulda. A man that became like a mother to her. He'd shepherd his flock of one away from all the things that might hurt her.

For him, couldn't nobody care for her the right way, couldn't nobody do it as good as he could: couldn't feed her right, couldn't hold her right, couldn't watch her close enough.

Everyone was to blame if she caught cold, so up until she was three years old, he wrapped her up at night hisself and worked hard in the day to get back before them gossiping women let her fall in the stream. And when he labored, he never looked no one in the eye, never gave nobody half a reason to whip him. Never spoke.

By the time Josey was five, everybody could see that his love and Josey were the same thing. The pair of 'em was as wrong as a dog nursing a kitten. And if he knew it, he never said and everybody else was scared to tell him. So at seven years old, when Josey asked him if he was her momma, Charles said, "Love is just love."

They would talk like that. Honest-like. As if the world had no boundaries and the lush green of East Tallassee, Alabama, was all there was to it. It was the place that became home. The place that became home to me, too. Like a sister to me, Tallassee is—the dirt, the trees, the river, the hillsides. For Charles and Josey, it's home, where the real world disappears beneath forests of perfectly placed vines. They flow through these woods like silken hair, running over treetops as if they were shoulders and along the ground where pink flowers sprout and get tucked behind her ear. Pretty.

Charles and Josey would walk along her creek—Stone Creek— far enough away from cotton fields and mills, hands carrying whips. They could dream of a future here, even though people say negroes are dreamless.

Stone Creek was just a man's skip wide but Josey couldn't make it across without Charles's carry. She was five years old the first time she saw the past there—red beads and pottery. Tallassee would let the past seep in that way, through overflowed waters from the fast and wide Tallapoosa River, scooping buried things and rearranging 'em. Resurrected. Drag marks of black sand and brown mud led to where old things ended up—the storms' treasure turning over lame in the swampy banks. Charles would lower Josey over the water so she could reach down and pick 'em up, the back of her dress knotted in his fist.

"Creek Indians," Charles told her. "Chased out."

Josey wondered why they'd gone and left such pretty things. And before she could ask the question, Charles would answer. "The Creek

Indians lived here before the Spanish," he told her. And he told her how the French came, then the English, then the English again, the second time with a dream to build a new nation.

Men rode the Tallapoosa River almost three hundred miles from Georgia to Alabama. Then just above Tallassee, thirty miles upriver, they built a dam in Montgomery. They came for the water's strength—the waterfalls. They could power a mill with 'em, wet a town. They carved up Tallassee like cuts of meat. Sold her with the promise that she was theirs.

The river splits her in two so the men named one side of her East, and the other West. But she still see herself as one. Be silly to cut a person in half and call 'em now two peoples, treat 'em different. But they did. On her east side, bluffs hold groves of magnolias and oak trees like a fistful of flowers, and plantation houses. The west holds the mills and the workers.

Tallassee didn't say nothin when they split her up. Of course she didn't. She's a piece of land. A mute spirit. Any voice she may have had went when the last Indian tribes left. But you can feel her fury. Angry at how she was tricked over the years—slow and steady. If it was done to her quick, she might have noticed.

These settlers weren't forceful, at first. They were charming-like. Whispering sweetness in her ear as they passed through. Coming back more and more regular. Mapping things. Told her they were drawing pretty pictures of her. It's how they do. Capture things on paper. Would catch the spirit, if they could. Would capture music, if they could. But some things you just got to be there to see. It's why I thank God for making the spirit like running water. Even captured water will steam away. It's what the Creek Indians believed Tallassee was—a spirit, uncatchable 'til she was caught.

Maps is how they did it. They separated East and West Tallassee on their papers, marking squiggly lines that meant "Tallapoosa River." And on the paper, two waterfalls—the power that would turn the water wheel and give life to the mill. A mill that first made cotton cloth. A mill that would last make bullets. Even the gray bedrock that the river tumbled over was drawn in, unmoving. Proof you can't capture everything. 'Cause in real life, the waterfalls splash on the green moss blanketing rocks and spray red berries stuck on leaning branches. But that didn't matter on paper. And what don't matter, don't survive. Nothing survives its usefulness to white folk.

The Creek Indians were driven away (they got Africans and poor whites instead) and the waterfalls were made mules, and the river's rocks were used to build stone buildings. Only gravel remained in the water, mostly unbothered. That, and the animals they couldn't catch.

"The past always got a way of coming back," Charles told Josey, pointing at the beads in her hand. "And this land got a memory." It's why Charles thought the bridges went down over the Tallapoosa River regular.

Tallassee would always start that happening the same way. She'd send the morning gusts first, high above the ground, rushing it through the treetops that covered the whole five-mile forest like a God-made roof. Even when heavy rains came, hardly a drop got through.

The wind would rush like water above the town, uncatchable, bending trees south. The limbs would lean, layering a thick cover of roof over the world of folks and things underneath, not disturbed.

I once watched a dried orange leaf hang from a branch by a single thread of shimmery web. While it stormed above, the leaf played in the calm space below, spinning, unaware of the darkening skies, nudged only into rocking by a bluebird seeking shelter. By the noon hour, it had been plucked away, stolen like everything else not rooted in the earth, then shoved into the wind-made tunnel that burrowed a pocket through Tallassee.

"This is a day of reckoning," a white man said, standing on the wet cliff above another fallen bridge. Another said, "You can't contain this landscape. Can't beat her back. These vines are relentless growing in." But people must beat it back, and they do to live here. Those who been here long enough call Tallassee the green-skirted gypsy of the South.

Full of illusions. She'd set clouds on her hilltops like floating pearls. Even on days when no weather would call for 'em and no storms were on their way, she'd put just one cloud above a cluster of three or four oaks, making it look like the nesting jaybirds were smoking.

Good weather.

"Fertile and stable ground," visitors would say, while a torrent simmered beneath her trick of "perfect place to make a life and start a family." The Creek Indians knew her better. A thousand years they respected her, the way Charles and Josey do.

Those men shouldn't have cut her up. Shouldn't have tried to own her. Define her. Not with their caught pictures, their maps. The Creek Indians wouldn't do it until they were forced to. The Creek landmarks became borders. Their asking her permission to stay became demands. Their maps, their boundaries, meant the end of the Indians' world. It's always how white men came to own things: "If you can define it, you can own it," they'd say. "If you can define it, it can be fought for, killed for. A woman, a slave, a cow, dirt, an idea." And it is what happened. Thousands lost their lives. The Creek Nation fought the new United States of America. The unshapeable spirit had been shaped into Tallassee's pretty picture. And the lines of her cheekbones became battle lines. And it wouldn't be the last time. There's a civil war coming.

"If you lucky," Charles said, pulling a broken plate from the water, "when the past comes to greet you, all it want to say is, 'I remember you,' then smile from longing."

6 / FLASH

Conyers, Georgia, 1846

THE LAST THING I remember is Hazel telling me, "Run!" And I ran with all my soul, I did.

Then walked some.

Rested beside a stream and drank water. Ate some stale bread Hazel gave me. And when the bread was gone the second day, I used Hazel's fire poker to kill again. But I prayed over that coon. Prayed over it with my Bible, started a fire the way Hazel taught me to. Roasted it, ate it, slept 'til daylight and ran again. 'Til nightfall, I did. Three more days this way. Three more days with Hazel's voice in my head telling me, don't stop. "Go north," she said. So I kept on, under the cover of rain-wet leaves and gray clouds.

By nightfall on the fourth day, I found that North Star. But by then, I was too tired for it to matter. Had been climbing up and over and up and over, the backs of my arms were sore and my muscles were burnt to cinder.

The rain had started again, was overflowing, making the ground a stream of cold. I was slipping over rocks, walking more than running, catching myself from falling. I tied big green leafs around my bleeding bare feet but still felt every grounded thistle like a blade.

Rain kept pelting my face. Was soft tickles at first, then turned to hard pinpricks from hitting the same spot again and again.

I stumbled into a road, soaking wet, turning myself this way and that way. The light of two buggy lamps showered me and the sign in the road next to me. It read: Conyers, Georgia.

The buggy's horses were coming my way, snorting, their hooves pounding. That's when I threw myself off the road.

Now, I don't know how long I been in this room.

Or how I got here.

Or who put me in these dry clothes.

Or why I feel full. I don't remember eating after that second night.

My whole body hurts and my eyes is swole shut. I cain't see. Puss and blood is squeezing around 'em, pushing my eyeballs out, slicing pain behind 'em. Whoever got me here put piles of sheets on top of me making it hard to move.

The sheets bend and make a space under my neck between my chest and chin like a roof's peak, where hot is puffing out and blowing steam over my face. A wet rag is sagging down from my forehead to my mouth, almost dry from fever, rubbing the thin skin on my top lip raw.

Shivers send my teeth chattering. My jaw is sore and my ear holes are plugged like they brimming wit water, muffling noises outside of me.

My imaginings got me thinking that some man's standing above me with a knife, ready to cut me up 'cause he know I cain't move. For a hour, I been facing the spot where I think he is but he ain't killed me yet.

Throw-up's racing to my mouth, bitter, 'cause I'm thinking 'bout Momma killed. I swallow it back down, breathe slow, keep it from coming again.

Lord, I miss Hazel.

✛

THE SCENT OF a woman is on me like lavender and sugar. Must be a negro 'cause she clean. But somebody oughta tell her she wasting her time trying to save me 'cause I think God mean for me to die here.

My eyelids is lighting up red so I reckon God's coming for me now. I peel 'em open, peek through to see God, but it ain't Him, just an open window above me burning my eyes with light and dust.

I close 'em, don't deserve to see the light no how, gon' accept my punishment, stop getting better. Sleep.

✢

I BEEN UP a long time today.

Tears for Momma and Hazel's keeping my eyes from burning.

The musk of tobacca smoke is in my hair. Must be what yellowed the wallpaper, turned its tiny pink flowers brown. I been catching a corner of the paper wit my fingernail, flicking it up and down, give me something to do 'til I die.

I reckon I got in this room yesterday or the day before cause the moon outside the window ain't changed much since the last time I seen it. The round of it looks like Mama Dean's spinning wheel, hanging in the sky, stuck on nothin.

The clouds are stretched across the moonlit sky like ready-to-spin cotton across a dark tabletop—pulled apart, kneaded back together, its different little pieces tangled into one. Mama Dean once told me, "We're all like this spinning cotton. A God-made thang. Blended together the pieces are strong. Apart, the wind gets them, blows them away, makes them dirty before they have a chance to make something beautiful." I reckon I'm like that cotton, blown-away dirty.

I can move an arm now. Can almos' touch the bed next to me. I ain't on a bed, though. What I'm on is something hard but dressed like a bed, with a pillow under my head and these heavy covers. I reckon it's a trunk cause I can feel a big latch on the side. It reminds me of the door knocker Hazel made for me. She'd carved a woodpecker from pine and put a string through its beak and a separate piece of wood so when you pulled the string, the bird would peck the wood. She said, "See, ain't all knockin bad."

My neck's sore from my jaw ache but I can move my head, can see the pattern on my sheets—more yellow flowers. I cross my eyes to fix 'em on the dry, gray stain below my chin. I take a big sniff of it but it don't smell like nothin. It's clean.

Across the room, a white chair stands in front of a vanity, a shawl with red feathers hangs lazy down its middle. The vanity holds perfume bottles, two drankin glasses and a washbasin. Wax is sliding down a lit candlestick there, too. Its holder got a pattern etched in it like Hazel's fire poker got. It brings my tears back 'cause I don't know where I lost hers.

I'll wait. Let Him take me peaceful.

⊹⊹

THE KNOCKIN SOUND woke me up but it ain't Momma and it ain't this trunk.

A white woman is on the bed in front of me with a man.

There ain't a wall, nothin between us.

She's on all fours, looking at the ceiling, grunting. Her face is a schoolteacher's but her act is a slave.

Her blonde hair is spiraled to her wrists and rocking back and forth. The naked man behind her is pushing, into her, cupping her tits with his hands now, rubbing her nipples with his fingertips. It's making me shamed to see so I close my eyes.

The man say, "Is she watching us, Cynthia?"

"Frank, just finish."

"I'm just saying. If she was, it would be sorta nice."

"*That* would be extra."

⊹⊹

THE DOOR ACROSS the room swings open and pushes a gust of wind over me, bringing men and their voices near to my bed. Their hot-whiskied breaths rain moist on my cheek. I keep my eyes shut. Pretend I'm dead. Let their funk, spit, and sighs blanket me. I won't move.

"You sure she out of it?" one of 'em say. "I ain't had one of these black whores in years."

"You think Cynthia mind?" another one say. "If we just . . ."

"She'd be making money, wouldn't she?"

The blood's pumping fast to my head now, my face is swelling, lips tight, eyelids sealing from swell, cain't open 'em if I wanted.

I hear a woman's voice: "You think that black bitch is better than me? Hell, I'm good enough for the both of yous."

"That sho' looks nice, Cynthia," one say.

My blood keeps rising. Everything go black.

⸭

THIS MORNING, A woman's humming a peaceful song and dancing nice with a little boy. He's barely tall as her armpit, standing on her shoes.

I ain't never seen hair so red.

She say, "I love you, Johnny."

⸭

I MUSTA BEEN sleeping good 'cause she changed my clothes and gave me a new pillow stuffed with mint.

The boy's gone.

A man's there in the boy's place, sitting on the corner of the bed with his back turned to me. His red neck looks like not-done meat with white lines creased deep and jagged across it. His grayish hair is lined with a razor's edge above his neck. I see him in the mirror smiling and when he laugh, his shoulders bounce. When he ain't laughing, his teeth poke out his mouth like a egg halfway out a chicken. He covers his mouth with one hand to hide it, lets his buckteeth wet his palm. When he pulls his hand away, he stretches his lips over 'em to cover.

The woman slouches in her chair, painting her makeup on. Her silk gown clings to her curves. The man was fixing to say something but took a deep breath instead.

Finally, he gets up and goes to her, puts his hands on her shoulders, squeezes. "Cynthia, I wanna take you away from here. Give you the good life."

Cynthia laughs out loud. "And make a good woman outta me, Nate?" She throws her washrag in the basin. "Take me away from my kingdom?"

She squats above her chair, smacks the wet rag between her legs, and swishes it around her privates, then stands up and sprays a burst of perfume there, too. She slides her frilly britches over her hips.

He puts his hands back on her shoulders.

"Come on, Nate. I got a headache and another customer. Just pay me and go."

"I'm serious," he say.

She clears the snot from her throat, hocks it in her rag, and throws it back in the basin, then falls back in her chair and takes a fancy silver box off the table. She pulls out a cigarette. "You still here?"

He grabs his hat and coat from off the dresser. Hiding under 'em is a bunch of yellow flowers. She smiles. "You gettin soft on me, Nate."

"I know you like yella," he say. "I could bring you flowers every day, if you let me. Be the man you want me to be." He crouches on one knee, holds the flowers out to her. She lets him rub her thigh. He say, "I love you. You know that. I could look after you. You could stop what you're doing here and just be mine."

Her expression softens.

"Hell," he say. "I'd even look after your bastard. Every boy needs a daddy."

She stiffens, lights her cigarette, sucks it started, and blows the smoke over his flowers, say, "I'm allergic to little dicks and spare change. So like I said nice before, get the fuck out."

His fistful of flowers slam across her chin and her hair spreads across her face. Yellow petals twirl across the room and blood rises from her split lip.

He say, "I . . . I try to do s-something nice for you. Look what you m-made me do."

She don't look at him.

"Just leave my money on the dresser," she say, her voice crackling. She picks up a glass of water and drinks. Blood rushes in.

The door slams when he go. It makes me jump but Cynthia don't. She keep puffing on her cigarette, then eases down in her chair and lets her legs gap open like a man. The strap of her gown slides off her shoulders, flashing bruises on her back. I ain't never seen a white woman with bruises like that.

Between her puffs, she spits out bits of blood from her lip, sprinkling her gown with dots of red. She wipes her mouth with the back of her arm, leaving a streak. It makes me scared for her.

"Don't look at me like you better than me," she say.

I close my eyes fast.

I can hear her turn her chair around to me.

"I've been keeping these dogs off your ass for twelve days."

I ain't never heard a woman talk like that.

"What brings you to Conyers, girl?"

I don't answer. Keep my eyes closed.

"Then let's start easy. . . . What's your name?"

I open my eyes. Don't say a word.

"How about my name is, 'Thank You For Saving My Black Ass.' Yeah, that's a good name."

She puffs on her stick again, glares at me, throws her feet up on the bed, slides back in her chair.

"Albert found you in the woods thirteen nights ago. Thought you was a wild pig, grunting and groaning so. Nearly stabbed you dead. Felt sorry for you since you busted your head wide open. Caught yourself an infection. Lucky for you, it was nothin I hadn't seen before."

Must be a nurse.

She exhales a line of smoke. "What was you doin out in them woods anyway? Ain't no town closer than forty miles. . . . What? Was you runnin north?"

I don't look at her.

"You people always tryin to run north like y'all ain't niggas up there, too."

I don't want to talk.

She throws my Bible, spinning it toward me, I catch it with my strong hand.

"Only thing you had on you 'sides this fire poker." She picks it up from next to the mirror, sucks on her cigarette. Smoke seeps out her nose. "No money, no papers. Like to have thrown you back. Where you from?"

It don't matter. I cain't never go back but when I get my strength, I'm gon' leave here, too. So I ain't got to listen to her. I press my Bible against my chest real hard, close my eyes real hard and start praying cause Hazel told me that God can understand me even if I cain't talk.

"Ain't gon' do you no good," Cynthia say. "The gods are dead. There's only us."

My ears pop open for the first time and sound rushes in, forcing me to sit up and pay attention. I can hear knockin all around me, behind these walls. I didn't hear it before, didn't feel it, smell it—the liquor, the perfume, sweat, reminding me of the times when Massa made Momma dress up and smile.

"This is my house," Cynthia say. "God don't own a half cent in my dime." She blows a funnel of white in the air.

I push myself against the wall 'cause I know God put me in hell. She laughs at me with bloody teeth, the taste of it turns her 'round to the mirror and she leans into her reflection, rolling her lip over and stares at the cut. She licks off what's left of the blood, then pushes her cigarette back in.

She stares at me through the mirror. "So you a runaway?"

I don't say nothin.

"Hell, girl. We all slaves to somethin." She turns herself to me.

I press myself straight against the wall, the furthest I could go without breaking through. She say, "I tell you what . . . runaway or not. You gon' need to earn your keep."

My body gets tight cause she gon' force me.

She reaches under her bed and throws a white sheet at me. A dress. Long and plain. "Here, you wear this."

I ain't gon' be Momma for her. Momma died so Hazel didn't have to be her, neither.

In one quick move, she grabs my poker from against the wall and shoves it far behind the dresser and relaxes back in her chair. She say, "That dress is the only thing I got decent. Wore it at my momma's funeral. It's clean. Mop and pail's in the closet down the hall. You gon' be cleaning up after us."

I wasn't expecting her to say that.

"I might get used to you," she say. "Keep things interesting around here. And don't you mistake it for kindness, cause when losing people get angry, they first turn on the kindest hand. You a loser?"

I shake my head.

"Good. Letting you stay here is no more than my good fortune of finding a slave for nothing. My pappy used to say, 'everythang cost somethin.' But you ain't gon' cost me, are you?"

I costed Momma.

Costed Hazel.

She grabs my arm and yanks me to her. "Law say, I should send you back where you came from. But I tell you the truth? . . . You steal from me . . . or run, I kill ya on sight."

7 / 1855

Tallassee, Alabama

LIFE CAIN'T BE taken for granted. 'Cause in the end it'll leave you with the worst kind of wanting. Like being desperate for something that came and went an hour ago.

That day, the word would rise and stretch and breathe sweetness from her mouth like warming dough. Then it would sink back down into her throat, undone. Just one and a half years old and Josey wasn't ready to speak her second word. Her first was "yes."

She'd fallen down that day, scraped her knees and elbows, had hit her head and started growing a knot in that place. When I got to her, I hung over her, listening and praying while she oozed blood and cried. I wanted to hold her, to kiss her where it hurt. And that moment is when the word fully formed in her mouth and she spoke it out loud. That m-word, that mmmm, that rounding, that calling to me, that kneading, wanting me to heal her bruising things, smear her tears away and cool her knots 'til they were all better. But this word wasn't served to me.

It was Annie Graham who came running. It was Annie who lifted her from the ground. And rocked her pain away. And I could have died again in those moments, quaking from this side of living. Wanted to steal it from Annie, take back what was mine, give back the name I died with—birth mother—trade it for plain Momma. But the choice had already been made for me. When they took my life, they took everything.

I've found peace in these years just watching and listening. I've swallowed the separation and been floating through this plantation, watching everybody, waiting, and hopeful that my baby's death far in the future won't be our first chance at reunion.

Truth is, I hadn't always intended to stay.

I meant to leave that first night I was killed, wanted to go and find my own Momma since we was both dead. Had said my good-bye to living but it's hard to leave when the person you saying bye to is still talking back. My baby was my hesitation.

There were things I still needed to tell her.

That she's beautiful. That she's loved. That there's a God who loves her.

That there's me.

But I cain't tell Josey none of that now. All I have is this.

It was her cry the night I died that got my attention. Not the smell of gunpowder in the air or the bitter taste in my own mouth. I was still near the place that I died when I heard her. Could see my blood on a broken branch. The moon was still full and merciful. I was on my way to find Momma. I needed to tell her I was sorry. Tell her I shoulda loved her better in the living. I was wrong to want her to be somebody else. Wanted her to be like them other mommas who were thanking God every day that her babies weren't sold and were kissing their fat cheeks. I wanted Momma to show me love that way, sloppy wet. I didn't understand life then. What it meant to be wrung dry. But I never found Momma.

The crying found me first.

I followed it through the woods into a warm and humid space. A scattering of footsteps overtook me. It was a white man carrying my baby and she was crying out for me. The man was Bobby Lee, escaped from his cousins on the promise he'd turn my baby into a profit.

Instead, he went to Annie's with her.

AFTER THE FIRST few weeks, I thought I'd leave Josey's side when I knew she was safe. Then I decided I'd leave after I saw her lift her head for the first time. Then, after she'd rolled over, then babbled, then walked, then ran. Then when. Then when. Then when.

Then, it got easy to stay.

And Josey's my reason.

Since daybreak, I been watching the sun shine on her seven-year-old body. Watched its light climb high to heaven, then pour itself over acres of green like spilling lemonade rushing to the floor. It drenched white plantation houses and seeped through trees and through me, splashed down on rows of chalky brown slave shacks, soaking through all of Tallassee, Alabama, and over the brown skins already busy in the fields. Bent over like broken stems, slaves are picking and washing and cleaning, chanting a melody of low tones and sopranos, a harmony set to the drums of palms, clapping. This is how I wait every day. Up in these trees watching the cool lips of morning kiss everything and start new.

This morning, the laughter of young children erased the echo of the bullet that took me. But trees don't lie so the hole's still there. My blood on its branches, long dried. Negro children are running past it, a group at a time, escaped from their fields, crunching leafs, swishing ground, and blending earth and the past together. The wind of 'em pass by me, their shapes come in glimpses and blurs—two boys, three girls, four boys, two girls, all of 'em seven-year-olds, all slaves, but the feel of 'em is free.

And there's my Josey. Happy. Happy 'cause God gives all children laughter. A time for happiness. To be joyful. A time before they learn who they are and what it means to the world—a woman, a slave, black.

What you've missed of her life so far only matters to me.

Not you.

Not yet.

"Nobody likes to listen intently about somebody else's child," Massa Hilden said to Momma about his sister's new baby. "Nobody care. Not unless it fucked up or it's dead."

Maybe Massa's right. Not about the harm but the gist.

JOSEY TALKS IN her head sometimes. She pretends to be a boy some-times, too. She once stood above the pissing pot, holding a short stick at her belly button, and just let her bladder go. It got all down her leg and around her thigh, stopped herself mid-flow to clean up after what girls ain't supposed to do—stand.

Being a woman means always having to bend at the knees even for the simplest relief.

So she ain't a bad girl. Just different, is all.

She don't curse but she spit. Digs for bugs but not boogers. She make knives and doll babies, wear trousers under her dress. Considers things most girls wouldn't. And certainly not at seven.

Even her singing voice is manly. She'll puff out her chest and hit low notes like an old black man. She's out in the field now singing "Swing Low, Sweet Chariot." Notes as slow and as deep as she can manage. Her "chariot" sounds like "cherry-uh-uht."

"Josey, please!" Ada Mae say, plucking the cotton from her ears. "Ain't enough cotton in da world to keep dat dyin dog noise out dees ears." Josey grins through her blonde strands and opens her mouth to start again, trying not to laugh or run out of breath before she gets the whole verse out.

I used to think she could see me.

I thought the both of 'em could.

Turns out Josey was just recalling the things her daddy had told her in the day and would repeat aloud like she was talking to somebody: "Read my lips," she'd say. "No." And, "Didn't I say no?" And, "No means no."

I was always near Josey then. Just a step away in her daytimes, and in her nights I'd be standing next to her bed, watchful. Waiting. Now I keep to the trees where I stay, mostly. Back in the corner of her room at night.

"Where'd you learn that horrible song," Ada Mae say.

"This song? Swing loooooooow. Sah-weet, chariot-ut . . ."

Josey chases Ada Mae, sucks in big breaths as she go, sending the air back out in song. They slip-slide on slick purple leafs and around a berry bush, scraping thin lines on their legs and arms from thorns. Ada Mae escapes in a twirl around a tree trunk. Her dress gathers between her legs from speed.

"Stop it, Josey! Promise me you gon' quit it or I tell you the truth, I'll leave you here and let the Witch of the Woods get you."

"These are my woods," Josey say. "Cain't nobody find me here if I don't want 'em to. And if you leave me here, you'll be here by yourself. Honest, Ada Mae . . . who would carry you but me?"

Josey's laughter becomes hard coughs. "All these negro children out here alone, about to get ate up," she say, coughing through it. "But you safe, Ada Mae. The witch would need a big ole mouth to eat you."

"Well, she ain't gon' eat you, neither. You ain't a negro."

"I'm black just like you!" she say. "Just not so colored, is all."

"Fine!" Ada Mae say.

"I'm negro, too!"

Josey's cough becomes barking. She squats where she is, hard-breathing like she just finished a long race. She closes her eyes and slowly lets air in and out of her throat. Swallows a few times. A whistle joins her exhale. I know these signs.

"You a'right?" Ada Mae say. "Need some water?"

Josey grabs her chest, clawing at it to squeeze a bit of air. Ada Mae pats Josey hard on the back, and each swat brings a short whistle. "You need some water?"

Josey's eyes redden with strain. She fixes 'em on Ada Mae and they roll back behind her closing lids. "I'll get Charles!" Ada Mae say, scared now.

But Josey grabs her arm, stops her, mumbles raspy words in a whisper. "Stay. Please."

Ada Mae sits and holds Josey's hand, wipes the sweat from her cheeks, hoping that Josey's panting will fade.

But her whistles rise. "One day," Josey say, "I'm gon' marry me a black man . . . dark as blue. . . . Then there ain't gon' be no mistakin who I am."

A whistle.

A whistle.

A whistle.

8 / FLASH

Conyers, Georgia, 1846

LAST NIGHT I took off running in the dark, escaping Cynthia.

HER CUSTOMERS LURK in dark corners here like shadows, except the whites of their eyes show and move when I move. Their voices call to me in whispers, hissing, one at a time and all together, "Hey! Pss . . . Gal. Come 'ere." I made the mistake of turning toward the sound last night and saw a man with his trousers down, his hand at his crotch, rubbing and tugging there. That's when I stole some shoes and ran. A month here's been long enough.

I had my Bible and Hazel's poker with me. Found the poker behind Cynthia's dresser before I left to follow the North Star to Boston where negroes belong to themselves.

I started running from 'round back of this brothel where Cynthia never go, then on the road past Albert's blacksmith shop. It was glowing orange from the furnace inside. The color traced every gap of the building. Grit from the road rolled under my soles and wet grass lapped my ankles. I was only five steps into the field when a sharp pain shot to my head and forced me to stop.

Blood shot out my nose in rhythm with my heartbeats. I pinched it and spat out what trickled in my throat, then staggered my final steps. I looked to the sky trying to find my North Star but there were so many. Their pinpricks of light grew to suns, blinding and burning. The world spun around me: Albert's shop . . . black space . . . Albert's shop . . . black space. I fell to my knees, needing to throw up. It was the last thing I remember.

I woke up late last night and found myself back at this brothel, laid out on the front steps with Cynthia's foot in my ribs. "What's wrong wit'cha?" she said, shaking me awake. "Still cain't talk?"

She kicked my shoes off and said, "Next time you choose whose shoes to steal, don't let it be Bernadette's. She got the foot fungus."

THIS MORNING, CYNTHIA woke me up before daybreak shouting, "If you well enough to go outside in the middle of the damn night, you well enough to cook breakfast."

So I got up.

A line of blood had dried and cracked between my nose and top lip. She threw a wet rag at me, said, "And I don't like the way you been taking certain liberties around this place. From now on, you keep to the side yard. And only in the day." So that's what I been doing since breakfast.

I keep to this patch of garden at the side of the house, and from here I can see most of everything east. And since we the last establishment on the east end, we must be double east. The rest of town is built west where I cain't see. But I got these rolling hills to look at and that empty green field across the road where Albert's workshop is.

Cynthia used to let me walk far back as the barn where I could get my tools. Now she keep my tools upside the house. Won't even let me go to the shed across the road 'cause she cain't see me good over there.

She watch me through her side window, always makes sure I'm working. But I don't mind. I love this garden. It gives me a reason to come outside and breathe. Cain't let her know that, though.

She's watching me now so I gotta look busy. I bend over the garden with my hand on my back, pretending it hurt. I touch my knees like they sore, squint my eyes closed, hem and haw out loud so she can hear me miserable.

She still watching.

I'm still gon' leave here and go north. But I got to get better first. Get all the way healed.

It ain't been all bad here. I cook sometimes and clean for all the nice ladies and Sam, too. Sam's the bartender. He always looks clean even though he got hair on his face—a beard trimmed short and square around his mouth. He keeps it closed most of the time—his mouth— only listening to customers tell him the same stories he's heard a thousand times. Sam nods anyway, pretends it's new, lets 'em keep him company while he wipes the insides of glasses and along his countertops, ready to ask the next would-be talker, "What can I git cha?"

Cynthia likes Sam 'cause he don't talk much. Maybe that's why she don't mind me, don't wanna hear too much lip from nobody and I don't talk.

I look to the window, slow. Cynthia's laughing at somebody but ain't looking this way.

She owns this brothel.

Said she bought it with family money. I ain't seen none of her family, though. Not even a husband. She told one of the girls that she too old for marrying, be thirty again next year. But that don't keep men from asking for her hand 'cause she's mostly pretty like my sister Hazel was. And if Hazel were here, she'd tell me she loves me, tell me she scared for me, tell me wait before I try running away again 'cause I coulda died last night.

I hear Cynthia's voice loud behind the window. Her chair's scooting like a duck honk across the floor. I sneak my eyes over to the window again.

She gone.

I put my hand on my back, lean back and forth trying to crack it and search that window while I do, just to make sure she gone. I hear my name gettin shouted. Again and again, "Naomi! Naomi!"

I run to the house, through the side door, toward Cynthia's call. I find her after going to two other rooms first. She in Bernadette's room, the old washroom. Sam followed me in.

Bernadette is screaming crazy in the corner and Cynthia's trying to hold her down, talk to her. A man, a customer, is standing next to both of 'em with no shirt on.

"Didn't you hear me call you!" Cynthia say to me. "Get me some towels."

I go to the cupboard inside the room, can see Bernadette shaking now. She got throw-up on the front of her dress and in her brown hair. She ain't much older than me. Cynthia found her at the train station with no money, no food. Been here two months working but she cain't stand no man touching her if she ain't had her medicine. Cynthia make it for her by mixing coca leaves in a shot of whiskey. Said Bernadette cain't live without it. It's the only thing that stops her from rubbing her arms and from being afraid of the dark, and men, and makes her *yes* come easier.

"What'd you do to her, Jessup!" Cynthia asks that man.

"I swear I ain't touched her, Cynthia. I took my shirt off and she started screaming hysterical. I swear it!"

"I told you she wasn't ready to come off it," she tell Sam.

I hand her the towels.

"Damn if I don't have to go back to that apothecary every month for you."

Cynthia wipes Bernadette's face. Her hair. Bernadette whispers something.

"I'm sorry," is what I think she said.

"Oh, you will get off it!" Cynthia say. "This ain't a drug den and you ain't staying here free. Sam, watch her 'til I get back."

Cynthia gets up and starts past me through the door. She stops. "And you don't go nowhere but upside this house working 'til I'm back. You hear me?"

"Yes'm," I say.

THIS MY GARDEN.

My piece of life.

When I'm in, I feel like it belongs to me.

That's how I pretend. How I know I belong someplace. 'Cause one day, we'll all be dirt again.

I fill my apron with all my vegetables. Two sweet potatoes. An onion. I don't move when a shadow slides across the ground in front of me. I've learned to ignore the fools who taunt me here—name calling, cursing, and those that hide in dark corners.

I hold tight to the sides of my pregnant apron, close my eyes.

He touches my shoulder.

I still don't move. I hear his footsteps come around in front of me. Just Johnny. The eight-year-old boy that Cynthia dance with. Her son. He squats down beside me with his hands on his knees. Got painted clay marbles peeking between his knuckles like dry fish eyes.

Sunlight floods his red hair and bursts an orange halo around his head while joined-together freckles start a stripe of brown across the center of his face, exploding in specks of auburn and sticking to all the white skin I can see. Even his bare feet are singed.

He picks up my sweet potato, flashing three of his knuckles, all of 'em got picked-off scabs. He puts the vegetable in my hand.

I don't know what to say.

I hold my throat, show him I cain't talk to thank him, nod my head instead.

He rubs his tired eyes. The bags underneath 'em are purple and black. Like he ain't slept in days. Cat naps is all he get and when he's behind the bar asleep on the floor, he'll shoot straight up awake sometimes,

probably reliving his daytimes in his nightmares—because daytimes is
when most the men come for his momma. Men, he cain't stop.

I saw him attack a grown man once.

I came in from fetching eggs; started my day in darkness and found
him waiting like a cowboy at high noon. He had readied hisself for the
man to come out his momma's bedroom, had his painted clay marbles
between his knuckles then, too. He caught me watching him so I smiled.
He turned away from me, focused.

I hid myself behind Bernadette's door. From there, I watched the
boy watch the man through the crack of his momma's door. Her noisemaking wasn't motherly. Only the parlor music that spilled in the hall
offered relief.

But when Man finished his pleasure inside Cynthia, Man held her
the way she holds Johnny at night. So when Man walked out, Johnny
beat him around the waist with both fists, caught one in Man's crotch.
Man twisted Johnny's arms behind him. Told Cynthia, control your
son, said, have a nice day.

Happened so fast, Cynthia didn't do nothin.

Johnny lets men walk by now.

He watches 'em go in her door one way, buckling their belts on the
way out. They step over him in the doorway like he ain't a boy wanting
his momma.

We all hear her good reasons through our thin walls and empty
hallways. She yell, she got bills to pay, his mouth to feed, clothes and
shelter Johnny needs.

We only grumble. Go back to our own hard days and hard nights.
I tend to my swollen and parched brown ankles—be on my feet all
day—got to shut up the voices in my head telling me to leave this place
and go north. But Johnny, he's tracking years, thinking of the future,
wanting his momma's touches, remembering the present as if it's time
already gone.

So sometimes, he'll hang on her arm when a customer comes, wanting her to touch him, even if it's to push him away.

Sometimes, he'll kick and scream 'til she picks him up—an accident hug—before she sets him at the end of the hallway.

Sometimes, when she in the middle of doing her business, he'll walk in on her. Stand next to her. Asking for water.

"YOU CAN HAVE it if you want," I tell him. It's the first time I've spoke since I got here. "The sweet potato," I say. I speak because I know what it's like to wait behind walls the way he do, to listen to a mother's music. But I had Hazel. He ain't got nobody.

He smiles. He don't talk, neither. Maybe he a real mute.

"You don't go tellin nobody I got a voice, you hear me?"

He laughs like a old man, in hoarse shrills.

"What's funny?" I say. He fixes his happy face on me and his expression reminds me of those times I seen him dance with his momma. Dance 'cause they both hurting. Dance 'cause she save her sinless moves for him.

He shrieks again and the sound makes me laugh the loudest I have since I been here. And it feels good, too.

Our laughter is the only thing we own.

9 / 1855

Tallassee, Alabama

AFTER THE VAPORS got Josey, Charles brought her here to the Graham house where she been resting. Got hisself sent home to wait 'cause he was pacing too loud and Missus Graham don't like to be near him long on account of his burn scars. Some people get nervous around bodies that move or look different, deformed or retarded. She's one of them. But I ain't leaving. Been passing time rushing 'round this big house and through its downstairs corridors, along dustless floors and hand-carved finishings. Been in the grand ballroom twice, along its papered walls and white moldings, and up to the ceiling where clear crystals hang.

I settle in this darkened hallway. Useless pretty furniture line the path to the room where Josey is. I go through its closed double door. The sun through the window casts a yellow mist of color, tinting everything. There's a stillness here. A quiet. This sound of *nothing* strikes me like deafness.

There's a chaos here, too. The way things been put together wrong. Like across the room, there's a statue of a naked baby angel on a white column and its base teeters on the thick edge of an African rug colored a mess of orange and red and green patterns. Above the fireplace, a gold frame holds prisoner the likenesses of a sad white woman and sad white man dressed in black. And next to it, muted green curtains climb the heights of two tall windows. Between 'em is a redwood bed shaped like a dead horse on its back. Mosquito netting swoops down from where the hooves would be and touches the floor.

A tapping near the window brings the sound back to the room.

Missus Annie Graham patters her foot below the hem of her blue satin gown making the fabric bounce and the light reflect off of its sewn-on silver flakes, spitting sparkle. The flakes follow the dress's neckline and make a trail down her shoulder and her crossed arms, where the white dots of light cast freckles on her angry face. Annie looks broken and old even though she ain't more than twenty-nine.

"Bessie," Annie calls to a dark-skinned field negro she's trying to train to be light. Light, 'cause most housework's done by the offspring of the raped: mixed-raced and birthed out of broken wombs. "Bessie," Annie say again, this time with her voice raised. She steps in front of Bessie and puts her hand near Bessie's neck. The touching makes Bessie shiver like a wet dog, drenched—a common condition for older slaves that Annie buys new. They must have never been shown mercy.

"How many times must I tell you?" Annie say. "Your collar needs to be pressed down. The ends are intended to remain straight throughout the day. Properly ironed and cared for. Not curled up in this fashion."

"Yes'm, Missus Annie." Bessie starts crying.

"There's a particular way to do everything. A right way," Annie say. "Do you understand me?"

"Yes'm."

"Why are you crying?" Annie say, stepping away. "Am I harsh in my instruction?"

Bessie puts her head down, shakes it slowly, "No, ma'am."

"When you do it right the first time, there's never a need to cry. Never a regret. It's either right or it's wrong. The sooner you learn that, the better. This will be what's required of you if you are to remain in this household. Do you understand me?"

"Yes'm, Miss Annie."

Annie snaps a loose thread from the second buttonhole of Bessie's blouse. "Everything in its right order." She puts the string in Bessie's hand. "Discard it properly," she tells her.

"Yes'm."

"And I don't mean for you to drop it along the way."

"Yes'm, Miss Annie."

Next to the bed, water trickles into a basin as a light-skinned slave twists a wet rag in it. When the rag stops dripping, she slides away the mosquito netting that surrounds the bed and lays the rag on Josey's forehead. Her body is drowned in covers, her head sunk into the pillow. Only the tip of her nose and her cracked pink lips show. She breathes lightly.

A lanky old white man, a doctor, sits down on the bed next to us and puts his big head on Josey's chest, listening. He sits up and puts his fingertips on the center of her ribcage, massaging around in little circles. He say, "It's not my intention to call to question your methods, Missus Graham, but I'd be remiss if I didn't say that it is highly irregular for this child to be in this house."

"Is her chest clear?" Annie say.

He lowers his head back down and listens just as Bessie comes back through the door carrying a cup of black coffee. "Place it there," Annie tells her, and Bessie sets it next to the basin.

Annie say, "Have you met Bessie, Doctor? She was trained by Mrs. Durand herself. Her coffee would stand against all challengers in these parts. Tea, especially."

"Training is one thing, Annie. But this gal in the bed . . ."

"She is my property, Doctor. I'll do what's best to see she's cared for."

"I urge you not to be so giving. This room . . . your good coffee. If Richard were here . . ."

"Bessie, try to wake her," Annie say. "Have her drink the coffee. It'll loosen her chest."

"Yes'm," Bessie say.

Bessie puts her hand behind Josey's head to lift her up to sitting, waking her for coffee. Josey takes a few sleepy swallows.

"I . . . I found that girl, Ada Mae," Bessie say to Annie. "She was peeking through the window downstairs. I thought you might want to have a word so I . . . She's in the hall . . ."

"You brought her in here?" Annie say, meeting eyes with the doctor. Doctor folds his arms like he told her so. "Where is she now?"

Ada Mae comes through the door slow and with her clothes still stained with berry juice and dirt from playing earlier. She stutters, "I . . . I was just comin 'round for Josey. See how she was. She got the vapors when we was playin and . . . I ain't too sure how it started. Could be the berries or could be . . ."

"Do you think it's acceptable to come in my house dirty?" Annie say, her voice rising. "Like some naked African fresh off the boat. Some kind of vile creature," she yell. "Answer me!"

"No no, Missus Graham."

"Then why have you insisted on bringing your filth into my house? Get out! And the next time you try to kill another one of my slaves, I'll have you and your momma strung up like runaways. You hear me?"

Doctor seems pleased.

"Yes'm," Ada Mae say, trembling.

"Well go!"

The wind of Ada Mae's sprint makes the door yawn and Josey comes wide-awake. Annie leans over Josey's bed. "And you. If I have to spend another dime to treat your carelessness, I'll sell you off!"

"Yes'm," Josey say, breathy.

From the other side of the doorway, hands clap together, loud and slow. "Bravo," a man's voice say before his muddy black boots stomps across the threshold shaking brown chunks to the floor. Newly growed to manhood, about eighteen, George is two feet taller than he was the last time I saw him but he still small—the same size as Annie is now. "Brilliant," he slurs, drunk. "Wonde'ful."

"Bessie, come and clean this up," Annie say, pointing to the mud.

"Was that little performance for the doctor's sake, or yours?" George say. "It was . . . quite amusing." He burps, then covers his mouth, dainty and polite-like, making hisself chuckle. He steps out of his boots, front ways, over the tongue of 'em, kicks 'em back into the hallway with his heels, then staggers toward Annie in his stocking feet, swaying from side to side.

"George, this isn't the time," Annie say.

He grabs her around the waist and lifts her up, grunting as he do. She stiffens in his skinny arms, her pretty puffed dress crushed to a wilted flower. "That's enough," she say, shoving her forearms in his chest. He holds on to her anyway, pulls her closer.

"I can't show my big sister how happy I am to see her? Been back three days and you haven't even hugged my neck yet." He swishes his sweaty hair in her chest, laughing, while the sweet funk of alcohol rises off of him.

"I told you to stay out of the cordial," Annie say.

"Always telling me what to do," he say and drops her directly. He reaches in his coat pocket for a metal flask, undoes the lid and swallows a few gulps of something strong before teasing the flask under her nose. "It'll sweeten your disposition."

"Doctor," Annie say, clasping her hands in front of herself. "Wouldn't you like to use the washroom? Down the hall. Last door on the right." She waits for Doctor to understand that her question wasn't a question and when he finally do, he nods before he go.

George strolls around the room, drunk-grinning, pretending to ponder the sad people on the wall. "When's your husband supposed to be back?" That's the third time he's asked about Richard in as many days.

Richard's been gone for years and with no word to Annie on when he plans to come home. George has known the fact since the first time he asked, but annoys Annie with the question anyway.

"Bessie, come and help me fold these clothes," Annie say, reaching for her basket of folding.

Annie shoves a blouse into Bessie's hand and takes a pair of bloomers for herself to fold.

George twists his flask open again but before he sips, he stops and squeezes out gas from his backside. A shame, really. George used to be a pretty boy. Striking, even. And polite. The sight of him—dark-haired with eyes the color of purplish stones—used to be enough to stop me from doing my rounds through this property. I'd stop just to stare at him.

He was twelve years old when I first took notice. It was the year after I first come. He had an odd beauty about him, his features verging on manhood, even at that age. He was slim like a boy, and poised like a young man, but his Adam's apple was pronounced like full-grown, his lips a dark-pink rose. Girls had noticed him before he'd noticed himself. At twelve, his focus was still on building forts and wooden trinkets. Inventions, he called 'em, and his imagination took him everywhere he needed to be, gave him a place to escape.

Josey coughs from the bed, hard and will-less, the bout sending coffee through her nose and out her mouth. Annie tells Bessie, "Give her a cloth and a little more coffee. Slower this time."

George takes a sip from his flask, then strolls around to the bed, sits down on it, falls back like it's his, stares up at Josey. "Goddamn, they're looking more and more like us every day. Pretty soon we'll all be coons."

"Off the bed," Annie says.

"*Me*, off the bed," George laughs. "What in the hell will your husband say when he finds out you've been having niggers in the guest bed?"

"What I do in my house is nobody's business," Annie say.

"Hell," he say, getting up. "If you like it, I love it. Just keep it out of my room." He takes a mouthful of drink and squints from the burn.

"I heard about what happened in Montgomery," Annie say, folding a pair of britches.

George's manner changes. He slowly puts the lid back on his flask and slides it in his pocket. He walks back to the sad people like he ain't seen the painting before. "Is that right?" he say.

"I know what the authorities said . . . ," Annie say.

"All I did was give the girl a toy."

"You were the last one to be seen with her."

"Prove it," he say, leaning back against the wall. "You believe 'em?"

"Doesn't matter what I believe. No one is asking anymore and that other girl, the Humphrey girl from up the road, moved away years ago."

"That wasn't true, neither. Children will say anything."

"She was five years old, George!"

"More reason for her to lie. Play make believe. Children will say anything." He pushes hisself off the wall. "I'm beginning to believe you'd trust strangers before your own brother."

"I never said I believed them."

"Is that why you sent me away?"

"That school was good for you," Annie say. "Besides, it wasn't me who sent you."

"You didn't stop it either . . ."

"Our parents knew what was best for you."

"They're dead," he said. "But I'm still here, Annie."

"That school was supposed to make you . . ."

"Distant?"

"Happy."

"You used to hate that place as much as I did, Annie. You used to say it kept us apart. Best friends, remember? Then you let your husband send me there again."

"University is not the same. That was a privilege. You could have come home anytime."

"That's funny."

"Before then, you were a child. You needed something we couldn't give you. It helped you to mature . . ."

"You stopped writing—"

"To become a man."

"Never an explanation why."

She shakes a pair of trousers from the basket. "I'm happy you're home now. That's all that matters."

"That's *all*? You mean, that's all for you. You didn't have to go through it. That's all. Telling me that I need to move on, that's *all*." His face reddens and his cheeks quiver. "Eight years, Annie! Three weeks it took for me to get the news that Mother and Father died."

"They were my parents, too!"

"And you didn't send for me . . ."

"You'd only been there a few months. With everything that had just happened to you, your state . . . I didn't know what it'd do to you. It was the best decision . . ."

He rips the trousers from her hand. "What happened to you?"

She closes her eyes. "I wanted to protect you. You weren't ready. You needed to mature. Children have to grow up sometime, George. That's what they do."

"I suppose I didn't do that right, either." He flicks the trousers to the floor.

The doctor knocks on the door, opening it at the same time as he knocks. He walks in and leans over Josey, laying his head on her chest, listening. "Her vapors have gone."

"Thank you, Doctor," Annie say.

He gathers his tools.

"And, Annie?" Doctor say. "You should reconsider your position on the matter. These negroes have no place in the house like this."

10 / FLASH

Conyers, Georgia, 1847

FOR THE BETTER part of this week, me and Johnny been shooting marbles. We mostly play in secret and only after my chores is done. Mostly. Johnny's good at keeping secrets.

His momma's been spending more and more time running to that store for Bernadette's medicine and been rough-sketching something she wants Albert to build under her house. She been gone for most of the day already so Johnny drew a circle in the dirt hours ago. We just dropped our marbles in. All but one of our little ones and a big one. Two each.

The big one is called our shooter. I painted mine blue and it got three stick people on it, holding hands—me and Hazel and Momma. But it mostly look like a spider.

Johnny's shooter got all sorts of colors—blue and black and white and tan. He used all the pots of color Cynthia gave him to do it. I think his is pretty.

I drop my shooter outside the circle and lay my body down in front of it, my flat chest in the dirt. I put my thumb behind it, close one eye to make sure it's all lined up. My breaths make the dust putter.

Johnny snatches my shooter, laughing.

"You cheatin'!" I say. "I was about to shoot."

He holds out his hand, teasing me with my own marble, and closes it before I get it. So I wrestle him for it, both us laughing. I twist his arm and shake it from his limp hand. He lifts his chin toward the barn and smiles.

"What?" I say. "Your momma kill me if I go out that far. And if you keep going out to that barn after she told you not to, she gon' kill you, too."

He raises his brows, daring me.

I admit, the risk-taking makes me want to go. It feels like freedom. Reminds me of Hazel and our dusk runs.

I take off with Johnny. Close my eyes and pretend I'm back with Momma and Hazel, pretend that Johnny's one of Momma's gave-away babies here to let me be a big sister one time.

I let the grass brush under my feet, the cool air swish over me, half-waiting for Cynthia's voice to yell me back to my place and keep me from this stole happiness.

The barn meets us.

Its tall front doors are dark-brown masses, three times my height, streaked black and wet. They gap open wide enough for us to slide through sideways without touching.

We hold hands and shuffle our feet through the hay spread on the ground, then around a column, past another, 'til Johnny stops us near the back of the barn where there's a broken baling machine. Wood planks lay atop two hay bales there like a roof. He lifts the planks.

Four yellow puppies are trembling inside. The runt ain't moving much, though. That's the one Johnny picks up and holds to his chest. Johnny smiles and nods for me to pick one up, too, but I shake my head. I ain't got nothin to give it. "Where's the momma?" I say. He raises his shoulders, rubs the sickly one again. It moves for him.

"You probably shouldn't get attached to that one. It don't look well."

He turns his back to me, presses the puppy into the crook of his neck, and kneels down to a pail of milk ready for churning. He takes a cloth from his pocket and dips it in the milk, then holds it to the pup's mouth. Squeezes.

"Johnny, you steal this milk?"

He don't hear me.

"Johnny?"

Cynthia's voice rumbles from up the road. She loud-talking, yelling to somebody. "We in trouble now!"

Johnny puts the pup in his shirt and points ahead to a open place in the barn wall and waves for me to follow him. We climb through the space, then run across the field, keeping low to the ground. My legs move as fast as they can go, leaving Johnny behind. I wait 'round the side of the brothel house, can hear the clinks of glass from Sam serving, so I take my chance and run toward the center of the garden, my head held back, my fringe bangs flying straight up in the air. I dive, sliding to a stop, pretend I been here all along, looking at something in the dirt. My knees are scraped and burning but I stay cross-eyed, focused on a clover, waiting for Cynthia to see me.

Instead, I hear her on the porch talking to somebody, but this time, from here, it don't sound quite like her. Pete is standing where she should be with a voice that's high, like a woman's. He's yelling and talking to Jessup using Cynthia's tone. I laugh and thank God it weren't her and spit the dirt out my mouth, stand up and bend over to brush my clothes down.

A man's voice behind me say, "I like the look of that."

"Um-hm," another man say.

"That makes three," comes a third. My breath catches.

I turn around and see 'em close to me.

All of 'em are tall and lanky. Brothers, maybe. It's their voices I remember. That night in Cynthia's room, when they came ready to take me in my sleep.

"Why you reckon Cynthia's been protecting you so much?" the first one say.

I don't answer.

"What brings you to Conyers, girl?"

I cain't speak.

The second one comes over to me, walking wide-legged. He slides his hand down my backside, pinches my ass with his whole hand. My lips quiver but I ain't gon' cry.

"It's about time we had a go," he say, unbuckling his pants.

"Right here? Right now?" the third one say. "In the broad daylight?"

I cain't move.

"Let her 'lone!" I hear her say. Cynthia is running down the stairs coming this way with her two pistols popping in the air. "Let her 'lone!"

The first man, the leader, backs up with a hand in the air. With the other, he pulls me close to him, say, "Whoa now, Cynthia," and puts me half in front of him.

She waves both pistols across everybody. She say, "I said, let her 'lone, Jonas."

"Just having some fun, is all," Jonas say. "We'd have paid you."

"She ain't one of my girls."

"Then this ain't none of your business," he say.

She fires in the air again. "I reckon it is."

"You crazy," the second brother who had his hand on my ass say.

"I'm crazy, Tommy?" Cynthia points her pistol at him. "That wasn't what you was saying three nights ago when you were crying on my shoulder about the bitch that stole your shit and you still want her back."

Tommy steps behind Jonas.

"You hiding, now? Way I see it is I made it a fair fight. It was three on one and now, me and my Walkers here make it three on three. The girl don't hardly count."

Jonas tears a pistol from behind his waist and points it at her.

Cynthia gets real still.

Everybody do.

I hear us breathing.

"We at a stalemate," Jonas say.

"I don't reckon so," Cynthia say, keeping her eye and one pistol on him.

She dumps all the bullets except for one out of her other gun without looking, and snaps the chamber closed. "Sometimes, the only thing between life and death is luck. Ain't no rhyme, no reason, no God to come save you, just Lady Luck."

"Don't give me your bullshit, Cynthia. You can take the girl and we'll go."

"How lucky you think I is?" she say.

She takes the pistol with the single bullet and presses it against her head.

I close my eyes.

She fires—click, click, click.

I open my eyes, breathing hard. She points the pistol back at the men.

"There weren't no bullet in there," Jonas say. "Some kind of trick. Tommy, grab her guns!"

Cynthia flicks her wrists, daring him.

Tommy don't go.

"This ain't none of my business," the third man say, straightening hisself like he just stopped by to say hi. He say, "So I'll just go . . ."

Cynthia stares at 'im with dead eyes and tilts her head sideways, enough to make him want to stay.

"You ain't gon' shoot," Jonas say. "How will that look to the law? A whore shooting upstanding citizens like ourselves."

"Regular pillars of the community," Cynthia say, laughing. "Hell, law can only take me to jail or hell, no place I ain't already been."

She keeps the fully loaded gun on Jonas. The other one she holds directly at Tommy's head.

Jonas say, "Don't worry, Tommy. Ain't no bullet in there." But Tommy don't move.

Nobody moves.

Cynthia lowers the pistol she got pointed at Tommy and fires. Its sound is like rocks hitting together, but louder.

Tommy screams, grabbing his hand where the bullet grazed, blood spills through. He clinches his hand between his legs, knees the dirt, whining and rolling around.

Cynthia don't flinch. "Jonas?" she say. "Now how lucky you think you is?"

"You bitch!" Tommy say.

She fires her pistol near him again, burying a bullet in the ground. "Shut up. It's just a graze."

He opens his hand, sees the flesh ripped, holds the wound closed and clinches his teeth, swearing and spitting through 'em.

Jonas lets go my arm. He pushes me to Cynthia, his voice shaking. "I'm trusting you now, Cynthia. You know we was just messing around. G'wan and take her. We don't want no trouble."

He backs away, pulling the third man away with him, and nudges Tommy with his foot. Tommy's still whining.

"Quit yer crying," Cynthia say. "You can pay me with the other hand." She keeps her pistol on 'em when she grabs me and together we snake our way backward to the brothel house.

I think Cynthia's gon' keep me safe, after all.

11 / 1860

Tallassee, Alabama

THE WIND SWISHES through ancient treetops, spraying leaves from their perches, tumbling the gold ones to the ground. They roll along green fields, tickling thin grasses—a soft touch to the hard ting of Josey's daddy, Charles, blacksmithing. Three weeks of rain has brought every living thing to the surface. Worms and even roots are ground cover now, flattened 'cause everybody's trampling over 'em.

A dirt road runs between Charles's shop and the cotton field where rows of negroes are bent over and reaching for the next burst of white on a cotton stalk. Their dark faces and hands seem to sprout from their muted clothing—men in gray overalls and women in long gray dresses and headscarves. The children's hands sting from pulling weeds 'cause their palms ain't calloused like Josey's. Two years 'til she's a teenager and she's careless with her picking, careless with her sitting, careless with her running. She rounded a corner this morning, headed toward the slaves' quarters, going too fast to see the black boy who was carrying the basket of food. She hit him whole-bodied, his spilled cabbage heads rolled, and Josey crawled after 'em but they were already ruined, he said. "Cain't sell 'em like this," he said. Sheets of cabbage leafs peeled away.

"You all right?" Josey said. He didn't answer.

The boy was about Josey's age and, compared to her, harmless. I gave him the name Wayward years ago because of the way he comes and goes on this plantation without much notice. He don't belong here. He takes shortcuts through this property three or four times a year carrying vegetables and fruits bound for market trade across the river. If somebody asks, he'll lie and say he's selling for the Graham household. Confusion and his look of purpose—his *look-busy*—keeps people from asking more questions. But I do. I do 'cause of how he stops and stares into Josey's yard sometimes, waiting for a glimpse of her. And when he get one, his expression turn to mush.

Josey's legs are splayed open now like a boy. But she's covered and sitting next to Ada Mae and near the other negro children. From here, she looks like a white watermelon seed among the black ones. Frail-looking and out of place.

She sings a made-up song and pulls without looking, belting out another note now, the longest that ever was, and Ada Mae looks to the sky for mercy.

Across the field, Slavedriver Nelson stands in the dirt with his steed and no hat on letting the sun beat down on his blood-orange face. His lashes shade his pale-blue eyes as he squints through the sunlight to see his negroes in the field. When the light hits his eyes directly, their color disappears, then reappears when the full shadow of his towering horse passes over him. I float around 'em both, watching how Nelson runs his fingers through her mane like he's petting a dog. Calls her Maybelle.

The offbeat trot of another horse draws our attention. Up the road, I can see the rider coming closer. It's George. He bobbles on top of his horse seeming lightweight and as small as a ten-year-old. His bobble becomes quick ticks when his horse picks up speed, jerking George this way and that. Like George cain't control it. He's headed right this way in a hurry.

Nelson yells, "Whoa! Whoa! Whoa!" But it don't slow.

Maybelle neighs. And again.

George jolts awake and pulls the reins late. He's laughing when it stops in front of Maybelle. "You shoulda saw the look on your face. You thought I was going to run y'all over."

"You had me, sir, Mr. George. Didn't know if you was well or sleep or . . ."

George's eyes draw closed, falling asleep, the musk of alcohol rises from under his clothes. "Are you saying I drink too much?" George say with his eyes still closed. "Are you my sister now, boy?" He calls Nelson "boy" even though Nelson's an old man. Still, Nelson don't flinch at it.

"Naw, sir, Mr. George."

"Well then. I did it 'cause its funny. That's funny, ain't it, boy?"

Nelson say, "Maybelle can spook easy, is all. Didn't want her running off."

George falls off the side of his horse, sliding in an almost split. Nelson tries to catch him but it's too late. George lie on the ground like he dead this time. Nelson goes to lift him. "Get away from me," George say, brushing hisself off and pushing up to a stand. His knees give out again and Nelson reaches his hand out to him. George gags. Covers his mouth. Gags again like his tongue is pushed all the way down his throat. He throws up, keeps throwing up, spraying warm mud made of runny food, alcohol, and dirt on his shoes. "That's what I get for eating second," he say, dry heaving now.

Nelson gives him a mug of fresh water and a cloth that George runs around his face. He swallows a gulp of water, then swishes the next around and spits it. Behind him is a hay bale that's twice as tall as he is. He leans back on it and catches his breath. "I bought my first horse when I was eight. A saddlebred mare, died just before I got sent away the first time. Broke my heart." He reaches under his coat, pulls out a silver flask, puts it to his lips. A gust of wind sweeps his eye and pushes a tear out.

Nelson watches it roll down George's cheek. Nelson say, "I know how hard it is to lose one, sir. I can tell you bonded with her, let her get you on the inside, made the magic happen." Maybelle nudges Nelson with her nose, blows quick snorts. Nelson tugs her closer.

"When I look at my Maybelle," Nelson say, "I know she could trample me at any second if she wanted, out muscle me, but on the road she let me control her every move. I'm her master. We understand each other. Me and Maybelle connected." A low tone rolls from Maybelle's belly. He trades her affection with a rub along her neck. "I love her more than I like most people."

"You are one sick bastard," George say. "It wasn't the damn horse that broke me, it was getting sent away. And how in the hell could you love a goddamn horse?"

George bends down and picks up a small rock, hurls it at a squirrel in the road that was twitching to break a nut. When he misses, he throws his mug at it, too, tries to chase after the squirrel and sends it up a tree. George bends over gagging and breathing hard but no throw-up come this time. He looks over his shoulder, say, "I reckon if that squirrel rubbed your leg, you'd move it in your house, call it best friend."

Nelson only mumbles under his breath, shimmies the saddle 'round Maybelle. Don't talk to her this time. Don't stroke her, either. Don't show no care. He climbs up on her and just sits.

George shuffles hisself to the center of the road where he staggers back and forth in a circle, looking for something out in the field where Josey is. He say to Nelson, "Where's that washed-out negro girl that's supposed to be working?"

"You got a few that look like that, sir."

"I mean, the one that looks like you."

"Beg pardon?" Nelson say sharp. "Ain't one drop of me nigger!" George don't pay him no mind, staggering in a circle again, working on keeping his head the right way 'round.

Nelson say, "All of 'em out there working, sir. None missin. I flog the stragglers."

"The children?"

"I do my job, Boss. Don't need no nigger setting his mind to mischief, five or fifty-five. Let one get away wit something, they all start. I only got one whip."

George reaches back to his horse and unlatches a large cloth bag. It falls to the ground from inattention, tumbling white shirts and woolen trousers to the dirt. He say to Nelson with a newfound joy in his tone, "I'm here to distribute the negroes' clothes. Came from England on Monday's shipment. Give 'em each two shirts and a pair of trousers for the year."

George unlatches a pine hoop from the side of his horse. From the ground the hoop stands to his waist. He unties a matching pine stick, too. It's about the length of three middle fingers high. He starts to the field with 'em.

"I wouldn't go favorin' none of 'em," Nelson say. "They get jealous, making more work for me."

George keeps in Josey's direction, walking like an old man or like one leg is shorter than the other. He uses the hoop as a walking stick over the moist and uneven ground. I get beside him, follow him in.

He stops in front of Ada Mae and Josey. They get to looking busier than ever like they don't see him. He slaps the hoop on Ada Mae's closed bag 'til the bag blossoms open and shows its brown, dying weeds.

"Massa George?" Ada Mae say. "We was workin so fast, we didn't see you come up."

"That's good work y'all doin there," he say to Ada Mae, pretending not to notice Josey. He dabs his throw-up rag on his fo'head, clearing the sweat. He talks to the air around Josey. "I got this here wheel. It's a game, see, a toy called a rolling hoop." He taps the hoop on the ground in front of Josey with it. "You push it with this stick, make it go."

Ada Mae sits up but Josey keeps her eyes low, working, and only say, "Yes, suh."

"I was looking for some good worker to reward. Any idea who deserves it?"

"No, suh," Josey say.

"Yes, suh," Ada Mae say.

"Nobody?" he say to Josey, nudging her with the hoop, then dropping it down in front of her.

"Don't think it be right for you to give it to me, suh," Josey say. "We all work hard."

George's face flushes red and he grabs the hoop, "It wasn't for you no how!"

"Yes'sa," Josey say, keeping to her work, her head down.

"I got better things to do!" he yell. "You just remember that I'm the one who decides who gets and who don't."

"Yes'sa."

"I own you!" he say and yanks Josey's bag from her hand, drop-kicks it across the field, spilling weeds. But his kick snatches his other leg from under him and he lands flat on his back, moaning in the dirt. He rolls over and grabs his hoop before hopping up to a stand. He tosses the hoop to Ada Mae and hobbles back across the field to the road.

"Look it, Josey!" Ada Mae say. "Look what I got."

"I thought he was gon' pass us," Josey say, bitter, brushing dirt off her knees. "Where'd my bag go?"

Ada Mae squats down and rests her hoop on her thigh and reaches for a weed, pulling it careless, then slices her hand with it. She yelps and sucks the edge of her palm but Josey don't ask if she's all right. Instead she say, "Cain't nothin good come from him favorin' you, Ada Mae. Not all gifts is good gifts."

Cotton castaways float up from Ada Mae's bag and get pushed away by the moving silence of her breath.

12 / FLASH

Conyers, Georgia, 1847

I AIN'T ALLOWED IN the garden since what happened yesterday.

Cynthia say from now on I got to wake her up in the morning before I start my day's chores, but, "Yours ain't the first voice I want to hear in the morning," she said. "So just tug on my toe before you go."

She left for a date on Bernadette's bed a little while ago. Said Bernadette ain't making her money no way so I've been making the most of my time in here alone. I been sitting in front of Cynthia's mirror, twirling her tiny pot of red lip stain. Stroked her small brush across its mouth.

One of the legs on this chair is missing a bottom piece, broken. It wobbles from side to side, like a gimp man dancing.

I read my Bible.

But, if I'm honest, I'm just laying my face on it, crossing my eyes to see the words. Candle wax is cooling in bumpy lines down the candleholder. I scratch my nails down it, let its softness pack under my nails and push back the meat. I flick it out with my thumb and drop the clump back in the candle's flame. It falls through it but don't melt much. Just enough to stick and harden when it slides to the tabletop.

The flame stutters again when the door blows open. I sit up quick, pretend I'm reading.

It's Albert, the negro. He say, "Sorry, didn't know nobody was in here," and starts closing the door back on hisself.

"It's all right," I say. "You can come in." But he don't come. He stay on the other side of the door speaking to me.

"Cynthia sent me to fix that chair. But I do it some other time."

"Naw, come in," I say. "I wasn't doing nothin."

He creeps the door back open and I slide off the chair and go to my trunk. When I sit, my thighs bulge and spread under my dress like rising pancake batter.

"It's good to see you better," he say.

He kneels next to the chair and rocks it back and forth checking which leg's broke. Its wood shoe is split. He takes out some sort of grinder from his satchel, some binding glue, and a wood piece from his pocket.

I watch him while he busy hisself fixing it.

He got big ears.

They cupped like hands on the sides of his head. I don't know why they like that 'cause he ain't one to listen in on other people's conversations. His wild reddish hair is so puffy and high, he must got some other blood mixed in him worser than I got. But his eyebrows is black. And thick. He got freckles, too.

Cynthia call him the "Scottish Banshee" on account of all the red. She said when she took him in a few years ago, she did it cause she felt sorry for him. He was a free slave who never made it north. She reckon he afraid to leave, afraid he's gon' get stopped, afraid some white fool gon' ignore his papers and send him back to slavery anyway. Sometimes she say she never shoulda treated him so good in the first place 'cause now she cain't get rid of him.

But he helpful to her.

He fix things, do all the blacksmithing around here, cleaning sometimes, too. Me and him ain't never talked even though we both negro.

White peoples don't like to see black folks together no how. Always suspecting the worse like we plotting, or must be lovers drawn together by some black magic they don't understand. So me and Albert keep our distance.

He reaches for his glue from the floor and smears some on his new piece of wood, then puts it on the broken leg.

"Thanks for saving me," I say.

He don't answer.

"Cynthia told me you did."

He nods, holds the new foot in place.

"You do a lot of things 'round here," I say. "You should know you appreciated, is all."

He still don't talk.

"Why you don't cut your hair?" I say.

"'Cause it's mine," he say. "My hair's my freedom. I can do what I want with it, when I want. I'm a free man."

"If you free, why you here?"

"You ask too many questions that ain't none of your business."

"You slept wit Cynthia?"

He stops working. Rolls his head 'round his neck like he cracking it and just stare at me. He starts working again.

He's funny.

Easy to bother.

I say, "A young man like you should be finding a wife and a home."

"I'm thirty-seven years old," he say, stopping again. "Ain't been a young man a long time. What you? Sixteen, seventeen? I got at least twenty years on you, girl, so don't fool yourself into thinking you know somethin."

"I know you here," I say. "But you say you 'free.' Been here five years and still do what you told, eat when you told to, sleep in the field. 'Free.'"

"Child," he say, smiling now, like I'm the one who said something funny. "How you know I ain't saving my money, readying to go north?

Buy some land, build a house, find a strong, feisty woman there and make her my wife."

"I'll help you find her so long as you take me north with you when you go."

"Naw, the woman who'd marry me ain't north," he say, closing his glue pot. "I reckon she's south already. Over the border in Mexico."

"A Mexican?"

"A negro. Runaways and freed men been escaping south of Texas for years. Even the ones that go into Mexico as slaves is finding their freedom there. It ain't like here."

"You mean negroes ain't slaves everywhere?"

"Not in Mexico. We got a kinship with Mexicans in Texas. They like us. A captive people, too, but on their own land. This country's their homeland. They didn't migrate here or been stolen and brought here like us. They been moved out, off their land, piece by piece. So they don't allow slavery."

"Freedom's north. Everybody know that. You said Mexico's south."

"Freedom is wherever you find it."

"Then mine's north. Always been north. Always be north."

"You don't know everything," he say. "There are men. Good men. Quakers from out east. God-fearing. Risking their lives to get negroes to Mexico. Got the burning in their hearts to do so, and the fearless-ness of a child who'd defy his own hunger to free an animal being led to slaughter. They're what you call zealous men. Doing God's work."

"And taking slaves to Mexico?"

Albert packs his stuff. "Like I said, you don't know everything."

The door shuts soft when he go. I sneak over to his fixed chair and sit in it. I go easy on it at first so I don't mess up his work. I lean back in the chair to see if it's still lame but it don't clunk no more.

I bring my Bible back to me and start reading from it, catch my reflection in the mirror again, see my top lip disappear when I read the word "thee" or when I smile big.

I'm still flat-chested.

Hazel promised they was gon' grow but they never did. If I knew
back then that they never would, I woulda been stuffing my dress with
stockings so Hazel wouldn't feel bad that I weren't a woman.

I still pretend that Hazel is sitting with me sometimes, talking to me,
reading with me. I slide my Bible to myself again, imagine Hazel saying,
"Now you read."

"The Lord is my Shep . . . Shep . . . hard. Shep . . ."

"Shepherd," Cynthia say coming in, slamming the door. She throws
her money down next to me. "So you can speak."

I get up quick and grab my Bible on the way back to my trunk.
Cynthia pulls her bra straps down from her shoulders. She rolls down
her britches and steps out of 'em, then throws 'em across the room to
her pile of soiled things.

I clear my throat. "Thank you for what you did yesterday."

"Um hum," she say, taking off her dress. She slips her silky gown
over her head. Lights a cigarette.

"You weren't scared?" I say.

"Scared? They was the one's who needed to be scared. Jonas was
glad he wore his tight pants so his shit didn't fall out near his ankles."

She folds her dress and with her shoes makes a stack. I take 'em,
when she finish. Carry her dress to the basket for washing and her shoes
I put with the others. I say, "The way you used them guns . . ."

"Asshole charmers," she say. "You heard of snake charmers? Snake
charmers hypnotize snakes with flutes and shit. My guns do the same
to assholes."

She blows a stream of white.

"And they're a good distraction," she say. "Keeps 'em in a trance
long enough for my girls to pick a pocket, shop, and be back with empty
wallets by the time the game is through."

"But you could kill yourself."

"And?"

"You could be dead."

"And by the time of my funeral, my girls would be best dressed. Now, if you finished with your concern, gon' and get my bath water ready."

"Naomi," I say. "My name. It's Naomi."

"All right, Naomi . . . get yer ass up and fix my bath water."

"Yes'm."

I run across the hall to the bath where I already put her water. I pour flower oil in it 'cause she like that. I always bathe her and wash her hair. It's nice hair.

I make sure it ain't too cold, pour in a little more hot from my kettle, then cool from my pitcher. It's just right. Five lit candles make the room yellow and warm. I give it one spray of perfume to clean the air and float a lily on top of the calm water.

Cynthia bursts through the door, drops her towel, and stomps in the bath, splashing water everywhere. Her cigarette bounces from her bottom lip, she say, "It's always them little-dick mother fuckers that want me to make the most noise."

She pushes herself forward in the water so a wave of warm flows back over her. She stops to take a drag of her cigarette, turns to me like she gon' ask me something, but blows out smoke instead.

I mumble.

"Speak up!" she say.

"Christian?" I said. "You Christian?"

"Nope."

"I mean . . . was you one? You seem to know the Bible and all. The verse about shepherds. I thought . . ."

"Ain't one. Never been one. Ain't gon' be one now, so don't try to sign me up. Here, wash my back."

I don't want to ask her no more questions.

"I want to show you something," she say.

She's still wet from the bath and wraps her towel around herself. The oils I put in her water are steaming off her, smelling like a face full of roses. "Where we going?" I say.

She kneels down next to the bathtub and reaches her arm under it, huffing. "Help me with this."

I follow her around and get on my knees, too, look under the tub and see her fiddling with a copper latch laid on the floor. It looks like a door knocker but I don't see no door.

She taps the knocker with her fingertips trying to lift it. It slips away. She tries again. It flips over this time. Thuds. "There," she say. "Help me move this tub."

"Be easier we get the water out first."

"We gon' move it. Just like it is." Weren't a question.

I roll to my butt, put my feet against the tub with hers and we push with our legs. Grunt. Push. It moves. We push it all the way back past the latch. She crawls over to it, holding her towel tight against her chest. I sit up on my knees.

The latch is in the center of a square door etched in the floor. Cynthia pulls the door open. Dust rises while clumps of dirt, stuck to the bottom of the door, crumble down the passage and rests on the top step of disappearing stairs. Piano music swells up from the dark hole—an echo of what's going on in the saloon out front. Cynthia starts down the stairs. "You comin?"

I shake my head no. "It's dark down there."

"Come on," she say, not asking.

I say a quick prayer and follow.

My white dress powders brown in the dirt as we slowly walk under the brothel. Above us are all of its rooms. Light shines through the floor boards touching our faces. A woman's high-heeled shoes tap and shuffle in the kitchen above us—Bernadette's in there bent over the sink with her boyfriend behind her. She's supposed to be working. Cynthia huffs and keeps walking, steps over some lump in the dirt. I kick whatever it was out the way, thought it was a stick at first but it's a stiff dead thing. My knees buckle and Cynthia grabs my arm. "It's up this way," she say.

Above us, the slits between the floorboards become wider because of the warped boards. "Water damaged," Cynthia say. "Fools laid the new floor right over the rotten joists." Some of the wood boards under the bar don't even touch. They're opened like a gapped-toothed man, teeth staked in the gums, showing everything inside—food and drink and tongue and voice. I can see everything up there.

Men dance to the fury of fast-playing piano. Their steps hard-fall as they move with hired women captured in their two-step twirl. The bottoms of the girls' dresses make them look like caught butterflies. Prisoners who still smile 'cause it's for the money.

"They cain't see us," Cynthia say. "I bet if they blew out the candles upstairs, they'd be scared if they looked down and saw us spooks staring up at 'em from under the floor."

I laugh a little.

Across the room upstairs, a thin man, vested and white-button-shirted, leans over Cynthia's piano with his back to us, hiding the black and white keys but unmasking notes. Cynthia looks back at me and her face is bright like a little girl's—giddy and happy, like she ain't ever been a day in this whorehouse. She covers her mouth with her hand, giggling.

She takes a few steps and swoops her backside down on a bench just ahead. She dusts it off and slaps the space next to her. I sit down, too. She whispers, "This used to be my secret place. Still is. You got to do the secret handshake to be here." She grabs my hand and hooks her pinky finger around mine, then shakes hands with me.

"I used to come down here all the time," she say. "At first, to watch my business." Her voice raises, "People always trying to steal from me. Gotta have eyes everywhere."

A new couple shuffles a two-step above us.

"After a while," she say. "When Sam came to work for me, 'bout four years in, I changed some things around. Didn't need to be there all the time. I could be at peace down here. Think." She smiles, lowers her eyes, like she's embarrassed she telling me this. So I smile back at her to let her know it's all right.

She say, "I imagine some whore before me, before I owned it, snuck down here and did this, too. Watched. Maybe she waited for her prince to come rescue her." She points to a door behind us. It's wonky and broken like the floorboards above us. I can see clear through the crooked pieces of the door to the porch steps outside. "Right through there is the front porch. I reckon she made it out that way."

"You think she found her prince?" I say.

"She ain't here, is she?"

Cynthia hugs her knees to her chest and watches the dancers do another pass above us.

"Why didn't you leave?" I say.

Her legs drop from the bench. "You dumb or something? This is mine. I ain't never leaving. Maybe you ought to be the one going. I been taking care of your ass too long."

"I'm sorry," I say. "I didn't mean to . . ."

She act like I'm not here now.

I really am sorry.

Sorry I said it. Sorry I made her remember we ain't little girls. Sorry we ain't in a secret club and we ain't innocent.

"Ain't nobody comin for me," she say, and draws her knees up again. "Don't need nobody to, neither."

I don't say nothing else. I wait and watch her relax to the swirl above us where red curtains and dim lights paint the room. I could fall asleep right here.

The brothel door at the top of the steps swings open into the room and behind us new feet stomp up the porch steps. But by the time we turn around to see, the shoes have disappeared. They appear again in the doorway. New customers.

Cynthia leans forward in her seat to see who it is—"Mayor of Otalika," she say. "How old you think he is?"

"Sixty."

"He's forty-five. One of those whose face ages in dog years. But I reckon with all the drinking he's done, he's pickled himself to live another forty.

"And him right there coming in and can't find a seat . . ."

"I see him. But there's at least ten empty chairs up there. A seat's a seat."

"For you and me, maybe. Difference is a serial asshole will walk in any party and look for the one person he hasn't shat on yet. Anybody else would look for friends."

Before the mayor finds a seat, one of the girls is on him. He don't fight her off. Meets her instead with his hand on her thigh.

"And him there," she say, pointing to the corner of the room where a husky old man, dressed rich, laughs hearty. "Our new house dealer. Charlie Shepard. He been working up at the McCullen's for years. They fell out. Probably 'cause of a woman. As long as it wasn't stealing, I don't care. He starts here tonight.

"Everybody calls him Mr. Shepard, even his wife. That's her next to him. Soledad."

She's pretty and brown but not black like me. She got red yarn braided in her long hair. Maybe she half Cherokee.

I met her my first week here. I was pushing my broom by her opened door after she'd flown into a fit, and was slanging ceramics through her door hole. They shattered against the wall.

She was yelling in something Percy called Spanish. When she saw me, she grabbed my arm. Tears and sweat had drenched her face and hair. Her cheeks, chin, and mouth were hanging loose from anguish. So loose that it was like there was a whole other face underneath hers, and this one was a mask glued on. Her hot tears were steaming it away. If I pinched and pulled her bottom lashes, the whole thing would slough off.

She held me and shook me, not trying to hurt me, but for balance— drunk—then yelled up the hall, "These games get old, I quit, Cynthia! I quit you. I quit these men! I'm never coming back!"

Then she said to me, "You're just her toy, you know that? She *will* get sick of you. And when she does, you come and see me. Hummingbird Lane."

"She used to work for me," Cynthia say, but I already remember. Though Soledad seems delicate now, dainty and feeble but put together smooth like the ceramics she smashed before she left. She smiles shyly at Mr. Shepard.

"He bought her a house," Cynthia say. "Gave her things she could never earn for herself. And now she's religious, too. You'd be surprised how many women find God for money. Mr. Shepard had the most. He did me a favor."

I fly across the room when gunshots pop over the music, put my back against the broke door. But Cynthia ain't moved. "That's just Ray and Henry's stupid asses. Cain't hit shit. Always shooting and fucking up my ceilings. You can come on back over.

"Bounty hunters," she say. "Hunt their own selves if it meant a payday. But they gon' pay for that one . . . like the last ones. Look at 'em . . . damn fools." They're pulling at one of the girls nearby, rubbing themselves on her like it's dancing. "The only one with any sense is the one sitting. Bobby Lee. All of 'em cousins, though."

He's slumped over his table, drunk or tired, his face hidden. His blue shirt is rolled up past his forearms where thick copper hairs look brushed.

"He lost his wife and firstborn, just a month ole," Cynthia say. "Both of 'em on the same night. Bandits. He been looking for 'em ever since. Folks say he scratched his own eye out trying to stop the tears. He only comes here to drink and to not be by hisself. Good-looking, ain't he? Hell, I'd give it to him for free."

The girl that Ray and Henry was pulling sits on Bobby Lee's lap. He nudges her off him but Ray and Henry grab her. Bobby Lee shoves 'em all away and they tumble to the floor, jump up ready to fight. Bobby Lee ignores 'em both, walks past 'em and brings the girl with him, toward us.

"Get back!" Cynthia say. We step back into a dark patch.

Bobby Lee stops at the bar just above us. Girl's gone. She's already working another table.

From here, I can only see from Bobby Lee's ankles to his knees so I take a step forward and see under his nose. Even from here he's good-looking. He fumbles in his pockets for change. Sam say, "What can I get cha?"

A nickel falls, hits the floor, bounces, flips, flutters, then lays flat, teetering on the end of a plank right above me. Bobby Lee bends to pick it up.

I don't move.

I swear he's looking me dead in my eyes.

Cynthia pulls me all the way back, next to her. We hold our breaths, then I whisper under the music, "I thought they cain't see us."

"They cain't."

When Bobby Lee stands again, I can see the whole flat of his face. He gulps his shot of whiskey, spreads his lips to stop the burning, says to Sam, "Tell Cynthia she got rats."

13 / 1860

Tallassee, Alabama

JOSEY MOVES SLOWLY into the newness of the woods. This is
the furthest she's been from the slaves' quarters since five years
ago when Charles found her 'sleep on the dark ground, glowing white under the moon. Underneath her feet, once-green brush has
turned to a dead gray like no rain's been here. Except for this next step:
soupy mud splashes under the soles of her bare feet while the smell of
mildew and rot steams from the ground. Josey looks around lost, lifts
her damp foot and turns it over where peaks of mud have splotched and
mixed with something sticky and binding, eggy and brown. She scrapes
it with a stick and leaps back on a small patch of grass, an island in the
muck. She wipes her feet there.

Ada Mae has been trailing behind Josey, looking nervous, carrying
her rolling hoop. "We shouldn't have come out this far," she say. "I've
never been out here."

"You said you wanted to practice with that hoop where nobody
could see, didn't you? The place I found was just up here."

"I don't want to no more."

"You scared?"

"I don't feel so good, is all."

"There's a good bush right over there."

"You ain't scared?" Ada Mae say, her eyes widening.

"No. Yes," Josey say. "Maybe more."

A glint of white catches Josey's eye in the distance—a house between the trees. "I just want to see what's out there."

"Then take my hoop," Ada Mae say. "Practice with it and I'll catch up."

The house sits on the edge of the woods with its paint peeling and its porch worn by too many steps. Josey holds her arm up blocking the sun when she steps out of the tree line. Sunlight catches her blue eyes and forces her head down. The warmth rolls over her shoulders, then goes cold like a blanket yanked away. My gut is telling me that Josey should turn around 'cause I feel the dark of this place. No birds are singing. No green's growing. And now that the sun's passed, everything looks hollow and drowned.

Josey stops.

I reach for her. Hesitate 'cause I cain't touch her.

Something darts between us, startles us both—a man with the sun behind him so all we can see is a shadow—eyeless, mouthless—a paper cutout in the sky. We look at him where the eyes should be.

When the sun passes, flaring nostrils meet us. She's a woman. Old and hard-breathing, taking a mouthful of air through her nose, trembling her top lip when she breathe out.

The curly man-hairs on her neck are there like they've always been—like they were almost nine years ago—moist like they sweat-glued on. She starts circling Josey, hunched over and slow. Her long dress sways, the back of it is butt-lifted higher than the front. She goes 'round Josey and Josey don't move.

She holds her breath, hoping the woman will pass, but it's too late to play dead.

The woman leans into Josey to get a better look. A faint blue circle traces the colored part of her eyes where dried tears chalk the creases in the wrinkles packed underneath her bottom lashes.

She churns her lips, moving something in her mouth—a bit of old food on her tongue—a small yellowish ball like a piece of nut. Her quick blow sends it flying to the ground.

Josey's cheeks redden.

"Well, well, well," the witch say. "After all this time. There you is." Her jowls quiver and her lips clinch together.

"You . . . you work on the Graham plantation, ma'am?"

"I should cut you to pieces," Witch say.

I swear to God, she touch Josey, I'll learn this moment how to kill a woman.

Josey watches her circle and disappear behind her. "Forgive me, ma'am, I don't believe we know each other."

"No, no. You don't know Miss Sissy, do ya'?" She stops behind Josey. "I know you."

"Ma'am?"

"You almost made it, didn't cha, darkie? You thought you was one of them, didn't cha, coon? But you just like the rest of us."

Sissy moves herself in front of Josey, staring with dead eyes. "I never thought I'd see the day. Nine years I been waitin for you."

"Me?"

"Look at cha," Sissy say. "I've seen some get through. Yes, suh. Seen some like you make it pass. And you pretty good. I admit that. But you had to have it all, didn't cha?"

"I don't know what you mean?"

"I was up there in the big house, too. Servin high society. Eatin good, dressin good, like a good house negro should. Then you came. A nigga tryin to be a white. Tryin to get for free the place and respect that a lifetime could never get me. But I seen't ya, didn't I? Your skin golden all year long, your curls . . . the way they fall. Just one drop. One drop, law say. One drop of our blood can ruin any God-created man, poison so strong that maybe we don't even know our own power. It's what got white folks scared. But one thang's for sure . . . when I saw you

poisoned in her arms, I knew who you were. Takes one to know one."
She flicks Josey's hair and grins.

Sissy's aged much faster than she shoulda. Another fifty pounds have
reworked her into a different woman. But she's still in there. Twelve
years since the day we first met. Twelve years since the night Annie
Graham was given my baby; the same night Bobby Lee left my dead
body and his cousins for the road.

He had been pushing forward in the dark for over an hour, following a light a long way off. Bobby Lee's fear was opening his senses,
widening his sight, helping him to see in the dark. To smell sharply. He
could smell a fox that had been that way hours before. His dry mouth
tasted the sour of leaves that split as he passed.

I could hear what he heard. Hear him talking in his own head.
Felt his doubt and the tricks his mind was playing. He was hearing
shuffles behind him that he didn't make, started seeing mysteries in
the dark.

It wasn't long before something *was* following us. At first I thought
his cousins, maybe, keeping him honest, but it was something else—a
living thing tasting birth in the air, smelling it on him. Cain't be sure.
We had to find somebody quick, somewhere to take my baby. But there
wasn't no place but that hell.

The jagged parts of wild trees and bushes tore into his thighs,
scratched his neck, dug in his eyes. He twisted 'em away and threw
their broken pieces to the ground. Bugs were sticking inside his clothes,
tangling in the material and in his chest hair. They bit at his arms, his
ankles, his face for food, but he kept my baby in a world her own, floating her on a cloud inside his coat, sacrificing his own body for hers—not
a scratch, not a bite, not a cry.

The light was finally getting close.

He pressed her against himself and thought about the lie he was
gon' tell when he got there—this is my baby. And the parts that
weren't a lie—my wife is dead. But he was gon' keep hisself one

secret, though. Like how Ray never let him see his wife and baby after they got kilt that night. How he fought Ray and Henry to get through the door where broken chairs and dishes littered the floor and blood pooled but his cousins wouldn't let him through.

Bobby Lee settled it in his mind to never forgive Ray for not letting him in the door to see his family, dead, and now he can't accept the empty place in his remembering where he never saw 'em newly deceased. He only saw 'em blue and strange-looking in their caskets.

He put in the place of their death memory his own imaginings, a lie, pretending they ain't really gone. Instead, he remember how his wife fought off the ones that tried to kill his baby and that she ran away, hiding in the woods with his child until her new husband, a hero, a man who woulda never let this happen, saved 'em both.

So that night with Josey, Bobby Lee got it in his mind to be that man he never was. Be that hero and save my child.

The light from the distance covered us. We were five steps to the porch when he stopped to take a deep breath and a sudden tug at his coat startled him. An old slave woman was peering at him.

She told Bobby Lee, "The plantation mistress is barren. She'll have the baby."

Just then, Josey started crying. Bobby Lee bounced her calm. His last chance to be the daddy. And when he looked back for the woman again, she was gone.

He knocked on the front door with his knees bent two inches low, trying to make hisself seem small and pitiful. Knocked again and hugged my baby close, half-wishing nobody never come.

When the door opened, a young white woman stood behind it. Her small voice said, "Good evening, sir. May I help you?" Her thick dark hair hung to her waist, half pin-curled from earlier in the day and the moonlight made her skin blue. Another young woman, a negro girl, cowered behind her, watching Bobby Lee's tall frame go from bent-kneed to hunched-back, smaller. When the light caught his scarred eye, the negro girl pushed the door closed and said. "I'll have you know, suh, the man of the house is here."

"Please, ma'am," Bobby Lee said. "I don't mean no harm. I have here this baby that needs tending to."

It was Josephine's broken cries that finally sent Annie out to her without caution. Annie searched Bobby Lee and found Josey under his coat. She peeled his coat away from Josephine's face and we watched my baby yawn.

The cool air made her cry again.

"Quickly," Annie said. "Come in. Please."

"I don't like this, Miss Annie," the negro girl said, trotting close behind.

"Sissy, please . . . fetch a few clean blankets." Annie tugged the coat from Bobby Lee's arms.

When Sissy came back, Annie snatched the blankets and wrapped my baby in 'em. She bounced Josey in her arms, twirled her around. "Please. Sit down, sir."

"I don't have much time, ma'am," he said to Annie. "Are you the plantation mistress?"

"I am."

"My wife," he told Annie. "She . . . she didn't make it through the birth."

"Dear Lord, Mr. . . . ."

"Smith," he said. "Bobby Lee Smith, ma'am."

Annie gazed at my baby, sorry for her. "Mr. Smith. I'm so sorry."

"We been traveling a full day, ma'am."

"Sissy, fetch the wet nurse," Annie said sharply. Sissy mumbled on her way back through the kitchen and out the back while Annie put her pinky finger in my baby's mouth.

"Ma'am . . . Missus Graham?" Bobby Lee said. "I know I'm just a stranger to you and I appreciate your kindness but I got to be honest with you. . . . I heard you might take this child."

"Mr. Smith?"

"I ain't got no place else to go," he said. "She's healthy, far as I can tell. But I cain't do it on my own and . . ."

"Don't you have family?"

"No, ma'am. None to speak of, ma'am. My wife. She was all I had. And now . . ."

Annie held up her hand to stop him talking.

She paced with my baby. Her happiness at a chance to be a momma was guarded by her fear. She carried Josey near the warm fire, looked into Josey's eyes and it's like she fell in love. She said, "I don't have no money to give you, sir. Don't have anything of value, no place for you to stay. Nothing."

"And there's nothin I want from you, Missus Graham. Just your kindness. For you to say yes." He sat down slowly in her big armchair, scooted to the edge of it, his knee jumping. He held it still with both hands. "I don't want to push you none, Missus Graham. But I'm afraid that if you don't spare me this, this baby won't make it another night."

"I will!" Annie said.

"You will?" It was the first time I saw Bobby Lee smile—all his straight yellow teeth flashing between his thin lips. Josey cried as if for joy, too.

"Thank you," he said. "Thank God for you."

Sissy came out the kitchen with a full-bosomed slave. "Miss Annie, she here." The nurse hurried to my baby and scooped her from Annie's arms, quieted her with her breast.

"Cain't no good come from this, Miss Annie. You cain't help God. You cain't just *give* a baby. If God wanted you to have a baby, He'd give you one. Look at me . . . he didn't give me one befo' Paul pass. Ain't nothin wrong wit not havin' one."

"God's giving me one now, Sissy." Annie shook Bobby Lee's hand like they made a deal, said, "I'm sorry for your loss, Mr. Smith. Sincerely, I am. But I think God sent you to me."

"No, ma'am," he said. "God's blessing me. You're giving me and this baby a special gift."

Annie sat down on the sofa next to the wet nurse and touched Josey's forehead, swept her wispy blonde hairs aside, watched her suckle. She said quietly, "Mr. Smith? What do you call her?"

Bobby Lee washed his hand around his head, smiled. "I didn't want to name her 'til I knew she was gon' make it."

"Josephine," Sissy said, bitterly. "I woulda named mine Josephine."

"That's a beautiful name, Sissy. Yes, we'll call you Josephine."

"HOW YOU THINK your daddy got you, huh, Miss Josephine? You weren't always his. You used to be white." Sissy paces around Josey, clinching her teeth, rabid.

"It's 'cause a you I'm here!" she say. "I'm the one Annie blame. I'm the one she told, 'Don't come back,' like I was a stranger. All my years she lied. Said I wasn't like the others. That I was her friend. That I was like her. Just born unlucky. So where's my reward?"

Tears smear down Sissy's cheeks. Her grunts of emotion almost cover the crunch of coming footsteps from somewhere behind us, not near enough to see.

The front door of Sissy's house swings open. "Mama!" a boy's voice calls—the black boy who belongs to nobody—Wayward. "Mama!" he say again.

The footsteps from the woods stop behind Josey. Ada Mae. She grabs Josey arm, and tells her to run.

"Come back here!" Sissy yells. "I know who you are. You owe me!"

14 / FLASH

Conyers, Georgia, 1847

BLACK NIGHT SURROUNDS us—Johnny and I—as we sit near Cynthia's back door. It's open, a little, and the new gambling parlor is just on the other side. At dusk a triangle of light seeped out and soaked the porch floor where it got trapped and spread to the steps and out to the dirt where it colored our game. I can see better now.

I get down on my knees, balance myself on one hand, and shoot my marble across the dirt. Missed the one I was aiming at.

As much as I love our games, I know me and Johnny cain't do this forever. Cain't play forever. Johnny'll grow up soon and go the way that we have to—blacks and whites. I spoke to Albert last week about his South. About leaving here once and for all like Hazel woulda wanted me to.

He said we had two choices. The Railroad, north, or these Freedom Fighters, south.

"Both got problems," he said. "The Railroad's made of good people with safe places to get negroes out of this country. Not to Boston. Negroes is slaves there, too. *North* means Canada.

"Problem is, the Underground Railroad, north, don't start 'til Virginia. Who gon' get us to Virginia from Georgia? There ain't no secret maps to show us how. It ain't organized for us here. We're too far south."

Albert had heard of a newer railroad to freedom that comes twice a year, fall and spring. And that's only maybe.

"It can take us up to Virginia," he said. "More dangerous and a longer journey. Could leave us worser off, too."

Our second choice was these Freedom Fighters going south.

"Law ain't looking for negroes heading to Mexico like they do for ones going north. But the way south has been weakened in the last two years. Slave owners are getting wise to the trick. Fighters used to go around asking owners to hire their slaves for the week. Paid top dollar for borrowed labor, but not enough to buy a slave outright, and when that slave never got returned, the Fighters and their property had a one-week head start.

"Didn't take long for word to spread that owners was getting duped, their slaves kidnapped, for the cost of a week's wage. So for a long while, couldn't nobody—a kidnapper or employer—hire out a slave. Not even for a day.

"The Freedom Fighters had to change their method 'cause nothing was gon' stop 'em from risking their lives for God's will—to set the captives free—so they started taking 'em. Outright stealing 'em. Took whole families. Made their own meshwork of willing men, and fed and watered steeds, lined the way from here to Texas, racing the devil. That became the fear of slave owners, the threat—having their property kidnapped.

"So Fighters started moving into communities, building relationships with owners, would hire a couple of their new neighbor's slaves for the day, return 'em back. Hire 'em for two more days, return 'em. A week, return 'em, kneading the leather soft so that the next time they hired slaves, they'd take 'em. Weren't no going back, neither. For nobody. To the life they built or the people they knew.

"The Fighters are more careful now. Don't go near places they been. They ain't been through Conyers before. Are set to do it in the next six months. A pass through only," he said. "An arrangement made by the Mexican girl, Soledad."

"I know her," I told Albert. "I mean, I met her." She left here raging at Cynthia with a mask of grief and the devil in her eyes.

"Her father was a Freedom Fighter in Mexico and she said when these men come, we'll know who they are by the orange stripe on their satchels. Orange, like sunsets and sweet fruit—the taste of fought-for freedom."

JOHNNY HUNKERS DOWN next to me and shoots his marble. It flies past mine skipping a trail over the soft dirt. It leaves a dotted line behind. Click.

I squat on the last step behind Cynthia's brothel. Inside, a handful of customers hoot and holler every time dice shake or get flung across the floor. Fists slam down and glass cups jump from broken tables. Crumpled dollars wave in the air to get in on the next game. A voice yells, "Seven!"

A young man is cheering 'cause he bet against the roller. The rest of the men inside moan 'cause they lost. An angry man throws his hands up and yells to the only winner, "You cheated! You and the roller in it together."

The accusing starts a scuffle of flat shoes sliding back and forth on the wood floor. I bend over the last step and lay on my side, stretch further to see better, see who the winner was. The new house dealer, Mr. Shepard, say, "Jeremy, g'wan git yer money. You won it fair and square." The low light hides his face but even through shadows his walk is confident. Jeremy steps into the light.

He takes my breath away.

He strolls out onto our porch in no particular hurry, lights a cigarette, and leans over the railing above us. His skin is buttery smooth like a pot of sweet cream. (Everybody else here is plucked chickens.) Everything on him is perfectly placed—his square jaw, his crinkled and full lips. They look like they belong on a black man, soft as pillows. He licks 'em and I tingle inside.

"How do?" he say.

I turn back around. I don't want to see his pretty lips no more.

I point at Johnny so he would hand me a marble but Johnny don't know what I'm talking about 'cause I already got both mine.

Jeremy say, "I've never seen a pretty girl play marbles."

My mouth drops open. I close it.

He comes down the steps, flicks his cigarette out his hand, and stoops down next to me. "Can I play?"

I cain't talk, cain't move my head to look at him. Johnny hands him his marbles.

"So what do I do?" he say to Johnny. "Just flick it?"

Johnny nods.

He say to me, "How about you, beautiful? What do you say I do? Is there a secret?"

"I don't know a secret, suh."

"Everybody's got secrets. Even the boy here's got a secret."

"Yes, suh."

He sticks his hand out near mine for me to shake it. He say, "Not 'sir.' Just Jeremy."

I shake his hand and a giggle slips from my mouth. "Naomi, suh. I mean. My name is just Naomi."

"You been out here the whole time, Naomi? I reckon you my lucky charm."

My cheeks lift on their own.

"Pretty smile," he say and stands up, lighting a new cigarette.

He reaches in his pocket and pulls something out. "Want to see 'em?"

Before I say yes, he kneels next to me again, shows me a set of dice in his hand. "Bought 'em in Louisiana," he say. "Can you believe they're carved from knuckle bones? Made into perfect little cubes."

One of the dice got four black eyes showing, the other got two eyes up. I touch one—without thinking.

"Would you like to roll?" he say.

"Yes, suh . . . I mean, yes."

He puts his knuckle bones in my hand and I clutch 'em and get ready to throw 'em but before I do, he grabs my arm, tugs me up. "Come with me."

I rein back on him straight away, almost make him fall down.

"I just want you to roll one for me," he say.

"I cain't go in there!"

"Aw, come on. I won't let nothing bad happen."

"You asking or telling me to go?"

He smiles the softest, most kindest smile I ever did see and say, "Asking."

I look back at Johnny and he nods and smiles for me to go. Jeremy tugs me again and I let him take me. When we walk in the parlor, it goes from loud to quiet. "Fellas," Jeremy announce, "this here's my lucky charm."

A man yells something but Jeremy puts his hand up and speaks over 'im. "I know women ain't allowed in our game."

"Or niggers," another man shouts.

"But as my lucky charm, I'm including her."

"I ain't playing wit no nigger," the same man say.

Dealer acts like he cain't hear none of what's going on. "Put your bets down," he say, starting the room into a frenzy of noise again. I step back into the corner, listen to all of 'em yelling numbers, waving money. Arguing starts about who's s'posed to be the next roller. Two of 'em get to shoving. Dealer say, "The girl's g'wan roll."

I shake my head, tell Jeremy, "I ain't really the lucky charm."

"All you have to do is throw, Naomi. Bubba," he say to his chubby friend. "Give me a few more dollars so we can bet on my lucky charm."

Bubba hesitates.

"You know I'm good for it," Jeremy say. "And you only here one more night. Let's go for broke."

Bubba throws his money down.

"Then, go!" somebody yell. "Roll the dice!"

I flinch.

Everybody's watching me.

My two bones is laying on the ground, waiting. Jeremy say, calmly, "Go ahead. Pick 'em up."

But I'm scared to.

"You'll just shake 'em in your hand, then throw 'em out there and make sure they hit the back wall."

I cup the dice in my hands, close one hand over the other, and shake.

"Can't use two hands!" a man yell.

I drop 'em both. They scatter.

Dealer say, "No roll."

"Let somebody else do it," another man say.

Dealer picks up the dice, gives 'em to me again. "Come on, darling. Your roll."

Jeremy leans over me, touching me with his body, whispering in my ear. "Just relax," he say. "Feel 'em in your hand. Shift 'em around in there. You feel 'em?"

"Uh huh," I say.

"Now shake 'em. However you want. A little or a lot." I move 'em a little. Rock 'em in my hand. "You shaking 'em?"

"Yeah."

"Now, think seven or eleven. You thinking it?"

"Yes."

"Good. Now cock your hand back."

I do.

"Throw 'em!" He push my hand forward and I open it, let the dice fly out, blurring their dots in twirls. They crash into each other, hit the wall, roll back and finally on their sides.

Four eyes. Three.

"Seven!" the dealer shouts. Jeremy hollers, excited.

CHEERS BOUNCE OFF the walls. Johnny stands in the doorway jumping up and down. I do, too, 'cause almost everybody's cheering. Jeremy points at me, tells the crowd. "My lucky charm."

"Let her roll her number," say the man who didn't want me to roll in the first place.

I roll an eight—my point, my number. Now, I got to keep rolling my number to win for those who bet on it.

Jeremy puts everything on eight. He say, "Eight is good. Real good. There's three ways to roll an eight."

Most everybody else in the room bet on eight, too. I roll eight four more times.

I get the dice again.

"Ain't no way she'll roll another eight," a old man say. "I'm moving my bet."

From the front part of the brothel house, I hear Cynthia's voice calling, "Naomi!"

"I gotta go," I say to Jeremy.

"You cain't go."

But I do.

He looks in my eyes, smiles that smile. "Well, you cain't go without this." He unfolds his wad of money, separates out about half his winnings, gives it to me.

"I cain't take this," I say.

"Could be your ticket outta here," he whispers. "Besides, we're a good team. You and me. I can't cheat my teammate." He yells to the men, "Y'all ain't gon' wear out my good fortune. Say bye to my lucky charm."

"Naw, no," the old man betting against me say. "She gotta keep rolling and crap out like the rest of us."

The dealer picks up the dice. "She say she's done. Who's next?"

"Dealer, you ain't fair," the old man say.

Jeremy pulls me up to a stand and goes with me to the door, pushes it open ahead of me. Johnny's waiting across the yard, playing marbles with hisself.

"Naomi!" Cynthia calls again.

Jeremy comes all the way out to the porch with me.

"Thank you," I tell him.

"So . . . you think it's wrong?" he say.

"For a negro to gamble wit whites?" I say.

"For a man like me to fancy a beautiful woman like you."

I hide my smile with a turn down the stairs. He catches my swinging hand, stops me, and say, "I won't tell."

Everything inside me flutters.

The back door bursts open and Bubba comes out holding the note of a long burp. He bear hugs Jeremy, lifts him up, and carries him back through the door. Jeremy's eyes stay on mine 'til his door closes.

I teeter on the stairs. Filled.

15 / OCTOBER 1862

Tallassee, Alabama

T HE "AMERICAN" CIVIL War started a year ago, April, and I don't know what it means to be American.

I'm not.

The war began when a Frenchman, Pierre Beauregard, a one-star general, ordered his troops to open fire on Americans with fifty cannons at Fort Sumter in Charleston, South Carolina.

Even though folks in town proudly call Pierre "Little Napolean" nobody calls him French but me, 'cause I'm fair. They don't call him French here 'cause he white and rich and born here . . . mostly. His family was of a French colony in Louisiana, and that French family line led him there from France. He didn't speak English 'til he was twelve.

So, I don't know how many generations on American soil you got to live before you're called "American," or if English has to be your first language.

No matter, negroes may always be foreigners.

But I'm here.

And tonight, the fall of white light and gray shadow from the moon showers me as I pour myself through the slaves' quarters—one-room shacks built in a semi-circle around a patch of dirt. I coast along a path of balding grass, trodden over and worn by cats and people. The wispy blades shift as my body brushes by.

I pass door after door. Ada Mae's is the third one on the right. Charles's and Josey's is the seventh or eighth—the last one on the end.

The path continues on without me, leading from Josey's to a hole in the woods where everybody dumps their leftover food for the critters to finish.

I pass through Josey's door and round the corners of the main room, blowing by a sheet that hangs from the ceiling. It divides Charles's part from Josey's. But right now, they're sitting together at the table eating hot stew.

Charles gets up and checks the shuttered window, makes sure it's shut, puts a blanket around Josey, then sits back down. She brings her legs up on her stool and crosses 'em there, pulls her blanket tighter.

The dull scraping of their wooden spoons catch most of the stew left at the bottom of their bowls. The chicken bones have been slid out of the way to get to the vegetables. Charles finishes his meal and waits for Josey so he can clear the table.

She say, "That boy, Everett, made Ada Mae fall again today. Can you believe she call him sweet? Sweet!"

"Nobody knows the ways of the heart," Charles say.

"That ain't heart, that's just dumb."

"Well, boys are good at that."

"Be better if they was good at somethin else."

Josey slides her spoon across the bowl, back and forth while Charles reaches under his chair and sets a soft, burlap-wrapped mound of cloth on the table. It's topped with a blue bow. Before Charles can speak, Josey swipes her gift off the table and got her fingers swishing around the bow.

The bag blossoms.

A button-down blouse, matching white stockings, and a pleated blue skirt tumbles out.

"It's the fashion up north, I heard," Charles say. "If you don't like it I could . . ."

The hanging sheet that separates the room billows as Josey runs through it, behind it, already undressing. She rolls her new stockins up her bug-bitten legs, then buttons her skirt, her blouse, twirls on her way back through the sheet. She poses. Her blouse is hanging lopsided off her shoulder, her stockings are sagging at her knees, and her skirt is slid down on one side.

"There," Charles say, satisfied. "A young lady." She holds out the bottom of her skirt and spins. "Yes, ma'am," Charles say, his voice quivering. "A young lady."

She hugs his neck and his chair tilts back from the love of it. "Best birthday of my life," Josey say, picking up the gift wrapping from the floor.

"The happiest day of mine," Charles say.

"Two years old when you come. Could hardly talk. Only in pieces. Potty trained you myself that first day. You cried the whole first week."

"Happy tears, I bet," Josey say. "You think it was hard for whoever had to give me away?"

Charles starts stacking their mostly empty stew bowls. "Don't time just fly by?" he say. "Fourteen years ole . . ."

"I love you, Daddy," she say, leaving her first question alone. She takes the bowls from his hand and nears the front door where she steps out of her stockings and into Charles's big shoes barefooted. She throws her blanket over her shoulders.

"Happy birthday," Charles say.

By her third step outside, the cold air finds its way through Josey's skirt and the gaps between her heels and Charles's shoes. She lets her blanket slide further down her back and around her legs and waist. She catches it there, ties it around her hips.

She scrapes the tiny bones and smeared food from the bowls and into the hollow of the bushes where critters wait eager and hungry for their turn at it.

A snap of thistle turns her around sudden. She hooks her arm around the neck of a person—a boy—and pulls him to the ground, straddling him, pinning him, lifting her bowls above his head.

"Wait!" he yell.

It's the boy, Wayward.

"What you doing in my yard!" Josey say.

"I didn't mean to scare you."

"You watching me!"

"I . . . I was just . . ."

"You want to hurt me?"

"I . . . I'm sorry!" His voice trembles and his body is limp in surrender but she don't get up.

"We done talking," she say, pushing herself off him finally. "You go home and don't you come back ne're." She dusts her knees and puts her blanket over herself, collects her bowls and starts back to her door. He brings hisself to his feet. Tall as she is now. His light-colored clothes against his black skin and the night sky makes his shirt look empty. It's been months since I last seen him.

"Josey?" he say.

She pause.

"I'm here to see you. To talk to you. To say happy birthday."

"How do you know my name?"

He opens his mouth to speak but no more words come out.

"How you know anything about me?" She points at him with her bowls. "What plantation you from?"

"N . . . none."

"So you don't live no place, ain't from nowhere, but you know it's my birthday? How long you been coming around here, liar?"

"Not a liar."

"For sure a peeper."

"We met before," he say.

"Never."

"Twice."

"Liar."

"I promise we did. My momma is Sissy."

Josey laughs. "You the witch's son?"

"Ain't a witch!" he say.

"Evil," Josey say.

"I shouldn't a come."

"I'll be dog gone, if you ain't the witch's son. Wait 'til I tell Ada Mae."

Before she finish laughing, he's gone back across the slaves' yard and path, nearing the woods.

"Good," she yells from behind him. "You leave. You shouldn't be coming 'round here peeping on folks no way." She yanks the blanket around her shoulders and watches him. But she don't go inside right off. She keeps watching. Watching the way the moon rests in the cleft of his neck beneath the round of his head. A perfect scoop, smooth and hand-shaped under the nap of his hair.

She studies his blue-black skin and her heartbeats slow. He's an impressive color, the kind of shade that Josey had already wished for in a husband, in the father of her dreamed-of children. And now he's disappearing deeper into the brush. Her own color leaves her face as she stares, confused now, at that empty space where he was.

"Wait!" Josey yells, breathless. "Wait!" she say to the shadows, coughing now, her breath lost.

When she breathes deeply and puts her hands on her knees, dropping her bowls, her blanket slides off her waist. "Come back here!" she say, coughing.

Nothing.

A wheeze. She pats her chest to clear the sound. She coughs and finds relief.

She reaches down to collect her bowls and picks up her blanket. Wayward say, "You all right?"

A fleeting smile graces Josey's face but she pretends not to notice him, sets her bowls on a stump of cut log, and takes her time tying the blanket over her shoulders. She coughs again.

"You all right?" he say.

"What do you care?" she say.

"Well, if you're all better, I'll go."

"You haven't even told me happy birthday."

"You ain't gave me a chance to. Not properly."

"Go on. Here's your chance . . ."

"Happy birthday," he say.

"'Bout time."

"Awnry."

"You like it," she say.

"Maybe."

"Josey!" Charles calls from the doorway.

"I have ta go," she say in a hurry, bunching her bowls against her chest.

"Wait," he say, reaching into his pocket and pulling out a braid of wound-together red string.

"Josey!" Charles calls.

"Coming, Daddy!"

"I made it myself . . . for your birthday. In case I . . . Can I put it on you?" he say.

"I don't even know your name."

"Jackson. Jackson Hayes."

He smiles and reaches for her hand and she lets him tie his strings around her wrist. He scoots the knot around and down her arm.

"This is silly," she say.

"Can I see you again?" he say. "Tomorrow?"

She only smiles.

"Eight o'clock?"

"Good night," she say, running toward Charles's call.

"Good night," Jackson say to the closing door.

16 / FLASH

Conyers, Georgia, 1847

THE MUSK OF burning wax is seeping through Cynthia's bedroom door. I knock.

No answer.

I press my ear against the cool door. Cain't hear nothin.

My hair tumbles over my shoulder. It smells of Jeremy. Makes me smile.

I knock again, ease the door open. "Cynthia? You call me?"

Flames atop two candles sway above their silver holders. The holders are pushed back on the vanity, painting soot on the mirror.

Fancy plates that Cynthia usually keeps under her bed wrapped in a velvet cloth, is out. One of the plates is on the floor, half-pushed under the vanity, mounded with gray chicken bones, thin as thistles. Rib bones are branched off a greasy spine. A leg bone's still got the white crunchy gristle on the end.

I take a step in.

An empty bottle of wine lays tipped over next to the bed. And next to it is the rest of that chicken—bones piled on a book beside a knocked-over, empty wine glass.

Her naked white toes wiggle off the end of the bed while the rest of her is crumpled on the trunk I sleep on. She got one arm against the wall, propped straight up in the air like she's waiting to be called on. Her head is sunk in her shoulders, her body is draped in a man's undershirt pushed up above her stretched-out belly. I pick up the glass near her foot and put it on the vanity next to another bottle of wine. My hip bumps her chair, knocks her hanging dress to the floor. When I reach down to pick it up, her eyes shoot open. "What the hell you doing walking in on me?" she say. She pushes herself up but falls back, pointing a bread roll at me like it's gon' hold me in place.

"You called me?" I say.

She washes her hand over her face, says, "I called you a long time ago. Where were you?"

"I knocked but you was 'sleep."

She strains her swollen eyes open, bends over her lap with her elbows on her knees.

"I was shootin marbles," I say.

"I can tell you lying. The way your voice just rose."

She stretches both arms above her head, cracks her back. She sticks her finger in her ear and wiggles it around, snorts at the same time. "Next time you see me not waking, you come see if I'm dead before you go and wait over there with my wine."

"Yes'm."

I take the half-full bottle of wine from the vanity and pour her a glass before she even asks and watch the dark-purple color slide in. I give it to her, sit back at the vanity, and work at pushing the cork back in.

"Just so you know," she say, "I wasn't sleep. I was praying. I don't never sleep. You remember that."

"Yes'm," I say. The cork is stuck sideways.

She finishes her wine like a shot of whiskey. She say, "You think my momma's in hell?"

My cork pops.

"If there is one, I reckon she is," she say.

She reaches her empty glass out to me to refill it. I say, "I thought you don't believe in heaven or hell?"

"I said *if*. And I don't. Come on, have a drink with me."

"No, that's all right."

"So you don't drink, neither?"

I don't answer.

She raises her glass. "A toast—to all you bitches that don't drink and think your shit don't stank." She chugs a big swallow of wine, continues with a loud burp, laughing now. "You know what special day it is today? Go'n and guess."

"Your birthday?"

"Guess again."

"Johnny's?"

"Know what Yom Kippur is?"

"No, ma'am."

"A religious holiday," she say. "Thas today, started at sundown." She raises her glass again, sips.

"I thought you weren't saved. Didn't believe in Jesus."

She laughs. "Christians ain't the only ones that got religion. I'm a pure country Jew. And this is *my* Day of Atonement. "

"I thought you was white?"

"I am. Wrong kind of white for these parts."

"And you said you didn't believe in nothin?"

"I can give God one day . . . most of it, anyway." She drinks again, leaves a gulp at the bottom. "I'm s'posed to be looking at things I coulda done better this year. Repenting and asking God for forgiveness—saying things like, 'I'm sorry I slapped my child, I won't do it again,' and apologize to people I wronged." Her breath catches, "If you think I wronged you, sorry."

"You gon' give up whoring?" I say.

"I'm talking about the shit I done wrong. What I do for them out there, I do right," she laughs. "God understands a girl's gotta make a living. Thas my job, my business. Ain't nobody gon' give a woman work unless it's doing dishes and I don't do dishes. I sure as hell ain't getting married, neither. I'm doing me and my girls a favor. A chance to earn a living for ourselves." Her foot knocks the chicken bones off her plate and onto a book she got on the floor. She reaches down and picks it up, wipes the bone grease off. "What I hope is for God to forgive me for my wrongs," she say. "Write my name in his Book of Life. Everybody's fate is sealed tomorrow."

"What about me?"

"What about you? You ain't Jewish."

She fans open her book. It looks like a diary inside. She thumbs through its handwritten pages without reading it. Closes it.

I say, "So what you s'posed to do on this Yom Kippur?"

"If there was a temple around, I'd go to it and pray all day like my father did when I was young. As it is, I'm a woman. So *this* is my temple. And after the shit I done this year I got a lot of making up to do."

She puts her diary down, rests her head back on the wall. "Already fucked up, though," she say. "I shoulda been fasting since sundown— no food, no drink, nothin. But you best believe I'm gon' finish off this bottle of wine unless God hisself tell me I cain't."

The glass in her hand slips through her fingers, spills on my trunk, the wine gathers in its creases, near her book. She yanks her book away and leaves everything else.

I rush to clean up the wine, wipe it with the edge of my dress—the only thing I got but she don't move except to plop her thigh over the last part I got to clean. It stains her own leg purple. She looks at her spilled glass. "Well, goddamn—a sign. I'm done. Can't spend much time in contemplation if I'm loaded."

I take my dress to the basin, soak it in the little bit of water left over at the bottom, scrub my dress between my hands. I dip it in the basin again, but all the water's used up.

Cynthia don't apologize to me, like she don't care, even though it's her fault my dress is ruined. "Is there something you called me for?" I say, and throw my hand on my hip.

She lays back against the wall closing her eyes. "You think I'm gon' be saved, Naomi? In the end, I mean?"

I want her to get up off my sleeping trunk.

I say, "Ain't for me to decide."

"Why I even ask you?" she say like she's mad at me now. "What do you know, exactly? Nothing." She gets off my trunk with her book, plops down in the chair in front of me. "Why don't you go over there somewhere, make yourself busy. Better yet," she say holding her hand up, "if this is temple today, gimme some scripture."

I don't want to read to her but I go to my trunk anyway and pull my Bible from under my blanket.

"Old Testament," she say.

"Why you worried about damnation now, anyway?" I say, and sit on my trunk.

She leans into her mirror, wipes the sleep from her eye, pinches her cheeks to bring back color. "You believe in the sixth sense?" she say. "Reading the past, the future, and all?"

"Only God knows the future."

"Well, when I was seven years old, He told me mine. Told me I'd die before thirty-five. Come October, I'll have my curtain call. Maybe I'll slip into a well and break my neck or get some disease that eat me away."

"Cain't nobody know when they die," I say. "Or how."

"I can and I do. Now, read me something."

I open my Bible. "'The Lord is my Shepherd, I shall not want . . .'" I can feel her watching me. Maybe she seen me talking to Jeremy. Maybe she know I been talking to Albert about south. The worry makes me lose my place reading. I start again. "'The Lord is my Shepherd. I . . . I shall not want. He maketh me to lie down in green pastures.'"

"I grew up around yer kind," she say. "My daddy bought and sold peoples like you all the time. Charleston, South Carolina. Charles Towne. Big office on King Street. When the trade dried up he sold whatever he could. Didn't want to go back to New York with nothing." She lights a cigarette. "Go on, read."

"'He leadeth me beside . . .'"

"'Still waters,'" she say, finishing my verse and staring into her mirror. "My momma wrote hymns and ran Sunday school. She never could get over what Daddy done."

"Sunday school? I still don't understand how you ain't Christian."

"Y'all ain't the only ones that go to Sunday school and got scripture, neither. We had it first." She puts white powder all over her face.

"There used to be a whore that worked here," she say. "Always reciting the Bible like it made her better than everyone else, even her customers. But there was only one holy of hers these dogs were interested in."

She blots color on her cheeks, changes her mind and wipes it all off. She draws in her eyebrows straight and plain.

"Is there many of y'all 'round here, now? Not-Christians, I mean."

"Used to be plenty of us in Charleston. Mostly from Europe. A beautiful continent it is. You even heard of Europe?"

I shake my head.

"You even been outside Georgia?"

"Alabama," I whisper.

"You runned all the way from Alabama!" She leans back laughing. "You must got some kind of spirit on you, girl. Ran all the way from Alabama and ain't been nowhere."

I put my head down in my book, pretend to read so she shut up asking me questions. She reaches over from her chair, flips my Bible closed, got a sly look about her. "I bet you ain't never been wit a man?"

I don't say nothin.

Her voice fills with excitement. "Not even a kiss?"

I try to reopen my Bible. Cain't. She falls back in her chair laughing. "I knew it! Soon as I saw you. Shit girl, you ain't done nothin."

I get my Bible open again, put my finger on my verse, follow under the words, look busy, and watch her out the corner of my eye. She grabs her silver cigarette holder, shakes one out, and lights it. "Been with my first when I was ten. Paid a debt for my daddy."

"I'm sorry."

"Hell, he had lots of debts, sold everything. Before then, I was like you, didn't know nothing about nothing. Didn't know a dick end from a fork end."

"I'm sorry."

"What's wrong with you? Who the hell are you to be feeling sorry for me? Why don't you go back to reading."

Sometimes, I think me and Cynthia is friendly, but most times, not. She likes to remind me of who I am in the world. I read, "'He res . . . restoreth my soul.'"

"I killed him, you know. My daddy. One slice across the neck and he was dead, just like that. Ain't nothing like taking a man's life."

She stares up at the ceiling, folds her hands on her chest. "Nobody ever suspected his little blonde baby girl done it." She laughs. "Shit, I feel better already, confessing. It's good to get some thangs off your chest. Don't you get no ideas, neither. Nobody would believe you no way."

The law believes us sometimes.

They must.

I have to tell myself every day that they believed Hazel when they came looking for Massa and she had to lie about what I done.

Memories of that day flash in my mind like they real again—blood around my fist, the toughness of his skin when I pushed that poker through.

My hands start shaking and I hold them together on my lap.

"My momma kept this here diary," Cynthia say, flicking her book. "Probably talking about her nothing life. I ain't read it though, ain't going to, neither. She don't deserve for me to hear her explanation why." She tosses the book at the mirror. "She was dead by the time I killed Daddy. I guess that mean she didn't mind I did it. It wasn't like she tried to stop him when she was alive, anyway. You reckon they both in hell?"

"I don't know," I whisper, trying to keep myself from crying about Momma. Hazel was so strong in everything she did and Momma was so strong when she saved us, but I'm so weak.

She say, "I wonder if my momma ever asked God to forgive her for what she done to me? What she let happen? I woulda chopped him up and thrown him in the river if somebody did to my baby what he done to me. Instead, she took her own life." She flicks a glowing orange clump from her cigarette. "If I saw her again, I'd tell her, 'Fuck you for killing yourself and leaving me.'"

I say, "Not every woman got the same strong."

"What'd you say?"

"Your momma had the strong to give birth to you, to raise you, to put the strength inside you to do something she never could. Maybe she couldn't be your strong. In the end, you saved yourself." My eyes brim with tears, regretting my weakness.

Cynthia brushes her hair in silence, starts her makeup again—plain white. She finishes with something shiny and clear on her lips—no color nowhere today.

My tears tip over and run down my cheeks.

"Why you crying?" she say.

I wipe my cheeks.

I try to stop thinking about what I done, hang my head low over my Bible but she keep staring.

"You done a little dirty of your own, didn't cha? Where? In Alabama?"

I close my eyes, let new tears slide out.

"I knew it! My sixth sense never lie. What you do?"

"Why you want to know?" I say.

"Hell, girl, you already told it."

I won't look at her.

"You kill somebody? Another slave? No, no . . . This is something big. Somebody that mattered." She gets excited again. "A white woman? A man!"

My crying quivers out of me.

"I don't believe it!" she say, and rushes her face close to mine, almost touching my nose with hers. "You did!"

She lifts my arms, pulling me up to a stand. "Oh, let me look at you. Yep, you a killa. I didn't see that one right off. Well, one thing's certain . . . you better not try that shit with me."

After a moment more of her threatening look, she gets excited again, hurries back to her vanity, zips opens her special drawer, and unlocks the silver box she keeps inside. Her funny-smelling tobacca is in there. It looks like dried grasses.

She takes a pinch and pokes it along the middle of her smoking paper, adds tobacco, and rolls a fat one. She lights it with her burning candle and takes a long drag, relaxes.

"Them plantation owners is bad news," she say. "Always messing around in their henhouses. Thas what happened, isn't it? Good girl like you. A little rebellious. About sixteen, seventeen. Still a virgin. I say you was overdue." She takes one, two, three puffs, like she's swallowing the smoke, then blows it out, coughing. "Don't worry," she say, "he deserved it."

"You gon' kill me now?" I say.

"Kill you? Hell naw, you gon' save me. See, what you got is special. Something God sees as honorable—a virgin. I'm gon' do for you what my momma never did for me. I want God to see me protecting your innocence so he write my name in His Book."

She puts her hand on my shoulder and shakes me like we got a deal.

But I ain't got nothin. Less than nothin since I lost Hazel. Momma.

Like all these days here, alive, have been extra time for no reason—a judgment so delayed that even telling Cynthia what I done didn't bring it. A confession wasted.

There's no mercy here.

17 / 1862

Tallassee, Alabama

Y OU CAIN'T REASON with a fifteen-year-old girl who's convinced she's in love.

Seeing Jackson last night on her birthday was all the sure
Josey needed. She was awake before eight this morning, smiling before
she opened her eyes. She twirled Jackson's red bracelet around her wrist,
then buried her face in her pillow, laughing in it. Took her 'til now to
get out of the house and on the road. It's almost noon.

Her white headscarf is tucked in a bulge above her forehead, wonky,
so a single lock of her blonde hair is swaying across her face.

She spent twenty minutes buttoning her skirt but still she skipped
two buttonholes, so there's a bulge there, too.

A sweaty stem of a yellow flower is in her hand. She plucks one of
its petals and sends it to the ground where it joins a trail of other petals
and bald stems behind her.

"He loves me not," she say.

She needs to be thinking about eating and watching where she's
walking, not a boy, but this is love. She already stopped two people on
the way to the yard, asking if it was almost eight o'clock—the time she'll
meet Jackson again.

She takes the next petal off her crumpled flower—there are only two left—so with the first petal she pulls she keeps the odds in her favor and say, "He loves me not."

Rain begins to splatter on the ground, spreading dirt into tiny circles. Her new-plucked petal falls, adding color to the mud.

"Josey!" Ada Mae calls, running toward her from the top of the road. Her thousand-toothed smile is like a white corncob set sideways and bent up on both ends. "You hear the rumor?" she say, squealing. "We free!"

Josey's confused.

I'm confused. Could it have finally come?

Everett overruns 'em and almost knocks 'em over. "More than a rumor," he say, shouting. "The president signed papers!"

"President?" Josey say. "The man nobody like?"

"But everybody got to do what he say. He make the law. Make the whole world mind him."

"So, we could just leave?" Josey say. "But what about this war? The war's still raging."

"It's safe, ain't it, Everett?" Ada Mae say. "But, you think they just gon' stop the fighting and let us walk on through their battlefield, north?"

"'Not even a chicken could survive those fields,' is what I heard," Josey say.

"Maybe they give us guns to protect ourselves," Ada Mae say.

"And shoot white peoples?" Everett say. "Well . . . maybe if we join our Southern armies. Fight 'longside our masters . . ."

"And shoot white peoples!" Josey say. "You think Nelson will turn his back on you with a loaded weapon?"

"Maybe the president will come get us," Ada Mae say.

"If he could get this far," Josey say. "If he could win."

"I ain't never seen the president before," Ada Mae say.

"Well, I don't know if he come, or if he send somebody . . . ," Everett say.

"And then take us where?" Josey say. "He'll be our new Massa?"

"No, we free!"

"I don't know what you mean, free."

"Free mean free," Everett say. "It's what Mr. Sam's gon' say. He about to make the announcement. Tell us what the 'Mancipation Proclamation paper mean. What we got to do to get it . . .'"

"When Mr. Sam gon' tell us this?"

"Now!" Everett say. "Everybody going to the meeting now."

"Now! I gotta tell Daddy!"

"But the meeting's about to start," Everett say, grabbing her hand. "Why don't you come with me. Your daddy's probably there already."

"He wouldn't go without me."

"I'll go with you," Ada Mae tell Everett, smiling full of teeth.

Josey don't wait for them to leave before she does. She darts between trees, using 'em for shelter from the new pouring rain. She steps out of the hollow near her front door and gets a running start to slide herself across the muddied way to the door with her arms held out to her sides to keep from falling over. "Daddy!" she yells.

No answer.

"Daddy!"

Charles ain't inside.

Just as Josey pushes the door open, something catches her eye in the woods behind her. She touches her bracelet, whispers, "Jackson."

I wait at the door when she goes back to the place she first met him.

She walks inside the hollow and I hear her calling to the boy, "Jackson?" I go with her.

A bright green frog hops across her path and she shoos it. I wish I could shoo it, too, chase it with her, hold her hand, enjoy this rumored freedom 'cause there's hope in it right now even if its meaning is lost.

If I could talk to Josey, I'd tell her to always enjoy the present. To live in it. I'd tell her about love, too. I'd tell her the love she has for this boy, she'll feel again. I'd tell her about real love. Tell her to not be fooled by what feels real. Tell her to get married like I never could. Tell

her to marry someone who's kind. I'd tell her to make herself kinder
by learning to care for people with bad attitudes and nothing to offer
'cause the kindness she measures to others will be measured back to her.
I'd tell her that in the end, we'll all need somebody to take care of us, if
we live long enough. If we get old. That's when it'll matter most. When
we're living the consequence of our old yeses and nos. And if you're
lucky, I'd tell her, your caregiver will be your own spouse because you'd
have paid for that privilege with your commitment. And if not your
husband, let it be someone you love and loves you.

I take a look around and share this present with her.

"Massa George?" I hear Josey say. "Somethin I can do for you,
suh?" I hear her muddled scream before I can reach her.

His hand is at her throat and her eyes are wide. She grabs his hand
and a squeak like a quick-blown whistle shoots from her mouth but
cain't nobody hear her but me. She swings her hands, her feet, at his
body but he sends his fist to her cheek. She's limp.

Jesus! I don't know what to do! Tell me what to do!

He grabs her by her blouse and drags her moaning along the ground.
Her headscarf unravels, her blouse rips away. He holds her under the
armpits, pulling her deeper into the woods, then drops her in a patch
of dirt he already prepared for this. George straddles her, pulls his belt
from his loops one-handed and wraps it around her throat, pulls it tight,
then loosens it.

Josey wakes and flails wild on the ground, tugging at the belt, her
nails break against the leather, the sharp broken bits scratch down his
arm, slicing thin lines. The belt strap slips from his hand. She screams
hoarse, out of breath. He finds the strap again, pulls harder, like reins.

A smirk grows on his face as her fight weakens. He double loops the
strap around his whole fist.

Josey stops. Her eyes roll back. He loosens the leather and moments
pass. She takes a life-saving breath. Coughs. He say, "You scream again,
I swear I'll kill you."

Something nearby in the bushes moves and George looks over his shoulder. Just for a second. Enough for Josey to kick him square in the jaw. She leaps up, confused and running in the wrong direction. He dives on her back, puts his full weight on her, anchors her down 'til she shrinks to her knees. He puts his hand on the back of her neck, pushes her face down in the ground, presses her cheek in the dirt. He bites her shoulder through the skin. She screams. He rolls her over, puts his knee in her stomach. She reaches for his face. Too short's her arms. She only huffs beneath him now. A whistle joins her exhales.

"Please," she say. He reaches for a low branch and runs his hand down it to rip the leafs off. He shoves the leafs in her mouth, turns her over, face down in the mud, sits on her spine, both his hands pressed down on her shoulder blades. Tree roots, like dead fingers, have risen from the wet ground and press against her throat, crushing her windpipe.

He shifts her head and she breathes.

"Please, God," I say. "Please kill this man right now. Burn him up. Stab him through the heart. Please!"

Josey cries loud and hollow. He pushes her back on the root 'til she cain't make a sound.

I kick up the wind, make tornadoes of leaves and dirt, send it to his face. He only brushes them away. "God, have mercy. Please kill this man! Please, God? Please?"

Josey stops moving.

Only he's moving now. Grunting.

The only thing I can do: I lay down on the forest floor with her. See her breathing. Just enough. We lay together. Stay still together. I imagine I kiss her tears. I imagine I stroke her forehead. Whisper, "You ain't alone."

Part III

18 / FLASH

Conyers, Georgia, 1847

THE HOT GEORGIA sun is beating down on all of us, 'fectin me most 'cause I'm the only one that got to walk in it. Cynthia sent me to the apothecary to get some medicine for Bernadette. I forgot the sheet of paper with the medicine's name written on it but I already know. It's the same as always. Coca leafs.

The heat is keeping the streets mostly clear except for the white children playing in 'em, a few shades darker than usual, their winter skins brown. White women are posed under the shade of storefronts with their pink and blue dresses on, fanning themselves softly like it ain't that hot. But in the shack far behind the shops, black women are sitting side-by-side across the porch, wide-legged and perched back on their hands, welcoming a breeze. Their skirts are scrunched up to their waists showing their hand-washed britches.

White men roll by on horse-drawn wagons crumbling rocks beneath 'em and spraying out dirt, stinging my arm. Some old bits of grass get caught on my face and stick to the sweat. And other men are walking around with no shirts on, or thin garments with their nipples and nuts showing through their clothes. It ain't fair they tell women to wear something like a baggie sleeve from neck to ankle even in a heat wave.

The religious ones tell her it's what God wants. To honor her body. When really it's to make women servants to those men's sin because they cain't see women the way God intended—not everybody's a possible lover—sisters and brothers, maybe. But those men blame her instead of asking God to cleanse and fix them. Around women, those men are always halfway in hell. Double-minded.

I stagger up the porch steps and into the brothel. Inside's as hot as out and Cynthia's complaining in the corner like it's gon' make God turn off the heat.

"It's about time," she say to me. "Put it on the counter and go wash your hands out back."

I love the way Jeremy play piano.

He looks like a stray cat sitting over there all spit-cleaned and skinny. He's playing a slow and easy melody, erasing the stains of this place. Even though Cynthia hired him to play for the house, I think he only plays for me.

He's real good with his fingers.

Cynthia told him she gon' cut 'em off if she catch him touching my hand again when I pass him by to serve drinks. So I don't go near him this time. Instead, I pass Bobby Lee and another man sitting at the side table near the mouth of the hallway. It's the first time I've seen Bobby Lee this close without his hat pulled all the way down and his arms crossed high on his chest.

Down the hall, in the back room, the washbasin is filled with already-dirty water but it's cleaner than me so I rinse my hands in it. I can still hear Cynthia yelling, "It's too damn hot to screw!" and, "Percy, move over. It's already hot as hell in here. I don't need you breathing on me, too."

But Jeremy's music stirs. It covers the squeal of her voice with the smoothest song I ever heard. It's the only slow song he know.

I bury my face in a cool towel, pat it slowly, then pinch my cheeks sore to remind myself not to smile too happy if Jeremy look at me 'cause Cynthia might see.

He don't never look at no other girls. The only reason he's here at all is the debts he got to pay off, even some he owe Cynthia. She told him he needed to stop selling his family heirlooms and get another job. It's why she gave him one. It's like she thinks she's part responsible for him. Knew Jeremy's daddy before he passed. His daddy sold her this brothel even though she a woman. Almost impossible to repay the favor.

When I get back in the saloon, Cynthia's standing across the room squirming in her low-cut dress, picking at her lace stockings. She cracks her toe knuckles when she takes her feet out of her heels.

I take a pitcher of water from near the front door and pour two short glasses full while I watch Sam through the window. He's out front talking to some plantation owners. Been out there since before I left. I don't know why Cynthia ain't called him in yet 'cause whatever news he getting cain't be good and he should be working. Ray joined 'em a second ago and already he riled up, pacing, and threatening to hurt somebody.

"Bring me some water," Cynthia tell me, keeping her eye on them outside.

I meant to bring her the water directly but I caught Jeremy smiling at me. It makes me flush.

I pick up the pitcher and pour water on the wrong side of the glass, drench my dress, splash the floor.

"I can damn well do it myself," Cynthia say, getting out her chair, coming for her pitcher. Sam and Ray come back through the door.

"Who you out there talkin to?" Cynthia say to Sam.

"Authorities," Sam say. "Found the body of a plantation owner over in Alabama. Don't know who did it. Got the rest of 'em scared."

My stomach lurches.

"Goddamn niggers, that's who!" Ray say. "And . . ."

"I didn't ask you, Ray," Cynthia say.

"Then *you* tell her, Sam. Tell her what some nigger did."

Jeremy's melody starts to fade from my hearing, and the sound of my own heart is loud as a drum at my ear.

Sam goes behind the bar, leaving Ray standing next to me and everybody else waiting for Sam's answer. Even Jeremy stops playing.

My hands tremble and I hug the pitcher to my chest to stop 'em. Without a word, Sam picks up a wet glass and dries it.

"The whole household was killed," Ray say. "The nigger stud, too. Three bodies, all . . ."

My hearing goes.

He spits as he talks. His words become noiseless sprays on my hands—soapsuds of colorless spit bubbles piled into tiny dome clusters there. They stretch and thin and turn from pink to yellow, then pop in rhythm, one after the other, leaving tiny white circles on my brown skin.

"No one knows who did it," Sam say, bringing the noise back. "Anything more is gossip."

"Ain't gossip," Ray say. "It's the truth. Somebody dark was seen running from the scene."

"Could've been a shadow," Sam say. "Everybody looks dark at night."

"Not as dark as the nigger who did it. I'd bet on it. Bounty hunters followed his tracks for miles. Damn near to this place."

"Wasn't nowhere near here," Sam say. "Happened ten miles from Faunsdale. That's still seventy or more miles from here. Could've gone anywhere."

I hold my breath, feel sweat on my face. Jeremy begins his piano again. His low notes like a funeral hymn inside me.

"So it was a *him*," Cynthia say.

"At least six-one, six-two, six-three foot tall," Ray say, stretching his arms up high like I did the night I ran with the coat above my head. "That's what the witnesses said. Broad shoulders. But I heard some of their females get big as seven foot in Alabama."

Ray reaches for the water pitcher in my hand and tugs at it. His quick movements almost send me out my damp skin. I want to let go of it but I cain't. My hands done taken root in it. Our eyes meet. Dead center. His brown eyes are cold blue. He say, "Where you say you from?"

"None of your damn business, is where," Cynthia say. "Five feet nothin, she is."

"She black. Maybe she know who done it."

"Give that fool the pitcher, Naomi, *after* you pour me the water I asked for twenty minutes ago."

"I'm puttin my hat in it," Ray say. "Me and my cousins. We gon' find who done it, get the reward."

I unstick my fingers from the pitcher and pour a glass for Cynthia and take a deep breath before I give it to her, feel my racing heartbeats slow—just a little.

19 / APRIL 1863

Tallassee, Alabama

IT'S BEEN SIX months since he got Josey.

Six months since he tore her apart.

Was six hours that day that didn't nobody come to stop him. Nobody heard nothing. Saw nothing. Nobody but me.

It was in those hours, those too many times, too many ways, that Josey had to surrender. Had to believe everything George was telling her. Had to swallow his words about herself. Her body. He said she was an animal. A dog. Not worthy of human decency. So when she disconnected from her mind and watched all those things happen to her own self, what was real was his voice speaking the truth about her, breaking her mind 'til she believed everything he said. And because she could believe it, she survived.

And now, her revenge is mine.

A kind of self-defense, I'd call it. A third kind. The first kind would be plain self-defense. That's what Cynthia once called it. "Justified," she said. "You ain't responsible for killing somebody if they trying to kill you first."

Self-defense is what Cynthia almost had to do about those men who came to hurt me in her garden. It's what I had to do the night I killed Massa.

But I won't let Josey be a murderer.

I'll do it.

And I don't need to be excused by the law: self-defense. 'Cause George don't need to be in the act for what I got for him. He's still alive and some danger is always with you. Its suddenness can arise at any time, you just don't know when. So I call it "defending self," a second kind of self-defense, a switch of words, a switch of position, where the victim takes control and beats the asshole to it. I need to make sure George never comes back; that I make him stop for good. I don't need the law to allow it. I don't need "justified." 'Cause it don't matter anyway. I already told you the truth. What I'm after is the third kind.

Satisfaction.

So for six months, I been visiting the spot in the woods where the dead walk hoping to find a soul to help me, to teach me what I need to know to touch the living. But I been unlucky. This evening was no different.

Now, the dark and early morning is sending a sliver of moon over me, following me into Josey's and Charles's quarters where it stops at the window. A thin curtain is tacked on it like a used napkin. It rolls from left to right. Wind trapped behind it is fighting its way out. A ripple flaps the edge away, finally letting go.

Charles sits on the floor, sleeping in the corner, wearing the day clothes he been in since yesterday. His arms and legs are crossed, his neck is hooked over, his back is against the wall. The whites of his eyes is showing through the slits, and every once in a while he'll swat his hand in front of his face and mumble. He chokes hisself awake on his slobber, then wipes it from his chin.

A sheet still hangs from the ceiling to the floor, separating Charles's part of the room from Josey's. I go behind it to where Josey's rolling in her bed covers, sleeping good. I wonder when the memories of that cursed day will stop haunting her dreams the way I suspect they never did for Momma. I imagine Josey keeps reliving it the way I do these flashes. The way Momma must have done before she went silent.

So I talk to Josey. Sometimes I think she hears me. Sometimes not. Maybe my words are just another thought, another voice in her head. I cain't be sure if it was me who talked her into getting washed up and dressed yesterday.

From first glance, or the second, there ain't much on Josey that would be a sign that anything happened. Except for the scars on her knees and elbows. She's even walking right again. But young folks can be that way. The worse thing could happen one day and the next be like any other. But, I know.

If nothing else, the proof of the horror is still in her eyes, even when she blinks, they don't move, still frozen from fear. Blues fixed in place like a doll's, painted on and empty, looking nowhere and somewhere or any place you make it look. "Chrissie Ann," Josey woulda said to her doll baby before six months ago. "See them fields and flowers. Them sparrows."

But she wouldn't say that now. Ain't seen her doll babies since it happened.

Charles been too busy to see her as she is. He's been sharpening his tools, putting together metal pieces, getting ready to show his work and be somebody's hired hand. He been running hisself ragged making plans for freedom, to start hisself a new life with Josey. You can pass for white, he told her. Got more chances, he said. None like I got.

And this broke her heart.

We work together, he told her. You buy supplies where I cain't. Say I work for you. White peoples . . . they can be your peoples, too. Tears streamed down her face as he told her.

She whispered, "I'm negro, too."

Charles was knocked out asleep on the floor from dreaming the future before Josey even finished the dishes last night.

A cricket is chirping in this room somewhere. I don't know where, but it's already on my nerves, creaking and calling for company. Before

I finish my thought, Josey sits straight up in bed and startles me, hollering, "Frogs!"

The panic in her voice shakes my soul. Charles rip the sheet down.
I'm already beside her. Won't leave her. Won't ever leave her. Her eyes
are wide open now, still screaming from her bed mat. "Frogs!"

She crab-walks herself back against the wall, kicking and swiping at
her bed sheets. "Get away from me!"

Charles swishes his hands around her mat, turns it over, reaches
under it but don't come back with no nothin. "They on me, Daddy! The
frogs is on me!"

Charles lunges for the floor lamp near the window, feels for the
wick, lights it, shines it on her covers. "Where the frogs, Josey! Where?
I don't see nothin."

He kneels next to her, holding his lamp, pressing his hands in her
sheets, back and forth. "I don't feel nothin, Josey."

"They on me, Daddy!"

"Nothin's here, Josey! Ain't nothin . . ." The lamp swings its light
on Josey's legs. Deep gouges and cuts are all over 'em, gleaming with
wet new blood. The wounds are still trickling. "What is this, Josey?"
Charles say. "How you get these?"

"Get 'em off me, Daddy," Josey say, tired. "Get these frogs off."

"Josey?" he say, shaking his head, confused. "Josey, these ain't no
thorn bush."

"Get 'em off me, Daddy. Please!"

"Who done this to you, Josey?" He grabs her arms, "Josey, who
done this! You fell down? You done it?"

"The boy," she cry.

"What boy, Josey? Some boy come in here?" Charles rushes the window, pushes the curtain out. "He come through here, Josey? Somebody
come through here?"

He holds hisself out the window hole trying to see as far as he can.
She hugs her knees to her chest, crying. He comes back to comfort her,

falls next to her. "Josey, what you mean, a boy? Was it your dream? Is that where the boy was?"

Charles don't know what to do, like I didn't. Like I don't. He looks too scared to touch her. Her cuts. Finally he say, calm, "It's all right," and pulls her to him.

CHARLES NEVER WENT back to sleep last night. He been sitting wide-eyed and quiet on the floor where the sun rose on him. In the center of the room, sunlight seeps through the wood plank walls, striping his face and the dirt-brown floor with white. Specks of dust float into the light like clear bits of lemon in a glass pitcher of sweet tea. He's been replaying last night in his thoughts. What it means for a slave to be sick in the mind. If that's what this is. If that's what he's been trying not to see in her strange silences.

There's a hundred reasons for a person to sit quiet and alone, he's been telling hisself. A broken mind ain't the only one. But now, these night terrors have come. The way they've come for other slaves he's seen broken in time. He knows what could happen if Slavedriver Nelson finds out. He remembers Sister Kate was killed after she confessed her bad memories and said they stick in her head. Said these things that stick pull off the skin inside, and show her the bad over and over again 'til she ache so bad she cain't see. She couldn't scrub it away like she did them floors so she blamed her hands and cut 'em in the kitchen where she thought nobody could see. The *stick* wouldn't rub off in a ball and get caught in the wind like it did for them slaves who pretended to forget. And she couldn't. And like them horses that broke their legs, them sheep that laid down too long, or milk left out of the shade, she cost too much to make better and wasn't worth nothing so she got ended quick.

But Josey was fine, he told hisself. A hundred reasons, he told hisself.

Last night's cricket is stamped dead in the corner of the room now. Its wispy gray stick legs are flat out. It didn't have a chance in the shuffle.

Charles gets up when he hears Josey stirring. He puts on food, his good face, and sets the table. When he sees Josey come through the curtain wearing a strained smile, he rejoices a little, quick to take it in as only joy. She's all right. He was wrong. He has hope again. And even more, today, they'll be free. Slaves from three plantations are meeting on this property. Even four months ago it wouldn't have been so 'cause all this was just a story.

Even Missus Graham never came to say if the rumor was true. Other plantations have. Some said it was true. Some, a lie. But here, Missus Graham never said nothin, ain't broke routine. Even when the letters started coming frequent last December, nothin. Nobody could read 'em but her.

And when Slavedriver Nelson never came back on horse or foot, everybody got suspicious that maybe we *was* free, but we decided it was safer to stay unsure than be a runaway.

So the ones of us in the field waited for somebody like Nelson to take his place and when none came, Seth took on the role hisself even though he was a slave, too. He ran a tight ship. One of decency and respect. He wanted to keep order for Missus Graham. Keep everybody fed and housed and working for the Graham plantation 'til there was an answer from somewhere, or at least 'til we got through winter.

Finally, we got that answer—a preacher from Montgomery County. He was a slave like us 'til January just gone. We are free, he said. The clay that was the Emancipation Proclamation had hardened and dried and was signed by the president of the United States hisself. The president has power over all us, he said, slave and free. So we could go and be sure. Many have. Don't know where they're going, though. They've passed through here over the months claiming north, and saying come with us, but we've said no, we'll stay.

But this preacher know what he's talking about. He got papers he can read and men with him to testify to the same. So finally, the *go* meeting has come. It's at noon. Everybody's gon' announce their intentions—where they gon' go and what they gon' do. We leaving, too.

"Come on now, Josey, put your birthday clothes on," Charles say, pulling his suspenders over his button-down shirt.

"Yes, Daddy," Josey say but keeps sitting at the table like she's done since the end of breakfast, stone-faced and staring straight ahead. She ain't touched her food. Ain't brought her hands up from under the table to take even a crumb to her lips. Sweat is beading on both sides of her forehead like it's hot. I go near her and listen to her breathe in pants. It ain't her vapors.

"I cain't believe it's official," Charles say, chuckling. "Four months we been free. I guess it's true what they say: the journey to freedom starts when you first believe it."

Josey's breathing quickens. A grunt. Another.

"April's good as any day to start," he say, chuckling. "But not good as God, though. He good, ain't He?"

Charles got one foot halfway in his sock, hopping away from the wall, and almost falls over laughing . . . at hisself, and this good news. The first time he heard the rumor of the president's order from Jacob and Jacob Jr. was when he got home at dusk on the day after the meeting, after what happened to Josey, those months ago. And that day, he had nobody to share his joy with 'cause Josey was already in bed when Charles came in shouting about it.

Josey didn't move from her mat. She didn't want her daddy to see her, didn't want him to know her shame, didn't want to explain to him what George did. So she closed her eyes and pretended to sleep. Rolled over when Charles came through her curtain. She moved just enough for him to see she was alive. So when he whispered that he was home and asked if she heard the good news, she didn't answer. Didn't say much the next day, either, or the next. "You all right? You sick?" Charles asked her. A week later he decided that not everybody take good news the same way cause that conclusion was easier than the other. And when he noticed her strange bruises, her eye, and her limp when she walked, he decided that maybe she'd hit her head. "Clumsy," she said before he could ask her about 'em.

What she shoulda said was, "Look, Daddy! Look what George did to me. Look what he done did." But she didn't.

She cared more about Charles than she did herself. Didn't want his anger to get Charles hurt or worse. You cain't be black and angry and not be punished for it. But I'm gon' find a way to tell him. He'd want to know. Or, better, I'd want him to know. Ain't fair that I'm the only one that got to go through this. He can do something. It ain't fair that he can choose not to see and make excuses for what he do see, and ask other people who don't know nothin.

"Woman problems," Sister Lestine told him. That was why Josey hadn't woke 'til noon three days in a row and was sleep again by sunset. Charles had gone to Sister Lestine when he first started worrying about Josey's silences. He stood behind Sister Lestine's house—the only woman on the row he trusted—wringing his hat, hiding, didn't want to give the other ladies reason to gossip if they caught him talking private to her. And when she came in from the field, he scared her when he grabbed her and pulled her behind the building. Said he was worried about Josey and she had to help.

"It's nothing to worry about," Sister Lestine told him. And nothing Josey would likely want to share with him. But if Josey wanted to come by, she'd show her how to care for herself. Charles was too embarrassed to talk to Josey about it. Asked Sister Lestine to do it on his behalf. But when she offered advice, Josey told her she didn't need help. She wanted to keep to herself.

See, Josey's sacrifice of quiet was for Charles at first. But she needed to tell him what happened.

Needed to tell somebody.

She needed to tell Charles so he could kill George. And needed to make sure Charles didn't get caught.

Charles could make a pretty metal flask for George and lace that gift with poison. Make the dying slow. A sickness. No. Make it look like an accident so there ain't no chance George would heal or that the poison wasn't enough. But I don't really want Charles to do it anyway.

I'm the one.

The night after it happened, I went searching for George. I don't know what I was planning to do but I was gon' make it matter. When I got to Annie's house, Slavedriver Nelson was already there. Annie was talking with him in her front room, told him from now on, he needed to come see her about collecting his weekly wage . . . 'til George got back. She told him that George "left for Virginia to join the fight in Fredericksburg," and she didn't expect him back soon.

I got time to plan better now.

"He's a young man," Nelson told Annie. "Not like me. He's fortunate to serve his country."

"Indeed, he is," Annie said.

"Still surprises me, though, that George would go so soon," Nelson said. "I thought it mighta been cause of what he done."

"What he did?" Annie said.

"Well I—I . . . I didn't see nothing, ma'am. Heard the two of you arguing and yelling last night, thas all. Heard you asking George about the scratches on his arms and neck. Heard you say, 'What you do?' More like, 'What did you do!' and, 'Who'd you do it to?' So I figured he left 'cause of something he done to a woman. But I see now that he left for something different entirely. A brave man, he is. If there's anything I can do in his absence, let me know. You always been so good to me and my family."

"The business in my house is none of yours," Annie said.

He grinned. "Like I said, you've always been good to me and my family. And now that times are getting harder with the war and all, maybe I could forget what I heard." His crooked smile rose.

Annie said, "You right about times being harder. War will be right here on this porch soon. It'll be a time for all of us to fight for what we believe, and age won't be a reason not to. Don't you agree?"

By the next day, Nelson was fired.

CHARLES PICKS UP his shoes and the sock he couldn't get on and brings 'em over to the table and sits across from Josey. He sets his shoes on the floor and raises a foot on top of the stool to put his other sock on. "I been waiting a long time for this day," Charles say. "Cain't hardly believe it. When I was yer age, this was a fool's dream. How many of us you think gon' be out there packed and ready to go? I bet you Miss Laura be first. She want to make up everybody else's mind about where to go. She need to keep to her own business, that's what. I reckon it's gon' be everybody from here to Montgomery." He slides his feet into his shoes. "And Jacob Jr. said some niggas who got free early been breaking into other slaves' quarters, stealing. Can you believe that? Who got less than us? You bet' believe that if they come 'round here, I'll cut 'em. So be careful. Especially when you out there alone. And only pack what you need. We'll get food as we go. And . . ."

JOSEY'S ARMS FIDGET under the table like she's opening a wrapped candy there. Charles say, "Come on now, Josey. Get up. Get ready."

She keeps sitting and her arms keep flinching under the table. I follow the line of her arm down and under the table to her lap. Her midnight blue dress is stained darker in the middle near the place where one hand is resting. In the other hand she holds a sharp rock. Its edge is red. Blood slides down her bluish ring finger, gathering at the tip, quivering. It drips.

Charles say, "Be next week before we go. I reckon I could make a few more thangs to sell. We can save up and buy us some land. Build something nice."

He bends over to pick up his other shoe from under the bench. "Josey!" he yells, finally seeing. He lifts her up by the arm 'til she stand.

"You do this?" he say.

The sharp rock falls. He turns her arm over, sees where she's been sawing at her wrist, other partly healed marks.

The same cuts as on her legs last night during the nightmare.

"Why I cain't feel nothin, Daddy?" she cry. "Why I cain't?"

"Why you doing this, Josey?" He rips the bottom of his shirt and ties it around her wrist, through her palm. "Don't do this."

"I ain't worth nothin, Daddy," she cries.

"Everythang," he say, hugging her. "Everythang, you worth."

"I'm sorry, Daddy."

He holds her away from him. "Are you sick, Josey? In your mind
. . . are you sick?"

"We free, Daddy."

"Does that scare you, Josey? You ain't got to be scared. I won't let
nothing hurt you."

"I was walking home . . ." Josey say. "I wanted to tell you. So many
years we'd wanted this freedom. When you came home, I wanted to be
happy, too. I didn't want to ruin it . . ."

"Then don't," Charles say flat. He hunches his shoulders. "Don't,"
he say again, tired this time. Tired of being tired. Tired of his sacrifice.
This one and the one he made for me the night I died. The night when
Charles's name was still Albert. The Scottish Banshee.

I had been dead for minutes or hours, I don't know. Found Albert
laid on the forest floor. He was wrung out from exhaustion there and
wishing for dead, teetering between sleep and passed-away 'cause that
night, Albert had followed me from the brothel and through the woods.
I didn't know then. He was chasing me, trying to reach me to save me,
was somewhere between me and them bounty hunters. By the time he
got to me, my labor had taken over and the dogs had closed in. He
called my name through the darkness. It was the last time I stood alive.
Saw him waving his arms for me to come his way when the spark in the
dark took me. His was the last face I saw.

Seeing me fatal didn't stop him from trying to save me. He shook
me to bring me back, closed his hand over the bullet hole in my head,
pushed down hard to stop the bleeding but it wouldn't stop. He almost
put his knee right on top of Josey when he moved from straddling me.
She had been so still, so quiet in my arms. That's when his face became
like twisted rock behind waterfalls, tears and sweat—one river—poured
over it. He grabbed a razor from his pocket and set its edge on the cord
that connected Josey to me but a weakness set into his strong hands and

he could hardly hold the handle, couldn't get the razor to slide. It fell out his hands.

All he could do was scramble to the shadows when the footsteps overtook us. Bobby Lee would be the one to cut Josey free.

I stayed with him for a while and waited for him to fall asleep there, heartbroken. Watched him wake and cry hisself back to sleep that night, empty. His dry tears had crusted a straight white line from one eye, over his nose. It was cracked when Slavedriver Nelson rode up next to him.

Nelson yelled something at Albert but Albert didn't move. The dark handle of Albert's razor was still resting in his open hand but Nelson didn't see it. Not even when he got off his horse and kicked Albert's foot. Twice. Albert sat up the second time, looked around wild, called out, "Naomi!" then, "Charlie!"—a man we both knew from Cynthia's.

From instinct, he closed his fist around his razor and slid it under his foot. Nelson shoved his shotgun in Albert's chest.

"Who do you belong to, boy?" Nelson said. "You a runaway?"

"Char . . . Char . . . Charlie," Albert stuttered. "A man was found dead in Conyers. Charlie Shepard, his name. Charlie . . ."

"I can't understand a word you saying, boy. Where your papers?"

Albert stood up slowly and reached into his shirt pocket, pulled out his wrinkled freed-man papers, then dropped 'em. When he bent over to pick 'em up, he lifted his foot off the razor and slid it in his shoe, gave his papers to Nelson. "So you free?" Nelson said. "Then you need to find your way off my property. I give you less than a minute."

Albert nodded and reached for his papers.

"Now, hold on, boy . . ." Nelson said. "These papers say Albert Pyle. But you said you Charlie. Which is it?"

Before Albert could respond, George came riding up. He was just about eleven years old then. He said, "A man just gave a baby to Annie! A girl baby. I'll be an uncle!"

"Must be the full moon tonight," Nelson said. "Folks just flooding in. Tell your sister I'll be there directly." When George snapped his reins to start his horse, Nelson turned back to Albert, said, "If you a runaway, boy, you got thirty days to be claimed. And if nobody come, you the property of the Graham plantation. So which is it, boy? Your name? You lie to me and you gon' have worser problems."

"Charlie," Albert said, lying. "My name. It's Charles."

"Well, Charles. You got thirty days for somebody to come claim you." And just like that, Albert gave up his freedom to be near Josephine.

Because he loved me.

"THIS A TIME to be happy," Charles now say. He takes her hand. "The choice is yours, Josey. What you do with it, is your choice. Tell me you're happy," he say, desperate. "Tell me you can be free. Tell me it's over. Tell me that makes you happy."

Tears flood her eyes. "I'm happy."

20 / APRIL 1863

Tallassee, Alabama

SWAYING FLOWERS THEY are. Women and children, men and babies being blown up the road toward the Grahams' slave quarters. They wear their oranges and yellows and bright blue garments like they been saving up a rainbow since Africa. They're from here and everywhere, all of 'em choosing to start their journey to freedom from this place. And it's real this time.

More people are on their way, through battlefields and their fires, filing up the road in a colorful funeral march, letting this past go. Four months of waiting since Lincoln's signed paper set us free. It's time for us to blossom the way God meant us to. Even in ash.

Charles pulls Josey through the rainbow sea of people. The two of 'em are the only ones dressed in white. The crowd peels away as Charles forces his way through, zigzagging around folks who won't move at his loud, "'Scuse me!"

His naked black head is a foot taller than everyone else dressed in color, so when he moves it's like a bee walking on petals. They make their way to the front where the preacher stands on top of a wooden box getting ready to speak. I float down to join 'em, stand next to Josey, find her po-faced and pale white. Her color matches the beam of Charles's smile.

A skinny brown woman in orange glides through the crowd and stops behind us. The baby on her hip is in orange, too. She drops her packed bag and stands on her tiptoes while a man in a straw hat shimmies around her and holds her waist.

Ada Mae and Everett wait across the yard handholding. They been a pair for a few weeks now and there are rumors they'll marry soon, rumors that the war is nearing, rumors that the North is recruiting negroes. We heard thirteen thousand soldiers lost their lives in Fredericksburg, Virginia, most of 'em Union soldiers, the North. It happened at the river crossing just before Christmas. A victory, folks here say. And a slaughter. So now, the North is recruiting any life, black or white, and when the fighting gets near enough, Everett say he gon' enlist, too. He'll join the escaped negroes that left months ago. But for those of us who are still here—black, white, and free, the war is all worry. 'Til it comes. At least Everett will have a weapon now. For the rest of us, our only weapon is hope.

Throughout this plantation field, folks got sheets knotted on the ends of sticks or thrown over their shoulders like satchels. Inside 'em are needed things—food, clothes, skins of water, and a few tokens, reminders that they are the only survivors of slavery. That said, more than one man's got nothin; ain't taking nothin, don't want nothin, they got all they need—their lives and their freedom.

The preacher say, "As we go from this place, let it not be in fear. The Bible say, God does not give us a spirit of fear, but of power, love, and a sound mind. We are strong. We've endured. And now, God has touched President Lincoln and softened his heart so that he be like Pharaoh and set us free. He's given power and bravery to the heroes that are carrying out God's will for our great land. I say to you, don't be afraid. We go with God to wherever he leads us. He has brought us this far in His love and grace and He will lead us home. Amen?"

Charles say, "Amen."

The whole crowd say, "Amen."

The woman in orange yells, "But where we go?"

Preacher leans toward her. "Praise God . . . that's the blessing," he laughs. "Go where you want. Federal law say you are free. But be cautious. There's still a war raging, north and south, and there's safety in numbers. Some of us from the Brown plantation are going north. Others going west." He opens up to the crowd, say, "Come with us to the lands of milk and honey, away from this place of our captors. Will you come?"

The crowd cheers.

"Make two lines," Preacher say. "On the right—those going north. The left—those of you who want to go west."

The crowd rumbles, excited, knocking into each other, going left and right. Charles leans down to Josey. "What you say, Josey? North or west?"

She points.

"West it is," Charles say, picking her up and pushing his way to the left.

Shots ring over the crowd.

Charles throws hisself over Josey. Other folks duck and scatter. Some clump together. Others lay out on the ground. But Preacher holds his spot on top of that box and let the gunfire come.

Slavedriver Nelson sits on his horse, Maybelle, with his gun in the air, his whip on his side. Twenty or thirty whites are with him. Nelson say to the crowd, "Since when are slaves allowed to gather around like this?"

A black boy yells, "We ain't slaves no more. We free."

"Is that right?" Nelson say, and trots out to him. "Where you from, boy?"

"Brown plantation. President Lincoln signed the 'Mancipation Proclamation and free us." The boy casts his arm out to Nelson. "Here's the papers."

"Right," Nelson say, pushing 'em away. "Maybe they free the niggers of the Brown plantation but niggers from the Graham plantation, the Henderson plantation, and the Reed plantation ain't going nowhere."

Preacher say, "You can't keep 'em here. It's against the law."

Nelson prances Maybelle to Preacher, bends down and looks him in his eye. He unbuttons his whip. "Is *you* presuming to tell me what the law say, boy?"

"Naw, suh," Preacher say.

"This here's the Confederate States of America. Lincoln ain't the law here. This war will prove that." Nelson trots around to the back of Preacher. "Now then. Take your nigras and you leave here before we punish y'all as runaways."

Preacher say to the crowd, nervous at first, then loud. "Don't matter where we leave from. We'll start our journey from the fields of the Brown plantation. If anyone wants to join us, we'll be there 'til morning. We *are* free."

"You disrespecting me, boy!" Nelson say, pointing his pistol at Preacher now. "I just said they ain't leaving and you just now invited 'em to come. Did I hear you right, boy?"

Preacher don't say nothin.

"You couldn't just shut your black fuckin' mouth, could you?" Nelson cocks his gun. "You inciting these slaves to run? Is that what you doin?" He knocks Preacher's hat off with his pistol.

"Naw, suh," Preacher say.

"Yes. Yes, you wuz."

One of the white men fires in the air. Its sharp pop sends all the horses in a panic. Maybelle, too. She rears up and throws Nelson. Maybelle comes down hard on one leg, shrieks and collapses, screeching in pitches that ears cain't endure.

Nelson scurries through the dirt and slides next to her. "Goddamn!" he yells. "Goddamn! It's broken!" The horse struggles to get up but cain't.

New commotion from behind the white men stirs the horses again. Annie's doctor, Dr. Mitchell, comes 'round on his horse, circling the group. "What the hell's going on here?" he say to Nelson. "I told you I needed ten minutes. Ten."

Maybelle shrieks.

"Shut up that damned horse," Doctor say. "I give you a chance, a job, and this is how you repay me?"

Nelson rubs Maybelle and she squeals. "Her leg's broke, suh."

"I said shut up your mare," Doctor say and pull his pistol. "She's no good now."

Nelson jumps in front of Maybelle, standing between her and Dr. Mitchell.

She keeps screaming, making too much noise, fumbling to get up, but it ain't no use.

"Naw, Dr. Mitchell," Nelson plead. "Don't do this. Please. If she got to go, I got to be the one that do it."

"I asked you to do a handful of things for me," Doctor say. "Notify the men of our meeting and wait for me 'til half noon. Don't you know this is a war, boy!"

Maybelle shrieks.

Doctor fires.

She don't shriek no more.

Nelson's eyes widen.

Dr. Mitchell waves his pistol toward the slaves. "Y'all go back to where you came from. Except for the ones that belong to Annie Graham or these men. You others . . . your owners are cowards."

Nelson whimpers next to his horse and Dr. Mitchell turns away from him.

Everybody moves slowly back to where they were going.

The lady in orange sings:

> "Oh! Go down, Moses
> Way down in Egypt land.
> Tell ole Pharaoh. To let my people go."

Others join her in song, walking past Nelson with pity in their eyes, watching him cradle his dead horse.

"Get outta here," Doctor yells to 'em. "Get." He pauses when he sees Josey and Charles unmoved. Doctor's strange expression is like he hadn't expected to see 'em anywhere outside a room where he treated her vapors, or where Charles wasn't waiting anxiously nearby for her recovery.

The black man in the straw hat throws his hands down and say, "I knew it! Lies!"

Charles continues to stand frozen with Josey's hand in his as the parade of other brown people pour around him like water past a big rock. His shoulders hang from hope removed, his once joyful face a blank expression.

Dr. Mitchell rides over to him and say, "Charles. I'm going to tell you this like I'm telling the rest. If you leave here, it means that you and Josey are both runaways. And nobody can protect you. We're at war." Doctor rides back out to the center of the yard and shouts. "All y'all belonging to Annie Graham. Get back to work!"

Josey looks up at Charles, waiting for him to say something but he won't look at her. He mumbles, "Let's gon' get back to work."

21 / APRIL 1863

Tallassee, Alabama

I T'S BEEN TWO weeks since negroes decided to leave without asking. They were wrong. Then last night, a man came to Annie's without asking. He was wrong, too.

I had been chasing after his black buggy since I first heard it a quarter mile down Annie's road. I wished to God that it was George. My hope helped make me swifter.

Falling rain was spreading around the buggy like tears, promising me it was George inside.

It bumped along the muddy road with its horses grunting and snot spilling, promising me George. And when the horses slowed in front of the Graham house, I was quivering for my satisfaction. Let me see him! I wanted to kill him.

A burst of firelight glowed from inside the carriage. Its door swung open where I was waiting, and a lamp came through the opening, then the arm of the white man. His whole body folded out. It weren't George.

The man hopped down from the buggy steps, limped in place to keep his balance, held the lamp out in front of him, and stabbed his burgundy cane between loose stones. He threw his coat over his head and his black hair flattened in the rain. Mud sprayed on his trouser as he began his hobble to the front door, a walk like an almost-tipped-over jar, rocking to find its flat bottom again. But he couldn't right hisself. He was a gimp. He shook his good leg on the front porch and the other he wiped down with both hands while I went inside.

Bessie was scrambling up the stairs toward Missus Graham's bedroom. I met her at the top of the landing and could've swore she looked right at me. But as soon as I thought it, she walked right through me. "Missus Graham!" she said opening Annie's door. She went in without asking, said, "Missus Graham!"

"What the hell's wrong with you, girl?" Annie said, sitting straight up.

"It's Mista Graham, ma'am. He here."

Mr. Graham's knocks returned to the door and Annie leaped out of bed like a child caught napping instead of cleaning and pulled a dress over her head, checked her face in the mirror, twice, rushed down the staircase, pinning her hair on the way. By then, Bessie was already in the main room, waiting for Annie's signal to open the door. But instead of giving the sign right then, Annie waited.

Fourteen years she'd waited. Fourteen years ago, Mr. Graham—her then best friend—left her in the middle of the night with Scotch on his breath and unspoken words on hers. And now, his knock was at her front door again, a stranger.

He knocked harder, surer. He said, "Annie, open this door!"

Annie grabbed hold of a chair, bracing herself, but still waited.

"Annie!" he said.

She took a deep breath, nodded to Bessie. When the door opened, he came barreling in. "Next time you hear me at the door," he told Bessie, "open it."

"Yes'sa, Massa Graham."

He was a beautiful man, Mr. Graham was. Like a garden statue standing there, five foot nothin. He threw his soaking-wet coat on the rack, letting its water rain on Annie's newly polished floor. Bessie got him a towel.

He looked around the room, puffed his chest out, held his shoulders
back, his legs spread in a wide stance like he weren't a gimp and put
his hands on his hips, nodded his head as if he was saying, yes, I live
here. . . . Yes, I own this house. Everything in it's mine.

"Get me some tea," he said to Bessie.

"Yes'sa, Massa Graham," Bessie said.

He took stock of the room, kicked off his shoes, and finally acknowl-
edged his wife. "Annie."

"Richard," she said.

He dried hisself off, then threw the towel on the floor, stretched his
back to cracking and something caught his eye on the grand mantle
over the fireplace. He limped over to it, then fingered the plain porcelain
figure and a matching white vase that sat in the middle of the mantle,
lonely and small, even though they was a pair.

Richard moved the figurine along the shelf one way, then moved
the vase the other. He stepped back to look at his new arrangement.
Unsatisfied, he switched the vase and the figurine again and stared at
'em. Finally, he grabbed 'em both off the shelf and said, "No, even you
can't fix empty, Annie," and laid them down like captured chess pieces.

"I wasn't expecting you," she said.

"This is my house," he said, looking at her for the first time. "I live
here."

"Not for years," Annie said.

"I'm not going to let you bully me out of my right, Annie. My property. My house. My place in it. I'm the head of this household," he said,
as if restarting a old argument new.

"I only meant that . . . I've missed you," she said.

"Psh," he said. "You couldn't wait for me to leave."

"That's not true, Richard."

Bessie came in with his tea. He waved at her to set it down the farthest she could from Annie and he went to it, took it, told Bessie, "Take
my shoes to my room." But instead of getting 'em right away, Bessie
looked to Missus Graham. Annie nodded and Richard raised his voice

and his hand at Bessie. "You do what I say do," Richard said. "I don't need Annie's approval."

"Yes'sa," Bessie said.

"Lincoln thinks he can infringe on our way of life," Richard said. "Has taken it upon himself to take away our rights, our livelihood, kill our brothers. Remove our property. He's freeing slaves to allow them to live among us as equals. Wants us to treat these mongrels as 'brothers,' too. It's wrong. Wouldn't you agree, Annie?"

"Is this about Lincoln?" she said.

"I intend to protect what's mine from any challenger."

"Do you intend to stay then?"

He sipped his tea. Then again while she watched.

"If Mr. Graham pleases," Annie said, "make a new bed, Bessie, and see to it that he's comfortable."

"That *we* are comfortable," Richard said.

"Yes. That *we* are comfortable. Clean sheets."

That's when he said it: "I have someone accompanying me."

"Oh. Of course. Make a place for him, as well."

"She's pregnant," Richard said. He used the word *pregnant* like it was some throwaway word, small talk, the same as saying, *it's night outside.*

"What?" Annie said, raspy.

"With child," he said. "She can help you to manage the property until it's time for the baby to come."

"And her husband?"

"Dead," he said. He wouldn't look at Annie.

"How long?"

"I wouldn't know."

"How long, Richard?"

"Two or three years."

"And you brought her here? You brought some pregnant whore to my house? Look at me and tell me, Richard. Is it yours?"

"You heard me the first two times."

Before he finished his words, Annie swung at his face and he caught her hand, threw it down, held his gaze on her 'til she was the one who looked away.

He left her there that way, went outside and brought back that girl wrapped in three or four blankets and a hood over her head. When it slid off, she was the spittin image of Annie but a whole lot younger. He said to the girl, "This is my wife."

"How do, ma'am?" the girl said, smiling.

Annie spit in her face but before her mouth closed, Richard's back-hand crushed Annie's lips. "Be a lady, Annie! You're still my wife." Annie covered her mouth with shaking hands. "If anyone asks," he told her. "This is your cousin, Katherine, visiting from Mississippi. Her husband, the father, is away at the war."

Richard put his arm around the girl to help her to the stairs. He called to Bessie to fix Katherine some warm water, some dry, clean clothes, and to re-dress his bed, Annie's bed, for Katherine. And for a long time, he sat in the chair across the room from that girl, watching her sleep. And Annie took herself into a guest bedroom where she stood 'til sunrise.

22 / FLASH

Conyers, Georgia, 1847

I WALK QUIET ALONG the path of a stream, pressing my feet softly on the spongy ground where the short grass and flooded water trace my footfalls.

Trout, brown and green and yellow, wade in place beside me, waiting for food. A few feet away, a lone fish jumps from the water and splashes down, chasing a bug or watching me. I take a step behind a tree, lean back further to keep my shadow off the surface. Upstream, Jeremy's hiding behind that mostly bare bush, but I can see him clear as day 'cause the small spring leaves ain't near enough cover for his blue shirt.

He signals with his hand for me to move down further, holds it up again to say stop, then points down to the water. I drop my fishing line in and my bright red salmon egg rides the running water, gliding toward him.

It disappears.

Jeremy shoots his thumb up from his fist, confusing me. What I'm supposed to do?

"Pull up on it!" he yell. "Pull up!"

The fish leaps out of the water and my pole shoots out of my hands, straight toward the waves.

"Don't let it get away!" Jeremy say, hopping over rocks and around a tree to get to me. I dive on that pole, pound my fist on the handle, jam it in the soggy grass. Water sprays in my face. When Jeremy gets to me, he grabs my pole and yanks the fish on the other end. "You all right?" he say.

I spit out the dirty water, wipe it away from my eyes. "It's that fish that gotta worry," I say.

He watches the place downstream where my line pierced the water.

"You got it?" I say.

"I got it."

He closes one eye and follows the line to where that fish should be even though it stopped moving.

It splashes!

Jeremy pulls up on our pole, the fish fights side to side. He winds the line around his elbow and hand, careful not to break it, and drags its fight to the shore. Finally, he lops it out of the water, puts his foot on its side to keep it from jumping back in. Takes the hook out. The hole where it was pierced trickles blood water.

He puts his finger through the fish's gills and holds it out to me but I shake my head. "I don't want it."

"It's your first fish," he say and raises it to my face. I cringe.

"Don't be scared," he say. "You grew up on a farm."

"Not a fish farm!"

"Come on, Mimi."

I like when he calls me that.

"I can't take your first fish."

"But it's alive," I say.

"Not for long, it ain't. Put some salt and pepper on this bad boy and . . ."

"You cain't eat it! You said it's my first fish. So I say put it back in the water with its brothers and sisters."

He hugs me with his free arm, laughing. "It's got family now?" The fish's neck fans in and out.

"Throw it back in!"

"What you gon' give me if I do?"

"My appreciation," I say.

He sets it down in the water. It only floats. Paralyzed.

"See," he say. "It don't even want to go." It jerks and disappears under the blanket of dark water.

Jeremy twirls me around and into himself, and rests his body behind me. He say, "Now that we're gonna go hungry, we'll have to find something else to do."

His closeness makes me nervous. "Cynthia will be back soon," I say, quick.

"Tomorrow. First thing. I know. She told me." He lays his head on my shoulder and kisses the side of my neck.

"Did she tell you where she was going?" I say, quicker.

He brushes his lips on my ear and whispers, "How about we stop talking about Cynthia."

"What you want to talk about then?"

"Whatever's on your mind. I want you to take me there."

His words make me shy. I try to make him forget about my mind, about being so close to me. I say, "We only got bread and butter now. What else we gon' eat wit it?"

"*With*," he say. "Not 'wit,' *with*." He turns me around to him, presses his belly on mine.

"With," I say, my tongue stuck under my front teeth now.

I feel frozen 'cause we touching this way and ain't nobody around to stop us.

"Can I hold your hand?" he say, and takes it without my yes.

He grabs my hand through the fingers like James used to do Hazel and walks me along the stream to where the sunlight is on our blanket. Our lunch sacks are there, too, filled with bread and no fish. He collapses on the blanket and leans back on his elbows, watching me.

I know what his watching means. How men, in their minds, take themselves on a magic carpet ride without us, imagining. That's what Cynthia say. But I don't know what it means. Not exactly. I've never laid with a man the way women like Cynthia do. Like Momma had to do. Or like Hazel would have done with James because she loved him.

I love Jeremy. But I don't understand how laying together feels good.

Don't understand how the screaming means *good*. Good enough to pay for. Good enough to lose your mind for. Good enough to spend the rest of your life submitting to because you have to or because of this *good*. It is a wonder of God's hands that He would put our greatest pleasure in our tools of creation.

I would like to know that magic.

And why Cynthia values it so. And how a man, in so doing, can change the substance of a woman forever. From virgin to something else entirely. Or, is that a manmade rule? That he can lie down with as many women and wives as he wants and still get up with his value.

I want to keep my value.

I don't want many men, I only want one. But manmade rule say I cain't marry him, neither.

I want to keep Cynthia as we are.

This is my body.

I want to decide my own value. I don't want a price tag no more. A slave or a woman. Valued twice. First as a woman and again as not white. I'm priceless. No matter what's been done to my body, by me or somebody else. I want to make my own rules . . . if I wanted. If I was sure.

Jeremy pats the space next to him so I can sit with him but I'm slow to go. "It don't matter to me that you a negro," he say. "All I see when I look at you is woman. Beauty is beauty." When I finally sit, I hold my knees to my chest, keep him far enough away. He slides one finger along my arm.

"People will hate to see us together," he say. "Me loving you. Our happy children."

"Children?"

He turns my chin toward his. "Could you risk it?"

I suck in my breath. Hold it. Cain't turn away 'cause he's holding me there with his eyes—the tiny red threads inside the whites are tying me up.

I see for the first time the tiny brown freckles that trace his eyelids above his light lashes. A single lash is out of line, bent and longer than the rest. He say, "Can I kiss you?"

I cain't breathe.

Before I can say no, his mouth is coming close to my face. I cross my eyes, watch his lips form a pucker—see 'em soft and funny looking, more crinkly than I expected. I cain't help but laugh.

"What?" he say. "Why you laughing?"

"You funny."

"You don't want my kisses?"

I put my hand over my mouth, catching my giggles.

"All right, but these some good kisses," he say, opening our lunch sacks.

He lays out the bread and a flask of something on the blanket. "I brought wine," he say, moving hisself over to make more room for me.

I try not to embarrass myself and eat too fast but I do. He twists off the metal cup on top of our flask, pours the wine in and offers it to me. "No, thank you," I say.

He drinks it hisself, pours another. "Come on, Mimi. Just one sip."

"I don't want none."

"You know I wouldn't give you nothing to hurt you. It'll help you relax."

I shake my head. I never had a drink before.

"Come on, for me?" His *eager* makes me want to try. I pick up the cup, sniff the wine, cringe at the smell of off grapes.

"That's it," he say. "Taste it with your nose. Breathe in the aroma."

"Aro . . . what?"

"Just taste it, Mimi."

I bring the cup to my lips, sip it, and spit it out, bitter.

He laughs at my coughing. "You all right? Was it that bad?" he say, taking the cup from my hand. He sips it. "No, that's good."

I keep coughing.

He sets the cup down next to him, says, "I thought you'd like it. It's supposed to be the best around. Spent yesterday's winnings on this bottle."

I think I broke his heart.

I reach over his lap and pick up the mostly full cup and chug it all down in one go.

"Whoa, Mimi." He takes the cup. "You ain't supposed to gulp it like that. Savor it. Take a sip. Put it down. When the flavor's gone from your mouth, take another sip."

I blush.

"You don't have to be embarrassed. Everybody mess up their first time. Here . . ." He fills my cup again. "Now try."

I take in a deep sniff of it. "Like that?" I say.

I close my eyes 'cause I think I can smell it better that way. Its scents breeze in me—pear, vanilla, a little cherry, maybe. I sip it and it runs in smooth, swishes between my cheeks, caresses my tongue, licks the roof of my mouth, and slides down my throat. The flavor seems to last forever. Better this time.

He say, "It was good, wasn't it?"

I open my eyes.

"I always want to make you happy. Whatever you like in this world, I'll give it to you."

I feel my neck and shoulders warm from the drink and my eyes bulge. A drip of wine rolls down my lip. He kisses it off. I don't stop him.

He say, "Was that funny?"

"No," I whisper, floating limp like that fish did.

He lays me down and scoots himself close to me, rests his hand on my side and presses his lips on mine again, holds 'em there this time. He opens his mouth, a little. His tongue touches mine.

"Did that feel nice?" he say.

I nod and raise up to his lips this time, want him to taste me again. He slides his hand up my side, touches my breast, spiraling his fingertip around my nipple. It tingles me everywhere.

I stop him. Slide his hand over to center, hold it to my heart. I don't want him touching me like that. No, Cynthia don't want him touching me like that.

"Let's go," he say, and grabs my hand to pull me up with him to leave but I don't get up. I keep his hand in mine and nudge him down 'til he kneels.

I want his touches.

I want to stay here with him forever.

He say, "I need to tell you something. I've kissed other women . . . been with others. Done more than kissing. A few."

I stop him talking. Kiss him open-mouthed the way he just taught me.

"Mimi . . . you're so innocent. You sure you want your first time to be with me?"

He's asking too many questions.

"I don't want to take nothing from you," he say. "Except to take you from here. Keep you mine. We could get married . . . well, not official, but . . . we could live like husband and wife. I'd never take another . . ."

"Yes," I say. "I do."

His face softens and every fine wrinkle in it goes. He's like an angel to me. I say, "Be my first time. Show me what to do."

23 / APRIL 1863

Tallassee, Alabama

BEFORE DAWN, I went looking for some body.

But bodies were mostly moving around this property in pairs, readying to work in the mill and seed the fields—tomatoes and beets—too soon for melons.

Some negroes were planning in secret—sowing turnips in the cow pen, burying silver spoons. While others were 'sleep or rousing, except for slaves like Charles and Josey who don't sleep much. Those are at home, defeated and afraid. But I ain't afraid. Not of the dark, not of taken-back freedom, and not of George.

I thought he'd come home last night. The pang of his arrival rose up in me a desperation. And fear. But it wasn't fear of him. But because I don't know how to kill him yet. How to touch the living with no hands.

I'm not ready.

That makes me afraid.

So I was looking for some body this morning.

Somebody to practice on. A weak vessel. A small animal. A fly. But I found Annie first.

The squeaking of her porch swing in the 5:00 a.m. darkness was like slow groaning breaths. Her rocking back and forth called me to her.

And she was alone. Her hands were warming around her cup of tea and her thick blanket was wrapped around her shoulders, swallowing her whole body like a soft turtle shell. Except her legs dangled outside it.

I NEVER TRIED to step in nobody before.

It didn't seem right to. Evil even. Possession. But I don't mean to stay. I just need her for a while. 'Til George gets what he deserve.

I stood beside her as she rocked. Watched her, considered how I might do it. Then changed my mind at first. But remembering Josey strangled on the ground made me do what I-did next: I stood in front of Annie as she rocked back, waited for her to rock forward again and I simply fell back onto her and waited to melt away inside.

But the pain came instant.

Like grabbing the handle of a hot pan, not knowing it was hot, then two seconds later dropping it 'cause your palm's on fire.

I fell away. I don't know what that was.

I was simmering after, but I was mostly fine. So I stood beside Annie again . . . for Josey. If I could be inside Annie for two seconds, I could stay longer if I tried harder, if I made up my mind to.

When Annie stopped rocking is when I did it.

She crossed her legs under her blanket and sat there, still as dead, and stared out into the nothingness ahead of her, so I braced myself.

It should have been such a small thing, like a toe to a body. But it wasn't. Or it was exactly. Like breaking a pinky toe on the corner of furnishings—a sudden, raging, tear-bringing pain, that takes your whole body to the ground. I fell inside her. I wouldn't let go this time.

But every time she moved, it was like something was stepping on that broke toe, breaking it again. She coughed—a new break. She swallowed—a new break. She reached her arms out to set her cup down and tears warmed my eyes.

And this heat! Her body on mine is like a boiling wet towel placed all around me. Lesser, when Annie stops moving, but wrenching still.

I try not to move.

Don't want Annie to move.

And when she does, I try to keep pace with her, move when she move. Move *like* she move. No rubbing against one another.

And now, through this heat there's a peace. I can feel Annie's skin as if it were mine. We rock on her porch swing together, in tandem, me and Annie, my form inside hers, the cold air sharp on her cheeks. But I'm still hot. Simmering.

I can hear her thoughts.

She's trying to clear her mind of the strangers in her bed. A new couple. One of 'em, her husband. She's lost now between her memories of him and the haunting sway of the skeleton-bare trees a ways off. "Empty," is the word her mind repeats. Her husband Richard's word. The word to describe their mantle. It comes to her first as an utterance—"Empty." Then a question—"Empty?" Then finally, a revelation—"Yes," she nods. "Empty." Even the sky's empty, she thinks. The only cloud in it is sliding out of sight.

I make Annie pick up her cup of tea, in pace with me now, and put two fingers into the loop of its cool thin handle. The heat inside her is rising on me like a coming rash. No, hotter. Like standing too close to a fire and not moving away. Skin tightening and fluid pooling to blisters. I feel heavy inside Annie. Weighty, from the swelling, the living of someone else's life. But I won't let pain be my excuse to give up. Josey didn't.

I need answers and George needs what's coming to him.

Annie pulls her blanket tight around her shoulders and brings her cup to her mouth. Mint vapors rush through her nose, washing it clean, clearing the way for the mint to come in, and the light scent of paprika or something like burnt chili powder. It's the burning of metal and flesh and gunpowder. The war is tracing the wind, its cannons and drum lines not far off.

Tallassee's already sent its able men. Who's left are women, the old, the crippled, and the good excuses. Somebody had to stay behind. Protect our town and the mill they made an armory. Tallassee Falls Manufacturing Company first made cloth, now makes bullets. It's the

Confederacy's now. So we get to wait for the war with carbine rifles. We're all waiting for what's next.

I make Annie swirl her finger in her warm tea water. Taste it. "What's happened to us?" she say to herself. "Isn't your marriage worth fighting for? Is it worth more than this land?"

Annie remembers the good years. The good things about Richard. The way he made her laugh. Her mind drifts to the day he asked her to marry him on a bended knee in the mud. See, Annie married Richard for love and not money. A fact that didn't matter 'til years later when she saw how he mistreated both. And her plan was to keep her family property in her name but when Richard had his stroke and lost all esteem, he needed something to believe in. More than that, he needed something to ground him here to this place when she felt him drifting away. She needed to build him back into the man he was before the stroke.

She never doubted that Richard would always care for her and for Josey and for the children they never had. And now, her hurt about it is sudden. He's been gone for fourteen years, and for the last four years of those, she had resolved in herself that an ending is what she wanted.

It's over, are powerful words, she thought. She's decided now that she won't be the one to say it. Speaking it is the same as killing a thing; can't pretend there ain't a dead body in the room after it's done. So Annie don't want to hear Richard's words out loud or on paper.

"If I can be a better wife this time," she tells herself, "he'll love me again. If I can show him that I'd sacrifice for him, be true to our vows, he will." Annie decides that she'll let Richard see her being good to that woman he brung home. Let him see his harsh words turn to loving kindness.

Annie needs time. Time to prove herself. Don't want to give him a chance to sit her down and say ending words. So she's gon' keep her distance 'til she's sure she's convinced him to start again. She'll volunteer at the mill. Stay out of the house all day or invite folks home. Busy is what she'll be even if it means parties in wartime. Her neighbors would still be pleased to call her friend. "Yes," she tells herself, "I am his wife."

Her thoughts make me sorry for her. Sorry that somebody's listening.

The porch door slams shut behind us. "You all right, Missus Graham?" Bessie say, leaving the warmth of inside. She pulls her sweater snug around her chest. "Can I get you somethin?"

"Thank you, Bessie. This tea is fine."

"Cold by now," Bessie say.

"It's fine," Annie say.

"I'll be nearby if you need me."

When I step out of Annie, searing pain makes my back bow. I fall to the ground limp. I cain't move now. A cool mist like aloe settles over me, rewarding me for leaving Annie alone.

But I have to do it again.

Get stronger.

I follow Bessie through the screen door and inside the house. I stay close as she strolls through Richard's study where last night he left a green-shaded lamp on his desk burning oil. It's fizzled out now. Red and brown leather books are lined side by side on his shelves and some are too high for Richard to reach without a ladder. White pages are spread open on his desk and black words, like smashed ants, are scattered on the page.

Bessie straightens a stack of books on the side table and picks up an empty teacup with a dried brown drip of tea down its side.

I follow Bessie down the hall, watch her pick up a puff of lint from the floor. She kneels and dusts the spot with her sleeve, stops sudden and looks over her shoulder at me. My breath catches. I flush with heat and don't know why. She's gone to the kitchen, now. I go there, too.

She sets Richard's cup into a sink full of already drawn water to let it soak, wipes her hands along the sides of her dress. A black kettle toots on the stovetop and smoke comes out of its hole. She lifts the kettle off the fire before humming a church song, returning to the sink. She swishes Richard's cup in the water. I move toward her. She say, "What you here to do?"

I look around the room, then back at her.

"What you here to do?" she say again, louder, and this time looking me right in my eyes. "Why you here?"

"You talking to me?" I say.

"Ain't nobody else here but us."

It's like the hairs on the back of my neck rise, my eyes widen, my nostrils round, my whole face gasps for the air it don't need. Years of nobody listening and she the first to speak to me.

"What you intend to do?" she say to me. I can hardly move, trembling.

"Haunt this place?" she say. "Haunt me? 'Cause I ain't gon' let you do that."

"H—how you see me?"

"You ain't getting inside me," she say, then lifts and slams Richard's cup in the water. Splashing. The cup breaks.

"Nobody sees me," I say.

"You ain't getting inside me!" she say again. "You understand?"

"Yes—yes'm," I say.

She gathers the three broken pieces of Richard's cup from the water, cursing under her breath as she do.

I say, "How you see me?"

"Look what you made me do," she say. "You a troublemaker!"

"I'm sorry."

"How I'm s'posed to fix this?" She's crying now.

"May—maybe Charles could fix it. He fix most things . . ."

"I know Char's," she say, huffing over the water. "You don't need to tell me about Char's. Don't tell me nothin about him. Don't need to talk to me!"

She wipes her tears with the underside of her forearm. "I cain't do nothin right."

She lays the broken pieces on the counter and I'm sorry about it. Sorry what Richard might do to punish her. I'll help her. Go to her to help her, but she pretend she don't see me now. I reach out with the hope to touch her like Annie but a searing pain shoots through me.

"How you see me?" I say.

"Feel you more'n see you. Feel you angry."

She takes a wet cloth and calmly rubs the drip of tea from the outside of the broken piece of cup.

"It's not meant for you to be inside people. It'll kill you more than dead you keep trying. You keep doing what you do, you won't even be a mist. You people always trying."

"There's others here?" I say, and take a step toward her.

She takes a deep breath, "Why you botherin me?"

"Can *you* help me? Show me how to touch the living?"

"Y'all are all the same. Always finding me. Trying to hurt me with your questions."

"I don't want to hurt you."

"Don't you?" she say. "Want to hurt someone, though."

She don't know me. How can she know that?

"Forgive," she say. "There's the answer to your question. If you ever plan to go home, you got to forgive."

"This is home."

"For now. But one day it ain't gon' be, that's the truth. You'll be back here like the others. Asking how to keep away that hellfire you feel when you try to live somebody else's life. Somebody else's body. You're all selfish!"

"You don't know nothin about me. Answering questions you ain't been asked. I ain't here for me."

"The girl you follow, she'll die one day, too. Everything that lives do. Then what reason will you have to be here? What you gon' do then?"

"She's my daughter! I won't ever leave her."

"That's what you think now. It's not true. One day you will leave her, by your choice. It's what you're supposed to do. At some point, every mother has to let her child go."

I don't want to talk to her no more.

"You got to forgive. If you want to help her. If you want to be stronger. Whoever it is, you've got to let it go . . ."

"You don't even know what that man did to her! I ain't giving him shit except what he deserve."

"Don't matter. 'Cause don't nobody deserve forgiveness. Nobody. Not even you."

"What you know?"

"It's a gift. Not for him. Forgiveness is a gift for you. For the girl you follow."

Richard calls from the top of the stairs, "Bessie! Bring a cup of tea to my study. I'll be there momentarily."

"Yes'sa," Bessie say and hurries to get a new cup down from the cupboard. She takes a small pouch, smaller than the inside of her palm, and packs it with fragrant leaves. She drops it into his cup and pours hot water over it.

"Revenge ain't for you to do," she say. "What's done is done. Ain't no justice. Only grace. You gotta decide if you want to help her."

"Of course I want to help her."

"Then leave her be." Richard's footsteps come down the stairs and Bessie leaves me standing in the kitchen, alone.

She's wrong.

She cain't know. Not about me, not this burning, not what I'm gon' do to George.

She don't even know me. She's probably not even a mother. Probably. Advice as old as time: Don't never take advice about raising a child from somebody who ain't got none. They cain't even fathom the kind of crazy a good parent is able to ascend to while still seeming normal on the outside.

There ain't even no children here. So she can save her advice for somebody else.

But . . .

I don't know how she see me.

24 / APRIL 1863

Tallassee, Alabama

AWARENESS HAPPENS IN stages.
    Not all at once.
    It comes by age.
Experience.

Or 'cause somebody told you something and you believed.

Before then, you didn't know better. Couldn't judge the consequence right.

But I cain't judge this.

I cain't figure how Bessie could see me. And how she might know something. Maybe what she told me is true. That walking into others to touch the living could bring about my end. I've felt the pain. So if it's true, it could make it so I don't spend another day with Josey. And I want to believe Joscy'd feel the difference if I weren't here.

I've got to count the cost.

RICHARD SITS AT his desk thumbing through his papers. Even from here, as I drift in his hallway looking in, I can feel his body warm, like running a hand over a candle. Being in Annie's got me weak. And if what Bessie says is true, I'm deciding that I ain't ready to die.

I pass Annie on the other side of the porch door, making my way home to Josey. But see Annie there, awkward looking, hunched down inside her blanket, staying out of Richard's sight. She cain't let him see her. Cain't have him come out and give her final words that'll end everything.

The porch door creaks and Bessie's in the doorway. Got the door only slightly opened and she's standing square in the middle. Richard's mistress is standing behind her. Bessie say, "Ma'am, Miss Kathy's here to see you. It's all right I bring her out?"

Without waiting for permission, Kathy shoulders Bessie to the left and brushes her pregnant belly against her on the way out. "Good mornin, Miss Annie," she say, wide-mouthed and loud. Annie's eyes close directly and she sits up straight. "Mind if I come outside wit'cha?" Kathy don't wait for an answer to that, either, before she starts lowering herself into the swing next to Annie. Annie say, "Please . . ." and holds her hand out to the cushioned chair next to the door. "Better on your hips."

"Thank you," Kathy say, smiling. She shuffles across the porch, holding her back with one hand, then thuds back into the white wicker chair.

"Bessie?" Annie say. "I'll have more tea now."

"Don't mind if I do," Kathy say.

"Yes'm," Bessie say to both of 'em.

Annie stiffens when she sees Richard staring at her from inside the house. She puts on a smile big enough for him to see.

Kathy waves and smiles at Richard through the window and lies back in her chair. "Ain't nothing like an Alabama winter," Kathy say, loud as before. "It can't decide if it'll rain or snow. Good thing it don't do nothing. That's what I call patience. Don't nobody got none where I'm from. Miss'ippi. There, if the weather cain't decide what it want to do, it does something anyway. Slush," she laugh. "Cain't hardly do nothing with slush. Cain't work in slush. Children cain't play in slush. When they go sliding in slush, water sprays this way and that. Makes grass flat. In Mis'sippi . . ."

"Do you mind if we sit quietly for a while?" Annie say, turning her head in such a way that Richard can still see her smiling.

"Oh . . . yes ma'am." Kathy lays her head back, closes her eyes. "Cain't even have a doggone snowball fight in slush." She pauses, "Oh. I'll be quiet now."

Kathy starts tapping her fingernails on the armrests, clicking and pecking. "What is this, wicker?"

"It is wicker," Annie say.

"Sure is chilly out here," Kathy say. "Mind if I share your blanket?"

Annie pulls her blanket tighter under her chin, but keeps her smile on. Bessie comes out the house with two steaming cups of tea and a feather-filled blanket for Kathy. She lays it around the pregnant girl's shoulders but Kathy don't thank her.

When Bessie goes, Kathy whispers to Annie, "I woulda spit in my face last night, too."

Annie's smile leaves her.

"Maybe we can try again," Kathy say, with one hand out. "Be friends."

Annie crowds her fingers around her cup and nods. Grins. Kathy say, "Most people call me Kathy, 'cept your husband. He likes to call me Katherine. But my good friends call me Kat or Kathy or Pooty Kat. I respond to most things, though."

Annie looks beyond Kathy as she talks and searches inside the window where Richard was, while Kathy takes in the fullness of Annie— her poise, even sitting, the soft lines of her mature beauty, the fall of her auburn hair . . . the silver wedding band on her finger.

"In Mis'sippi," Kathy starts again, "summer got three kinds of hot that time of the year. The kind you can sleep in, the kind you cain't. And the kind you get pregnant in. That's when I met your husband."

Annie's listening now.

Kathy lays back in her chair, closes her eyes and snuggles into her blanket, like she's 'sleep. Annie sips her tea.

With her eyes still closed, Kathy say, "Must've been hard running a place like this all on your lonesome, without a man's hand."

"I managed well," Annie say. "While I waited for Richard, my husband, to come home, I did just fine."

"Not what I heard. Richard said you was bringing niggers in the house like family. Your hand, Nelson, told Richard this morning. Said it was over his objections. And it was why you fired him."

"That so?" Annie say.

Kathy leans over and whispers, "I thought you should know Richard hired Nelson back."

The porch door opens and Richard comes through it. "Are you all right out here, Katherine?"

"Fine, Richard. Fine," she say, waving him away.

"Annie?" he says. He and Annie hold a friendly gaze. She's the first to turn away. "Well, when you're done out here, Katherine, please join me in my study."

Kathy nods as he closes the door. She say, "Some people say I talk too much . . ."

"'Silence is golden,'" Annie say. "It's what the Chinese believe."

"Then I reckon they don't have bats in China. In Mis'sippi, silence means a dead bat. Bats are blind, see. A bat has to make noise and send it out, so when the noise bounce back, it knows what's in front of it, what it's dealing with." Kathy stretches her arms. "Besides that, bats keep the mosquitoes away."

"How old are you again?"

"Twenty-one come my birthday."

"A baby," Annie say.

"Same age as when Richard married you."

"A child."

"Worse mistake of his life, he said, on the account you couldn't have babies. He'll have his first Graham soon. Be happy when this one comes." Kathy rubs her belly.

Bessie comes back through the door and picks up Annie's empty cup. "Another, Missus Graham?"

"Two," Annie say.

Kathy watches Bessie as she ambles back inside. "Savages, they are."

"Or people."

"A dirty subject," Kathy say, resting back in her seat. "Hard to even trust 'em with tea. I wish we could find a way to get rid of 'em without war. Cutthroat abolitionists push the issue. I may not know everything, but I know they cain't free such a people in our midst. Richard understands the order of things. He'd never trust 'em the way you do. They're disgusting, they are. I once saw one of their babies playing in muddy water. Like a giant earthworm, it was. Rolling around, brown and slimy and . . ."

"Maybe you're right," Annie say. "Maybe you don't know everything. Even things you should."

There are secrets, it's true. Like the ones between Annie and Richard that Kathy'll never know. Some matters are so private between couples that even the bitter end of love won't give 'em away. Little pieces that meant something once and nothing now. And one of theirs is the accident. Another is Josey.

Josey had just turned one year old the day it happened. That day she was having her birthday party. I had been watching Annie make her house pretty. She hung streamers from ceilings and gathered pins for the paper donkeys she'd stuck to the walls. There was cake and cookies. Lemonade and a beef was killed. But she wouldn't start the party 'til Richard arrived.

According to witnesses, he'd been speeding in his carriage that afternoon. His horse was out of control and Richard's face and body was seized. The animal was killed after plowing the cart into a tree. Charles was the first one to come running. Found Richard thrown from the wreckage, face down in the creek, drowning in two inches of water, his leg gashed open, his speech was slurring after he coughed out water. Paralyzed from a stroke is what the doctor later said. He might not make it, he feared.

Charles carried him over his shoulder that day, back to the house, and into his bed. Told Annie he thought Richard mighta had too much to drink. But Doctor said Richard had bleeding on the brain and the same could happen again at any time. It was lucky Charles got him when he did.

Richard lost his memory for a while, everything he knew before the accident. He didn't recognize most everybody including Josey, who he once loved. He wouldn't let no one come near him except for Charles. He thought the doctor was trying to steal his money. Annie, too. He wouldn't talk to neither one of 'em unless Charles—the man who saved him—was present.

Charles was the only one Richard let care for him and Charles became a blacksmith turned nurse and Charles did his job with the most care, everything with great patience and concern—the wound care, the measuring out of medicine. He helped Richard walk again.

Charles earned Richard's trust, never asking for nothing for hisself in return, only that Mr. Graham would learn to love Josey and his wife again, the way he did before the accident.

Eight months later, when Richard decided he was leaving from the prison Annie made of their house—against doctor's orders—and said he was recovered, he gave Charles larger living quarters, nice shirts, trousers, and a thank you. And when he discovered that his adopted daughter, a stranger to him now, was negro, he gave her to Charles, too. Told everybody else his precious child died. So after the funeral, the deed was done.

See, some secrets are worth holding onto. And Annie seem secretly proud that Richard hadn't given that one to Kathy. Had she been told, Kathy would have known her baby wasn't the first. Josey was.

"ANNIE?" KATHY SAY. "You mind me calling you Annie? You feel like a mother to me. Really. I'm out here on my own, and you're treating me as if I belong. Can I ask you a question, Annie? Did Richard leave you 'cause you couldn't have babies or 'cause you're old? Don't get me wrong. You're pretty, I guess. But I wonder if what my grandmama say is true. That men don't want to die next to an old woman and that young widows are happiest of all. You reckon that's true?"

"Sweet Kathy," Annie say. "Maybe your question should instead be, 'How do I keep my baby from being a bastard?' What did your grandmama say about that?"

Kathy grips her armrest. Quiet finally. A look of anger washes over her face, then the weight of worry. A sadness. Her spine curves behind her belly as she sinks in her seat. She whispers, "I didn't know he was married, you know. Those damned Yankees are murdering us in cold blood, taking our property because we own slaves. All that's left out there are cowards and liars. Same thing, maybe. I wanted to be the wife of a military man. The wife of a brave man.

"Far as I'm concerned," Kathy say, "Richard shoulda went to the war, gimp or not. Done anything he could to help on the front lines even if that meant cooking for those brave men, one of the good men my baby deserves to have as a father. I deserve a nest for us. A safe place to raise my family. We're women. We need for this war to be over."

"Is that why you came here?" Annie say. "To take my property?"

"We can't survive in this world alone," Kathy say.

"Then your grandmama should have told you. Whores survive. Women live."

25 / FLASH
Conyers, Georgia, 1847

CYNTHIA SITS OUTSIDE on her porch fanning herself while the heat ripples the air near the ground like a clear running stream with no bottom. I bring her a drink, spill a little in the doorway.

"What's wrong wit'cha?" Cynthia say.

"Just hot, is all."

Truth is, I cain't stop thinking about Jeremy. Last night, I snuck out after Cynthia fell asleep drunk. Walked a quarter mile down the road in the dark, trying to talk myself out of turning around, going home. We had tried intercourse twice before and failed. It hurt too bad and the pain lasted too long. Don't make sense to my body to allow a hole to be dug where there weren't one. So we laid next to each other with all our desire and no follow through. Not 'til last night.

When I got to Jeremy's, he met me at the back door of his manor, grabbed my hand, and hurried me inside before anybody saw. The smell of lavender soap wafted off him, tenderly. I thought that even if all we did was kiss and sleep, his scent on me when I left would be my heavenly reward.

He whisked me along a darkened hallway and past rooms where his boarders stay. Gray paint and paper peeled from the walls there, but not upstairs. Those walls were clean and tidy 'cause the second floor he keeps for hisself.

He opened his bedroom door where candles burned next to a fancy bed. Wine was already poured in silver-tipped glasses and set on an end table. When we finished drinking—two full glasses each—he told me he wanted to try something different, something to help me relax.

He picked me up easy like I was as lightweight as a house shoe and sat me on his soft bed. He kissed me and asked me to lay back.

He kneeled on the floor just in front of me and bent my knees up, cinched my hips forward to the bed's edge. He put his head between my thighs and skipped down 'em with kisses. When he got half-way, I shivered with nerves and clutched my legs together, held his head there.

He looked up without a word, his blue eyes asking permission, and rocked his head from side to side, wedging my legs apart, leaving kisses on each thigh—left side, right side, left—all the way down 'til my legs were butterflied. With two fingers, he spread me open, sucked me gentle, and rolled his tongue along the middle. I held my head back and lifted my hips to him, smothered him flat against me . . .

"Hey!" Cynthia say, bringing me back. She points out to the road. "Will you look at that?"

In the distance, splotches of color stained the landscape, reshaping itself into a figure on horseback coming toward us. A white-haired man in a black shirt and white collar stops his horse a few feet from our porch.

Cynthia say, "Ain't that nothin. A priest in the South."

I ain't never seen a priest before. I lean over the railing where Priest is tying his horse to our plank of wood while Cynthia pulls a chewing stick out of her bra. She shoves it in her teeth, then yells to him, "Despite what we look like, we ain't a house of God."

He laughs a little and checks that his loop's tight.

"And if we was . . ." Cynthia say, "we for damn sure ain't Catholic."

He smiles and opens his saddlebag, unfolds his money from it.

He walks up the porch steps and past me to the front door where Cynthia's sitting. She throws her leg across the doorway. "I got the right to refuse service to anybody."

"Ma'am, I'm just here for a quiet drink."

"The end is nigh, right, Preacha?" she say. "I need to get saved, is that it, Preacha Man?"

I can tell the priest is tired. His shoulders sank with her question and his eyes closed. "Ma'am, you looking to give a confession?"

"By the looks of thangs, you going to hell same as me," she say. "Can I take yours?"

Preacha Man only nods slow like he understands something. Exhausted-like, he say, "If there are no other fine establishments around here, I hope you don't mind if I have a drink?"

Cynthia puts her leg down. "So God didn't send you here for me?"

"Not unless your first name is Jake, last name Beam-Bourbon."

"Funny, too," she say, standing up, stretching and cracking her back real good. "Go'n in."

Cynthia like to control everybody.

Everything.

Who come in and who come out of here. What people do. Say. She'd control God if she could. Tried to control me. But I made my decision last night, lying there with Jeremy, his body in mine—an ending like a thousand purple butterflies fluttering on my eyelids.

I did what I wanted.

These are my choices.

My body.

No longer a slave.

If I did what she wanted, I'd be living her life, not mine. I cain't save her. Cain't nobody save another person that way. She say she's trying to protect me, keep me from the hard choices she made. But we have to choose for ourselves and our sacrifices are our own to make.

"Can you believe that bastard!" Cynthia say, unwinding a tightly folded sheet of paper in her hand, smaller than a playing card. I go to look, too, and see the image of our bartender on the paper. But only if he was wearing Bernadette's long blonde wig. It's Jesus.

"Bastard had the nerve to leave his literature on my seat. Does he know who I am? Like he's gon' convert me . . ."

I hear him before I see him.

His clicking boots come up the porch steps.

My whole body flushes when he passes behind me, brushing my hand. My hip. The soft wings of last night awaken me. My eyes close and my knees buckle.

I open my eyes. I didn't know she was watching me.

In her sudden silence, my eyes peek open and slide toward her. Her eyes bore through me. "You didn't!" she say.

"What?"

She charges at me, grabs my arm. "Let me look at you! You slept with him?"

I shake my head. Fast as I can.

"You did! I can see it all over you!"

Jeremy stutters something . . . nothing . . . "Damn you to hell!" she tell him. "You've damned us all to hell! After all I've done for you!" She grabs him by his neck and throws him off her porch, follows him down.

"Cynthia!" I yell.

She slaps him over and over—his back, his head—closed-fisted to his jaw.

"Cynthia!" I race down the stairs.

She face me. In her eyes I see all the spite and disappointment. Whatever she was trying to protect me from, whatever protection she was giving me, is gone now. I don't even recognize her. "How could you give it to this mother fucker? How could you!" She's crying and I'm crying now, too, and I don't know what for. "Why this asshole?" she say.

Not an asshole.

"Naomi, you was pure. You were supposed to stay that way. For both of us."

I shake my head.

"What'd he give you for it?"

I don't want to look at her.

She backs away from me, throws her hands up, disgusted. She turns her back on me and her boots clap up the porch.

26 / MAY 1864

Tallassee, Alabama

THERE'S NO SUCH thing as justice when somebody's killed. Only satisfaction. The person cain't be brought back for no amount of punishment or cost. I cain't have the old Josey back and I've been long gone. My loss is worse when I think about how George got away with it. And how he did it. How he had to have been watching Josey before it happened. Watching her the way animals do prey. How else would he have known that Charles would be gone that day, or the moment she'd come home?

George was there waiting in the dark for her—black. Blending into trees—black. Squatting behind a bush—black. Pushing the leaves aside to make a space for his peeping eye—black.

There's no justice for that.

Bessie said to let it go but I won't. She should understand the pain of no justice 'cause she black, too.

And three weeks ago, George came back. Again, I got no justice.

His return was just a shadow of something I'd been waiting for, had hoped for, and crushing disappointment ain't sour enough a phrase. I was helpless but he was right there. Like needing to buy the life-saving medicine in front of you, but being ten dollars short and finding no charity.

His shadow stretched up Annie's porch steps and touched me before I knew it was him, shortened when he got closer.

Annie and Kathy were sitting at a stalemate—a woman and a whore, is what Annie said. That's when he took his first step up the porch and said, "I heard I had family in town."

A sudden fire started inside me and I rushed his body. The flames were from him. But I was grounded before I even started in. Was on fire, the way Bessie said I would be. Weak and broken, I could only watch him as he smiled from the bottom of the porch steps, popping sunflower seeds, his hair fresh cut and close. I was forced to watch this man who took so much from my daughter and God gave me no charity.

It ain't fair.

I despise him, and it ain't fair. I'm trapped this way. It ain't . . . fair.

He's the devil walking free. Didn't even look like half a demon when I saw him standing there, gentle in his disguise. No horns. No tail. Just a man. Annie's brother. And with joy, she sprinted down to meet him.

I was sickened.

Richard came fast-limping out the house and down the stairs, was laughing when he fell into George's arms and hugged him. "Bumfucker!" Richard called him.

"And you're my favorite asshole," George said, and asked him where the hell he'd been.

"I should ask you the same thing," Richard said.

"I'm done. I'm staying," George said. "Followed the fighting far enough. Heard they might go on to Winchester and that'll have to be without me. Not all my choice. And by the look of that hobble, you're done, too."

"It just means they need to bring the fight to me!" Richard said, and almost by instinct, excited to see George, Richard held Annie's hand. After a pause, he let go, introduced his cousin. "This is Katherine. Your cousin from down in Corinth."

"Corinth?" George said. "Now that's some fighting."

George went up the steps to greet her, and the whiskey on him turned the air drunk. He kissed Kathy's hand and said, "How do?" then held her gaze. "Corinth's a dangerous place for a beautiful young woman like you."

"No place more deadly," Kathy said. "You know Mis'sippi?"

Richard cleared his throat. "I could use some help up the steps," he said.

"Will you join us for tea?" Kathy asked George.

"Don't be ridiculous," Richard said. "George will join me for a drink in my study. A celebration. The brothers have come home!"

JOSEY WON'T LEAVE the house much now.

Not even to wash.

Not without Charles coming, too. He'll sit on the porch or a few steps away carving the ends of wood branches into sharp tips while he waits. And with Nelson around now, Charles goes to the field, too, instead of the blacksmith shop. Iron's scarce. It's all at the mill. But if there's something needing doing, he'll take Josey with him. But me? I'm useless. For the first time I realize: this must be what it feels like to be dead.

27 / FLASH
Conyers, Georgia, 1847

SOME OF OUR friendships won't outlast our usefulness to the other person. When their need for us is gone, so are we. But I cain't say for certain that me and Cynthia was ever friends. But she wanted something from me that shouldn't be given away on a handshake deal. A woman's body is hers, just like a man's is his. Every woman should make her own choices and consider what's up for grabs and the consequences. 'Cause she's priceless . . . 'til she names her price. I got wrapped up in Cynthia's ideas of salvation. And there was no good ending to something like that.

It's why I woke this morning in the dark, trying to be as quiet as I could. Didn't want to wake her. Cynthia don't keep nothing with no value. Worst, something with no value that cost her something. So I made my bed and pulled the curtains together so the sun wouldn't come in when it rose, put on my white dress and tiptoed around the room, and held the bedroom door to keep it from squeaking open.

Even though she ain't got one word to say to me, I keep showing up for work every day.

I don't eat her food.

Jeremy would feed me but he don't hardly keep no food at his. "A bachelor," he say. "In transition," he say. He got his place up for sale and don't want to make no rush decisions on what he'll do next but he said I'm going with him if he go. And even though no minister will marry us, we'll make promises to each other soon. But right now, we got to be patient. In the meantime, Albert let's me eat with him every morning and night.

I can already feel it's gon' be cold outside. This hallway's ten degrees colder than my room and it's even colder in this saloon. I bunch my clothes to my chest. I twist the handle on the parlor door—a shortcut to outside. It's locked. But there are men's voices coming from inside. Maybe another holdover that Mr. Shepard's making a fool.

I keep up the hall to the back door, slide out of it, feel the breeze of cold air blow my night stank off. I take off running toward the henhouse and through its door made of loose planks and wire.

Fallen feathers rise from the gush of the opening door and I take six eggs that Cynthia won't miss. Two for me and four for Albert. The door clanks shut behind me.

Dry thistles in the grass prick my ankles as I rush across Cynthia's field out front, then across the road for Albert's shop. It glows from inside. He's burning trash in a tin bucket, where orange and gray flakes lift their flat bodies and hang in the air. I fan them away from my face.

Albert pours a pitcher of water over his hands and head and into that bucket, wipes his eyes when he sees me standing in the doorway. He don't say a word. Don't like our morning ritual disturbed by voices.

When he finishes drying hisself, I give him the eggs. He cracks 'em over his metal tray, holds 'em over the fire, lets 'em sizzle. I sit behind him warm, watch him separate mine from his. He'll put mine on his only good plate—a shiny white platter with painted blue trees.

The firelight on his red hair makes it look ashy and dirty blonde. His hairless arms seem yellow. He flips the eggs with his flat tool and gives me my share. I wait for 'em to cool.

As soon as his finish, he spoons 'em up and eats 'em piping hot from his hammered-flat metal tray. When he's done, he holds his empty tray in his hands and don't look at me. He never does. Instead he stares out and around his shop where metal bits and shavings have spiraled to the ground like silver locks of hair.

Metal trinkets are pushed back on shelves. A grinder, a saw, and a sander's there, too. He got a water pitcher on the floor for drinking and it's covered with a pie tin to keep the black dust out. It's everywhere—that dust. A black handprint is stamped on the red-brick wall. Maybe it's from holding hisself up or bracing hisself to reach down.

After another second of sitting, Albert gets up and starts stacking his iron next to the furnace. That's his sign that it's time for me to leave. I take my steaming-hot plate to the door with me, about to push it open. "The Railroad's coming this week," he say.

My stomach snatches.

"I woulda told you sooner, but I just got told it last night. Might be the last time. Every time might be. So be ready."

I nod. Knew *happy* with Jeremy couldn't last forever.

My food was cold before I got back to the saloon. The whole room's freezing 'cause no bodies been in here yet to warm it awake and Cynthia's not due up for another couple hours. That's why this is my favorite part of the day. I dream about having my own quiet room one day. Not the house like Albert said, but after I marry Jeremy, it'll be the room we'll build together.

I sit in my favorite stool at the bar and rest my plate on yesterday's paper. I keep it there like a placemat so I don't ruin Sam's good polishing. The newspaper letters are showing from under my plate. I pull the top page away. "Wanted," it say. "Faunsdale Murder. Five hundred dollars." It got a line-drawn picture of a negro man. Big nose, it got.

There's chanting outside.

Tones like a song but more like a hum. I lean back on my stool. See out the window. Church people. Same ones that come most Sundays to have service. Young white women and one old one, too. All of 'em got

Bibles and babies and young children with 'em. Even the old one got a baby. This particular lot always comes before sunlight, telling us to burn in hell just after "amen." But they don't need to pray for me. I ain't like these whores here. We're alike in the way that all women are, but the root of us ain't the same. They value things that ain't worth nothin, throw away their lives for pretty things that Albert can melt down and burn up. They do what greedy women who want the easy way out do. Still trying to prove to their fathers that they was worth his love, after all. They have sex for money. But not money all the time. Free things, too. Gifts and special time. Time to be treated like somebody's spoiled child. But in private, they earn every bit of it, trading their God-made bodies for man-made shit. Exchange their everlasting souls for combustibles. "Free ain't never free," Cynthia say.

But love is.

Like the kind me and Jeremy got.

Ours cain't be bargained or paid for, it just *is*. Same way God *is*. He keeps me protected and above this place, shows me Hisself in the way I love Jeremy and the way Jeremy loves me. Keeps me outside their world but lets me wade through it.

So I ain't worried about them church ladies.

I stand up in the side window so they can see me proud and I tie my apron around my waist, watch the sun rise and feel it on my face.

The ones outside are shouting now. Their children are doing what the grown ladies do, scrunching their faces like they hate this place. Hate me. The old lady picks up a rock, slings it at my window. It clicks against the glass.

She ushers all the children up the road and turns around a last time to spit. It dangles from her chin and she wipes it with the sleeve of her pretty dress.

She should forget about us.

She should save her foul mouth for smiles and kisses on her grandbaby 'cause what Cynthia and her ladies do here ain't got nothin to do with her. It's not my business so I'll mind mine 'til me and Jeremy go. But for now, I'll bide my time.

It's my birthday today.

I ain't told nobody but Jeremy. I reckon he's gon' come and surprise me with something special 'cause he like to do that. Maybe sing me my own song that he wrote just for me, and that way every time he play the tune, it'll be him telling me he loves me, out loud to everybody, but only me and him know.

I pick up the last kernel of egg and poke it through my smile, sweep it down my throat with a wash of water, wipe my hands down my apron and leave Albert's plate on the bar top for when I get back from the toilet. I hop down from my favorite stool and start down the hall to the back.

The gambling parlor door swings open. I cover my mouth so I don't laugh. He's dressed in the same clothes he had on yesterday. He slams his fist in the wall and walks up the hallway the other way. I stay quiet. I don't want to scare him. And I want him to look for me first.

The sunlight from the saloon window traces his arms, between his legs, his straight hips. He still don't see me. His strut makes me want to touch him. But I stay quiet.

I tiptoe up the hall toward him, glance in the gambling parlor as I pass. Mr. Shepard's in there collecting money from the floor. His door shuts from a wind gust.

"Naomi!" Jeremy say, coming toward me. "Thank my lucky stars."

He wraps his arms around me like he don't care who else see. He pushes me against the wall the way I like it, kissing me.

Stops.

But I don't want him to stop. I smile and wait for him to say, "Happy birthday."

He say, "You got that money I gave you?"

I steal kisses from his cheek, his neck.

"That half I gave you?" he say, pulling away from me. "Do you?"

I straighten my clothes and notice how fidgety he seem. Not because of me. Not no surprise he hiding. He's worried.

"I need it 'cause of that asshole dealer," he say.

"Mr. Shepard?"

"He won't lend me anymore."

"Then maybe it's time to stop," I say. "You told me to save our money for Boston."

"I can win it back," he say. "I can feel it. One more roll and I'm back in the game. Get us a new home where we going. Boston is where you want?" He puts his hands on my shoulders like we pals. "I tell you what. I'll start saving the money for you. Investing it, like. For both us."

"I don't know what you mean, 'invest.'"

"Let me do the worrying. You trust me, don't you, Mimi?"

"It's my birthday," I say, smiling, stopping him talking.

"Oh, Mimi . . . I'm sorry. Happy birthday, doll." He grabs my face, kisses the top of my forehead. "I'm going to do something real special for you tonight. Something I planned. Jewelry? You like jewelry? When I'm done with you, you're gonna be sparkling like a Christmas tree."

"You don't have to buy me nothing," I say. "Maybe you could play me a song or . . ."

"Mimi. I need to get back in the game!"

I take our wadded dollars from my stockings and throw it at him.

Instead of asking what's wrong, he counts it.

"I gave you more than this," he say.

"I didn't spend it!"

"This is less than half!"

He finally sees my tears. He pulls me under his chin. "Come here, I'm sorry. Happy birthday. I know you didn't spend it. It's just not enough."

When he lets me go, he leans back against the wall. I go to lay on his chest, say, "What we gon' do for my birthday?"

"We can't do nothing now, we're broke," he say. "Isn't that what you said? That this is all there is?"

I shrug my shoulders. "I wish I had more to give you. I don't know what happened to the rest."

He kisses my forehead again, holds his lips there when he speaks. "You're my baby girl. The birthday girl. I wish I had more to give you, too. You know I'd do anything for you."

I know.

"And you'd do anything for me, too?" he say.

I nod.

"Anything?" he say, hugging me tighter now.

"Anything," I say.

"Then help me, Mimi."

I want to help.

"You like Mr. Shepard?"

"I suppose so . . . he's all right," I say.

"Suck his dick for me."

"What?"

"Mimi . . ."

I slap his face hard as I can.

He say, "He's always talking about how he never gets none. His wife is too mean. I'm not asking you to have sex with him. He'll pay you."

"Jeremy!"

"It'll be just enough to get back in the game and you said you'd do anything for us. I can win it all back."

"Get away from me!"

I'm light-headed. Like the wagon I was in hit a dip in the road and I'm sailing through the air, in flight with wheels off the ground, my stomach in my throat, and my mouth waiting for throw-up to come.

"I'm sorry," he say.

"I don't want to look at you!"

"Come on now, Mimi." He catches my hand and stops me. "I'm sorry," he say. "I don't know what's wrong with me. It's like I can't stop."

"You sick is all I can say!"

"'Sick'!" he say. "Sick?" His expression turns from hurting to pissed off. "My last gal used to say that. That's why she's my last."

I'm grounded now.

"I thought you wanted to help me. Help us." He walks away from me this time, back to Mr. Shepard's door.

"Thought you wanted to help us get out of here," he say. "Together."

"But I cain't do that," I say.

"I was gonna win the money back," he say. "Go to Boston, Mimi . . . take vows." He turns to me, "I've never asked a woman to be my bride."

I don't know what to say. He leans back against the wall, hanging his head. Won't look at me now. Instead, he turns to that wall, beats his forehead against it once, twice, rests it there, his arms fall to his sides, then he twists around forward, looks up at the ceiling. I grab his hand through his fingers. He's crying.

"I never wanted to do anything to hurt you, Mimi. I would've forgave you for it. I would've. Now you have to forgive me for asking."

I wipe my own tears. "I wouldn't even know what to do."

"Well, you don't have to worry about it now. There's nothing wrong with staying around this brothel all our lives and not getting married."

"You cain't sell more of your family things?"

"It's gone, Mimi. Everything! I bet it all for us. Guess I was wrong about you being my lucky charm." He throws my hand and walks away.

"Jeremy?"

My future leaving me.

"Jeremy!"

He's about to turn the corner into the saloon.

"Tell me what to do!" I say.

"What?" he say, sniffing his tears and coming back.

"Tell me how to do it."

I swear he's floating back down this hall to me, keeping his eyes on me like he loves me. Like we don't belong to this place, these women, this time. He takes my hand and kisses the back of it. "I guess it would be like tasting sweets," he say. "Like what I do for you all the time, but different."

I watch the floor.

"It don't matter anyway, Mimi, I won't ask you to do it."

"You want this money?" I say. "Just one more hand and you can win it all back?" I walk him back up the hall with me to the saloon.

"What are you doing, Mimi?"

I reach over Sam's bar and pour me a shot of whiskey and finish it like a drunk would, feeling it warming my cheeks. "You said you want this money?"

I start back to the gambling parlor and he reaches for my hand trying to stop me but I shake him loose, walk down the hallway alone. The walk feels longer this time.

I don't go through Mr. Shepard's door right away. I wait. Then open it. Let it close behind me. Locked.

It looks different in here during the day.

Empty with only Mr. Shepard here.

The chalk lines that were drawn on the floor last night from a game of craps look like a child's game in this light. The solid wood tables that were beaten by men's fists only hours ago look feeble and small and only fit for light reading. This room's a library. And I'm its newest fixture.

I stand on the wrong side of this door with my belly quivering, waiting for Mr. Shepard to greet me. He's counting his money, slipping bills through his pinchers. He folds a wad of dollars and slides it through a silver clasp and into his pocket.

I shift in the doorway, hope he see me move.

He don't.

He lops a deck of cards in his bag, his dice, then fastens it closed. I clear my throat. "Uh-hum," I say softly. Louder, "Uh-hum?"

"Didn't know y'all served breakfast," he say, and stacks his chips in piles on his table, then sits down. "You here for my order?"

"N—naw, suh, Mr. Shepard."

I try to think about Jeremy, the secret wedding we gon' have when he win, what I'm gon' wear when we promise. But just as I think it, the thoughts get ripped away, blurred and in pieces. I say, "S—somethin else I can do for you, suh?"

He sits back in his chair, puts his feet up. "It's a damn shame, really. Most men take at least a day, a week before they send their girlfriends, their wives, their sisters. But you . . . almost immediately. He did send you, didn't he?"

I don't say nothing.

"Twenty years and I've seen hundreds of gals like you. Chasing a chance for some man they think loves 'em. A sad occasion. I'll do you the favor of some advice. Leave him while you still got a soul."

I don't want to look at him.

I wipe my sweaty hands down the sides of my dress, whisper, "Can I do something for you, suh?"

"Speak up!"

I try to remember me and Jeremy, why I'm here . . . the way we love each other. How this can help us leave here and start a new life.

He say, "What makes you think I'd ever touch your kind?"

"I . . . I could take good care of you, Mr. Shepard. I'm experienced." I lean my back against the door, raise one hand above my head, put one foot flat against the door, pucker my lips.

He watches me. Finally, he gets up and comes to me. "Charlie," he say. "Call me Charlie."

"Yes'sa, Charlie, suh."

"Tell me what you'd do exactly," he say.

I lower my voice so it's sexy and raspy like Cynthia's when she charming. I say, "I'll make you happy."

"Then talk dirty to me," he say.

"Dirty, suh?"

"You do know how to talk dirty? With that voice you just made and all."

I fidget a little, lower my arm and foot, wipe my hands on my dress again, put 'em back on the door in place.

"Tell me what makes you special?" he say.

"I've only been with one man, suh. I . . . I ain't had no children so I'm still tight."

He puts his hand gently behind my head. I shiver as he kisses my cheek softly. Only Jeremy's kissed me there. That way.

He slaps it. Grabs my face around my cheeks, squeezing too hard. "Tell me you'd fuck me," he say.

I hesitate.

"Say it!"

"I . . . I'd fuck you, suh."

"Say, 'I want to fuck you.'"

"I—I want to . . ."

"Say, 'I like it rough.' You do that?"

"Y—yes, suh."

"Don't say, 'suh.'"

"Yes, Mr. Shepard."

"Charlie!" he say.

"Yes, Charlie."

"I got a big dick, too. You like that? Split you open?"

"Yes, suh . . . Charlie."

"You can make me hot? Make me come."

"I . . ."

He turns me around, pushes my face into the door. "Tell me you'd suck my cock."

"I'll tell you anything."

"Tell me!"

"I'll suck it."

"Spill my seed where I want to? Your mouth?"

I nod, my cheekbone grinding on the door.

"Your boyfriend want a chance that bad? Give up his tightness for me?" He clutches my ass, presses his face on the side of mine. I flatten to the door as he breathes in my ear, telling me things I don't want to hear. Telling me about me. About Jeremy. Nasty things I won't tell nobody.

He unlocks it, pushes me out the door, tells me to go.

I stand outside his door alone.

The morning light is stale now. Withered away. And I'm nasty.

My skin feels spitted all over, hocked and loogied, brushed on and stanking.

Jeremy's waiting for me.

I cain't go to him like this. Cain't let him feel me sticky and smell me this way. I smell of the breath of dead things. This hallway, an empty tunnel of bones.

"Naomi?" Jeremy say.

Don't come near me.

"Naomi?"

He holds me now. When my face hits his chest, the bitter taste of whiskey livens in my mouth. Jeremy kisses my neck but won't touch my sinful lips.

"I love you," he says, holding me tighter. "I love you so much."

He lets me cry there in his chest, rubs my back. "I love you, too," I say.

"I don't even care about the money," he says. "Whatever he gave you will never be enough. I don't even want it."

I don't want to talk.

He squeezes me. "How much was it?" he say.

I hug him back. Hard as I can.

He say, "It don't matter. I'm just so sorry, Mimi. I promise to God that I'll win back double. Triple. And we'll leave tonight. Get married like we meant to."

"Nothing," I say.

"What was that, doll?"

There's doll again.

I say, "He didn't give me nothing."

He throws his arms off me. "Bastard didn't pay you!" He turns away from me, headed to the parlor door.

I stop him. "He didn't want me. I tried but he didn't want me."

"How hard did you try?"

I cain't answer.

"I'm sorry," he say. "I love you so much, Mimi. We'll find another way."

28 / MAY 1864

Tallassee, Alabama

W E'RE ALL BORN empty. Got a empty place inside us that needs to be filled and refilled by something real. And if you believe as I believe, it's the seat of God. Love. God is love. But for these needy bodies, almost anything will do.

We start that way. Needy. Babies crying for food and drink and warmth. And as we get older, we fill our empty with anything promising wholeness, or peace from it—friends, alcohol, sex, money. But the only thing that quenches for a long spell—forever if we want—is love.

The love we choose.

And renewed love is as beautiful as new, I think. Like finding sweet things in old linted pockets, brushed off and licked new. Syrupy sweet, they are. The way they were first made to be.

I imagine when Mr. and Mrs. Graham were young they were filled with love. And the first time he saw her, he got a big lump in his throat while she ignored him completely.

I imagine his humor, his kindness, and the kiss he snuck on the day of a church picnic, made her give herself to him. That they exchanged letters that made her blush and she showed 'em to her friends.

I imagine he'd always find ways to skip fishing to see her, to hold hands with her, to waste time daydreaming 'cause nothing else mattered.

I imagine they laid on the grass near some stream when it was in full spring bloom and they shared wild dreams and the names they'd give their children.

I imagine they loved each other deeply, with every bit of themselves, they did.

But now, another woman lies in Annie's bed.

ANNIE WAS JUST finishing her wartime party, a fundraiser for some-thing-rather, when I came this afternoon and found Kathy upstairs in Annie's bed. Richard, who had slipped away from the party, was wait-ing across the room from her, and Doctor had his head on Kathy's fully covered chest. "Cough," he said.

When she did, he raised his ear off her chest and put two fingers at the side of her neck, said, "Missus Graham is gracious to allow you to utilize her bed. Her room."

"Yes," Kathy told Doctor. "My cousins have always been very kind."

Doctor rearranged his fingers on Kathy's neck like playing a small piano there, feeling for something. "Cough," he said again. "Sounds to me like Annie has her priorities in order now. Before today, I would've told Richard that he'd be right to divorce her. For her madness. Likely brought on by her barren condition. Especially after she's brought ill to the Graham home in the manner she has. Roll to your left side."

"Well, it's good to be home," Richard said and turned around into Kathy's gaze.

"Is it good?" Kathy said.

"It was the right decision," Doctor said. "It won't be long until the danger reaches Tallassee and this property. Annie shouldn't have to go it alone."

"It's dangerous everywhere," Kathy said.

"Union armies burned whole cities in Virginia," Doctor said. "Murdered innocent civilians. Lincoln is a war criminal, is what. Marauding and looting."

"Is that us or them?" Kathy said.

"Beg pardon?" Doctor said.

"I heard our own Home Guards are doing their fair share against the innocent. Harassing folks. Richard? How many times were we stopped at gunpoint on the road here?"

"Forgive Katherine," Richard said. "She's confused. Our Home Guards have important jobs to do. Protect my property—all civilian property—intercept stragglers, deserters, folks avoiding conscription . . . cowards."

"Is that what we look like to everybody?" Kathy said. "Cowards?"

"Disqualified," Richard said. "No one here's avoided service. It's been my misfortune. And every town needs a doctor on hand."

Doctor laid his head on Kathy's belly.

"See, she's simple," Richard said. "She believes everything is cut and dry."

"War is . . . complicated," Doctor said to Katherine, nodding with a look of *sorry*, as if he were explaining a dead pet to a child.

"I heard about what happened in Texas," Kathy said. "Sixty-five sleeping Confederates executed by other Confederates. You can't trust anybody."

"They were avoiding service," Richard said. "Escaping to Mexico."

"Deserters," Doctor said.

"Brothers deserving a fair trial," Kathy said.

"And I imagine they'll be plenty more," Doctor said. "Our army will be working long after we win this war to punish criminals. Our Home Guards and other military men will have to become bounty hunters. Have you heard the numbers, Richard?"

"Thousands," Richard said.

"No, tens of thousands of deserters," Doctor said. "Good thing there's no statute of limitations on cowards."

"Or murderers," Kathy said. "But that's not y'all. Y'all are good men. Richard, for coming home to be here with Annie. And you, Doctor, for ushering human life into the world."

"Unconventional," Doctor said. "It's what I do. Most folks believe the act of delivering babies is a woman's job."

"Unconventional, Doctor?" Kathy said.

"It means I can perform a job that most men won't," he said. "It's really no different than handling any other animal."

Richard laughed. "The biggest difference is that the other animals don't talk."

"Then it's our good fortune you've chosen the profession," Kathy said.

"She has an aversion to negroes," Richard said.

"The thought of one touching my baby . . ."

"It's understandable," Doctor said. "You'd be in your most vulnerable moments. A good white woman wouldn't necessarily want strange negroes helping to bring her baby into the world. My wife would have chosen the same, bless her departed soul."

He touched the other side of Kathy's neck, her back, and her ankles through her clothes while he talked to Richard. Told him that this was the End Times. It's what the Bible describes as the end of the world, marked by war and suffering. Doctor said he was ready to survive it. Made his home a blockhouse against enemies and weapons. Added rosebushes out front, said, "The bushes make good bullet stoppers. Most people think gunfights happen between the tits and naval. They don't. They happen twelve inches off the ground."

Doctor told Richard he should do the same to his house for Annie and Ms. Katherine in case the devil wins this war.

"They won't win," Richard said.

"Adequate preparation is the key to civilization," Doctor said. "Crops and fields could be destroyed in the battle, then the food shortages come. Anarchy. It doesn't take long for people to turn into animals.

Nine days of hunger could turn any good woman into a prostitute. Gold and sugar will be the only good currency. I've got both.

"Cough again," Doctor said.

He gently squeezed along the tops of Kathy's arms and down to her wrists. He pinched her fingertips, then her knuckles. Skipped back up her arms to her elbows and shoulders, tapped them there. "Roll to your right side."

Her thick auburn hair fell beside her and blanketed his hand, its reddish tones shimmered there. Even the doctor paused to notice. As he pulled his hand away, he rubbed her strands together as if sifting through grains of sand. Kathy caught him doing it before he moved on. "Please, roll flat on your back," he said.

Even though Kathy's not old, the loose skin under her chin sagged back as she laid on her back, leaving only a crease between her chin and neck and together it looked like a tree trunk. Strange-looking to me but not to Doctor. He was looking at her cleavage in the low cut of her sundress.

"Pretty dress," he said.

Richard said, "Folks around here don't usually wear clothes like that. All the fashion in Mississippi."

"Doctor?" Kathy said, pinching her cleavage to a bulge. "You reckon these are enough to please him? My baby, I mean. They're like blueberries, don't you think? Small and . . . a mouthful maybe. A teensy bit to suck on. What do you think, Doctor?"

He glanced past her chest like he hadn't already saw, and he stuttered, "They—they're plenty full enough . . . can please any baby."

"They're pleasing?" Kathy said.

"Sufficient . . . I meant. God created all mothers to feed their children. I don't think you'll have a worry."

He felt over her swollen belly from the outside of her dress, and just as he did, Kathy lifted her dress above her baby. "Will this be easier, Doctor?"

The doctor froze and stared at her nakedness.

"Katherine!" Richard said, and came near the bed. But when he saw the fullness of her veiny, white belly, he was struck and gagged and turned his head. "Put your dress down!"

"If he's gonna be my doctor," Kathy said, "he can't be afraid to touch me. You're not afraid to touch me, are you, Doctor?"

"Of course not," Doctor said, taking in a swallow of air. "Just like any other animal."

She reached up for Doctor's hand and pressed it into her naked belly. From over his shoulder, Richard said, "Don't go telling the doctor how to do his job, Katherine. I'm sorry, Doctor. They do things differently in Mississippi."

The doctor glided his fingers over her belly. "Perfect condition," he said. "I've seen many pregnancies, but you . . . no stretch lines, no discoloration, no absurd weight gain. Beautiful." He palmed her belly, held it with both hands. "I'll tell you what, Miss Katherine. Your husband is a lucky man."

"He's dead," she said.

Richard coughed.

"The letter came yesterday."

"Why, Katherine, you didn't tell me Billy died," Richard said.

"I asked Annie to give me a day or two before I let the family know."

"I'm sorry for your loss," Doctor said. His words triggered a flow of imagined grief in Katherine and she cried . . . no, wailed . . . like she'd lost the baby. Lost many babies.

"He was a good man, my Billy!" she said. "A soldier. Now, my baby'll be a bastard." She grabbed hold of Doctor and hung on 'im, cried beyond help. "No man'll have me now."

Doctor held Kathy the way doctors don't. "It's all right," he said. "You don't want to upset the baby."

"Yeah, you don't want to upset the baby," Richard said, mad. It didn't stop her.

"A pretty girl like you?" Doctor said. "You'll find a husband in no time at all."

"But so many good men are dead," she cried. "Like my Billy. What if they're all dead? But not you, Doctor. You're so kind. If only I could find a new husband like you. Then my baby and I would truly be blessed by God."

"Doctor?" Richard said. "Why don't you come back next week. Give Katherine some time to recover . . . from this loss."

"I reckon I should come back tomorrow," Doctor said and he took Kathy's hand, already a fool. "This baby is due any day now. I can keep a close eye on her and the baby."

"This is all such bitter news for us all," Richard said, somberly. "I assure you, Doctor. Annie and I will take good care of her. We'll call on you if we need you before then."

"As her doctor, I insist that I . . ."

"Doctor," Richard said, final. "That'll be all."

Doctor hung in the space for a moment and held tight Kathy's hand. "Thank you, Doctor," Kathy said, pitiful, before Doctor gathered his tools and went.

When the door closed, Richard rushed over to Kathy and said in an angry whisper, "What the hell was that?"

"My baby *will* have a father," she said.

"What do you want me to do, Katherine? Divorce her? I will. You just say it and I'll have her out of this house that minute. It can be just you and me and our baby—the nest you want."

"That's not what I want," Kathy said.

"Then tell me what it is so I can give it to you."

"Why should I have to tell you? Why do I always have to tell you everything?"

"Not everything. Just tell me you love me," Richard said. "Tell me you only want me. That you want to marry me so I'm sure."

"You already know I do."

"Then how am I going to marry you if you don't want me to divorce her?"

"I didn't say that."

He threw his hands up. "I swear I don't understand you sometimes."

"She ain't all bad like you made her out to be, Richard. She has this whole place to run. If I'm fair, I'm the one that took her husband, has his bastard baby, and she's been nothing but kind to me."

"You're simple, Katherine. You think everybody's got the best intentions, but she's a cold bitch."

"Maybe so. But I don't want to take this house from her. Live in this town. I don't want people pointing and accusing me of being the whore that stole you from your wife. Divorced or not, I can't get my good ending that way. Not here." Her real tears come. "I want to go somewhere where we can build our own memories. Raise our family together." She took his hand and laid it flat on her belly. He hesitated, almost pulled away, before he gave into it, ran his hand smoothly and gently over her.

"We'll need money," Richard said. "I'll sell everything. Anything that ain't tacked down. I promise I'll give you the life you've always wanted. A place for our family."

"When?" Kathy said. "And don't tell me after the war ends, 'cause that's never gonna end."

He swiped his hands down his clothes and hobbled to the door with purpose.

"Where you going?" Kathy said.

Without a word, he ambled down the stairs and to the outside porch where Annie was sitting alone. The last guest had gone. He stood over her and said those final words: "I'm divorcing you!"

29 / JANUARY 1865

Tallassee, Alabama

G ENERAL SHERMAN AND his Union Army—Lincoln's army— left behind a three-hundred-mile path of destruction, sixty miles wide, all the way from Atlanta to Savannah, the reports say. So Lincoln offered him Savannah as a Christmas present. Our freedom's coming. But right now, people are hungry, searching for work and food. Whites and runaways. And there's none—out of spite or shortage—and the reasons don't matter when you're desperate.

Almost everybody but us has moved on. Annie lets her hands take what they need from the fields, and leaves beef and pork for Charles and the twelve others still here. And me. I wouldn't miss this.

JOSEY OPENS THE front door and steps on the sun-wet porch, barefooted, and breathes in the smoke of burning pine and bacon. Her flimsy white dress wind-presses against her body—the winds change—but her sour expression tells me she cain't feel it.

Her pale skin is drained silver from sickness but not flu. She closes the door behind her and her pupils shrink to pinpricks from morning sun. A fly shuffles the thin blonde hairs on her arm as it staggers over strands, seeking a tangled yellow crumb of cornbread there. She rubs her arms with her bulby fingertips. Her nails are chewed down to the quick, swollen dark pink. A purple color traces the nail beds. She flicks her blanket, scattering crumbs caught in it, and they spread like chicken feed.

I'll call her name sometimes.

I'll hover out in front of her and watch her watch me the way a blind man watches someone, not seeing, but seeming so. This time, she looks through me, out toward the trees where those changing winds are bending the world. Naked-bare branches stretch to the left in some dancer's pose, and brown grasses reach upward from beneath the snow. She folds her blanket and goes back inside leaving me on her steps alone even though it felt like we was talking.

Josey asked Charles about me once.

Maybe more than once, but that one time, Charles's answer caused me to think Josey was asking about me, and not Annie. It's not strange for a negro to lose parents and for folks to move on in silence. And that day she asked about me, Charles had come home late from working hard. It was almost midnight when she woke him—a six-year-old rousing a giant of a man. But it was her that made him uneasy when she said, "What happened to my momma?"

She hugged her doll baby to her chest and stood doe-eyed, waiting. Charles told Josey that she needed to go back to bed and he'd tuck her in if she wanted. But she kept waiting and he was tired, hemming and hawing, then a rest came over him when she asked again. He said, "Your momma was beautiful," he said. "Free," he said. "Free because she decided so. Because she kept some sliver of hope guarded inside her mind.

"She had courage.

"And when she died, she left that courage inside of you.

"So beautiful a young woman, she was, that she glowed from the inside," he said.

I felt flush as I listened. Embarrassed that anyone would have those things to say about me. So I decided, no, Charles must have been telling Josey about Annie.

Inside, a fire roars from Charles's oven keeping the chill a step away. When Josey comes inside, the flames sway. A kettle boils on top of the stove while a wood bucket of warm water steams from the floor just outside the pocket of warm. Charles puts a tall metal rod in the bucket and stirs. The drowned garments wrap around his pole, layer after weighted layer. He lifts the mound and dumps it back in.

Josey sits at the table in front of a bowl of stew that Charles left her. Her parted blonde hair hangs over most of her face and she swoops it behind her ears neatly.

He's been keeping sharp things away from her. Because sometimes, she cuts. And sometimes, she lies about it. Because sometimes, things can happen that are so hard to understand, so violent in nature, that the mind abandons the body and not all of it comes back right.

It's what happened to Momma, too.

Charles keeps socks on her hands at night now in case her nails grow and make her dangerous to herself. Everything with jagged edges is a threat. It's what made her sickness real to Charles.

She spoons a mouthful of stew while Charles churns the clothes in the bucket, his pole knocking on the wood bottom. He lowers hisself to the floor next to the bucket and picks out a shirt. He wrings it mostly dry and does the same with the next piece and the next 'til his water bucket's empty. He puts the pieces in a wicker basket for Josey to hang.

When she finishes her food, she takes his damp things and joins the wind outside. It gusts in patterns of circles and crosses, blowing her stink off—onion and garlic of stew. Josey hangs clothes on the line to dry, hand-straightening them as she goes. The button-down white shirt that Charles wore for what was supposed to be Freedom Day still has a stain on it.

Josey reaches down for his trousers, her britches, and a dress when giggles of children and the sounds of running-away feet blow by me. Not real.

I hear Josey's thoughts sometimes. They're like her prayers spoken that I cain't answer. I'm not God. But I hear her just the same and I don't know why. Not just hers.

But those noises of running children ain't real. The voices, neither. They're only troubling thoughts. Thoughts like visions that come and go. Not real. Like this fog that she keeps seeing roll in, over the property. Not real.

The real and not real blend together for her like it's doing right now.

The sunshine. That's real. The melting snow. Real. These clothes. Real. That fog near the woods and that black shadowy figure sprinting across the yard. Not real.

Josey reaches down to grab her wet stocking from her bucket.

The bucket's gone.

Our clothes sway on the line to the rhythm of children's pitter-patter. Real. Not real.

The fog near the wood's a blanket. Not real.

A child walks out from the woods, between the trees, surrounded by a gray cloud of fog. She's just a girl. Eight or nine. She waves to Josey, then skips alongside the trees, got a brand-new rolling hoop around her neck. Not real.

The wind blows the hanging clothes and whips Charles's trousers into a split. Real. They flare and behind 'em is Ada Mae . . . when she was just nine years old. She stands alongside the rest of the trash gang. None of 'em are a day older than seven. They take off running, zigzagging, toward a start line finger-drawn in the dirt. They ready to race. They're holding handmade hoops—long broken branches with the leaves wiped off, bent backward and fastened in a circle, end to end.

I don't stop Josey from running over to join 'em. Our hoop is as nice as Ada Mae's was new. We stand on the start line a foot taller and years older than everybody else. We cain't lose.

Ada Mae teeters on her tiptoes alongside us with a white rag in her clutches. Her arm falls. "Go!" she yells. And Josey takes off, beating the top of her hoop with a stick, moving in front of the others. Ada Mae crosses my path to the finish line, waving us on. *Josey's gon' win! Josey's gon' win!*

A big-busted and big-boned girl runs up next to Josey, six foot tall and feral-looking. A challenger. But we move faster, more nimble, 'til that dusty girl curves around us and makes Josey lose her hoop and her balance. Josey slams into the girl and they both tumble over. Josey leaps up, grabs her hoop, and gets us ready to start again but the girl pushes Josey to the ground. "Don't hold me!" Josey say. "If you don't let go, we both gon' lose."

The other racers are on their way, not slowing down.

"Let me go!" Josey say, kicking the girl.

By the time she breaks free, the racers are passing us. Ada Mae is at the finish line, waving her white rag, but she's beginning to fade away. All the racers do. Our hoops do, too. Only Charles's trousers are billowing. Those, and the feral girl's.

She throws Josey to the ground and puts her hand on Josey's mouth. "I ain't gon' hurt you. Don't scream." Her words trigger Josey's memory of George sitting on top of her, strangling her, seething through clinched teeth. "You scream," he say. "I'll kill you!"

Another girl, a woman, runs out of the woods. Real.

She say to Feral, "You get the clothes. I'll hold this one down," and straddles Josey now.

Josey screams, "Da—!" But the woman slaps her hand over Josey's mouth. Her broken yellow fingernails are murky like grease-soaked paper.

"Stop moving, girl," the woman say. "We just need warm clothes."

"Mama!" Feral say. "I got 'em!"

Josey watches the shadow of a tree roll across the ground and touch her shoulder, her neck, all over her stomach. Her eyes widen and her body seizes, helpless from the memories of these trees that once held her prisoner.

"Come on, Mama!" Feral say, running away from our clothesline. She got Charles's shirt and all of Josey's clothes, except one dress. They disappear into the silence of Tallassee.

Scattering noises revive.

They're loud like a flock of nesting birds awakened. It's coming toward us. A space between the trees sweeps open. A gray Confederate uniform. A black man. Under one arm is a pile of her clothes. Jackson throws his bag from his back and lifts Josey over his shoulder, pushes forward to the house.

30 / FLASH

Conyers, Georgia, 1847

TWO WEEKS AND I haven't told Jeremy that I forgive him yet 'cause when you love the way we love, been through what we been through, you ain't got to say it. Staying is enough.

EVERY DAY SINCE that day with Mr. Shepard, I been waiting for him to come back to work. It's almost noon and he ain't been here today, either. I scooch back on his piano stool, slide open the cover, and fall on a key. It tings.

I press another lightly.

Ting.

I start playing the only song I know. The same song I learned from watching him play. He up to four songs now but his music never gets old. But my song don't sound like his.

That man with the satchel came by yesterday at sunrise. A Freedom Fighter. The one Albert told me was gon' come and escape us from here. He came a week late. When he rattled the door, I was hung over my broom sulking. The noise made me jump 'cause don't nobody come 'round that early. Almost 8:00 a.m. And we don't open 'til two on Mondays and Tuesdays. So when he knocked, I didn't answer.

I started sweeping my broom toward the door instead, leaned into the crack of it to peek at him. He must have heard me 'cause he took a step back, arms held up, a leather satchel in his hand, and let me look. He was a white man, plain as any but honest-looking—not like those around here. He had a boy's face on a man's body, the only giveaway to his age was the thin creases in his wide forehead. His blonde hair was groomed but not too much to mistake him for not-a-hardworker. Just cut nice, is all.

His brown leather vest laid over his blue-buttoned shirt and above his trousers the round of his silver belt buckle shined.

He said, "I'm looking to hire out a blacksmith and a nurse for the day." He went on about needing help for his young son, needing horseshoes. "Soon as possible," he said.

His satchel had an orange stripe across the flap where Albert said it'd be and he shifted it from one hand to the other as he talked, casual-like, made sure I saw it.

He pointed to the wagon behind him where two dark negroes was already in the seats, ones I ain't never seen around here before. Twelve or thirteen was the girl, and the boy was nine or so.

He asked if he could at least see who he was talking to so I cracked the door open and let him see a piece of me. He nodded. I remembered what Albert said, "Nobody'll suspect us if we travel this way. Not only are we traveling in the daylight, we're going the wrong way. Hired-out day laborers, we are. Fancy word for borrowed slaves. And by the time Cynthia realize we wasn't coming back, we'd be long gone and too far away for her to care. Maybe she wouldn't care, no way. She don't own us. But that fact don't keep some folks from acting like it."

"You do nursing?" the satchel man asked and shifted his bag again. "Is there somebody I can talk to about hiring you out? A blacksmith, too. I heard y'all had a blacksmith."

I looked beyond the man to out near his wagon. Albert weren't on it. He was standing out in the field across the road near his workshop.

I suspect he was waiting for me to decide. He'd never push me the way my sister Hazel did that night she told me to run, and this satchel man was my chance to make her sacrifice worth something, make James's and Momma's killings meaningful. Make it so I belong to myself and my future.

But I already got freedom here. With Jeremy. He's my future.

I can still smell him all around this room. On these piano keys, my fingertips. My face. His scent reminds me of how our love lingers.

Satchel Man said again, "Somebody here I can talk to?"

I didn't answer.

Don't need his help.

Freedom is where the heart is and I got the man who loves me. Whoever heard of running anytime beside night, anyway? And what am I supposed to make of him coming to the front door like this? Got negroes in the wagon. Reckless.

I closed the cracked-open door 'til there was just a line of light between us. I pushed my lips to the space and said, "We ain't open."

EVEN THOUGH THIS is the longest time me and Jeremy ever been apart, longest we been without lovemaking, I know he'll be back for me. I shouldn't have made him mad, said what I said. But I was mad, too, at what happened with Mr. Shepard. It stayed fresh in my mind. Dirty.

AND I WAS sorry that I couldn't get past my condition when we tried to lay together, pretended to be like we was. Jeremy went soft and I stayed dry.

I don't remember what I said to make him so angry, but he stormed out, dressing hisself as he went, had me running behind him telling him sorry, then good riddance.

But he'll be back for me.

He'll forgive me.

Nobody can love him like I can.

I'm wearing the pretty yellow dress Jeremy bought me. I'll wear it again tomorrow and the next day, if I have to. Every day 'til he comes back here so he can see me in it and know how much I love him.

This feels like the longest two weeks ever.

For now, though, I got to finish cleaning the parlor before Cynthia wake up and start yelling at me again for spending too much time pushing the broom. "Pretending to be cleaning," she say. It's one of the only things she's had to say to me. She mostly sit in her room 'til five minutes before opening.

Sometimes I catch her sitting on the edge of her bed mumbling to herself. She probably asking herself why she didn't stop Jeremy and me before it happened. I never promised her nothing and if God don't forgive her for the things she did wrong in her life, it's her own fault not mine. I don't see how she could think what Jeremy and I found has anything to do with her.

She do treat her son Johnny better now. Gave him his own room and put me in it with him.

I don't care.

I ain't got to hear her snore no more and I can pray in silence. I promised God that if he send me Jeremy back, I'll start going to church even if it mean going near those hateful ladies that curse us most Sundays.

Maybe I'll stop doing the things Jeremy and me already do and wait 'til we married.

The jingle and click of a turning key starts at the front door. It excites me 'til I remember Jeremy ain't got no key and we don't open for another two hours.

It's only Albert.

He stands in the doorway, his hair is red and wild as ever. I know what he got to say about me not leaving with Satchel Man yesterday and I don't wanna hear none of it so I don't start no conversation.

I wipe down the tables, mind my own business. I hear him sniffling like he sick. "They captured them slaves and the Freedom Fighter," he say. "The boy and the girl. The gal they maimed before returning her to her master. The Fighter they hung by his satchel. Tied it around his neck. Burned his body. Left it blackened and hanging. I don't know about the boy."

I cain't breathe.

"And I don't know what's worse, burning to death or being left up there with no proper burial. He's still there. Up the road."

I have to sit down.

I bow my head over an uncleared table, take a swallow of water left yesterday by somebody else. I whisper, "I thought you said it was safe? That nobody would suspect nothing?"

"He was turned in. Somebody knew the plan. The route. It's the only way it coulda happened . . ."

"It wasn't me," I say.

"You didn't know the route, Naomi. It was a risk for all of us."

"If he wouldn't have stopped here for me . . ." I say. "Oh! That little girl. That boy. Have mercy, I saw 'em. Jesus! It's 'cause of me!"

"'Cause of what he believed in," Albert said. "Cause of the freedom those children deserved. What every person deserves."

"We should've been with 'em."

"You saved both our lives," Albert say.

"You stayed 'cause of me?"

Heavy clicks of heeled shoes come up the porch steps behind Albert. Albert leaves directly, down the hallway. The back door opens and closes. The old priest—Preacha Man—is here. He's wearing a wide-brimmed black hat.

"How do, suh?" I say. "We not open. But Sam'll be in in another hour or so. I could help you, though. Remember you take bourbon."

"I came to see Cynthia," he say, sliding his hat off.

"She might already have a customer, suh. Or sleep. Folks don't usually come for her or the girls 'til after two. It's just noon."

"I'll wait."

"If that's your pleasure."

I step around the bar and pour him a bourbon. Slide it to him.

He takes a sip and stares at me like he gon' say something, got questions, maybe about Cynthia or this place. I don't want him watching me no more so I say, "I'll go and check on her for you, suh."

On the way up the hall to Cynthia's room, I can smell her liquor. I knock on her door. "Cynthia?" and push the door open.

She's still in her nightgown. Ain't been dressed yet.

"What the hell you want?" she say with gin spilling out her mouth.

"That priest is here to see you."

"What the hell for?"

"I told 'im you was busy but he said he'd wait."

She laughs too loud, snorting now. "A goddamn priest. That'll be a first. Help me up."

She throws her robe on and stumbles up the hall in front of me. I say, "Don't you want to get dressed first? Put some shoes on?" But she keeps walking, her drunken legs crisscrossing in front of her like sticks with no knees to bend with. She's been drinking more since we stopped talking, since she found out about me and Jeremy.

The first thing she say when she get to the saloon is, "You come for a piece of this, Preacha Man?"

He stands and wrings his hat. She go right up to him with her eyelids drooping, wearing a closed-lipped smile. She grabs his hat-holding hand and puts it between her legs, sliding it back and forth.

When he pulls away, her gin grin becomes a flat line.

"I've come to apologize," he say. "I haven't been obedient to the word of God and I failed you. I should have been a vessel for your confession the other day, not a hindrance."

"So you apologizing to me?" Cynthia say.

"Yes, ma'am," he say, wringing his hat again. "Even the faithful struggle sometimes."

"I charge by the hour," Cynthia say. "And since you confessing some bullshit, you're gon' have to pay upfront."

He reaches in his pocket and slides a wad of money across the bar, surprising me and Cynthia both. She flicks through it like she ain't impressed. "That'll do," she say and falls back on the stool in front of him.

From over her shoulder, she tell me, "Get me a drink."

I make her a shot of gin, the brand she already drinking so she don't get sick, and after she swallows it down, she say to the priest, "Proceed."

He unrolls his hat and peels a small sheet of paper from the inside flap and puts it on the bar top. He say, "It's the address to a temple nearby. Up the road. The rabbi there's expecting you. Got some from the women's group you might talk to. Could help."

"What the hell?" she say. Her whole face, her body, slouches in disgust. "What the mother fucking hell! You speaking for me now, Preacha Man?"

"Maybe you'll find what you need there," he say, putting his hat back on.

"You asking 'round about me, Preacha? You're the one up here in my bar. Drinking my drinks. Smelling the pussy I sell. You're getting God for me?"

"Have a good day, ma'am," he say, nodding to me when he go out the door.

"Well, goddamn," she yell to the empty doorway. "You don't know me, asshole. Come in here like you're God. Fuck you!"

She turns to me, grabs my wrist, ripping the stitches on the sleeve of my yellow dress, Jeremy's dress. My face flushes red. My tears come instant.

She point her long white finger in my face. "Don't you come get me for no more bullshit," and she starts toward the hall.

"You should be used to it," I say, before I can stop myself. Cain't believe myself, "That's all that ever comes for you!"

She stops.

"You think you smart?" she say. "First piece of ass you ever had and it's got your nose open. You think that Little Dick Jeremy is the shit and you the toilet? You think you got that, huh? Well, I been there, done that. That loser will sew you up and sell you for his first bad hand. He ain't all you think he is."

"You're jealous 'cause this *is all* you have. And you cain't buy me. You ain't got no friends, no family, no nothin. And now you cain't have what I got. "

"No. That's what I just said. I've had that. And like I also said, Little Dick will do whatever he can to get over another bad hand."

I spit in her face. She slaps me.

"Don't you touch me!" I say.

Before I can move, she's got her arms around my neck, throws us to the table. Drinking glasses crash to the floor. She's drunk and I pull her hair. She won't let go of me. I send my forehead into her cheekbone. Her hands follow to the spot.

I cain't see.

"Bitch!" she say.

I wriggle out from under her, wiping the wrinkles out my dress. "Don't you ever touch me again!" I say. "Not my dress. Not my body. Not ever!"

"This is my house!" she say. "I do what I damn well please and what I'm gon' do is send your black ass back to Alabama so they string you up for what you did."

"How about I send *your* cracker ass back to Charleston for what you did to your own daddy."

Her eyes widen.

Then a soft voice behind me say, "Mimi?"

I fall into him, crying. "Jeremy."

He smells of new cologne. This shirt I've never seen before. I kiss his lips, see his hair's combed different. He don't hold me the way he should. Loose, like. He don't look at me.

"Sorry I'm late," he tell Cynthia. "Had to finish helping Geraldine this morning. Was on the road back from Athens yesterday. I appreciate the extra money."

"Just get to them keys and play something fast and loud," she say. "Anything. And when you leave tonight, take this trifling whore with you. Ungrateful bitch!"

She staggers up her hallway, holding her face, still yelling, "Ungrateful! I don't care if I never see you again. In fact, don't you never come back here."

Her door slams shut.

"What happened?" Jeremy say.

"Where you been?" I say.

"What happened to your hair?" he say.

"How you like my dress?" I turn around in it for him. "I knew you'd come back and I wanted you to see me pretty. Don't mind this ripped seam. I'll fix it."

"Mimi, I'm leaving."

"What?"

"This is my last day."

I don't understand.

"They found gold in San Francisco. A bunch of us is headed up that way to try our luck. Get my head clear."

"You leaving 'cause of me?"

"There's some things I need to sort out. I need money. And . . ."

"I've never seen San Francisco before," I say.

"Mimi . . ."

"Ain't got much to pack. My brush. Some clothes. You use our money if Cynthia want you to pay for me . . ."

"Naomi . . ."

"A few pieces . . ." I say.

He grabs the sides of my shoulders. "You ain't comin."

I shake my head. I don't understand. If it don't make sense, it's a lie.

"I can't take you with me," he say.

"That's not true. You don't mean that."

He slides his hands down from my arms to my hands and holds them together.

"We getting married," I say. "Me and you fooling the world."

"People will know," he say, softly.

"We gon' have babies. A family. Our gamble, you remember that?"

"We can't hide our feelings . . ." he say.

"We're gonna make vows to God because we love each other. Jeremy, tell me you love me."

"Dammit, Naomi!" he say, throwing my hands. "Are you dumb or something? Can't you see me suffering here? I'm going to California without you. Why can't you just be happy for me, wish me luck? Give me a sweet word to hold onto?"

"We both escape," I say softly. I don't even recognize my own voice. "Both escape our suffering."

He opens the door and goes to the porch like I ain't even here.

He turns around to me, looking at me like he don't know me, then lingers there. One last glance. He's gone.

What's happening here? I don't understand.

I just gave up my peace for him.

My protection.

All those chances at freedom I gave up for him. My body—to him, almost to Mr. Shepard—for him. I left part of my soul in a gambling room and now I don't understand.

What's love supposed to cost? What's freedom cost? I've already paid it all.

And I don't understand.

31 / FLASH

Conyers, Georgia, 1847

I BEEN WAITING AT this door for two hours for Jeremy but he ain't come back yet.

Every time I get ready to go, I tell myself he gon' show up again, see me missing and think I don't love him. So I'll keep sitting here on my knees, waiting. I know he still loves me.

He could forgive me.

After what he asked me to do with Mr. Shepard, he owe me. He can forgive my insult. It wouldn't be fair if he found me unforgivable after all we been through.

When I think of unforgivable I think of how I killed Massa. No, God could forgive me for that 'cause I had to protect myself. Unforgivable is cold-blooded murder, senseless and with no excuse. Like what they keep writing about what I did in the papers that keep coming: "Faunsdale Slaughterer."

No, cold-blooded murderer is when somebody, for no reason, takes away everything a innocent man ever had and everything he was ever gone have. But what did I do to Jeremy? And who the hell's he anyway to make me earn forgiveness from him?

I could help him be better.

I could love him.

Lord knows, I do love him. I'd even forgive him for taking a life, cold-blooded, if he'd promised to love me again.

My sour stomach's making me sick and that's all right.

I want it that way.

I want Jeremy to see me sick for him, my knees black and blue for him, my eyes swollen for him. Want him to see me loving him the way he say he don't love me and regret it.

Throw-up's racing up my throat this time. I run out the door, shoot it all over the rail. "Jesus!" I cry and hollow out empty. The pain comes back again and I hang over the porch in the dark like somebody's washed and forgot clothes.

"Ungrateful!" I hear Cynthia say behind me.

I look over my shoulder, see her parading across the parlor with an armful of my things, talking to herself out loud, making sure I hear her, see her. "You're getting out of here tonight!" she say.

She kicks open the gambling parlor door, bumps around through the room, knocks open the side door, my things hurled from her arms: my fire poker, my clothes, my Bible, a jewelry box Bernadette gave me. They clatter when the heavy things hit the ground but I don't care. Most everything she got rid of was hers anyway.

ALBERT EMERGES FROM Cynthia's field coming my way. When he reach the bottom of this porch, he looks up at me. His expression is like he feel sorry but I don't need nobody feeling sorry for me, getting near me, except my man.

He takes a step up the porch and say, "Can I . . ."

"I don't want to see you," I say. "Not you! Not Cynthia! No part of this place. Get the hell away from me! And don't . . ."

A whoosh passes my ear and explodes a glass bottle on the porch, wetting the wood steps. Broken pieces fly and just miss Albert. My ankle burns and a thin red line appears there, just below the hem of my dress where my skin was sliced—the separation cries blood.

I bend down and hold the place with my hand, see Cynthia standing inside drinking from a new bottle she got. She cocks it back to throw it. I leap from the porch! "Ungrateful bitch!" she say. "You better not come back nowhere on this property! Albert, get away from her!"

I take off running.

Keep running.

Running again.

I ain't got nowhere else to go.

32 / JUNE 1865

Tallassee, Alabama

W E SURRENDERED.
April 1865 the Confederate States of America raised their white flags and gave up. Less than a week later, President Lincoln was murdered like it was done in trade.

"But slavery ain't illegal," Slavedriver Nelson said. We can still keep slaves, he reckoned. "It'll take a constitutional amendment to take away my rights as an American citizen," he said. And when he found out the proposal for the Thirteenth Amendment to end slavery was making its rounds in Congress last month, expected to be voted on and approved by the end of the year, he got on his new horse and just left, like most people. Slave and free. Nobody's stopping nobody, 'cause there's no extra food, no extra men, no extra ammunition, and no hope. Annie didn't want Nelson here in the first place.

George has been missing for months and Josey and Charles'll be disappearing from here soon, too. Go someplace where George could never find her. But she got Jackson's protection now.

For the last six months, Jackson's been keeping everybody here laughing, telling 'em his war stories. "We ducked down low like this. Me and Collins," Jackson will start.

He'll lay on somebody's floor or in the dirt, depending on who he's talking to and where, then flatten his belly and aim his imaginary rifle. "They caught me once," he'll say. "They weren't gon' catch me again. We wasn't going back without a fight. Northerners telling us they fighting for our freedom, then keeping us prisoner through the war. What kind of bullshit's that?"

Then he'll make a popping noise with his mouth, pretend-shooting trees and doors and people, then he'll drop his pretend rifle and scramble across the ground where he'll take the place of his victim and put one hand on his ass cheek, hollering like he was the one who got shot.

He'll get to carrying on and whining so that nobody can stop laughing. Josey's always the most tickled and loud, her laughing tears are showers no matter how many time she hears the story. Then, Jackson will run back to his place as the shooter and yell, "I don't want your freedom. I'm here to defend Dixie!"

The only laughter in all of Alabama comes from here on this plantation, a song because of Jackson.

The day he came back, the day them women tried to steal everything, Josey slept all day.

She only woke for a moment, drowsy-drunk, and Charles dressed her in clean bedclothes. Even the sizzle and pop of bacon fat from the stove didn't wake her the next morning, though the dead walls came alive, its wood pine oozed sap again. The fragrance cleaned the air and took away the dry cough Charles had carried for months. Jackson's a healer of the dead, the sick, the soul.

And it was like he and Charles were best friends from the start. Better, family. Jackson was some lost son and Charles the grateful father. And Jackson was a savior to Josey. Charles still cain't forgive hisself for not hearing nothin on the day those women came and tried to steal the washing. "You're a better man than me," he told Jackson. But Jackson said, "Only man better than you is God. I've grown up watching you."

"Don't burn it," Jackson said, laughing a little, just before Josey woke up the second day. He was leaning back in his chair, biting an apple when Josey dragged the hanging sheet over, showing herself to the room. He almost fell over.

"Here she is!" Charles said when he saw her. He rushed Josey, put his arm around her. "Don't be shy now, baby. Say hi to your friend." But she wouldn't speak that day. Only on the third day, when Jackson embarrassed her after he saw that she was still wearing the faded-to-pink bracelet he'd given her years before on her birthday, did she turn bright red and speak.

"I knew you loved me," he said, and smiled.

Jackson had gotten all their clothes back from Feral that first day. "Couldn't say much for my shirt, though," Charles said, laughing. Jackson had already tied what was left of it around his head.

"It's a blessing Jackson came when he did," Charles told Josey. "I can get another shirt. Cain't get another you."

Jackson brought with him all kinds of rations from war. Salt pork, sugar, flour. The bacon and coffee was already on. Charles drained the bacon grease on a clean rag next to the stove while I raced around the room, excited that Jackson had come home a hero. And for the first time my sprints caused the front door to open and they all looked at me. Not seeing. Jackson said, "Just the wind."

His words gave me hope that day. Hope that I can have hands again. For George.

BEFORE JACKSON CAME back, Richard left Annie with only doubt and questions and a rifle he won from the mill. He and Kathy took everything that wasn't tacked down, like they promised, except the gun cabinet, her gin, and the shutters falling off her empty house. But she's still holding on. Bedless. Without a place to set a dish, a place to eat. The emptiness inside her house is like poisoned air. The society ladies don't go around there no more. Not since word of divorce. And now that their world has surrendered, everybody's empty.

Hell is everywhere.

Annie will shuffle through her corridors mumbling and blaming herself for the things she did wrong. Like Josey. She cries in Josey's old pink-painted baby room, mumbles her regrets, the wrongs she didn't see. "I was so selfish," she'll mumble, and, "My baby," she'll say.

And now, she's lost everything.

Not Josey.

Not me.

Not today.

Brittle sycamore leaves cartwheel across the yard in celebration. One catches on the heel of Josey's bare foot, shifts, and gets swept away, chased over Josey's decorated broomstick.

The minister, maybe nineteen years old, and his wife and three children—the youngest, a baby of a few weeks—were just passing through on their way west. Whatever you could spare, they asked. We got plenty, Jackson said.

Jackson packed grains and nuts and canned beets, and Josey gave rest to the young mother, holding Baby Boy right, her hand behind his head. Josey swaddled him, bounced him. So natural with him. "We don't see many babies out in the community," Josey told her. "Most mother's don't come out 'til the baby's months old. It's scary to have a baby in times like these."

The minister asked Charles, "Why don't you come with us? We could use strong hands. Build a church. We need families. Bring your son-in-law, too."

"Oh, they're not married," Charles said, just as Jackson came up.

"Who's not married?" Jackson said.

Now, Josey's white dress mushrooms from a breeze. Her veil made of bed sheets whips her gold hair to the sky as she stands next to Jackson, hand in hand.

"With your permission," Jackson had said to Charles. "I'd like to marry her."

Charles had to choke back tears when he said, "It's her that has to say yes."

And now, Charles seems both broken and proud next to Josey while the young minister reads from his Bible. When he finishes, Jackson lingers in front of Josey. She pulls him into her and kisses him like she did her pillow before her life restarted.

I'm covered in sky.

It passes over us in a baptism of colors: blues, whites, and the yellow sparkle of sunshine.

I want to stay here forever.

Part IV

33 / FLASH

Just Outside City Limits—
Conyers, Georgia, 1847

T HE TINY LIGHTS in the night sky make me a believer. Make
me think I can wish on a star and all them wishes'll come true.

I close my eyes real tight, ball my fist . . .

I wish Jeremy never left me.

Wish I never made him mad.

Wish this day never happened.

I open my eyes.

It's still night.

I'm still sick. And Jeremy's still gone.

To hell with them lying stars.

I fall back against the side of Mr. Shepard's house, hoping Soledad,
the Mexican, will take me in. Hoping she'll remember her promise that
she would, 'cause I was wrong about her. About calling her the devil
when I saw her rage at Cynthia. She already knew something that I
didn't. Had a friendship with Cynthia that ended for a reason.

Her street sign across the road is rocking back and forth, squeaking
in both directions. The lamp above the sign is showering yellow light

on its words, "Hummingbird Lane." It's too bright for me to watch for long, already starting me a headache.

I'm crying 'cause it's all my fault.

Jeremy left me, my fault. I ain't got no place to lay my head, my fault. I shoulda just told Cynthia, yes and yes, ma'am. I messed up everything. My freedom. My peace. Messed up the chance Hazel risked her life to give to me. I should have stayed on the path she set me on. I should have kept running 'til I found North. Should have never stopped at this place, never met Jeremy, never loved him. I want to erase every moment 'til right now. Want to start again, build a new life. Go anywhere but here. But as it is, I've only gone three miles tonight.

I could go farther. South could be my new north like Albert said. But after I told him to leave me alone, I don't know if he could forgive me, either. Everybody hates me.

Except Soledad. She don't know me.

The odor of strange food is wafting out of her house making me feel sicker. My throw-up comes again—mostly spit and noise this time. I wipe my mouth, scoot back against the side of the house, lean forward over my knees, try not to smell it.

I had imagined Soledad's house would be like this. No houses for acres around, and hers, dainty and clean like it's new out a gift box. A carved blue sign on the front door say, "The Shepards."

I close my eyes because the light across the street felt like it was thickening and reaching over to me, touching me, thumping against my temples now. I'll keep 'em closed. No more wishes this time.

The screen door around the front of her house smacks open and I flatten myself against the wall.

"I can't do this, Sole," a man say.

"Yes you can, Bobby Lee. You're here, aren't you? Mr. Shepard'll be out of town until next week, dinner's almost done. We can have wine, make it special."

I peek around the wall, and see Bobby Lee standing on the front porch. She hangs over his back, climbing up on her tiptoes, pressing her

long, thin frame against him like a cape. Her sheer dress ripples away
from her legs and a thin strap slides off her shoulder. She kisses his back
through his clothes and say, "I can get you ready."

She swirls around and ends up between the porch rail and his body.
With her hands, she feels up the wall of his chest and he grabs both her
hands gently, holds 'em together in one of his.

"Don't worry about him," Soledad say. "Mr. Shepard and I understand each other. We have a special relationship."

She inches up on her tiptoes again, leans into his mouth, lips to lips.
I notice he don't kiss her back, though.

She pushes him. "Look," she say. "We've already shared a bed so
there's no reason for you to go and get righteous now."

When Bobby Lee don't say nothin, she shoves him again. It only
moves him slightly.

She say, "Everything's not good and evil, you know. You're always
looking for somebody to protect. Last month, that person was still me."

"'Cause no man should hit a woman," he say. "Not Mr. Shepard,
not nobody."

"See, then you know what kind of man he is."

"I talked to him, Sole," he say. "You had me pinning that man
against the wall, threatening to kill him, and he still swore he never did
nothing to you."

"You're taking his side now?"

"It's not about sides, Sole. There's right and wrong no matter what
side you on. What we did was wrong. I know it. I take the blame. You're
married. I . . ."

"It's that dead girl, isn't it? Your wife."

In one stride, Bobby Lee clears the porch, throws his hat on. "I
shouldn't have come back here," he say.

He comes in my direction and I slide back a little further in the
shadow, flat as I can go.

"You can't mourn her forever, Bobby Lee," Soledad say. "You
deserve to feel something. Anything."

He stops in the dirt next to me, don't see me.

Almost pleading, she say, "I can make you feel good, Bobby Lee!" But he keeps on up the road, out of sight.

IT'S GETTING COLDER out here and I'm hungry. Soledad didn't go back inside 'til long after he left. I huddle my legs to my chest and wrap my arms around 'em. That stanky food is smelling good now. I close my eyes and imagine it's Momma's cooking. Something *savory*, she called it—stew beef. Or maybe pigs' feet. A side of greens. Some biscuits. Smothering gravy with onion and pepper, poured thick and rich over everything.

It's only been about three hours since I left Cynthia's and I'm already half starved to death, slobbering in my mouth for the food I imagine be inside. I finally knock on the door and take a whole-mouth swallow of spit.

I knock again.

I can hear Soledad sing-songy from the other side. She say, "Coming." When the door opens and she see me, the smile she had goes. "Naomi?" she say, 'cause she'd hoped for Bobby Lee, then, "Darling," like she'd wished it was me all along. "Come in," she say and grabs a blanket from her arm chair. "You could catch your death of cold out there."

She puts it over my shoulders. "Let me get you some warm tea. You must be hungry."

"Thank you, ma'am. I didn't have no place else to go."

"Then you've come to the right place."

She takes my hand and guides me to her dining table like I'm her little girl, helps me sit. She takes a pink apron laid on top of the table, hooks it over her neck, then ties a bow around her waist.

"You don't have anything to worry about now," she say, and glides toward the back of the house, swaying from side to side as she go.

If she ask me where I been or where I'm going, I'm gon' first say, "For a walk."

She's in the kitchen where I can see her cutting some green vegetable I don't recognize. She say, "You look like a girl who can handle a little spice. This soup is my family's recipe."

From on top of the stove, she lifts a wagon wheel–sized lid from a deep black pot. What's inside steams over her face as she stirs with her wide wooden spoon.

I feel so small sitting at the head of her big table in her big house. Even the vase on the table is big. Its fresh flowers reach out in every direction like a frozen and colorful explosion at the center of her table. The longest stem points to a wood and glass cabinet where little clay people are faceless. The painted-on clothes is how I can differ the boys from the girls. The porcelain dresses are green, yellow, and red, and the boys got wide hats of the same colors.

"Make yourself at home," Soledad say.

I don't even know what "home" means.

"I hope you're hungry," she say. "When we're finished here I'll fix a bed for you in the guest room."

"No, ma'am. That would just be too much."

She peeks around the wall at me. "We've got a bond, Naomi. You may not know it yet, but I understand things about you because I know who Cynthia is. And I know what it's like to escape mistreatment. To be alone out there. Not a friend in the world."

She jots around the kitchen area.

"Stay as long as you need," she say. "Charlie won't be home for another week or so. And when he's home, he'll agree to your staying."

I want to feel what it's like to stay.

I'm tired.

Tired of all the running.

"Do you drink spirits, Naomi?"

I lie and say, "No, ma'am."

"Then you're a good girl." She sets two bowls on her countertop. "I'm sure you've never had any stew like this before. It's from Mexico. My mother's recipe. It's called menudo."

"No, ma'am. I haven't ate that."

"Then you're in for a treat."

I fold my hands together on the table, trying to act like I been taught some manners. The crocheted placemats feel lumpy under my hands and these silver spoons and forks is catching light. I put my fingers in the diamond-shaped holes of the tablecloth, give the net a little tug, slide my finger inside the scoop of the spoon, pick it up and see my reflection.

"You'll like the bread, too. Finely ground corn, water. A few seconds on the griddle then . . ." She walks in slowly. "Mexican flatbread. We call them tortillas."

She balances two bowls of soup in one hand and a stack of flatbread covered mostly by a cloth in the other. She slides a bowl to me and sits down in front of hers. The steamy red stew washes up the side of my tan clay bowl and settles.

"My father used to eat menudo all the time. My mother said it was to cure his hangovers but he said it was to stop her nagging." She laughs, unwrapping the cloth from over the stack of tortillas. "Menudo reminds me of family."

The smell of simmered onions and garlic, tomato, and something sweet and green, unfamiliar, rises from the stew's fog. White balls, like lumps of grits and brown meat, peek out of the juice like little mountains in a lake of red. She watches me bring a spoonful to my opened mouth.

"You want to know what's in it?" she say before I eat.

"I'm not picky," I say, shoving it in and swallowing it down. I fill my spoon again.

"It has stomach in it," she say.

I stop the next spoonful midway to my mouth.

"Beef stomach," she say.

I send it on in and muddle, "I eat chitlins, too—pig intestines." If she wasn't watching, I'd tilt my head back and drink it whole.

"I like you," she say. "We'll get along just fine. I'll show you how real friends should treat each other."

All I want is that.

No promises I cain't keep for her. No nothing. If I could find somebody like me and Hazel was, I'd be better. And for now, I could help out around here.

Soledad stirs her food and her face lightens with a memory of something. "Cynthia hated menudo. I used to make it for her anyway."

"Cynthia can't stand anything to do with something's insides," I say. "Bits neither."

"Is that right?" Soledad say.

"Yes, ma'am. If she tastes the grit of black pepper in her food she'd spit it out."

"So you know her pretty well, then?"

"No, ma'am. Not at all."

"Well, it sounds like you ate with her."

"Sometimes."

"Sounds regular to me if you knew how she liked her food." Soledad twirls her spoon and sighs. "She'd be satisfied giving me what was leftover after she ate."

Soledad starts saying grace: "Dear Heavenly Father . . ."

When she finishes, I watch her long fingers move along the table. They're dainty soft, like their ends are made of swan feathers, brushing the spoon to lift it from beside her bowl. She dips the silver in the stew and puts it to her mouth in a smooth stroke. So light those fingers are. Weightless, they seem. Her thin lips, delicate, too. Like egg shells sipping spice on her tongue and into the pockets of her cheeks.

"It wasn't the leftovers that bothered me," Soledad said. "It was sleeping on her floor where she put every drifter or any of her girls who stopped working. Hurt my back that way. In fact, it was a splinter there that caused an infection. She spent ten days treating it. That floor was the last thing we argued about before I left her. Did she tell you?"

"No, ma'am."

"How's that floor treating you?"

"I sleep in her son's room. The second bed. His dog's got the other half of his."

"She allows you to take care of her son?"

"Nine years old and he's like a brother to me."

Soledad stops eating altogether. She sets her spoon down on the side of her plate like she's re-setting the table.

"So you do sleep in a bed?" she say.

"Not at first. Before, I slept on her old trunk that she made look like a bed."

"Well . . ." she say, blinking too much, making me feel like I said something wrong. "It doesn't seem like you had it so bad after all." She picks up her spoon again, runs it into her stew, pushes the meat to the sides of her bowl, stabs the meat with her spoon, and shimmies it in half. "Would take me all day to make this," she say. "Never a thank you. She'd just keep reminding me of the stomach inside." Soledad rolls her tortilla and dips it in the stew, bites the top of it. "Cynthia has a way of turning any good thing to nothing."

That's true.

"How was she when you left?"

I lift my shoulders. Don't want to talk about Cynthia no more.

"Well, we shouldn't be speaking of her anyway," Soledad say.

"All right," I say.

"Too much good food to waste, right?" Soledad spoons her stew, eats it, and taps her napkin to her lips. "Tell me," she say, "do you have a boyfriend? Or someone?"

I nod. My heart hurts again. I say, "But he don't love me no more."

"Men are that way, aren't they? Get what they want and go," she say. "No matter. There will be others."

"Yes'm."

She flattens her napkin on her lap. "See," she say. "I'm not all the bad that Cynthia makes me out to be, am I?"

I don't say nothing. A couple people said Soledad was crazy and others said she was right to leave the brothel when she did. But I don't know if you can be crazy and right at the same time. Or maybe we're all a little crazy.

"She probably speaks horribly of me," she say.

"No, ma'am."

"She never has anything nice to say about anybody. But maybe you wouldn't tell me what she's said anyway."

"I would. Honest. But she don't talk about you."

"Talk bad about me, you mean?"

"She don't talk about you at all."

She stops eating.

"I mean, she don't talk much about nothing."

"Nothing, huh?"

Soledad pushes herself away from the table. She's back in the kitchen, clattering around in it.

I shouldn't have said nothing. I need this place to stay. So I'm just gonna sit here and be quiet.

She comes back in tossing three steaming tortillas straight on the table, mostly dried out. They crumble into pieces and catch in the tablecloth. She sets a fresh bowl of soup on top of 'em, reckless, so some of it laps over the edge.

"I left them on too long," she say, and sits back down, breaks the hot tortillas with her fingers. "You consider Cynthia your friend?"

"I don't know," I say.

"How close?" she say.

I lift my shoulders and keep eating.

Soledad drags my bowl from under me, leaves me holding my spoon above the table. "So what do you do for her?" she say.

"Do?"

"What do you do to earn your keep?"

"I clean."

"Clean?" she say. "How much does she sell you for?"

"I never . . . I mean . . . I only clean."

"Sounds to me like she's a better friend to you than she was me."

She slides my bowl back, picks up her spoon and taps the table with the wet end of it, making a moist spot on her tablecloth. I can feel her watching me. All of this talk is confusing. I feel like I keep saying the wrong thing.

She say, "I'm glad you and Cynthia are friends. Did she tell you her family owned slaves?"

"Yes'm."

"Tell you her daddy beat 'em, killed 'em, sold 'em?"

"Yes'm."

"So I guess y'all talk about a lot but nothing at all."

She stands straight up and goes back to the kitchen.

I don't look up but I can hear a drinking glass clunk on the counter-top followed by the familiar ting of glass touching glass, then the gurgle of alcohol pouring in.

Soledad comes back to the table holding a drink. I can smell it's gin. Cynthia's favorite.

She say, "I'm sorry. I ask too many questions, don't I?"

"No, ma'am."

"Just making conversation, is all. But right now you need to eat and we've already promised not to waste a good meal on Cynthia." She laughs a little, smiles at me. I do, too. Take some more of my soup. I can eat this every day even though it burns my throat from spicy. It's good, though. Something maybe Hazel mighta made to kill a cold.

She say, "So where are you from? Your family?"

"All over," I say, lying. Jeremy used to say that it's easier to not have a beginning. That way new friends don't judge you too fast. I want Soledad to be my friend.

"Of course they would be," she say. "Keeping negro families together has its challenges, doesn't it?"

I don't say nothin.

"Did you hear about those murders in Faunsdale? Black people killed, in a horrible way. Their owner. Did you know them?"

"No."

She say, "I heard Cynthia found you. You'd come from some place else. Had an infection or something. She nursed you to health. Probably just a rumor."

I hold my spoon over my bowl. I don't know if I should answer.

"Eat," she say. "I'm just making conversation. Sometimes a good conversation makes a better meal. Wouldn't you agree?"

"Yes'm," I say, even though I thought we weren't gon' talk about Cynthia.

Soledad smiles and stirs her stew. We both eat in silence this time. I wish I had some good conversation to say. I feel like she wants something from me but I don't know what it is.

After another ten minutes of slow eating and noticing how Soledad's watching me still, she takes the last two gulps of her gin. She sets her glass down in front of herself and starts picking the tortilla crumbs from the table. Finally she say, "Why are you here, Naomi?"

"Ma'am?"

"Since everything's so perfect between you and Cynthia—she trusts you with her son, you sleep in his bed, eat at her table, she nursed you to health, saved your life—what are you doing here? I think it's more than 'no place to go.'"

Escape is what I want to say but don't. I'm afraid of my words. Afraid to ask her for what I need. To help me go south to escape Cynthia, and Jeremy . . . or . . . maybe west to find him.

"What have you heard about me?" she say.

"Nothin."

"Nothing?"

"Just rumors, is all," I say.

"Rumors?"

"Yes'm."

"Thing about rumors is they can be true. Tell me what you've heard and I'll tell you what's true."

The back of my neck's getting hot.

"Go on," she say. "Everybody should get a chance to clear their name. Isn't that fair?"

"I heard you help people," I say.

"People?"

"Negroes. You get them south."

"Is that what you've heard?" she say.

"Yes'm."

"Then when are you planning on going?"

My gut drops.

"I could arrange for you to get there," she say. "Over the border through Texas. Is that why you've come? You want to start all over again somewhere else? Leave this behind. Take you and your friend Albert."

I run my finger through the holes of her tablecloth.

She leans forward, "Is that who told you about me?"

I want to say, help me get away from here. Take me south. West. I don't care. I look up at her to say something and notice how her brown eyes are fixed just above mine—somewhere on my forehead.

I know that look.

I've seen the look of the lie before—cain't look me in the eye. Seen it too many times. Jeremy.

"No," I say in a hurry. "I have no reason to leave here. Albert, neither. Any negro who would is a fool."

The expression on her face changes suddenly. "Indeed," she say. "I'm not like my father. Freedom Fighter. Revolutionist . . . a fool." She sits back in her seat, picks up her spoon, scoops her red broth. "It took me this long to finally have something in common with him," she say. "The way he and I feel about Cynthia."

She picks up a tortilla, hangs her wrist from the edge of her stew bowl. "Did Cynthia tell you she kidnapped me?"

I shake my head.

"I guess she didn't tell you everything, after all." She drops the bread in her stew, gets up and goes to the cabinet where her colorful dolls are.

She lifts one out—the girl figurine—and comes back with it. She sets it on the table next to her bowl.

"I was young," she said. "My father was a Freedom Fighter. Rescued slaves and took them to Mexico where they had a chance to be free. He took in everybody. Even Cynthia. Cared about other people more than he did me.

"Cynthia was a teenager when he found her, covered in blood, her father dead next to her. I was only seven when she came but it was the moment my memory started. I remember her presence from the beginning. Powerful and bold, she was. Almost a decade older than I. Unlike any woman I had ever seen before or since. Beautiful in a different way.

"I wanted to be her. Did everything I could to make her my friend but she didn't want me around. For years, she shooed me away. Then one day, when I was fourteen, my mother asked me to choose the material for a dress. My coming-of-age celebration. And a celebration it would be. I decided that I'd be more beautiful than any girl who had ever become a woman. And I was.

"The night of, I went to my celebration in Cynthia's dress, painted my face like hers, my hairstyle, hers. And I did a dance that my father will never forget. I *was* Cynthia.

"By the end of the week, my father had arranged for me to marry a farmer. An old man. My father wanted him to take me away, thought he could save me but it was already too late. I was already lost to her. So on my wedding day, I begged Cynthia not to let that old man take me.

"We ran off together, Cynthia and I. Took with us everything her dead father had left. She spent every penny of it to buy that brothel and to send me to a school for girls just east of here. See, she thought she could save me, too."

Soledad slouches lazy in her chair. "She should have never taken me." She lifts her tired eyes to me and say, "I don't know what she sees in you."

I don't say nothin.

"We was lovers. She tell you?" Her breath wafts across the table, strong as onions but smells rotten, turned sour by the liquor. It makes me sick to my stomach.

"May I have some water?" I say.

"Cynthia could never love nobody but herself, Naomi. I don't care how perfect you say you two are. Isn't that what you're saying?"

I shake my head.

"She saved your life! Took you in. Cared for you with her own son. Isn't that perfect? Funny how somebody can do one wrong thing and suddenly all of the good they've ever done is wiped away that minute." She stands up and pushes her chair in, takes her glass with her to the kitchen, and pours water from a pitcher into it. When she comes back, she sets it in front of me. I drink the water, taste her gin mixed in it.

"You look feverish," she say, and sits across from me. "Puffy around the jowls."

I cough in my water, put my glass down.

She eases back in her chair. "I finally got away from her," she say. "I married Mr. Shepard. He's a good man but you don't always know everything about a person when you marry. You want another water?"

"No, thank you, ma'am."

"Are you saved?"

"Saved, like being a Christian, saved? Yes, ma'am."

"What scriptures do you know?"

"The Lord is my . . ."

"What does John 1:1 say?"

I can't remember that verse.

"'In the beginning was the Word,'" she say, "'And the Word was with God, and the Word was God.' Romans 6:23?"

I shake my head.

She leans into me and say, "'For the wages of sin is death.' Death is the punishment for sin, Naomi. You can't be saved if you don't know the Word." She kneels to the floor and sweeps the fallen pieces of tortilla into her hand, starts praying from there. She stops and looks up at me, and say, "I don't think I have a bed for you tonight, after all. Since you already have a place with Cynthia in your own bed, I think you should stay there."

I slide the blanket from my shoulders. "Yes'm," and get up for the door. When I get there, I turn around to thank her for the food but she's already got eyes on me.

"Look at you," she say. "Cynthia doesn't love you any more than she does me."

I reach for the knob.

"And, Naomi? No more messengers with orange stripes on their satchels will be coming to your door."

I let myself out.

34 / JUNE-NOVEMBER 1865

Tallassee, Alabama

I STAYED BESIDE 'EM, Jackson and Josey, as their wagon rocked from side to side, bumping over weak stones making gravel. Charles had tied a yellow ribbon above the back wheels to mark a special day—their wedding made in freedom. It meant they could own their coming babies now. And each other, never parted.

Charles stood with his hand in the air behind them as their wagon rode away. His good-bye faded the further we got away from him, 'til finally he disappeared. Not because he left that spot, I imagine, but because our wheels kept churning. He probably stood there another two days a statue, perched on the edge of his empty nest.

Josey lowered herself down into her seat and hid on the wagon's floor with her forehead laid on her arm like a child's counting game while the trees seemed to walk toward us. Their shadows casted themselves across us, staining and restaining us gray with colored-in outlines of leaf bouquets.

We rolled over short hills separating the slaves' quarters from the Graham plantation house. The house's white face rose and its windows were like eyes watching us. The broken shutters hung off 'em like the saggy lids of an old man. We veered right at the bottom of the road and the trees around us thickened and our path thinned. This is the way to our new home. Two miles of road patterned after the scribble of an unsteady hand drawing a half circle. Less than a mile in a walking beeline.

Our final slow roll led us into the yard. A place Josey and I had been before, long ago with Ada Mae. The drowned dead garden and worn steps of the house were still there. No longer just the witch's house. This was ours now.

Jackson started cutting a path out front of the house the morning after they'd first arrived a month ago. It's wide enough now for no tree, no shadow, no nothing to come near Josey. It's almost done.

"Another month or two and it'll be finished for good," Jackson told Josey and his momma. "A shortcut straight back to the old slaves' quarters to Charles," he said and then took them around back to show 'em the space. Stumps of half-cleared trees erased a space ten feet wide by twenty feet deep, leading into the woods.

"In case of fire or any trouble," Jackson said. "Josey could go out this way. You, too, Momma."

"Does that make me second?" Sissy said. "An afterthought?"

"Aw, Ma, I'm just talking. You and Josey or Josey and you . . ."

"Um hm," she said.

Sissy was first, she'd been reminding him. First to wipe his nose, his butt, to put clothes on his back. Only yesterday, Sissy told him how she was first to come and see the fishpond he'd built above ground when he was eight years old. She reminded him how he had carried bricks home for months and stacked 'em into a jagged circle and packed the inside of it with mud. Eight-year-old Jackson told his Momma, "Mud is what's on the bottom of any stream. It'll stop the leaks!"

The retelling of the story made Sissy laugh.

"'You gon' eat fish all year long,'" Sissy said. "Then he filled his pond with water and stocked it with a half dozen fish he caught and brung home alive. He was counting his fish eggs before they hatched. Before they were even laid. But by morning, the water was missing. Cats had eaten all but the heads of two, and the flies were settling on leftovers."

Sissy laughed loudest about the leftovers, mocking Jackson, "Every Sunday'll be a fish fry!" But Josey was still proud of him. Proud of Jackson's trying. For building. Proud of how he wanted to make her happy. But now, to Sissy, it seemed he only wanted to make Josey happy. So she took more notice of the words he'd use and their ordering, and even who he'd first pass the bread to at supper. And now, Sissy sees these cut-down trees they never needed before Josey, and this path Jackson made.

"You an idiot, son, I swear it," Sissy said. "You ain't grown from the boy who tried to hold water in sand. Ain't got the sense God gave you. Cain't do shit right. What we need is light in this house. Some windows. I shouldn't have to sit outside all the damn time. When you ready to do something for me, get yourself together, get some training, and help *me*—the one who raised you—then you let me know."

Jackson bowed his head like a boy chastised, weak and ashamed of hisself in front of Josey. But Josey held his hand. Told him what he did was beautiful. Couldn't nobody do it better. And she loved him for it. Would always love him. It's why Jackson loves her, too. For who she's not.

Not-Sissy.

Not a yeller, not a curser, and she don't pinch him when she think he's done wrong. Don't talk down to him, call him lazy, ugly, or need to wash his ass that stink. Josey don't make him feel bad about hisself, don't argue, though she say what she need. And when she do disagree, she gives him understanding and words of encouragement. Love. Jackson thinks Josey's touches are love alive.

So for her, Jackson was willing to cut down all the trees in Alabama. Was gonna reward her love with his love, and with his appreciation, and with whatever it took to make Josey's sickness never come back. 'Cause sometimes, still, she has bad days.

The first week of their marriage, he found Josey standing half-naked and white on a mound of dirt and trampled tomato vines shouting at the top of her voice, "1:00 a.m. and all is well!" She was counting the time. It was 2:30 a.m. when he finally got her inside.

Even on these bad days, when Josey would turn up paralyzed by the edge of the woods 'cause a tree got too close, he would show her enough love to woo her back, to calm her anxious thoughts. And when she would recover, she'd show him love more than Sissy ever could. And two weeks after Sissy treated him bad for making that path out back, Jackson rewarded Josey's love by starting to build an outhouse inside.

It took him a month of hammering all day and not letting anyone in the house, near the cupboard, where it was going. He made 'em enjoy the sunshine outside during the day and kept the cupboard door closed at night. "A surprise," he told 'em every day when they asked what he was building.

On the day he finished it, he guided 'em back inside the house with their eyes closed. Then he pulled open the cupboard doors and walked inside, stood next to a wooden bucket tipped upside down on the floor. "Ta-da!" he said.

The space inside was wide enough to fit hisself plus two or three more people. He put his hands on his hips and smiled.

"Where's all my food gone?" Sissy said. "What you do to my cupboard?"

"Don't worry, Momma. Your food's safe. What you think?"

He turned in the space, smiling hard, shook a shelf that hung on the wall where his two hammers and nails were, and said, "See, you can put your girly thangs up here. Or clean rags."

From the doorway, Josey leaned into the room but wouldn't go in.

"This is the real surprise," he said, lifting the lid of the upside-down bucket on the floor. Sissy took a step inside and peered over the lid. Josey finally went in, too.

The bucket covered a hole in the wood floor and the hole went clear through to the dirt four feet underneath the house.

Jackson lowered his backside on the seat and covered the whole of it with his skinny butt. "See," he said. "It's a outhouse, inside."

"Oh," Josey said. She forced a smile. Sissy didn't bother.

"You got all the privacy in the world," Jackson said. "Ain't gotta go outside in the middle of the night with a bad stomach or pull out the pot. Just sit right here and let go." He wiggled himself on the seat. "It won't move, see. I bolted it down. Comfy, too."

"Ain't the smell gon' come up in the house?" Josey said.

He hopped up. "Just close the lid like this when you done and that's it. No smell. We just got to make sure to shovel under the house every day, thas all."

"And who gon' crawl under there and do all the shovelin, you?" Sissy said.

"Well . . . Josey or me."

Josey laughed, "I'd rather use the one outside."

"Come on, Josey." Jackson said. "People do it all the time. When I was off to the war, I seen books about these people a long time ago. They made holes like this . . ."

"I ain't gon' use it," Josey said. "Clean it, neither."

"Well, you cain't clean it now 'cause you pregnant, of course."

"Pregnant?" Sissy said. She rolled her neck, slow and long, like it was on wheels. "You wasn't gon' tell me, Jackson? I don't deserve to know?"

"Aw, Momma. We was just waiting for the right time. Make it special."

"When Jackson? How far 'long?"

Josey whispered, "Just two cycles I missed is all, Miss Sissy."

Sissy wouldn't look at Josey.

"Two months of knowing and you couldn't tell me?" she say and limps out of his cupboard and back into the room.

"Momma, I'm sorry. I . . ."

"That's your problem, Jackson. You waste all your time on shit. I coulda had my windows. Only a fool shits where he eats and sleeps." Jackson clears the shelf with his forearm, grabs the bucket and rips it from its hinges. He heaves it out of the cupboard and across the room, past Sissy. He scoops his hammer from the floor and storms out the front door.

"Jackson?" Josey calls, following him. "Jackson?" But he kept on out.

"Jackson Allen!" Sissy say.

He stops directly on the porch steps and was breathing hard and tearful when he spins around to his momma, whimpering like a boy told he couldn't go out and play.

Sissy limps past Josey to stand on the steps next to him. When she get there, she and Jackson turn their backs on Josey. Josey tries to join 'em but they take two steps down the porch.

"Jackson?" Josey say. "I'm sorry. It's not your fault." But Jackson don't turn around.

Sissy rubs his shoulders and the back of his neck with her thumbs. She whispers in his ear. He hangs his head low and listens. Josey backs away. She picks up his tools from the corner of the front room and the broken bucket. A shard of wood stabs her hand making her drop the hammer. Just missed her toe.

She rips off the extra shards still stuck on the bucket and carries it back through the cupboard door and sets it over the hole in the floor again. She closes the lid. "I miss you, Daddy," she whispers.

Josey snaps off another piece of splintered wood from the bucket, then another, then all around the lid 'til the bucket is smooth again. She sits down on it and drops the fractured pieces of wood into a short pile there. But the biggest shard she keeps. She rolls it in her hand before sliding it back and forth across her thigh on purpose, grunting as it reddens, then bleeds. Her eyes roll back in pain. Or feel-good.

35 / MAY 1866

Tallassee, Alabama

B IRTH IS NOT the work of a conscious mind any more than a heartbeat is. It just happens. In its own animal way, it do. Through God. Its own magic. And in its own time.

Josey crawled her way into Jackson's cupboard—the outhouse, inside—alone and in the dark, then squatted over his broken toilet seat and started pushing.

Jackson never meant for the bucket to be used as a birthing chair but nobody had the nerve to use it in any other way.

The lid's been kept closed all the time to stop things from crawling up and into the house.

Except right now.

There's a hole in the floor 'cause Josey dragged the bucket across the room. She's softened the bottom with the clean sheets and linens, wadded and stuffed inside the bucket—a safe landing for the baby. Now, she hovers over the bucket, pushing alone. Pushing because she is alone.

JACKSON LEFT TWO months ago for the new war, the Indian War west. Wasn't the same man he was when they married. Everything got to be too much for him—Josey's sickness, the work needing doing, and most of all, he missed war. Most of the able-bodied men did, black or white. The ones who weren't flinching at every loud sound and sinking into madness, seemed like they needed guns and to be afraid and needed somebody else to pay with their lives for new anger.

And this condition became a dependency of men.

The same way trousers *needed* suspenders, instead of finding harmony in a pair that fits. We're not the same, they tell us. We're different, they say. We don't fit together.

The world is too big and too strange now, they believe, and without a conflict or war holding us up, leaders are uneasy. They have the weight of the world on their shoulders and they need straps. Without them, they feel something is wrong. They could be exposed as naked at any time. Vulnerable. They need to feel secure in something familiar and taut. The strain of one thing pulling against another. This is what the new America needs to feel normal, with the wrong question being asked over and over again, "How can we have peace without suspenders?" Not, "How can we have harmony and not need suspenders?" A silly question to too many, so we get more suspenders. And now, our men and their strain are inseparable.

JACKSON NEVER DID finish Josey's path out back and never started Sissy's windows.

He told Josey, "You ask, but I don't know what's wrong with me. I don't wake up in the morning saying to myself, 'I'm not gon' do nothing today.' I think I have time to, or I don't think about time 'til night falls and it's too late and all I want to do is go back to sleep. So I don't know what's wrong."

But he knew.

In part, he did.

In the first months of Josey's pregnancy, Jackson was strong. Even when she went in and out of good health—made worser by her morning sickness—Jackson was still eager to love his wife.

Jackson found her more than once naked and standing on that mound squawking like a hawk, or just plain lost. He got good at not staying too far from her. He liked how much she needed him. The same way she had needed Charles. "You can count on me," he'd tell her. "You don't need to do nothing. Just sit here and rest your feet."

By the third month, he was doing more than his fair share of work, the hunting and skinning, the cooking and some cleaning, while able-bodied Sissy did nothing but moan about not having her windows.

By the fifth month, Jackson spent all his time praying for Josey. Twice a day, every day, for healing. That started after he'd snuck up on her in the kitchen, went to hug her, and felt the wet red lines she'd sliced across her forearms. It broke his heart that his love stopped helping her, stopped being the healing kind.

He prayed straight through a week. If his lips weren't moving to talk, they were moving to say, "Thank you, God, and amen." Then one day, he stopped.

It was the day he found Josey sprawled out at the edge of the woods, not moving. He didn't even check to see if she was dead. He just stood there in place, staring at her.

Then he collapsed.

From the ground he cried an ugly cry. Full-bodied, up in the shoulders, cry.

And it made me sorry. Sorry for Josey. Sorry for him. Sorry when I knew he couldn't care for her. Sorry for his broke heart when he knew it, too. He was ashamed of hisself for wanting to give up. Then devastated by his own fleeting thought: that if Josey were dead, it would be a relief.

I wish Charles were here.

She'll always have me, but right now she need a Charles.

Charles had spent almost five months living between Sissy's house and his old slaves' quarters. In secret, he'd walk the shortcut that Jackson had partly finished so he could see Josey most days, waiting to overhear her tell Jackson she missed her daddy but that never came.

But mostly, Charles wanted to be sure that Josey was safe and properly cared for. That Jackson could be the man to do it. That he could be trusted. Charles needed to know how Jackson would be when he thought no one was watching. Needed to see the character of the man he called friend. And Charles missed Josey.

For weeks he cried every night. Had decided that lonely was the disease that Josey left him with. Incurable. A leprosy of the soul. And that first day, Josey's wedding day, he was falling apart inside. When Josey and Jackson would come to visit him on Sundays, it was the only day he'd dressed hisself all week. And when they'd come, the house was full again with her laughter and the deep ocean of joy in her smile, only ebbing when she saw in him something like sadness and asked, "Daddy? Are you all right?"

He didn't want to be the reason for her to stop smiling.

"I'm going west," he finally told her. "Join the preacher and his family. If they won't have me, I could join the fighting against the Lakota Indians. The west is wild. I won't die a useless old man."

But Josey couldn't let him go.

She told him so.

The first time he left, he walked fifteen miles back home because of his second thoughts and her voice is his head. But when he got back and saw again how well Jackson cared for Josey, it hurt him some. He thought maybe Jackson could do it better than he could. And he didn't want to be a burden. So he left. He held the healing vision of Josey in his mind ahead of him so he wouldn't turn back.

BY THE SIXTH month, Jackson stopped believing Josey could be better. Her sickness wore on him like thighs on inseams. But maybe it wasn't just her. Maybe it's the nature of things. How men cain't stay at home and do the work of women. How he was stuck at home, instead of the war. Some women are bred to be trapped in a house. Caged animals in their housework who feel free.

Not Jackson.

Not for long.

Not since he heard from Charles about the new war against the Indians out west. So when them "negro representatives" came down our path recruiting new federal troops to help re-occupy Texas, Jackson said, "I will . . . but I gotta talk to my wife."

JOSEY SITS ON the ledge of the bucket with her leg bent up on the seat. Her pink-white toes are stretching long and bulby, double creased at the knuckle as the pain of her labor rises.

It hits her hard and she grips the bucket's seat with all her toes and fingers, bearing down, chin in chest, grunting and groaning. But not like she's about to have a baby, though.

Quieter. Lot quieter.

Like she's straining out some solid block of the bowel in private. Guarded.

All of this quiet is to keep Sissy unaware and asleep in the other room. Josey don't want this moment spoiled by her.

"You a whore," Sissy told Josey the day after the wedding. "Brides s'posed to bleed on their wedding night," she said. "These sheets stayed clean. And if you try'na pass off your cycle blood as something different . . . know that new blood don't smell the same."

WHEN THE PAIN lets go of Josey again, she leans back and lets her legs gap open, waiting for the next wave to come. She's calling for Jackson. Not for me. It wouldn't be me. Why would it ever be? Even now?

"Nobody's going nowhere," Sissy told Jackson the day he announced his leaving. "There's a lot here that needs doing, a baby coming . . . you ain't leaving me. You promised the last war was the last time. What about these windows, Jackson? What about the sowing that needs doing? What about what I need?"

JOSEY SCOOTS BACK on the bucket and undoes the top buttons of her dress, tugging the material away from her neck like it's too hot even though there's snow outside.

Her panting hot breaths push smoke through her thin lips, drying the soft skin there to clear flakes.

I hover next to her, pacing back and forth, wish I could go get somebody, wake Sissy. "Jackson," she whispers.

"WE ALL DESERVE freedom," Josey told him when he said he wanted to go back to war. "We'll be all right. It's your turn."

"Don't listen to this fool," Sissy said. "She's trying to get rid of you. Probably got somebody waiting down that nice path you cleared for her."

JOSEY BRINGS HER foot back to the toilet ledge, biting into her lip, shutting her eyes and rolling her head to one side. For the first time, she screams. And again. Pushing.

Screams!

The cupboard door bursts open, "What the hell you screaming for!" Sissy say coming in. "All this damn screaming!" Sissy drops a bucket of warm water on the cupboard floor. "Two hours you been in here grunting. This ain't no proper place to have a baby. Get up!"

Josey staggers to her feet and lets herself get pulled along. Every step she takes looks painful.

Sissy sets her down in the corner of the room on a birthing mat that she's readied for this. She take the cup and pours water in Josey's dry mouth but Josey coughs it up.

"You need to drink something or get this over wit."

Josey closes her eyes. "I just need to sleep," she say. "I'm so tired now."

"No woman's posed to sleep for birthing." But Josey don't open her eyes again. Only her parched sticky lips peel open and her head rolls. Sissy shakes her awake.

"My heart feels like it's running away from me," Josey say. "Scattering in my chest." Josey slides back down on the mat. Sissy nudges her again.

"You quitting on my grandbaby? Come on and get up. Drink your water." Sissy holds the cup out but Josey don't move.

She wakens sudden, grinding her teeth and balling the sheets in her fists from the coming pain. When it releases her again she slides back down, grimacing with closed eyes.

"What's the matter wit'cha?" Sissy say. "You ain't the first one ever birthed a baby. And you ain't gon' be . . ."

"Shut up!" Josey say. "Just shut up! I'm sick and tired of hearing you flap your lips! Get away from me, woman!"

Josey hollers from new pain and pushes at the same time. Her body twists in a strange position, her hips one way, her torso the other, wrung out from the pain. When it ends, her eyes are red like each socket is its own tiny pool of blood, the colored part a blue marble dropped in.

Josey forces her way to a stand. Walks wide-legged across the room, holding her belly. Sissy's voice trembles behind her. "I . . . I just wanted you to drink your water."

Josey stops at the farthest wall next to the cupboard, too tired to open the door. She leans back against it instead, takes a deep breath before sliding down the door into a squat. She undoes the middle buttons of her dress, tugs at the material, finally rips it off and over her head, leaving her buck naked and pearly white.

"Good Lawd!" Sissy say, blocking her eyes. "You fixin to go to hell."

Josey's breaths quicken and her teeth grind again. She rolls onto her hands and knees, meeting the coming pain on all fours this time. Her face reddens and the muscles on the sides of her belly lurch forward and center. Tears run down her cheeks. Breathless now, she tell Sissy, "Throw me my sheets."

Sissy gathers 'em quickly from the mat and tries to stand with 'em. "No!" Josey say. "Just throw 'em over. You don't need to come."

Josey catches 'em one-handed and tangles the sheet into a ball and places it on the floor beneath her. A new nest. She squats down over it, her back flat against the wall and grunts and waits for the next push to come. Her eyes draw closed.

A drip of blood dots the sheet. Then another. A steady stream of red patters from between her legs, wetting the path where the baby'll come. But blood like this ain't supposed to happen.

Josey's head flops forward, her neck sinks into her shoulders, her upper body droops between her legs but she don't fall.

All the muscles in her belly jerk to center like before but Josey don't make a sound. I try to touch her face. Of course, I cain't. I call to Sissy for help but she don't hear me.

"Josey?" Sissy finally say. She shuffles slow across the room, puts her hand on Josey's shoulder and shakes her. Leans toward her.

Josey slumps forward into Sissy's arms. Josey's head tilts back and Sissy slaps her face. "Wake up, Josey!" She sees the blood soaked through the sheet and sees Josey's belly lurch to center again. "It's comin!" Sissy say. "You gotta wake up, Josey. Push!"

Sissy searches the room for something to use.

Nothing.

She lowers Josey in her arms, cradling her like a baby, then reaches for the mat one-handed, catches the edge of it with her fingertips, then drags it over, puts it under Josey's hips, perches Josey's legs up and open. "I can see the head, Josey! It's right there. Push! Josey, push!"

A black mass rises between her legs like a bubble of dark—baby hairs coated in gleaming white and red. "Push, Josey!" Sissy say, trying to help it out. No use. "You got to push, Josey! Or else this baby gon' choke to death."

Josey's belly tightens and the head comes. Sissy gives it a gentle twist to one side and the curve of its shoulders seep out. With speed, the whole body, too. "We got a boy!" Sissy yells over his stuttering cries.

She cuts the chord, joyful, and crawls to Josey with him tucked under her chest. "You gotta wake up, Josey. We got a boy to take care of."

Josey grunts but her eyes don't open. The sides of her belly lurch instead, and a new bulge rises from between her collapsed knees—not the gray mass of afterbirth, but something bluish and striped with strawberry colored hair.

"Sweet Jesus!" Sissy cry and lays the boy down. No sooner than she do, the next baby's delivering itself right into Sissy's waiting arms. Silent.

"Come on, baby," she say, flipping it over on her forearm and patting the back. "Come on!"

Nothing.

Finally, a sputter. A cry. Might as well have been the voice of God.

"It's a girl!" Sissy cried.

And this girl, this boy, Josey would name in freedom. So the last name she chose for them was not Graham who'd owned her. Owned Sissy. It was Freeman.

36 / FLASH

Conyers, Georgia, 1847

I WAS TIRED WHEN I left Soledad's near midnight last night. Spent two hours resting three times, was sick once, and had to talk myself out of saying fuck it to everything, and letting myself die in the cold. And now, the smoldering embers of Albert's blown-out fire are glowing in his furnace, waiting to be resurrected, warming me still. It'll be sunrise soon.

I lay across this bench alone, in the dark, and in the soot of his workshop. A pop from the furnace starts the fire to life again, tinting the air orange and yellow, and casting the black shadows of Albert's tools against the wall. They throb and change shape in flickers.

I snuggle down into Albert's burnt-smelling clothes and shift his big leather gloves that I made a pillow under my head. I roll onto my back and stare at the beams on the ceiling, all four of 'em are mostly black from layers of up-floating smoke that stuck.

My hands slide to my nothing belly. I do it because I should have started my monthly cycle ten days ago. And almost thirty days before then. But it ain't come. I tell myself that it don't mean pregnant because strain and pressure in life can stop any peace. Any normal. And I've had some. And anyway, I don't feel no different 'cept this sour stomach. Sick

287

every morning, though. And we was careful. Jeremy pulled hisself out of me before he finished every time. And if something was growing inside my body, I think I'd know. I'll bleed. Cycles come late all the time. I could just be sick and dizzy and weak for no reason. My breasts could be tender for no . . .

"If you gon' stay in here," Albert say from the doorway, "I'm gon' have to let Cynthia know."

I sit up. Nod. Saltiness fills my mouth, directly. I spit.

"I think I'm pregnant," I say. I'll be sure soon. And I'll have to provide for it. Make sure we got a place to sleep.

"Even more reason to tell her," he say.

"Jeremy's the father," I say, wanting to get everything out in the open.

"I brought some eggs," he say.

"I'm not hungry."

Albert sits on the stool nearer the furnace, breaks the eggs into his pan, and they sizzle over the fire. The slimy clear whites look like snot—nasty!—from a big sneeze—sick!—and he's about to eat it. I throw up red broth menudo.

"I'm sorry," I say. Albert gets his shovel, throws dirt over it, then scoops it all together and tosses it out the doorway. "Thank you."

He sits back down and flips the eggs over without a word, can hardly hear him breathe. I lay back down and look his way but not at him. I don't want to talk about last night.

I shift his gloves under my cheek, then roll on my back. He dumps the cooked eggs on his plate. The yellow pieces are charred brown. He say, "Now that you're empty, maybe you've changed your mind about being hungry," and holds his plate out to me.

He's right. I take it.

"Fork?" he say.

"A big spoon be better," I say.

I finish before he starts his and I rest back on the bench, rub my belly. "Jeremy'll be a good father," I say. "We almost made it out of here. He just needed another good hand, is all. Could've had our new life right now."

I think about the way me and Jeremy gon' love each other when this baby come. When he see what we got. "If I could've helped him more, he'd have got that hand."

"Is that what you believe?" Albert say.

"You just don't know about the world and how it goes 'round. Every family needs money."

"The greatest wealth is time and health. Love."

"And family," I say.

"You can always have family," he say. "You live in health long enough . . ."

"And I got one. When Jeremy gets back, we're gonna be family. You'll see."

He takes my plate. "You're welcome to stay here for as long as you need," he say. "'Til the baby comes and only if Cynthia will allow it."

"I have other places I can go."

He slides my plate in a bucket of sudsy water under his seat and say, "I'll make sure you have food, water, that you'll stay warm."

"And what do you expect me to do for it?"

He runs a wet rag over the plate, takes it out and rinses it in a second bucket.

"Don't take me for a fool," I say. "No man gives something without expecting something else in return."

"Then you've got me mistaken for somebody else—maybe your baby's father."

I don't want to stay here.

Albert sets the wet plate near his furnace to dry, takes his plate of food and moves hisself to the small stool against the wall—just big enough for one butt cheek. I don't care. I don't need him to do nothing for me. I just need to stay somewhere 'til Jeremy see what he done wrong and come back for me.

I get another egg from Albert's basket, crack it over his hot pan and watch it bubble. He say, "You need to stand back from that fire. Could flash."

My egg's already done.

I put it on my plate and take a bite before I sit where I was. "Why didn't you leave?" I say, making conversation. "When the Freedom Fighter came to take us to Mexico, how come you didn't go with 'em? You said before it was 'cause of me."

"I didn't say I stayed because of you. I said you saved our lives. Your indecision. It wasn't the first time I didn't leave," he say.

"You were leaving before?"

"That first night I found you was one time." He piles some eggs on his spoon. "I planned to join the Railroad north that night."

"I thought you said you was going south?"

"South. North. But only twice a year the Railroad comes this far south from Virginia. Only once I found them guides to be organized and timely. They stop here for my canteens, things I'd give 'em to trade."

"Why didn't you go then? On that day you found me?"

"Unorganized. A dozen negroes were in their party and their guides couldn't decide who was in charge. Get everybody killed. All their signals were right, though. Their whistle first. Then the second—a strange sound like no night bird you've ever heard. Then the three flickers of light from the forest's edge. But that's where their good planning ended. On my way back I almost stepped right on you."

He gets up to clean his plate. Takes my plate when he passes.

"Thank you," I say. For good measure, I get up and go over to him, hug his neck, let him feel me real close.

"I already said you could stay," he say.

Tears start coming out my eyes for no reason I know, except sorry. Sorry for all this.

Sorry for having this baby inside me. Sorry Jeremy left. Sorry I'm desperate.

He say, "I reckon the best thing for both of us is to not say nothing else. I'll talk to Cynthia. And if she won't have you, I can't."

37 / FLASH

Conyers, Georgia, 1847

IF IT WERE up to Cynthia, I'd have been gone three months ago when Albert told her I was here, and *pregnant* was my excuse. "So long as I don't have to see her wretched ass nowhere on this property," was Cynthia's compromise after she finished with her hell no's and that bitch this 'n' thats.

So most days I stay out back in the garden behind Albert's workshop. I can stretch my legs back there and run in place to keep myself well. It's what Cynthia prescribed. Not to me. But I heard her tell it to her hand, Sarah, before Cynthia sent her off: "I don't care what that doctor say. You gon' regret the two days of labor if you don't get strong now."

I walk far.

Four and five miles each way, zigzagging across Cynthia's backfields and back roads like a mule plowing, getting stronger by the day, my belly bigger. I stopped trying to suck it in after Albert caught me standing sideways in the glass looking at myself and taking in deep breaths to make sure it weren't just gas.

It weren't.

ALBERT'S BEEN HEATING his black metal rods to an orange glow
so he can reshape 'em into something new. Beautiful things. His
hammers have tapered his metal into delicate flowers and leafs and
scalloped coat hooks, turned skinny metal pieces into the thick feet
of end tables, and spread fat pieces into thin fishtails and scoops of
spoons. He's twisted metal staffs into the braided hair of banisters,
and punched holes to join two pieces together . . . and split 'em apart.
His anvil is the iron table where he bangs out the story of life—that
with vision and fire, we can all be something different. And this is
what he gives to Cynthia to sell so we can keep our place here. I sew
and hem dresses. Men's trousers and shirts. It ain't much but it's
something.

Negroes on horseback pass through here a few times a month to
water their steeds so Albert built a metal trough for 'em. It's prettier and
more watertight than the one Cynthia got but she don't want to pay him
for a new one.

Summer's been a bouquet of green fields and cherry blossoms. The
last buds of the season showered me in pink. The scent of Jeremy was in
'em. It reminded me of long days along the stream and our secret nights
of quiet hallelujahs.

I imagine him coming home to me. That he'd pick me up and without a word, kiss me—long and open-mouthed. That when he saw our
baby boy looking just like us, he'd love us both.

But it's no time for remembering.

Not now.

Now, I got to keep Albert alive.

THERE WAS SCREAMING when it happened.

So much screaming.

I took off running in the direction of Albert's scream. He flew out
his shop door with his hands on his head, his hair on fire, and his shirt
and neck was smoking. He threw hisself in the trough and flailed in the
water like it was deep and he couldn't swim.

He lifted out the water, took deep breaths, dunked back in again. I scooped water on the parts of him that he was trying to drown.

"I cain't see!" he screamed, throwing his hands at me.

"You got to calm down!" I said. "I cain't help you like this."

He hummed and jumped up and down, dumped his head in the trough again and again. I got next to him, scooped more water over him, saw the edges of his shirt burned down his back, his neck. A burning ember must have got him, a flash of fire. The new lotion he was gifted, a trigger. The top of his head and face was bleeding, his skin was peeling away in gray sheets.

I ripped my dress to try to put it on his burns but he grabbed my hand before I could touch him. With his voice quivering, he said, "You touch me with that cloth and it'll melt in my skin."

I backed away from him. Didn't know what to do but give him room.

He bent over the trough clinching his jaws together while the smoke piped off of him smelling of burnt meat. I reached into the trough and got a hand scoop of water, threw it on him, but by the time the cooling wet reached him, it was only sprinkles.

"Just let it be!" he hollered, desperate. Dunked his head completely, baptized.

I can only sit with him now 'cause water don't heal.

It only stops the worsening and gives us time to think about what went wrong.

For the last three hours since he ran out on fire, I haven't done nothin. I guided him back into this shop and went and got Cynthia. Thank God she was home and would come tend to him. But ain't much she can do but wait with me 'cause right now he's like lava, she said. His skin is red underneath with blackened skin on top. He's cracking and recracking, shivering on his bench slouched over. Blood and sweat drips from his face, skipping like a picnic fly from his chin to his shoulders. He squeezes the neck of the whiskey bottle in his hand.

Blisters on his face and neck are swollen, red, and weepy, and little white bumps have broke out on his nose and under his swollen shut eyes. Patches have spread on the sides of his face where his brown skin was and is gone now. Cream-colored splotches have risen there, too.

"Albert?" Cynthia whispers. "Let me see you." She barely touches him and he grunts.

His eyebrows are gone. A slimy film has smeared in their place. The ridge of his top lip is rippled black and dry. Cynthia say, "I think you look better like this," but Albert don't laugh. Neither do I.

"I brought you something," she say but he grunts, no. "I know you don't like my medicine but it's the best thing for you right now. One time won't get you hooked."

He grunts louder, shakes his head, bringing hisself terrible pain.

"Have it your way," she say.

She raises white sheets around him like a tent and tells him, "It'll keep the soot in the air from blowing in your wounds."

She wrenches the bottle of whiskey from his hand, turns her back to him and pours something else in it—a syrup—and shakes it up. "Drink some whiskey," she say and tilts the bottle to his lips while keeping the flow of it away from his burnt top lip. The double heavy syrup is already separating from the liquor and it snakes though the neck of the bottle and into his mouth.

After a few minutes, he stops shivering.

We wait for him to sleep before she asks me to help wash him. Real gentle. Tapping him with warm water. Took us both a hour to do everything. But she the only one who could help us now.

"Don't burst the blisters," Cynthia say, getting up to leave. "Don't use healing oils. And don't move him 'til tomorrow. But tomorrow he's gon' need to walk. Just back and forth to the end of the shop. Outside, if he can stand the light. You'll have to hold him up by his unburnt parts—his forearm . . ." I start crying when I look at him again. He's hurting and I cain't do this. I cain't take care of nobody.

Cynthia looks at me softly and waits for my tears to finish and when they don't she say, "The stuff I gave him is gon' make him wrong in the head so when he wake up, he might want to fight you. You need to protect yourself and the baby, so give him more of that drink the second you hear him waking."

I wipe my tears, nod.

"And it's fine to double the amount of syrup if you need to. It'll keep his face numb, stop him from cracking the blisters and skin. He don't need an infection."

She gives me the vial of her syrup and stops at the door before she go. That soft look again but she say, "This don't make us friends."

38 / FLASH

Conyers, Georgia, 1847

ALBERT AIN'T WOKE up for more than thirty minutes in the last week.

I walk him and give him more medicine, change his towels and sheets, bring him a pot to empty hisself and wipe his messes away. I can hear him rustling under his tent now. He'll need some new water.

I go to get it fresh 'cause I fell asleep and left the cover off the pitcher. It's already filthy with soot so I hurry outside with it, pour it out, and fill it again.

When I walk back through the door, Albert's sitting up. He's got his tent off, huffing. "Who's there?" he say, his eyes still swollen. He groans from speaking. "Don't come no closer."

"It's just me," I say. "But you don't need to talk. Your scabs need to heal."

His lava face has stretched out on one side and his skin is pinned up and back by hardened puss crystals like crunchy new skin. He shifts in his seat.

"I have water for you," I say. He raises a hand to take the cup. His hand is trembling and his arm he brings up only halfway. I stare at the freckles on the back of his hand. The shaking seems to join the dots together in a line. Tears crowd my eyes but I won't cry for him again. He deserves better than weak.

I put the cup in his hand and sit next to him, help him hold it to his bottom lip only. He can hardly part his lips to drink. He swallows.

"Cynthia's been by to see you," I say. "Took care of you on and off. But now you just got me."

I don't want him to die.

I cain't see his eyes good enough to tell if that's what he wants to do.

Hazel used to say that you could tell when a person's ready to go. There's a stepping away from their own body that happens and you can see it in their eyes. She said people know when it's time.

Like I know.

I know I'll die by thirty-five because I'm not worthy of more than what Momma had.

I've been thinking about what Albert said. About the most valuable thing—time and health. Love being what we leave behind. Family, what we make it. Maybe when this baby comes, I'll go with the Railroad. And maybe, if Albert's well enough, the both of us, all three of us, could go together and be family. North, south. No matter.

I give him another sip of his water and he flinches 'cause the cup touched the wrong part of his lip. I cringe, too. He takes deep breaths to calm his pain.

"Here," I say. "Drink some more whiskey."

He pushes it away.

"Don't you want to get better? Not get the infection?"

He tries to speak.

"Don't talk. Just scrunch your eyes . . . blink once for no, twice for yes." I look at him. "You understand?"

He blinks twice.

"Good. I need you to drink your whiskey. Just 'til you're better, then you don't have to drink it no more."

He looks around his shop one-eyed. A line of gray puss is caught on his lashes joining the top and bottom together. He starts huffing and crying.

I say, "I been keeping it clean for you. I plan to do more sewing and hemming work from Cynthia and maybe when you're healed, you can show me how to do what you do. Make pretty metal. Don't matter I'm a girl."

He blinks once, then shakes his head, a little, then forces words out even though he promised not to. "I don't need no more of your help," he say.

"Stop talking. You gon' crack your face and get the infection."

"You don't owe me nothing," he say, his words cracking the skin at his temples. Blood starts running down the side of his face.

Damn.

39 / 1870

Tallassee, Alabama

I BELIEVE IN REDEMPTION.

And Tallassee, Alabama, is redeeming herself, making the bad things that happened here better. Greening it over with her vines folded into walking paths, and climbing them up tall and wide things, erasing the brown of dirt and dead with the living. Full trees and bushes are crowding open skies, turning once-blue spaces to shade. Everything around her is coming back. Sagging limbs and leafs of many kinds—square and round, prickly and straight—are weighty on her branches like jewelry. Her mosses are furs. Tallassee is finding her way. Reclaiming her land. There's no one to cut her to pieces or temper her spirit now. Five years since freedom, just over four since my grandbabies birth, and now benches and tools are swallowed by her rising tide. Fence posts and garden statues consumed. Redemption is taking place. It's what happens to a plantation with no slaves. Where there were once fifty bodies and a hundred hands, there are now only four—two hands for Norah and two for Gwen. They're sharecroppers who used to be slaves and still live on this plantation but get paid with crops and are free to leave.

It's her time and Tallassee don't owe nobody nothing.

I follow Josey through her, along a double-wide path worn by possums and prey. Possums, 'cause don't nothing eat possums but people.
Possums have nothing to fear 'til it's too late.

Josey fast-walks beneath low-hanging branches that have grown
back since Jackson's ax last touched 'em. Their shade makes darkness
here now. They're only cut by white-tailed deer in winter while they're
shedding their antlers for summer horns. In the end, those horns'll look
like the unclenched hand bones of giants.

Josey keeps her head down, pushing forward past pine. She's got
paper stamps hanging out the side of her shoe that she'll use at market
to pay for food. The drought here has lasted too long.

She still got Charles's three coins that he left her with before he
went. She won't spend it. She's made her own money trading stamps
for things she make with cotton—socks and under clothes. Cotton is
everywhere and the cost is free.

A family of wild turkeys spur Josey's children—almost five now—to
get up the path faster, chasing stick legs as they windmill beneath puffy
balls of feathers.

The children don't look like twins.

They are as close looking as two strangers could be. Rachel's milk-
white skin and mousy blonde hair are Josey's, but Squiggy's browner
like Jackson but with golden-brown eyes and his hair made of big loops
of shiny copper.

And he's slow-learning.

What Squiggy can do puts him about two years behind where he
should be. Two years behind Rachel. She stood up to walk before one
years old while Squiggy was still scooting at three.

He was just a month old when he started showing signs of his lag-
behind. He wouldn't move his head from one side to the other, or move
his body the way Rachel would. And when Josey would lay him on the
floor, his legs would splay open like a dead frog. Was mostly expres-
sionless except for the two times he smiled. His limbs would just hang

down when she held him. He wouldn't lift a fist to rub a eye or a cheek, but Rachel would punch your neck from stretching.

He seemed lifeless, but he was breathing, and got so behind in the things Rachel could do easy. There was only one conclusion: "Will he look retarded?" Josey asked herself. Not because she didn't love him but because she knew what he'd be up against.

THE FAMILY OF wild turkeys escaping the children get swallowed by the brush off the side of the road except for one lone turkey crossing behind Squiggy. Its face is featherless, bright red and puckered blue. A pouch of extra red skin hangs under its neck like a man's saggy parts. Squiggy goes after it in a clumsy walk. Don't know how to run yet. Then Rachel goes behind him, slower than she could because she wants to let him catch it and feel a victory. She and Josey have done most things for Squiggy all his life. They're used to picking him up and walking for him and taking turns talking for him. Josey'll chew his food to keep him from choking to death on a weak swallow. He always smiles on his own, though. And his good kisses are puckerless.

Josey passes the children up the path, then under an arch of tree branches and over grounded chicken feathers to meet the main road. Sunlight pours over the east field of the Graham plantation—Annie's new farm store. The Market.

Her children fall behind and that's good. It's about time she let 'em go. They've already healed her. Some children are born to heal us. To heal the holes we thought were forever or heal the holes we didn't know we had. Josey's sickness ebbed because of Squiggy and Rachel. They needed her. Especially Squiggy. And Josey stopped cutting when she decided that his suffering was more important than hers.

When he was born, she didn't lay him down on his own for months. She carried him in a sheet tied over her neck and it kept him taut against her body because she knew something was wrong with her baby. He was limp like I told you, and when she saw how his muscles were weak, she thought his heart might be weak, too. That maybe it would forget to beat. Maybe his lungs forget to breathe. She wanted him to feel her close, wanted him to mimic her body's moves. Breathe like she breathed. Beat like she beat. And if God were to take him, he wasn't gonna die alone like them babies who were laid down for a nap and let go.

"You crazy!" Sissy would tell her.

But some crazy is instinct.

Loud chatter and crowds drown Annie's market. Rolling wagons leave welts in the grass. A group of children chase a dog under a wagon and through tents. Negro sharecroppers put food baskets on carts same as whites. Two buyers slouch next to a basket sorting collards and cucumbers, figs and something red.

Business is good for Annie. Like Tallassee, she's growing back, too. Husbandless. Annie don't say it, but her smile is proof. She rests atop her tan horse—biggest around—watching from behind the sidelines, pleased with what she made, a market for anyone to buy or sell or give free to anyone who needs it.

Josey wanders through the market, unnoticed by Annie, touching onions and ripe okra. She stops at a brown bag of sugar. *Her babies can't eat that.* But when they get here, sweets will be the first thing they beg for.

Bantam chickens outnumber the children here. There're little hens and chickens running around the whole of this market and through the streets. Annie bought two—a boy and a girl—a while back and now fifty of 'em are running all over this place. All her neighbors including negroes got bantams now. Josey and Sissy don't, though. Chickens too spooked to wander that way and into the darkness of unkept Tallassee. She's wild.

I cross the main road and back through the gap to the footpath to find my two grandchildren, taking too long. Rachel and Squiggy are laughing as Squiggy pulls hisself out and over the gutter at the side of the road. Rachel's behind him holding that turkey prisoner.

"Watch this," she say, lowering it to the forest floor. "Yah!" she yells, and sets the turkey free. It runs right toward Squiggy. I swear it ran over his head and now they cain't stop laughing. Squiggy claps his hands and say the only word he know—not, Momma—"Again!"

Behind me, an on-the-loose bantam stumbles straight in the road and gets runned over by a wagon. It gets up limping. Falls back down. Gets up again, fixed. I swear they live forever.

Three, four, five children are running after that wagon now. A man, half dressed in a soldier's uniform, rides in it with a knapsack on his back—one like Jackson had when he first come home. All these years and soldiers' bodies are still coming home. Not all of 'em dead. But no one asks anymore where these survivors have been. Only about the war.

"We don't need your help," Rachel say behind me.

"Just let me help him," a man's voice say.

Heat envelops me. Something I haven't felt in a long time.

"No thank you, suh," Rachel say.

I turn 'round to 'em. See what I've dreaded for five years. George's face hits me like a madness. And I remember everything. I rush at him, get set ablaze passing through, nerves inside exposed and wild. I've wanted this. Burning alive. And I don't care. Before he disappeared, I swore that no matter what Bessie said, I'd give my life for my daughter's justice.

But I stop now.

Hesitate.

Children change everything.

Heartbreak.

My grandchildren.

I don't make a move. Don't want to leave this place.

George drags Squiggy by the arm out of the gutter and back onto the path. Squiggy's knees scrape. "There," George say. "All better now."

"We fine, suh," Rachel say. "We don't want to bother you none."

"It's not a bother," George say and bends through me to pick up Squiggy but Squiggy arches his back, knees George in his sack but

George don't feel that, neither. "Calm down, boy," he say. "I'm just trying to lift you to the road."

"He don't like being helped," Rachel say, forceful.

"Is that true, little man?"

"He don't talk, neither," Rachel say.

"He don't need help, don't talk . . . You either a true gentleman or the perfect woman." He laughs and pulls his flask from his pocket and untwists it open.

He takes a swig, then wipes his mouth with his backhand. "Just water," he tells Rachel, screwing the lid back on. "I've been off the poison almost six years now. Then last week . . . a small backstep. You ever sneak a little drink?"

Rachel don't say nothing.

"Good girl," he say. "Type of thing can put a man in his grave. How old are you?"

"Be five my next birthday."

"Five years old! Whew! An old soul. Well beyond your years."

"Come on, Squiggy," Rachel say. "Momma's waitin for us."

"Squiggy? That's a strange name for a boy. I'm George."

Rachel pulls Squiggy along.

"You're Josey's children, aren't you?" he say. He lifts his flask to his face and circles the space around it. "I can see it all in here." He walks over to Rachel, bends down to her and sweeps her sandy blonde hair behind her ear. "Just like yer momma."

Rachel backs away.

"Hold on now," he say, kneeling and holding the back of her head to keep her still. "I'm just looking."

A loud-talking woman passes the mouth of the road a few steps away and a pear falls from her basket. She follows its roll down the short mound and meets eyes with George there. She pauses at what I see, too: George leaning too close to Rachel.

He flips a silver coin from behind Rachel's ear and shows it to her. Rachel gasps in delight. "Magic!"

The pear woman smiles, too, and George winks at her.

"Show me again, Mr. George! Show me how!" Rachel say.

"A good magician never tells his secrets."

"You can tell me, suh!" she say, holding his arm, begging. He stares at the place where Rachel is touching him and she lets go directly. "I'm sorry," she say.

"Naw . . ." George say. "You can touch me wherever you want."

"George?" Annie calls from the main road. "You saw him in here?" she says to somebody up on the road with her—the pear woman.

"Please tell me, Mr. George," Rachel say. "I won't tell nobody. Promise. Please."

"Another time," he say, and gives her the coin. "I'll see you again. And only because you're special."

40 / FLASH

Conyers, Georgia, 1848

ALBERT'S BEEN LOOKING different around the face since he got burnt up twelve weeks ago. Thick scars have risen from under his skin like it's been burrowed through. Other skin is yanked back in some places, slanting his eyes and spreading his bottom lip wider than it should be. The hairs left on his head are long and in thin bunches while the rest of his head's got shiny bald spots, like flat rocks in high grass.

Albert got his name from iron even before the fire. Before he was born. Iron is *black* metal. *Smith*, a craftsman. A blacksmith. But right now, Albert is just iron. I been doing the smithing. "Don't be afraid of the metal," he said. "It won't hit you back." But metal is not what I'm afraid of. I suspect he know that, too. He's been asking me to start the coal fire in the forge for him and it amazes me how forges can hold the greatest heat inside 'em. Like brick ovens, they are, turning the blackest iron orange-hot. Inside it, wild fire can be controlled. Bellows send large flames lapping and can send the same fire to a low burn. But if you get it wrong, there's only a bucket of water nearby.

Albert asks me to place the iron evenly in the fire pot, not on the coal. Asks me to give him his hammers, but some of 'em three pounds. "Don't be afraid," he said. But fire's already changed everything.

Albert made me give him a piece of mirror the other day. He stared at hisself, turned his head slowly from side to side, raised his hand to touch his face. He told me, "No use in crying."

And that time, I didn't stop myself crying for him.

I cried because I don't know what I'd do if I didn't have the face I was born to make.

I cried because being negro is hard enough.

I cried because I wished I had his courage. And because, in that moment, I was certain that even if he didn't want for me to be his family, I wanted him to be my friend.

Cynthia once told me that a man and woman could never be friends. Said, "Sex'll always get in the way 'cause men are lazy. A woman friend is what you call *convenient*."

But Albert ain't lazy.

And me and him rely on each other now. Every day and in most ways, we do. For things most men and women not related or married would never have the pleasure to share.

There ain't many secrets between us now.

That's my fault because I thought he was a dying man when I spoke to him honest and open about my regrets. And I figure his secrets are gone now, too, since I spent the first three weeks working on his toileting. "Life is funny," he said. "When the shame goes, what's left to do?"

I sneak up on Albert and slowly reach for a bunch of his hair with my scissor blades open. Before I can snip it, he spins me around, holds both my wrists in one of his hands, laughing. He say, "You trying to take away my power, Delilah?"

He crisscrosses my arms in front of me, making me hug my own seven-months-pregnant belly and he scratches in my armpit. "What you gon' do now, Delilah?"

"Let me cut it," I say. "Just a little off the top. Even it up." He keeps flicking his finger in my pit. We laughing. We take care of each other.

And this morning, he took care of me.

I had lost my voice in the night and had gone to bed speechless. I don't know if it was my talking too much that done it, or being out in the cold, or the coughing, but I lost it and Albert wanted to heal me.

I pretended to be 'sleep while I watched him tiptoe around our new living area. His back was against the stone wall he just built floor to ceiling to separate our new space from his shop. Ours is ten feet by ten feet, the ceiling is eight feet high to match his shop. "Mostly fireproof," he said, except for the doorway in the wall that leads to his work.

We both sleep on the same side of the door even though we ain't married. I sleep on my bed mat on the floor, and Albert sleeps across the room in a padded chair next to the oven. We eat and sleep on this side now.

And this morning, I was watching him go across the floor on the balls of his quiet feet. He started bothering his "secret" stash of liquor behind the box where he keeps his spare tools. This hiding place wasn't his best kept secret since all the bottle necks of his liquor stick up and over the box—a line of sight from my pillow—so I cain't say (and be honest) that I've never took my liberties with 'em. That's why when he woke me up this morning and only gave me a stingy swallow of his expensive Talisker whisky, I had to gag on it a little to pretend it was new to me.

"It's strong, isn't it?" he said. "Burns. But it's the best around. Tastes a little woodsy?"

"A bonfire in a glass," I said.

"And I already know I'm gon' regret giving you a taste."

"'Cause now I know where you hide your costly whiskey?"

"Naw, 'cause now I gotta hear you talk."

I LIKE THE way we think of each other—sister and brother. Adopted, maybe. It's like I can read his mind and know what he wants to eat or drink before he's hungry or thirsty. And he thinks of things I need before I even want 'em. Like the bag of candy he brought back from town this morning. He came in the door popping a piece of it in his mouth. The smell was clean lemon. He didn't even ask if I wanted some 'cause that's the difference between us—I give it freely and he wants me to ask. Teases me. "Sure is good," he said.

I wasn't gon' ask.

I tried not to pay him no mind. Instead, I focused on greasing my feet. Took the grease jar from under the bench and twisted it open. I scooped two fingers in it like a spoon, pulled back a clear wad, smooth as jelly, then warmed it by rubbing my hands together. That's when he got louder with his sweets, clicking that rock candy against his teeth, slurping sugar slobber.

I laughed, "Let me rub some of this grease on your face. It'll loosen your scars."

"Can't you see I'm working my mouth to enjoy this tasty treat?"

"Suit yourself," I said and widened my legs so that my big belly could fit between 'em. I swiped the grease on my right foot, then my left, took a deep breath and collapsed back on the bench, exhausted 'cause bending over winds me now.

"Why your feet need greasing again anyway?" Albert said. "You just greased 'em this morning."

I laid back, took some deep breaths. It's like I grew in a half second. "Albert," I said. "Come and rub some grease on my feet."

"I ain't touching your feet."

"I wiped your ass."

"Thank you," he laughed.

"You said it yourself, I'm eight months pregnant. I cain't do everything I used to. You could help me."

"Fine. But let this be the first and only time."

He came over and got down on one knee, lifted my foot to his thigh. He dug a finger in the grease pot and hesitated to touch my foot, said, "I don't think I can do this."

I wiggled my toes and smiled.

He closed his eyes and touched the grease to my foot, gentler than I woulda thought. He cupped my whole foot in his palms and rubbed his thumbs along the ridge.

"There," he said and dropped my foot. "Give me the other one."

"Thas all you gon' do?" I said.

"Fine," he said and lifted my half-greasy foot to his thigh again.

He buried two fingers in the jelly, rubbed it around both hands, slid 'em over my foot, then underneath it, kneading his knuckles firm but gentle into the flat of it. He twisted a hand around my heel turning it like a knob and moved up to the ball of my foot, then through my toes. They separate easily for him.

He ran two fingers up each toe, one at a time, a soft pinch over the bulgy tip, then back down again.

I didn't want him to stop.

But he grabbed my other foot.

He took his time with it. More time. Like he was discovering every crease. Gave me the chills.

He put my foot down softly and said, "Where'd you get this grease from?"

My voice quivered, "Bernadette said it'll make my feet look young and smooth."

"Don't make no sense . . ." he said.

I stuck out my leg to see my feet, told him, "Ain't everybody gotta walk around ugly as you."

He cleared his throat, got up from the floor, and sat up on the bench. He wouldn't look at me.

I put my hands on his forearm and shook him. "Albert? Don't be like that."

He kept his head down.

"I don't think you're ugly, Albert. Albert?"

For the first time since the accident, tears dripped from his eyes. Just one at first.

"Albert, I'm sorry. You ain't . . ."

"I know what I look like, Naomi. We've come too far to start lying to each other."

That's when I kissed his face. And kissed him there on the side of his lip, scabs and all—so rough on my lips. He stopped talking for my kisses and sat up straight.

"Not ugly, at all," I said.

And I kissed him again. Kissed his bottom lip that time. Gently. Felt it soft and unburnt, let him feel me soft, too. My lips were wet and I held myself there. I whispered, "I'm sorry."

SOMETIMES, WHEN *nothin* happens between friends, it changes everything. Like them Charleston earthquakes Cynthia describe. She say the *happening* is over before you realize something went wrong. Just a tremor along the porch at first. Like somebody was walking up the stairs—the beams sway, the wood creaks, and by the time you bother to look and see who's coming, nobody's there, the quake is already over, and the damage is done. But it also leaves you uneasy, knowing you was part of something big and missed it at the same time. It's what happened between me and Albert when I kissed him.

I'm guilty.

I started the quake that changed our normal—my kissing him and the way I let myself feel when he rubbed my feet. Those *innocent* things damaging us.

He's different now.

More different than what the fire did to him.

So I been avoiding him. Hard to do in this place so small. Three days and I already miss our card game. We cain't play no more. The way he looks at me makes me shy. I lose my words in his glances. I just want to get out of his way.

I hardly took a breath until a few hours ago when he went to town for Cynthia.

He'll be back soon and we'll start our strange dance over again—
he'll step forward, while I'll step back. He'll go right and I'll go left.
Yesterday, he bumped into me in the space between our sleeping quarters and his shop. Started us both rambling off apologies. For a second
I thought he wanted to say something more but before he could, I took
off into the shop. I thought, maybe I could clean something in there.

In this shop is where I spent last night sleeping and didn't get up this
morning 'til I heard him go out the side door next to me.

THE SIDE DOOR jerks open.

I make myself look busy in the shop. I grab my broom and start
brushing the metal scrapings across the floor. I can feel him staring
at me.

I don't say hi and stay busy, turn my back to him, hear him walk
into our room. From the corner of my eye, I can see him holding a sack
of potatoes. A few seconds more, I hear 'em thud against our cutting
board in our bedroom area. One, two, three of 'em. We need five. Five
potatoes for stew. And before I think to stop myself, I walk my broom
over to the doorway and fix my lips to say, "We need five if the stew's
gon' turn out right."

But when I get to the doorway, he's already walking straight to me.
No dance.

Damn.

He say, "We cain't keep doin this, Naomi."

I sweep. I keep sweeping. I swing my broom over the edge of a thin
piece of metal that's melted and froze to the floor.

"Naomi?" he say. "You listenin?"

He grabs my broom from my hand and I don't stop him. Instead, I
look around to see what else needs doing.

He say, "I don't want to keep playing these games."

I think I'll start the kettle for tea.

I go in our room for the kettle. He follows behind me.

"When I come in," he say, "You go outside. Or you go out before I'm up."

I pour pitcher water in the kettle and go back to the shop, set it on the grates near his furnace.

"We cain't keep going around and around like this."

I think the dust on the windowsill needs wiping down.

I take a cloth and wipe the sill.

"Is this about the kiss?" he say.

Ain't that somethin. All of that dust came off in just one wipe.

"Naomi?" He's too close to me.

"Get away from me!" I say, harsher than I shoulda. "I just don't want nobody touching me!"

"You mean you don't want me touching you?"

"I'm going outside to stretch," I say and grab my coat off the hook next to the door, reach for the doorknob, but he reaches around me and holds the door closed with the flat of his hand.

"Open this door, Albert."

"Why'd you kiss me?"

"Step away from this door, Albert. This baby . . . this baby . . ."

"Just stop avoiding me and listen . . ."

I don't want to.

I cross my arms over my belly. "I need to go outside and walk for this baby."

"Just be honest with me," he say. "Tell me why you kissed me?"

"Why'd you rub my feet like that?"

"Like what?" he say. "How am I supposed to rub somebody's feet? I just did what you asked me . . . I don't know."

"Then I don't know, either."

"You do know. Tell the truth."

"How can I?" I say. "There's a lot of questions in just that one. If you don't know why you touched me different, I don't know why I kissed you."

"I want to spend the rest of my life with you," he say.

I wish I could disappear.

"And if you feel this way, too, let me know now."

He unblocks the door.

I cain't look at him.

"Do you?" he say.

I wish we could go back to the way we was.

Wish we could erase the lie my kiss told. It's easier if you don't love me, I want to say but don't.

"Naomi?"

"You're a good man, Albert. But ain't no more room in my heart to love. Jeremy took all I had with him. And I'm sorry for it."

He nods his head.

Clears his throat.

"Don't be sorry," he say. "That's all I wanted to hear. The truth."

I want to take it back. Take back everything I just said and lie. What's wrong with somebody believing they're loved in every way? I shoulda lied. Made an excuse for why we couldn't be together like that. And that way, he'd always know he was loved.

"And this baby?" he say. "Could you let it love me?"

My heart breaks at his asking. Must be what sorrow is. Not being able to change the truth. Not even for love.

"I know what you're thinking," he say. "The child ain't mine. But seeing as Jeremy's gone, you can let her love me."

"I cain't make somebody love somebody else, Albert. I cain't promise that."

"But you're the mother. Mothers can set a child's heart to the way she should go. So set her heart on me."

I don't know.

"Say yes."

His softness right now—the way his eyes plead and his shoulder sag, defenseless—remind me of the way James was with Hazel. His surrender.

"All right," I say.

He hugs me like his body ain't still in pain or my belly ain't a bridge between us. And for the first time, touching him this close feels right. For the first time since Momma and Hazel, I feel like I'm where I'm supposed to be.

41 / FLASH

Conyers, Georgia, 1848

THE KNOCKING ON the door is hard and wild.

I hobble to a stand on my swole toes. Cynthia yells my name from the door and pushes it open, barges in. She don't never come out here. Not for months.

"Gaw-lee, look at cha," she say. "Ain't grown a pinch. Belly's still small as four months pregnant. Not the six or seven you claim. Albert, you sure this ain't your baby?"

"Can I get you a drink?" Albert say.

"No," she say.

"Can I get you something else?" Albert say.

"Privacy. With Naomi."

I don't want him to leave. Albert reads my thoughts and don't go. He say, "Let me get you whiskey. Or bourbon?"

"I just want a minute with her," she say.

"What you need?" Albert say. "Naomi can't do nothin for you in her condition."

"This is something I need to say to only her. Wait outside the door if you want to. What you think I'm here to do, Albert? I'm the one helped save your life."

"The past is the past," I say, final. I nod to Albert. Let him go out.

"You should sit down," Cynthia say. "Your feet don't seem right. Might be getting the swelling condition. Could make you seize if it gets too bad."

"I'm fine. I'll stand."

"Could kill the baby, too."

She helps me sit.

From her waistband, she wiggles out an old brown leather note-book. Her mother's diary. The same one she's held onto and cussed at on the nights she's drunk.

"Maybe things would've been different if I woulda read it before recent," she say. "Maybe not. I don't know." She opens her diary to a folded page. "I need you to read something." She sits next to me on the bench and holds the book out for me to take but I stare at it, think of all the private things I've ever done and never wrote down. But if I did, I'd never want a stranger to see it.

I say, "I cain't read this."

She flicks her wrist. "My momma wouldn't mind. She's dead."

I shake my head. I won't.

Cynthia lays the book flat on her lap, closed. "All right," she say. "My mother was dying when I found her. I was eleven years old. She had been in bed all day and into the night when she called to me. She took my hand and what I remember most is how cold she was. Middle of the hot summer and she was cold. Her grip was so weak. Even her tears were weak. They dried just as they fell.

"All she kept saying was, 'I'm sorry.'

"When she died, she left me with an empty box and a blade. The blade was on the end of a candlestick holder. The holder had a small lever inside that slid up and down. And when I pulled it down, a blade shot out the top of it and the holder itself became my handle."

Cynthia holds out her book to me again. "Please, Naomi. I want you to see. I need you to read it."

I reach out for it, hesitating.

She jerks it away. "I just want you to know," she say. "My momma was a saint. Remember that when you read this."

I say, "Cynthia, I don't have to read it."

"She didn't know much about nothing. Was just like you when you came."

"Cynthia . . ."

"Some women hid Shakespeare, mine had Fanny Hill. Wasn't her choice. A pauper gave it to her and Momma didn't know no better. It's all she had for literature. Pornographic novels have story, too. So don't judge her. It gave her permission, I think, to write what she did."

"You giving me pornography to read?"

"That ain't what I said. I said my momma's a saint."

She puts the diary in my hand.

I don't want to read it.

I sit with it on my lap, then open it slowly, turn it to the creased page halfway in and start reading it to myself.

21 October 1818

Dear Diary,
I fear I am with child.

For a bundle of rags—I am.

But I want to remember. Recall every moment of the happening so as to never forget what happiness feels like.

I was drying my hair when the rag salesman rattled my door. I should have covered my head but I did not. It had been a long time since we welcomed company here, over a year since we settled, the first time I had been alone in our home for so long—just over a fortnight.

He stood behind the haze of my screen wearing his out of place business suit, his silly smile, and his almost ugly face, saved only by his pretty blue eyes.

Just twenty-five cents, he said, and pulled from his leather bag a bundle of thick pink cloths.

I opened my screen door though I'd already decided his fee was thievish. But I thought my husband and I could have used some color, some softness, to make us alive again so I agreed he could attempt to sway me.

After a moment of salesmanship, I bent over to look into his bag and—I'm almost ashamed to say, but—I smelled him. Not on purpose, but—I did. Maybe my inhale was, at first, a sigh but I certainly breathed him in and smelled him fresh like jasmine.

I sorted through his bag pretending not to notice, chose the fluffy yellow bunch and smiled. He said, pure cotton.

I liked the sweet smell of his breath. It was not like my husband's—whiskey laden and cigar stale. His was like honey, his lips full, drawing me in too long. He touched my chin and told me I was pretty.

I dropped his rags and told him I was married. He said he understood and asked if he could show me how well his rags dry. He unfolded a gold one from behind the fastened compartment of his bag. He touched it to my damp hair.

He dried it slowly while I watched his hands squeeze down the length of my brown hair and near my breast. I did not pull away when his slender fingers returned to my cheek, grazing it . . . and again. I closed my eyes. Felt the hairs on my cheek rise from his strokes and hold themselves there after his pass. My head rested on his hand.

I allowed him to step through my door and felt the hard and soft of him brush by me. In an instant, he woke the whole of my body.

I closed the solid door and waited there. He dropped his bag, pushed me against the wall. His lips were as sticky-sweet as they promised.

But I had to stop him, told him I could not. He said he understood, adjusted himself and picked up his bag. He said he knew what I needed, said, "I can be your first."

I had been married since I was thirteen, I told him, ten years since my wedding night—he was too late to be first at anything. I put my hand on the doorknob, ready to pull it open when he took my other hand and kissed it like a gentleman's good-bye.

When he raised his head from my hand, I was captured by the bliss of his baby blues.

In my hesitation, he pushed me against the door, his tongue pressing on mine, then he released me, asked if I still wanted him to go.

In one motion, I lifted his shirt over his head, let him tear my dress, pressed my body against his, and I crawled up him 'til my legs were tethered around his waist; my backside seated in his hands. His trousers fell away.

I let go of my grip around him, rested my feet gently on the ground, his hand cupped between my legs, my pantaloons the only barrier between us. He tore up their seams, from my knees to the crotch, slid his thumb along the ridge of the torn material at the top of my thighs, dragged what was left of it, over to the side, feeling me wet. I wanted him to touch me again.

His weight on my body was light, his kisses like bites. He ran two fingers between my legs and inside me, tapped my warm spot in short pulses. Felt myself engorge.

My hips found his, surrounded him inside me, his size stretching me to my potential. Suddenly, a pure pleasure paralyzed me and I clinched down around him, my eyes wide, my body releasing everything in this world that's lovely.

I let it happen once more. And again. The third time, we finished together, rocking in each other's laps.

I fold the diary closed and say to Cynthia, "I'm sorry."

"Did you get to July, yet?" she say. "I was six years old."

"I've read enough."

"Just read July."

"No . . . that's all right."

"July," she say, nudging the book.

I open it again, slump down in my seat, flip through the pages.

8 July 1825

Dear Diary,

More and more my good husband has remarked that our child doesn't favor him—But of course not, she looks like me, I tell him. At seven years old, her features are still developing.

I don't think he believes me.

He spent most of last month with varying versions of the same accusation. "We all look alike in my family," he said. "Men in my family can only have boys." So I asked him who he thought his sister belonged to? He slapped me—deservingly—I told him I meant that anything was possible and maybe being out here, detached from our community, has put us both on edge.

I think my good husband prefers to keep me isolated. Only in the fall does he allow me to go into the heart of Charles Towne, the nearest temple, for the Days of Awe and occasionally to teach children in return for good favors from the congregation. He is committed that way—he is. But otherwise, he manages his hidden affairs out of their sights, except in those days when he allows everyone to see I am fine.

Today, he told me our child has an "independent spirit" like no woman in his family. I told him, maybe she has mine. But that only confused him because he does not know me. Not even after nineteen years. He thinks he does, but he does not.

*Then yesterday, he asked me the question that prompted
this entry. "Why in thirteen years of trying had you never been
pregnant before? Or since?"*

*I told him I'd prayed and he should not question a gift that
God has seen fit to give.*

He stopped asking questions.

I close the book again, this time for good, and hand it back to
Cynthia, say, "It must've been hard for you not knowing your daddy.
White folks tend to know."

"You're missing the point," Cynthia say, opening the diary to the
back pages and pulling out a loose piece of folded paper. She unfolds it
and hands it to me but I won't take it. I tell her, "I won't read no more."

She draws it back in and starts reading out loud. "'Seventeenth of
September, Eighteen Hundred and Thirty.' I was eleven."

> *Dear Diary,*
>
> *I am writing to you on this piece of torn-out paper because
> the good husband found you. He was sitting in the outhouse,
> taking too long, when I found it missing. He had been reading
> page after page of my life, taking the shortcuts to secrets he has
> not bothered to learn from me. Thank God he started from the
> beginning, our fifth anniversary. When I ripped it away from
> him he only knew enough to ask, "Who's this rag salesman?
> And what happened when he came to our door worth writing
> about?"*
>
> *I ran away with my book and buried it under the house.
> But by then, it may have been too late. Things began to come
> together in his mind—the date, the birth of my beautiful
> baby girl.*
>
> *Our anger was equal at first—mine and the good husband's.
> His, for what he was almost sure I did years ago, and my
> anger because he stole something so personal to me. The only*

difference between us was his hate was unimaginable. So when
he said to me two weeks ago, "This girl is not mine, is she?" I
should have corrected him immediately, kept up my lie, been
forthright about it. But I did not. I took pause.

In the second and a half that it took me to tell him he was
mistaken, it was too late. He struck me. And though I lied
again, it was my pause that he believed.

I was blind when the beating ended. And in the midst of it,
I did not expect to survive. He nursed me to health over the
course of a week. But I still do not expect to survive.

I'm leaving him tonight.

Cynthia flips the page over, keeps reading. "'First of November. My Dearest Leah. I have tried and failed. If we never make it away from your father, I want you to know the truth. You are my daughter whom I will love until the end of time. You must know that you came from a moment of beauty, my first and only moment of such. I do not regret you but I regret what you have suffered because of me.

"'Dearest Leah. I hate myself for what my selfishness has caused. And now, for not being strong enough to protect you, brave enough to leave.'"

Cynthia folds the note, slips it back inside the diary. "Leah," Cynthia say. "I hadn't heard my name since I was a girl." She relaxes back on the bench, holds the diary on her lap.

"Point is," she say. "It's not who my daddy was. It's who he wasn't."

"I'm sorry," I say again.

"This book got a whole page dedicated to 'sorry.' Not really good enough, is it?"

She stands and stretches out her hand to me like she want me to shake it.

"I'm a different woman now, Naomi. I want you to know that. I'm different because I understand her. I forgive her. Forgive myself. And I know what I got to do for Johnny. For you."

She reaches her hand out to me again. "You're gonna need somewhere to have this baby. Come back to the house with me. It's safe. Plenty room for all us. Let me help you bring this baby into the world."

"And Albert?"

"This ain't no place to have a baby, Naomi. All this soot. Full of smoke. That can't be good for a new baby to breathe. Its lungs. Might get a breathing condition. So even if you don't want to come live with me for yourself, maybe you need to for the baby. What does Albert know about the labor of babies?"

"He needs my help."

"He's already healed and needs to let you go. Sometimes you have to tell your friends that this is where I stop on this road with you. And if they really care about you, they'll tell you thank you for coming this far and let that be the end of it."

"Then let this be the end of it for us," I say. "I won't leave without Albert."

"Then bring him," she say. "If Albert chooses, he can make a room for himself in the attic so he'll be close to you but still have his own space." She pauses, then laughs, "I guess y'all love birds now?"

I don't answer.

"You'll have to earn your keep," she say. "Serve in the saloon or something 'til the baby comes. Can't let people think I'm soft."

"Will I get my own room?"

"You can have Bernadette's."

"Can I go out when I please?"

"Just don't tell nobody I said so."

42 / 1869

Tallassee, Alabama

I DON'T KNOW WHAT'S worse: living in fear or dying. Before two weeks ago when George met Rachel, I would've said fear and only dying if the dying didn't last long. But now, I just say death.

I've been waiting and watching over Squiggy and Rachel, hoping for George to redeem hisself for better 'cause I have no choice. If Bessie's consequence is true, I cain't square in my mind not being here to see my grandchildren grow. To see Josey, a mother like me, grow. I can't end myself after all we been through. They need me. Even this way. 'Cause sometimes, just being there for somebody, wordless and present, is enough.

A few days ago, I think Sissy understood that, too.

She found a body floating dead in the stream. She'd gone down to fetch a bucket of muddied water 'cause dirty water is good enough for the crops, not good enough for drinking. The drought make it hard on everybody. That, and the war, end of war, and the new war west. New freedom. So bodies have been leaving Tallassee for years. And not everybody make it out alive. But something about this dead body spooked Sissy.

Her screaming is what brought us all out.

Josey went to her right away, leaving her children in the house but I got there first. Saw the body shifting in place on top of a bed of loose rock and water. It looked like a log at first. The body. But the smell was worser than the shit of two sick stomachs.

About three days the body had been there, I'd guess. It belonged to an old woman who'd been left behind near a worn path. Sissy kneeled, leaned over it, gasped when she saw the woman's bloated face. It looked just like Sissy. Coulda been her twin. No further than a cousin in rela-tion. Sisters, maybe. This woman could've been her long lost.

"Let's bury her," Sissy said to Josey with tears in her eyes. It was those tears that surprised me more than the body. She said, "Shouldn't nobody die with nobody to bury 'em. And I don't want to die that way, neither."

Since Sissy found the body, she's been helpful to Josey all week. Kind even. "Can I help you with the babies?" she'll ask. And, "I'll get that for you," she'll say. I swear it frightened Josey the first time. And today, Sissy's been downright confessional.

"I was wrong about you," she said. "And I ain't shamed to say it now. We need each other. Rely on each other. Even if all that means is waking up in the morning knowing somebody familiar is near."

"You ain't got to worry about dying, Miss Sissy. Or being alone. We're family."

SISSY'S RUSTLING AROUND in Jackson's old cupboard now. They keep their linens in there now. Sissy hired the sharecroppers' son months ago to come and put a lock on that cupboard door. She said it was to keep the babies from falling down that hole. But only she has the key to the room. It's hung around her neck on a string so Josey got to ask every time she need a new cloth to wash with.

Sissy comes out of the cupboard holding a wood chest they keep winter shawls in. She sets it down in the middle of the room and opens it. Inside are full tomatoes, still on a vine, plump carrots, runner beans, and potatoes the size of two fists. I don't know where she got all this from. Josey's eyes widened.

"I don't know why I kept it from you," Sissy say. She leaves her box next to Josey and shuffles over to the rocker, sits in it, and pushes into short swings. She closes her eyes like she praying.

Josey sorts through the box, puts one onion and one potato on the cutting board. Ties her apron around her waist before she takes her knife to dice them. "The world is changing, Miss Sissy," Josey say. "Even for us. And look at all this goodness. This is what matters."

"Perspective," Sissy say. "It's God's gift to the dying. And when I saw that dead woman, I think I got hers. I used to have people," she say. "Was married once. Can you believe that? Had good friends. Ms. Annie was one. My best. We used to play together when I was just older than Rachel."

"You two was friends?" Josey ask.

"Annie treated me better than any of the other slaves . . . always. We got into so much mischief together, found trouble wherever it be. If mudslinging was part of any game, we'd play it first. Her Momma used to come out and say, 'Annabelle Brown! You don't have no place in the mud with her.' A negro and a white. Unnatural how close we was. But nobody could keep us apart. Did a spit handshake to prove we was loyal. Best friends forever.

"Before we knew it, we was women. Sixteen and it was time for us to marry. Annie asked her momma if I could be her help to get her dressed and ready for courting. But Lord knows all we did was gossip and drink her daddy's stole liquor.

"We both married at the same time, was both trying to get pregnant at the same time, too. Wanted our babies to be best friends like we was. And even when my Paul passed on, I still had hopes for Annie. We were still gon' have a baby.

"But Annie wasn't getting pregnant. Months to years, then that knock met our door that night—the evening the night man, Bobby Lee, came to our door.

"You were her prize. She wanted to do everything for you herself. Y'all ate at the table together, she taught you to write at two years old.

You was already sewing beads on dresses by then. She'd praise you more than she shoulda, gave you more than she shoulda. Spared the rod even when you was breaking things, knocking things over, couldn't keep a room clean if you was in it. You were the reason Annie pushed me away. You left me with nothing except Annie's trust.

"It's why she listened when I tol' her what that night man had done to her. I was the one that saved her from kissing that black baby on the mouth. From the ridicule of this world. From them good people that despise nigger-lovers more than sin itself. But it wasn't them that Annie ended up loathing. It was me. I could see it in her eyes every time she looked at me after I accused you of being a negro. Eventually, she put me out like garbage.

"But I wasn't gon' let it end with me . . . no. And I'm sorry for it now. Sorry for what happened to you. 'Cause I'm the one who made sure rumors got spread. Didn't want to give Annie a chance to lie and hide it. I made her confront what you did to us.

"Her husband Richard had to finish the matter when Annie couldn't. He gave you away to Charles and soon your memories of Annie got erased. That was Annie's fear come true. You quit asking for Annie-Momma. You only wanted Charles-Momma to hold you and feed you and teach you. And Annie was heartbroke from being Forgot-Momma. Alone-Momma. But I wasn't gon' be alone by myself. And now I got you."

Sissy stops rocking.

"People need people," she say.

Josey wipes her hands down her apron. She goes to Sissy and kneels down next to her chair. "If all we got is each other," Josey say. "Let us be family once and for all."

43 / FLASH

Conyers, Georgia, 1848

BAND MUSIC WHINES through here for her party. "A celebration!" Cynthia called it. "Bat Mitzvahed!" she said. "My old ass has come of age!"

I think that means it's her birthday.

For certain it's a fancy way to have a barbecue.

I imagine a diamond looks like this brothel.

A jewel, clear-white and sparkly. Cynthia took the whole week to clean this room out and wash it down. The thrown-away things she changed for white tablecloths, white candles, sheer white curtains, and the floor shines. We could be on the ring finger of Georgia.

Cynthia's boy, Johnny, had a real birthday last week. Ten years old. When he saw me from the hall just now, he came running at me like I been gone for days somewhere. He hugged my neck and grabbed my head two-handed, pressed his lips on my cheek and a burst of slobber cooled there.

I love spit kisses.

They're made by folks with a reckless kinda love inside of 'em.

Cynthia started letting Johnny come in the saloon more often. She said she marking the beginning of their fresh start. But he's still careful with his permission, it's why he went after his kiss and I shuffled his red hair.

Cynthia paid a rabbi's son to teach her Hebrew and give her classes. She said she paid him for every vowel and every letter she learned. Cash money under the table and just between the two of 'em, 'cause girls ain't supposed to learn. She told Sam she did it 'cause she "Can't believe this body is all there is to me. I'm more than what feels good and makes me happy."

Bullshit is what Sam called it but said he respected her decision anyway. Then reminded her she's a woman of science.

"Exactly," she said. "Emphasis on biology. Living's a disaster with a hundred percent fatalities. None of us survive this. Maybe science should be more interested in known theories of what does. I chose this one."

She's completed her courses the way the boys do. It's why she got her wedding dress on to party in her own honor and only invited the people she like: fifty customers, and less than half her staff. So everybody's walking in and out here like they special. Chosen.

The ones outside are standing around the barbecue pit looking in it like Jesus is about to rise from the ashes. The only stranger here is the big white man guarding the door, asking Cynthia who can come in and who cain't.

Bobby Lee and his two cousins have already been by two times. Got kicked out once. It wasn't a mistake that they never got invitations. When they first came to the door, the guard said, "Cynthia . . ."

She stopped dancing to see who was at the door. That's when Bobby Lee took his hat off to show her it was him. "Only Bobby Lee can come in," she said. "This is a private party and his cousins don't wash their asses. I only want to smell barbecue pieces, not Henry's creases."

Since his cousins couldn't come, too, Bobby Lee wouldn't, neither. He put his hat back on and turned down the steps while his grumbling cousins put their middle fingers in the air.

Cynthia's twirling around the dance floor now, grinding her hips like she got something to sell, even though the invitations say her girls ain't working today. Maybe not ever. So they stand around the room in their party clothes, free.

This piano stool still feels like Jeremy's spot even though he's months gone and his piano's been covered in a white sheet. Cynthia keeps her mail on top of it now and Sam keeps stacking it there, too. Sometimes he try to make her talk about what's in the unopened envelopes, but she never do. A lot of 'em from the government.

This whole place has been decorated since yesterday but I put pink flower vases on all the tables this morning 'cause nobody would be able to see the small lit candles burning since it's day. We took down the dark curtains and let the light come in bright and clean like this ain't Cynthia's saloon. Even the mahogany wood chairs look pine from the sunshine. The smell of liquor's been traded for lavender. Streamers run down the walls, baby blue and white. At the top are paper-cutout stars, pulled open to a ball.

White men, dressed a little better than customers, make up the band at the front of the room tooting horns, twanging banjos, and sliding harmonicas. Except one man. He holds a wide-bellied bottle, got his top lip capped over the mouth of it, blowing. His deep base hums and gets everybody's fast feet stomping including Cynthia's.

In the middle of the room, tables and most of the chairs have been pushed away leaving space for Cynthia to throw herself this way and that way, dancing alone but wild in her wedding dress. Her hair that was all pinned up this morning's been danced loose on the sides, parting her unbleached strands, showing it brown underneath.

Sweet-smelling barbecue is wafting through the door now, full flavored and hickory smoked—chicken, beef, but no pork. Not because Cynthia won't eat pork ribs but because she's fond of the pig she call Doc.

She starts some kind of jump-back dance in the center of the room, hopping backward all the way across the floor and behind the bar. I meet her there with a glass of cold water. She grabs Sam and grinds her hips on him, laughing. She say, "Can you believe I graduated to 'woman'!"

Some old man behind her say, "You been all woman to me."

"Why don't you mind yer business," Cynthia say.

"You look beautiful," I tell her. "Better late than never."

"That's right," she say. "I'm officially responsible for my own actions. Six hundred and thirteen new laws not to break. I should teach a class."

A banjo player, his white face painted black with grease, takes a seat with the band. When Cynthia sees him, she grabs my hand and rushes us into two chairs already in the middle of the room. She starts hooting and clapping before our butts hit the seat. She smiles with all her teeth, tells everybody, "Ssssh. . . . Shut up!" then whispers to me, "This is for you. It's popular in New York."

Black-faced Banjo Man puts the pearly round part of his banjo on his thigh and bends one arm around it like he's holding a woman, pulling her close. He slides his other hand up its neck, along the four strings, and plucks one with his middle finger for sound. With the thumb of his other hand, he searches for the first note of his tune and his flat heel taps the floor. He shifts in his seat and closes his eyes. His song comes. It rises from deep in his gut like he mean every note.

Applause explodes when he finish. Cynthia is jumping up and down and clapping and whistling. "From New York!" she say, then shakes me, "How you like your surprise?"

"Mine?"

"Your gift . . . the Black-face man?"

"Does his face have to be painted that way? Do I look like that?"

"Go wash your face," she tell Banjo Man. "And come back and do it again."

THE PARTY ENDED an hour ago and the big white man that was at the door is paid and gone. It's calm and quiet here now except for the clacking of the band packing up. The orange-brown haze of dusk is pouring through Cynthia's uncovered windows while I stand in the way of one placing a golden platter, silver spoons, knives, and forks inside a cherrywood box, under a velvet cloth. I didn't ask where she got all these nice things.

It's just me and Sam left to clean up now. We don't talk much but we friendly. He gave me his last two days of tips, told me it was for the baby. Albert's only been up twice today from the room he building downstairs. Told me to stay off my feet and I told him I'd sit as soon as I finished serving the drinks in my hand. That was two hours ago. Now I'm just wiping down the tables. I saved him a plate, though. Barbecue sauce is coming off the side.

"Good job, boys," Sam say to the band as they leave. The bandleader tips his hat.

When the front door shuts, the side door near the gambling parlor opens. Sam shouts toward it, "Party's over. We closed." Then he say to me, "Drunks never know when it's time to say good night."

But footsteps from that side door keep coming up the hall. Sam say again, "We closed!"

"Evenin, Sam . . . Mimi."

My breath leaves me.

I grab this table, the only thing keeping me up. I'd know that voice and that word—*Mimi*—even in deafness.

"How do, Jeremy?" Sam say. "Long time."

I don't turn around. Cain't turn around.

"Let me get you something," Sam say.

"Water," Jeremy say.

Jeremy's hand squeezes my shoulder, squeezing the life out of me. My tears fall sudden—his touch the only push they needed.

Sam sets Jeremy's glass of water on the bar top. Jeremy don't take it. He grabs my hand, instead.

He say, "I don't blame you for not wanting to see me."

I cain't move.

He backs away and takes a seat at the bar. His reflection in the window across the room is like blurred vision in front of me. My tears giving me layers of lenses. He hunches over his water glass and slides it to his right side and rubs his thumb on the side of the cup, say, "I was hoping you'd find a way to forgive me. Maybe another gamble of mine that won't pay off . . . unless you think it do."

But I don't think nothin.

"I'm sorry, Mimi. I want to do better this time."

I can see myself in the window's reflection. See him. Feel this loss inside me swimming up to my throat and to all my surfaces.

In his reflection, his left sleeve is rolled up in a puff of cloth around his elbow. But below his elbow I cain't see nothing. No flesh. No fingers. Some kind of trick of these tears.

I swing around to him, confused. But it's true. His arm is gone, half-missing, a stub of what used to touch me, feed me. He stares at my big belly.

I say, "What happened to your arm?"

"You pregnant?" he say.

He rubs his good hand over his head of hair and smiles, "Mimi? We having a baby?"

Albert's voice comes too soon. "You save me a plate!" Albert say. I can hear the smile in his voice before I see it on 'em when he gets in the room. But it goes when Albert and Jeremy meet eyes.

Sam say, "Tell Cynthia I'll see her in the morning," and picks up his satchel from under the counter.

Jeremy say, calm, "But I didn't pay you, Sam."

"Water's on the house," Sam say.

"No," Jeremy say. "I said I'd pay you for it. For the good service. I'm a cripple, not a liar." He tosses a coin on the bar.

Albert say to Sam, "I'll let Cynthia know you're gone for the day," and he turns back up the hall.

Jeremy bursts out laughing.

Laughs longer than he should, slamming the countertop with his fist for funny.

He smiles at me, then at Albert's back. "Where you going, Papa Bear?" But Albert keeps up the hall.

"Funny thing," Jeremy say, smiling. "After that rockslide . . . when the doctors told me I had to lose the arm. All I could think about was the last thing I touched. Can you believe that shit? See, there I was dying, Mimi, and I thought of you." He bursts out laughing again, reaches over the counter and grabs a bottle of whiskey, pours it in his glass, sips it, and throws his legs up on the seat next to him. He say to me, "So when did you say you were due?"

"We're due next month."

"We? Who, *we*?"

"Me and you."

He starts counting his fingers out loud, "One, two . . . wait, I left, when? Almost nine months ago. . . . Whew wee, Mimi. This baby's overdue."

"Baby's supposed to be born after nine full months, not when the ninth month start."

"You don't look but half that."

He makes his voice soft and girly, "'I'm a virgin. Be gentle. Don't hurt me. It's only you. I love you. I want to marry you.' Bullshit, Mimi."

"There weren't nobody else," I say.

"Yeah. . . . So who's the lucky guy?"

"You, fool," Cynthia say, walking in, her wedding dress swaying above her sandals. "And by the looks of that arm, you sure as hell ain't lucky."

"You been lying on me, Mimi?" he say. "Been telling people that I'm the father?" He laughs again, picks up the whiskey bottle, and sips from it directly.

"Oh, hell naw," Cynthia say. "I know you ain't drinking straight out my whiskey." She rips the bottle from his hand and he throws a gold coin at her.

"Oh. All right," she say. "It's yours. You was fixin to earn yourself another bloody nub, though." She pours him a little more in his cup and caps the rest. "But I'll keep this bottle."

Jeremy finishes his drink in one gulp, then looks over his shoulder at me standing behind him, say, "If it's a girl, you gon' sell her, too?"

I slap him hard in his face. My hand is sore when I finish. He stares me down and Cynthia tells him, "This a private party and you weren't invited."

"My pleasure to leave," he say, putting his hat on, getting up.

"Wait! Just wait," I say.

He stops.

"Just give me a minute," I tell Cynthia. "Please. Just . . . a minute."

A look of sorry for me comes over Cynthia. She comes and stands so close to me, arm to arm, and in such a way that Jeremy cain't see her face. But I do. Her expression's not of pity, but of a mother. My mother. She say, softly, "Not everybody deserves your honesty, Naomi."

I nod. "I won't lie."

"You could be quiet."

"Just give me one minute," I say. "Please."

"All right," she whispers, then yells toward Jeremy, "One minute! Then we closed."

Jeremy brings his heel up on the footrest when she leaves. When I take a step toward him, he turns away from me. I grab his good hand, pull him back toward me, make him touch my belly. "*This* is our baby."

"Do you know what I been through? To get back here for you? How could you do it, Mimi? Whoring around?"

"You left me!"

"So you laid with the first man you see, some . . . some nigger?"

"You calling me a nigga, too?"

"I didn't say that . . ."

"His name is Albert. And he ain't a nigga. When you left, he was the only person to take care of me."

"Is that your story?"

"It's the truth."

"Well here's mine. You're a whore. Just like the rest of 'em. 'Cause no man would look after somebody else's baby unless he had a stake in it."

"He did."

He gets up slow from his stool and goes to the door. "Then Albert's a better man than me."

"It *is* funny, ain't it?" I say, these pasts we reach for like ghosts. Sometimes, we just got to be happy we survived. "You're right," I say. "Nobody can go back to what's gone. Like reaching out with a hand that's not there."

He holds the doorknob, ready to leave me again and I don't care. "Well, maybe when the baby's born, we can see who it favors."

"Albert," I say. "My baby'll favor Albert."

He opens the door. Gone. Gone again. And this time, it don't matter.

44 / FLASH
Conyers, Georgia, 1848

I BEEN SPINNING THIS gold coin around my fingers for most the night 'cause the worse thing about being pregnant is sleeping. Better, not sleeping. Cynthia gave it to me after Jeremy flicked it at her a few days ago. She said it was for the baby now. For me.

I told her I didn't want it. Not from him. Not for this baby. 'Cause there are things more important than money. Time is one. Peace, another. A good father for this baby. I've got all of that now without him. She said, "Don't let nobody tell you money ain't everything. Money keeps you from paying for things with your life."

Before this baby, I took for granted sleeping on my stomach or sleeping on one side for as long as I wanted to. Cain't even sleep on my back, now, for drowning. Like deep breathing through a reed. It's how I feel when I remember Jeremy.

Cynthia told me not to punish myself for him, for still feeling love for him. "If a person never loved somebody pathetically and unrequited, they haven't met themselves yet, so consider yourself introduced. And lucky. We don't always get to touch the ones we want without losing everything."

IT'S JUST AFTER midnight now, and I've been wasting time. Been folding clothes, counting unmatched socks. *How does that happen?* My mind's been racing with thoughts and feelings that pass and re-pass. Not just about Jeremy. And Albert. Or Cynthia. Momma. Hazel. A chaos of faces. Bernadette's, too.

Cynthia gave me her room like she promised. And in between time, Cynthia put Bernadette out in the shed across the road. Locked her in there for four days with only bread and water. Left her hollering and screaming like she was being murdered over and over again. When Cynthia finally got her out, Bernadette had throw-up all over herself, her clawing fingers were bloodied, and her screaming voice was gone. But she was cured of the leafs, though. Has been for almost a month and Bernadette say it ain't easy. Say, the first thing she think about when she wake in the morning is the leafs. Then she spends the rest of the day trying to forget 'em.

I FELL ASLEEP in this chair with my folding still in my hand. Might as well get up 'cause it's 3:00 a.m. and another couple hours of sleep won't make a difference.

I shuffle up the hall, gon' clean the saloon. Shouldn't be much to do 'cause it's been empty since Cynthia closed for business a few days ago—the day after her party. She's been telling everybody she's "renovating" but she tell me she need time to decide what she gon' do next.

Sam still comes to work every day. Been unloading them crates that he never got a chance to unload for five years. Some of the crates are more full than others, a couple of 'em only got one bottle inside from him cherry-picking 'em the last few years.

He built a new drying rack closer to where he wash. "Doesn't make sense to keep dripping across the floor," he said.

A few of the girls are still here, too, some loyal, some hoping Cynthia will come up with a new way a woman can make money without being a wife. Bernadette's making dresses. She's got a ball gown on a wire frame in the windows and when sunlight hits 'em, it throws sparkles of yellow and white light around the room, mixing with Cynthia's rainbows on the walls from her hanging crystals.

Cynthia and Sam are already up when I get to the saloon. "Evening, Sunshine," Cynthia say. "Or should I say, morning." She's sitting at the bar, nursing a drink, still wearing her wedding dress. Been in it three days. "It's about time you got up. Longest nap a person ever took."

"It's only three," I say.

"Yeah, but you was 'sleep at noon yesterday."

Cynthia's just holding her drink in her hand. Usually, pouring it in her glass is the same as putting it in her mouth. Only a two-second delay between 'em. But this time, we're going on a minute.

"I've been thinking," Cynthia say. "Maybe marriage ain't so bad. Maybe I *could* live with a man. A young sunflower like me gotta rethink her options. And Sam says he'll marry me."

"I didn't say nothing about marriage tonight."

He sets a glass of water in front of me.

"You don't want to marry me, Sam? I already got a ring. You can get down on one knee at sunrise or in front of the fire, romantic like, and . . ."

"See, that's the problem, you're too bossy. Most men find that intimidating."

"The people you want to partner with should intimidate you," she say, smiling. "Not because they're a bully but because they're that good and you know it."

"And what makes you think I'd ask again when you've already said no?"

"I'm a new woman, Sam. You never know. I could've changed my mind."

"All right," he say. "Marry me."

"No," she laughs and shoots her drink. "I cain't marry nobody. I'd eventually kill him."

"I know thas right," I say.

A look of calm rests on her face. She looks around the room. "Isn't this a good feeling," she tells me. "The stillness in here? Reminds me of the good ole days."

"Naw," I say. "Reminds me of the good days coming."

"So what you gon' do, then?" Cynthia say. "You welcome to stay here, make this house a home for you and Albert and Baby Peaches."

"Peaches'll be a boy."

"Then, Berry. And y'all can still be my good deed before I die. It'll make me look like a saint. A white woman caring for a black baby always makes her look like a saint."

"You ain't going nowhere," I say. "You got Johnny to take care of . . ."

"That's why I got Sam. You'll keep him for me, won't you, Sam? Be a better mother-father than me."

"I wish you'd gon' and divorce your death talk finally. Death, religion . . ."

"Then, what did you decide to do, Naomi?" she say. "You can be my backup for Johnny."

"I cain't even think that far. I just want this baby out."

"You say that now. Wait 'til it starts coming. When you cussing us all. I'll be sure to remind you of how bad you wanted it out—the baby and the old bag of blood that comes out after."

"Mercy!" Sam say.

Cynthia laughs. "Too much girl talk for you, Sam?"

"You could talk about these late notices instead," he say, opening an envelope.

"I don't pay taxes," she say, and slides back in her chair, puts her foot on the table. "What's the government done for me? I'm still a woman."

"Your problem is you always think you won't get caught for nothing. They could send you to jail."

"People don't get caught for the real thing they did wrong, Sam. They get caught for some lesser thing, some small offense. Taxes, jay-walking, a fine . . ."

She's right, I think.

'Cause I'm still free.

Only Jeremy is accusing me of a lie now. And no one mentions the murders in Faunsdale no more. Even the papers have quieted down. But in my heart, I know I got away with murder.

45 / FLASH

Conyers, Georgia, 1848

THERE ARE THINGS that happened to me when I was alive that I didn't know happened 'til I was dead. So I cain't place myself there now and lie about it, 'cause it didn't happen that way.

I wasn't there to know. Didn't see it. Didn't hear it.

It's the same thing that's happening to you.

Other people will make choices for you, about you—win or lose, work or won't, live or die—and you'll have missed it.

Choices that could change the rest of your life and you won't even know it happened 'til you're dead. 'Til you get your turn with the flashes.

And once you've been in 'em long enough, you'll get to see everything.

✛✛

I BEEN IN Cynthia's cellar below the saloon since daybreak. Ain't been back to sleep since before dawn. "Cellar" is what Cynthia renamed this secret place under the saloon. She gon' use it to store her good liquor. "It'll keep them skinny Irish from sliding over the bar top when Sam's back is turned," Cynthia said after Sam told her, "There ain't no way in hell I'm reaching into some man's drawls and retrieving the bottle they're stealing. Not even a twenty-dollar bottle."

So Cynthia keeps her good stuff down here in the cellar now. Daylight is seeping through the spaces around the door that leads from in here to under the porch outside. The weight and wobble of drunk folks, fat folks, and the occasional horse taking a step up the porch, has made the doorframe pull away from the brick walls. All connected.

It's already getting warm down here. It'll be hot by one.

Heat gets trapped in this cellar and turns even the cool shadows to coal steam. It's hotter in the corners where night-made cobwebs melt and break in their centers like little hands letting go. I brush those webs away with my broom, roll 'em in the bristles.

I've been picking up all the solid dead things around me, pinching my nose before I touch 'em even though they probably don't stink. The other trash that was never alive is easy—paper, napkins, and cigarette ends kicked through the upstairs floorboards. I put 'em in my trash bag and tie it up ready for outside.

One-thirty has me washing the walls 'cause it's hot like I knew it would be. The water feels cool.

Albert just laid this wood floor a few months ago so the nails are still flat against the boards and deep in the wood. They ain't been disturbed by shifting earth yet.

He didn't finish the corner pieces of the floor, though. That's where he decided to throw all the bothersome things I got to clean up now— wood scraps and tins.

The floor near the door under the porch ain't finished right, either. You gotta tug the door real hard to get it open 'cause it's warped and wonky. Cain't spy good in the saloon above because of its noise and the strength you need to wrestle it. Best to come through the trap door under the tub and close it quiet behind.

I yank at the door now 'cause there ain't nobody in the saloon to hide from. I barely get it opened and drag my bag of trash under the steps hunched over 'til I get beyond the porch and can stand straight. I scratch a trail in the dirt behind me now, erasing my wide footprints. I reckon my weight is half baby, even though everybody tells me I'm still small.

I can hear Albert at the side of the house hammering before I see him. Today, he said, is the last day he has to finish Cynthia's liquor cabinet before her grand reopening. Saloon and gambling only.

Albert's giving Cynthia a gift of metal finishings that he's melted to shapes—flowers and birds to work as doorknobs and drawer pulls. He made a big gardenia to be the centerpiece of the cabinet. I stand behind him, watch him nail it together.

⁜

YOU MAY NEVER know.

May never know about the choice somebody made for you that changed your life. Just like I didn't know about the choice made for me that day. By the time I was standing behind Albert, watching him bang those last nails in, my life had already changed.

Two fields over, down a hill and off to the left, Soledad's house had been sitting quiet for most of the morning even though Mr. Shepard had been home almost six days. He had been sick with food poison for three days of 'em and stopped eating. He started feeling better. Good enough, he thought, to finish that letter to his brother. Good enough to keep his promise to Cynthia to host her grand reopening the next day. Good enough, he thought. *But he rested instead.*

His shirt wouldn't get ironed.

His shoes wouldn't be shined. And his menudo would be left on the table cooling, then cleared from the table, thrown out rotting, then swallowed by the ground as if it was never there.

He had meant to pack his new deck of cards, pay his bills, start reading the book his gentleman friend gave him. So many things he was finally home to do, so much intention. All of it met by Soledad's decision.

She sat at her dining room table a full half hour after the choice she made, eating her stew. When she finally spoke, she said, "Mr. Shepard? You really should try this," and stirred inside her bowl of menudo. "You know it took me all day to prepare it. Just for you, dear."

She lifted the cloth that covered her pile of tortillas and took one, broke it, dipped it in. That was when she first seemed to notice the red stains smeared on the backs of her hands. She put her spoon down and snatched the cloth from under the pile of her tortillas, knocking them to the floor, crumbled to pieces. She used the cloth to wipe the blood, rubbed harder because it had dried. She gave up trying before they were clean, picked up her spoon, scooped her stew, brought it to her mouth.

Her fingernails were packed black-red and moist underneath.

✚✚

MY PLAN IS to help Albert lower his cabinet doors from the bathroom upstairs to down here in the cellar. His eyesight changed 'cause of the way his skin has healed at his brow. Above his right eye, the skin is pulled back tighter and thinner and it makes his eye water for no reason. So I'm his line of sight even though he want to do it all hisself.

"Shoo, fly," he say to me. "Get back."

He say he gon' use his ladder to guide the doors down instead of me since the last came rushing fast and almost hit me.

"You could hurt the baby," he say and shoos me again.

"I'm pregnant, not useless. How you gon' get it through this gap without me keeping it on track from down here?"

"I'll manage it. Just move."

He squats and lowers the long door along the ladder slide, got a rope tied around the gardenia piece, with the other end connected to his wrist. I reach my skinny arms up and help keep the door flat against the ladder so if the tie slips, it'll follow the ladder down, like tracks.

He say, "You not under this, are you?"

"No," I lie and step back. The new wood floor he laid creaks like old knees in an empty tunnel.

"You are down there. I can hear you. Get back against the wall." I squeak across the floor but when I reach the looser wood planks near the sidewalls, the squeak of the boards give out a donkey's hee-haw.

"All right," I say. "I'm all the way back now."

"Good. I'm gon' let it down now. If it falls, let it fall. You just watch it's fitting through and ain't caught on nothin."

"All right."

It slides smoothly as he lowers it, then stops. "What's in the way?" he yells.

I take a step forward—hee-haw.

"I said get back," he say. "I can hear you."

"How am I supposed to see, then?"

"Just look."

"You want me to help. Don't want me to help . . ."

"Forget it," he says and lets it go. It comes racing down the ladder, rocks forward, then slams back.

"You did it!" I say.

✚✚

SOLEDAD DIPS HER spoon in her stew again, raises it to her mouth, catches her reflection in the sweating silver water pitcher on the table. Her face is misshaped from the silver's bend. She notices the blood sprinkled on her cheek and large swipes of red across her forehead and neck.

Mr. Shepard gurgles from the floor. The stab wounds around his arms and hands were done after the chest wound that woke him from his nap, fighting. There's so many now. So so many. The second-to-last wound was on his neck, the worst in his gut, twisted more than once. The knife's still there.

Soledad say, casual, "I really did deserve better than you, Charlie."

He gurgles.

"But you never could see me. Always somebody else. So I asked myself, when do I get what I need?" She yells, "What about me?" She stops herself from talking, clears her throat, pats the tortilla cloth over her face, her hands tremble.

A thin flow of blood rises up from his mouth, then down the side of his cheek. She bends down to him, fixes his hair, combing it with her fingers, slicks it back with the flat of her hand, smiles. "Aren't you going to come and eat? I cooked this for you. Please, come and sit down."

She sits at the table without him, sits over her bowl, pushing meats to the side with her spoon, as always. She puts a spoonful of broth in her mouth, swallows, then turns back to him.

Charlie's eyes jot toward her, fix on her. She says, "You always did have pretty eyes." She lifts her whole bowl of stew to her lips and drinks it down like water. Chunks of meat fall around her mouth and to the table. She picks up the pieces and throws 'em in her mouth, smacks on 'em, swallows, wipes her mouth with her backhand. "No one keeps their promises anymore. You should've kept yours, Charlie."

An exhale like a man blowing his hands warm comes out of Charlie.

"Charlie?" Soledad say. "Charlie?" she say again, this time with worry in her voice.

☩

ALBERT PUSHES HIS new cabinet against the wall while I pick through the bottles of wine and whiskey.

I can feel Albert looking at me, can tell he wants to ask me about Jeremy's coming and going a few nights ago, but I ain't got nothing to say.

"I understand if you still want to leave," Albert say. "And be with him."

"You worry too much," I say. "What's Jeremy got that you don't?"

He smiles one-sided, all crooked-faced and ugly. Strangely beautiful, I think. I love him. But not the same as I did Jeremy.

"So I'm better than him?" he say. "'Maybe I'm somebody worth spending the rest of your life with?"

I smile. "Don't you gotta leave in an hour. If you stop talking now you could save your strength. It's a long trip."

"And if I gave my strength up now to ask, what would you say?"

"That Cynthia wants me to put all her liquor in order of their alphabet. But what do you think she'd say if I put the pretty ones up front?"

✢

"MR. SHEPARD!" SOLEDAD cries, trying to shake him alive.

She goes searching through her house like she looking for something needed to fix him with—in her drawers and closets, the bedrooms.

She gives up and finally bursts out of her front doors, hysterical and screaming, her bare feet scramble down her porch, leaving red footprints. They get floured with dust as she runs up her dirt road toward the main one, her hair heavy with blood and whipping from side to side. Her closest neighbor, a quarter mile away, comes out his door from hearing her scream.

"He's dead!" she say. "Mr. Shepard's dead! That slave girl killed him!"

Part V

46 / HOMECOMING: 1869

Tallassee, Alabama

THE LAW PUTS a limit on the time a person has to sue somebody. And if they don't do it in that time, the hurt person has to drop the matter forever. And there's a time limit on how long the law has to catch somebody for a crime, too, even if the person did it. And if the law cain't catch him in that time, it means the criminal got away with it forever.

Not murder.

Murder has no limits. So the death penalty is always on the heels of the guilty. And there's a lot of talk here about what to do with the treasonous, deserters, and war criminals. It's how I know about limits. It's how I know soldiers who desert are murderers according to the people here. Innocent lives were lost because of them. The death penalty, folks say, is the right punishment. But not according to newest president of the United States.

President Johnson signed an order giving "unconditional pardons to all Civil War participants"—on both sides—including war criminals. The order came too late for Henry Wirz, the commanding officer of Camp Sumter in Georgia where Union soldiers were starved, mistreated, and killed. Wirz was convicted of eleven murders and conspiracy and was hanged a war criminal.

He wasn't the only one.

There were at least two war criminals punished, but there are thousands of deserters, hundreds of them being hunted down and killed and murdered, all off the legal record.

As many as one in three soldiers deserted. So, one in three were eligible to die as cowards. Those men say they were scared or said they were fighting to save their families not a nation; they didn't sign up for this. It was the old president, President Lincoln, who said no to killing more deserters: "American people will not stand to see Americans shot by the dozens and twenties." But not everybody agree with Lincoln. The Civil War is proof they didn't. It's been over four years since the end of the Civil War and folks are still angry, Confederate flags still fly. And it's still true that the death penalty is always on the heels of a murderer.

Jackson came home three nights ago by surprise from the new war out west. Even with a son five years gone, Sissy's first question was, "You told somebody before you left, didn't you, son? Honorable?"

But Josey didn't ask no questions when she saw him standing in the darkened doorway, a hero with the night sky behind him. She collapsed with all her burdens in the spot where she stood. It's where his comforting arms would hold her 'til daybreak.

And now, they sit before the popping fire, Jackson's arms around her still, her body slouched into him. It only took Rachel and Squiggy a half minute three nights ago to find themselves lost in Jackson, too. They've been hanging on him like cares. "This is your daddy," Josey told 'em that first night, and now they move when he moves, follow him in and out the house, from one side of the room to the other. And right now, they're a step away, busying themselves with a piece of coal, coloring tree bark, and forming letters, but they're still keeping an eye on him. Sissy, too, in her rocking chair.

"And my daddy?" Josey say. "Any word from him?"

"I heard his regiment went north into Dakota territory the month before I made it to Texas," Jackson said. "They call negroes like him buffalo soldiers," he said.

"But you?" Sissy said. "You came home?"

"Negro fighters ain't getting proper shelter out there, Momma . . . food. Deal was we was gon' get guns and ammunition, new shoes and quality goods. Instead, we got rotten Civil War rations and cheap blankets that fell apart in the rain. They're the ones that broke the contract and don't care if we die."

"So they just let you go home?" Josey said.

"Put it this way . . . they know I ain't coming back."

"Did I raise a deserter, Jackson? Is that what you did, son? You telling me I raised a coward?"

"Momma, I ain't gon' kill Indians. Treat 'em the way white folks treat us."

Sissy shakes her head. "Oooh . . . they gon' come for you, Jackson. They gon' come and you deserve what you get. Always turning your back on folks that treat you right."

"Is that what I do, Momma? Huh? I mistreat folk?"

Sissy pushes back in her chair hard enough to set herself rocking in half swings.

++

FART SOUNDS ARE echoing from the bottom of the porch where Jackson got his face buried in Squiggy's belly, blowing. Rachel and Josey are beside themselves with laughter. It's been thirty-two days since Jackson's came home and it's like they've always been as perfect as a white family.

All but Sissy.

Jackson and Sissy ain't talked since a month ago when she told him she raised a fool. She finished breakfast without a word to nobody and stayed behind when everybody went outside. She don't say much to Josey now, neither.

"Daddy!" Rachel calls. "Look at me, Daddy."

Squiggy slides from under Jackson and tries running but Jackson tackles him by the legs.

"Daddy!" Rachel says, holding the edges of her dress out like she's about to spin. "Look at me, Daddy. Daddy? Look at me!"

"Just do it, already!" Sissy say, bringing herself outside.

"She's just excited to see her father," Josey say, hanging wet clothes on the porch rail.

"It's all right, Momma. Show me when you ready, Baby Girl."

Rachel starts spinning.

"Ain't all right," Sissy say. "You need to spend yer time with that boy. He can't talk, hardly run. Simpleminded."

"Ain't nothin wrong with Junior's mind," Jackson say. "He ain't simple nothin."

"Daddy, you didn't see me!"

"He just gotta catch up, is all. . . . Ain't that right, Lil' Man? You'll be talking soon, won't cha? Say, Mama. Say, Ma-ma-ma."

He don't.

Rachel skips over and kneels down to Squiggy, leaning too close to his face. "Say, Ray-chel," she say. "Come on, Squiggy. Say, Ray-chel."

He don't.

"Say, Da-dee," Jackson say. "Da-da-da."

Squiggy makes an *ah* sound, then blows his lips like another belly fart.

"He did it!" Jackson say. "He said Dada!"

"He did not say Dada," Josey says, laughing.

"You're just jealous he said Dada before Momma."

"He didn't."

"Say Dada again so Momma stay jealous," Jackson say. "Or say, Rachel."

He don't.

"What about me?" Sissy say. "You ain't gon' teach him 'Nana'?"

"Aw, Momma, we just messing around. And you know, 'Momma' or 'Dada' 'posed to come first, anyway?"

"First, huh? If I recall, I was first. Been here first a long time. Ain't I family, too?"

Jackson smiles, understanding something, and goes slowly to his momma, aching from sitting too long. He limps up the porch to Sissy and hugs her stiffened body. "Is that what this is about, Momma?"

"You turned on me, Jackson?" Sissy say.

"Aw, Momma. You are first. The only momma I got."

Sissy snorts.

She stayed on the porch mumbling to herself and watching Jackson and his family hold hands and walk in a circle, singing, "Ring a ring a roses. We all fall down." No one noticed when she went inside. They fall backward at once, laughing, and Jackson kissing Josey, more passionate than he should for the light of day or for children around. *Embarrassing.*

"Let's play another game," Jackson say, smiling slyly at Josey. "Rachel, you and Squiggy hide and me and your momma come find you soon."

"Hide?" Rachel say.

"Thas the game," Jackson say. "You and Squiggy hide and me and Momma come look for you and find you."

Rachel grabs Squiggy's arm and they take off running, veering right behind the house. After a moment Squiggy comes back on his own, and finds a side-lying barrel out front to climb into.

"Funny how he understands what we tell him," Josey say.

"People don't need to talk to be able to understand," Jackson say. "More people should be like him."

Jackson pulls her close and kisses her deeply.

Way back near the tree line of the woods, a sway of trees gets my attention. I haven't felt winds all day. I stay still and watch the spot. The tree limbs creep open, then shake closed. I go to the spot where I think it happened—close enough—and wait for it to happen again.

The bushes part to the left of me and a white man stands in the space watching Josey and Jackson. He's in a uniform. An old Confederate one.

He sees Jackson and Josey and turns around running through the woods. I chase after him but after two miles, he's still running fast as he can and only slows when we get about a hundred yards from an opening in the woods. On the other side of the opening is the top of a tent, and smoke is rising from a smothered-out fire. I rush ahead of Josey's snooper to the signs of life.

Two more soldiers are there.

One's fat, one's skinny.

They're wearing faded gray uniforms and sitting on logs, cleaning guns. But Fatty startles at the sound of Snooper's approach. He stands quick and drops his cleaned gun for another one in his trousers. Skinny do, too. Both of 'em point their pistols at the edge of the forest and before Snooper emerges, Fatty shoots, tearing the bark off the tree to the right of Snooper's head.

Snooper waves his arms, stomping out from between the trees, still moving toward 'em, like he ain't bothered by bullets. "This whole damn place gone crazy!"

Fatty and Skinny lower their pistols. "We didn't know it was you, Boss," Fatty say.

"It's madness!" Snooper say. "The devil's work, that's what! He's alive and well in Alabama!"

From behind the tent comes a third man, another soldier in butternut-colored trousers and he's closing the last button on his gray coat. His soldier suit got gold stars and a wreath sewn into each side of his up-perched collar. "Colonel," all the men say, saluting him.

There's a disquiet here.

I feel it immediate.

Like walking into a room of somebody else's best friends and when they see a stranger, everybody gets quiet.

A pack. The killing kind. Bonded by some hunger.

"What do you have to report?" Colonel say to Snooper.

"A nigger and a white woman, sir. They was kissing and hugging up on each other. Everything's all gone to hell, that's what," Snooper say.

Colonel shifts his trousers, signals to Fatty for his pistol. He say, "So what are you going to do about it, soldier?"

"Are they outlaws, sir?" Fatty say, giving Colonel his pistol.

His question makes Colonel red-faced. "Do you know what negroes do?" Colonel say, disgusted. "And what that nigger is doing to that white woman in bed right now? Sending our great nation to hell, is what. Next thing you know they'll want to marry. First, the government takes our property and rights and give it to niggers and then they give 'em our women, too." He cocks his pistol. "I'll show you what I'm going to do about it."

47 / JUDGMENT

Conyers, Georgia, 1848

I T'S PITCH BLACK down here tonight.

Mostly.

Only a teardrop from this candle keeps the light low—more wick than wax. And the light from the saloon above is sprinkling down on me.

Cynthia made me close the latched door in the bathroom floor 'cause she say these nosey women like to wander. So it's gon' take me forever to put these bottles of whiskey away since it's dark and I can hardly see. I finished the first rows—the letters A through E—put the pretty ones up front, like I wanted.

I sit here on my knees trying to read the shadows of labels, and wedge open the last cart of liquor. I run my tiny light across the first labels . . . doggone, another C, Cognac. Means I got to move the bottles again.

Dogs is barking loud outside, just beyond the porch, and men's voices are mixing in with 'em. I crawl over to the stuck-shut side door and peek through the gaps. The men there are tying their dogs to the porch.

Up in the parlor, Johnny's shooting marbles and Cynthia's still in her wedding dress, sitting on a stool, drying a glass.

Two of the men run up the parlor steps. A third set of clicking heels trail behind. Their knocks slam at the door all together.

"Sam," Cynthia yells to the door. "You got the key. I ain't gettin up."

"Open up!" a man's voice say.

"We ain't open," Cynthia yell back. One of 'em kicks the door.

"What the hell's wrong with you!" Cynthia say. "I said we ain't open."

"Cynthia!" the man say again, this time his kick almost moves the door open.

She hops up and I rush to see through the slats in the floor. She tell Johnny, "Go to your room and go to sleep. I'll be there directly." Cynthia grabs her pistol from behind the bar, puts it in her garter.

"Open up!" the man say.

Cynthia fixes her hair, sets two glasses on a table, and picks up a bottle of gin on the way to the door. She opens it calmly, relieved when she see 'em: Henry and Ray, and Bobby Lee follows 'em in wearing a patch on his eye now.

"Aw, damn," Cynthia say. "It's just y'all. Why you got to kick my shit? Bamming on the door like you the law."

She picks up the drinking glasses from the table with her fingers, takes 'em back to the bar. When she sets 'em down, she notices the men's silence. She pauses. Breathes. She says over her shoulder, "Ain't it a little late for you boys? Surprised y'all ain't at Sweeny's, Bobby Lee. Bernadette told me how y'all regulars down there now."

Cynthia picks up the drinking glasses again. She takes out two more and brings all four to the table in front of them with a bottle of gin. Ray and Henry take out their pistols.

"What's goin on here, Bobby Lee?" Cynthia say. "Y'all here to rob me?"

Ray and Henry start searching the saloon and disappear toward the gambling parlor while Bobby Lee waits.

He don't say nothing.

Ray and Henry come back from the locked parlor door, then Ray starts back through the hallway toward the sleeping quarters and bathroom. "There's too many doors," Ray yells back up the hall and comes back to the saloon with Henry and Bobby Lee.

"We can do this the hard way," Ray say, "and disturb everybody in here, or the easy way."

Cynthia steps away from 'em, pulls her gun from her garter as she does, and points it across 'em.

"I got my child in here," she say. "So if by easy you mean I take down at least two of ya, then easy. I ain't gon' let y'all rob me or hurt nobody in here."

"We not robbing you," Bobby Lee say.

"Where is she?" Ray say.

"Who?" Cynthia say.

"That nigra girl you used to keep here."

I don't move.

"What you want her for?" Cynthia lowers her gun and slides into one of the hard chairs above me to the left. Her shadow blocks the light from my eyes. I got to stay still. Don't want my floor to make a noise.

She pours four shots of gin. "Is this about my party, Bobby Lee? I swear y'all's invitation was in the post."

Henry stutters, "D-don't m-mess around, Cynthia. We know she here."

"Left months ago," Cynthia say.

‑‑‑

THE HOOVES OF Confederate horses click over mud-set stones while their riders—Fatty, Skinny, Snooper, and Colonel—let their horses' struts take over their sway. They ride slow and cautious through the tunnel of vines where Squiggy and Rachel chased turkeys into the thick.

"I swear it was down here," Snooper say.

A quick movement from the ground makes 'em grab their pistols and point 'em at the forest floor where George is. He's resting against a tree with his mouth wide open, snoring. Fatty taps Colonel and Colonel signals the others to stop.

Colonel jumps down from his horse and with his weapon drawn, he kicks George's boot.

"Boy?" Colonel say.

George flinches but don't wake up.

"Boy!"

George opens his eyes and blinks through the haze, squints at Colonel, then proceeds to take his time yawning and stretching his arms high and wide, cracking his back, straining, say, "How do, Colonel?"

Colonel lowers his pistol and slides it in his trousers. "You a soldier, boy?" he say.

"I much more prefer the title, *man of leisure*. Bum knee kept me from the 'honor' of war, of course."

"That so?" Colonel say. "I've seen one-armed men fight a hell of a fight for this great nation. Real heroes. And men like yourself, full of excuse and leisure, are insults to the Confederacy."

George wobbles hisself up. "If you don't mind me saying, Colonel . . . war been over a long time. And you and your one-armed men lost for all us. Thanks for nothing."

Colonel throws George against the tree and George laughs, flopping from side to side. Colonel lets him go. "You're drunk," Colonel say.

"Naw, sir. I'm George and *you* are on my land."

Colonel say, "We're looking for a white woman and a negro. They call themselves a couple."

George burps as he starts his sentence. "The only white woman 'round here is my sister. But now that you mention it," he say, "free negroes are more uppity than caught ones—talk how they want, sleep all day, and yep, probably take our women." George bends over a little, then thrusts his hips forward, back and then forth, making a humping motion. "And screw 'em like this."

Colonel slams George against the tree and this time George cries a pitiful "Ow," laughing all the while. "I promise you, Colonel," he say. "I ain't worth your time."

"We may have lost the war, boy, but the law still the law. God's law."

George holds up his hands like he surrender, "Fine. Fine," and brushes his clothes straight. "Since you and your . . . battalion seem like reasonable men, I think you're looking for Josephine and Jackson. Down the road a ways to the clearing. Bout a half mile on the right. A big new road points the way."

Colonel signals to his soldiers and hops up on his horse.

"What y'all planning to do?" George say. "My sister Annie isn't going to let you just come on her property taking things. You, of all people, should respect that."

Fatty spits on George's forehead and George wipes it off while the men trot up the road ahead. George slides back down on the tree, opens his flask and drinks.

✢✢

IN THE SALOON above me, Henry's angry. He's already searched behind the piano, under the tables. Flipped two. "We know you keep that nigra girl hiding here," Henry say.

"It's best you tell us where she is," Ray say. "Save the damages."

Cynthia holds up a glass. "Gin's your poison? Ain't that right, Bobby Lee?" She pours it in her just-dried glass, offers it to him but he don't take it.

She leans back in her chair, her legs fall open, for sale again. "Why y'all want her when you can have me?"

"Go outside to the workshop," Ray say to Henry. "Check the shed and the blacksmith's place."

I watch Henry go down the porch steps and disappear into the darkness on the way to Albert's. I still don't move.

Cynthia twirls the gin in her glass. "I ain't never known you to refuse a drank, Bobby Lee."

"She killed old Charlie Shepard," he say.

"Mr. Shepard?" Cynthia say. "Somebody killed Charlie?"

"This afternoon . . . butchered."

Cynthia sets the glass down, holds the table.

"It was somebody he knew," he say.

"I can't believe somebody would hurt Mr. Shepard," she say.

"Had to know whoever did it 'cause he let 'em in the house . . . let her in."

"*Her*? You think that little girl did this? You ask Soledad about that?"

"She told us she seen the girl running from her house just before she found him. Said Mr. Shepard figured out she was the one who killed those in Faunsdale. He was gonna turn her in."

"Naomi?" Cynthia said in disbelief.

"What you call her?" Ray say.

"Y'all crazy if you think that girl killed Mr. Shepard."

"Read the paper yourself," Bobby Lee says, tossing the wanted ad on the table. "Soledad said it's the girl."

Cynthia glances at it. Recognition slides across her face. "That ain't her." She picks up her glass, sips her gin.

"You know lies got consequences, Cynthia."

"Then why don't you go after the liar who's accusin."

"Soledad?" Bobby Lee say. "Couldn't hurt a fly."

"She's pregnant, you know that?" Cynthia say. "The innocent girl you trying to *kill*, Bobby Lee. She's with child."

"Don't listen to her, Bobby Lee," Ray say. "She just try'n to make you soft."

"You had a family, didn't you, Bobby Lee? A baby? A wife? Is that right?"

"Everybody heard his family got kilt," Ray say. "Point is, niggers can't go 'round killing white folk. Even the rumor of it got to be dealt wit. And ain't nobody gon' miss a nigger."

Cynthia sips her gin again. "Then like I said, she ain't here."

The floorboard squeaks under my foot and Ray looks down at me. His dark eyes get stuck on me but I don't move.

Another squeak.

Ray takes out his pistol. He signals the others to be quiet while he sneaks to the bar, then rushes behind it. Cynthia closes her eyes like she praying it ain't me.

"Aw, man," Ray say. "You damn near got yourself killed, boy."

Johnny whimpers there. Cynthia goes around the bar and grabs Johnny, yells, "I told you to go to bed!"

He's not crying but Cynthia say to Johnny, "No, no, don't cry," and pulls him into her body and walks with him to the middle of the room above me. She kneels down where I can see her face and tells Johnny out loud, "I'm sorry. I shouldn't be yelling at you," then hugs him, strokes the back of his head, looks down toward me, and slides her eyes toward the under-porch door that's all the way across my room. But I already know that door's stuck and there ain't no way to get across the floor quiet.

I shake my head at her. They'll hear me if I open it. But she cain't see me. Johnny rubs his eyes and walks sleepy up the hall.

"We all know about the story from the papers," Ray say. "Those black folk murdered in Faunsdale. The owner. That girl did 'em. Just like she did Mr. Shepard."

Cynthia picks up a new bottle of liquor from over the bar. She say, "You been spending a lot of time with Soledad, ain't you, Bobby Lee? Visiting her when Charlie was away. How do we know you ain't the one that done it?"

++

I'VE BEEN MOVING fast as I can to get to Josey before these soldiers do. I find her diving into a pile of leafs with Rachel so when the wind of my hurry meets 'em, the spray of leafs that follow go unnoticed. Squiggy and Jackson take my flied-away ones and throw 'em back on top of the girls, burying 'em under.

I yell to Josey, "Run!" but she don't hear me. "Josey!" I say, beating the ground with my feet.

Rachel grabs Josey's arm, say, "Momma? You hear that?"

"Hear what, baby?"

"Somebody calling you."

Josey listens. Waits. "Just the wind," she say.

"Or my belly screaming it's time to eat," Jackson say, throwing Squiggy over his shoulder on the way to the house.

++

"WHERE IS SHE, Cynthia?" Ray say.

Cynthia laughs and lays her pistol on the countertop. "Who?"

"Stop playin' games," Ray say. "We know she here."

"Is this what you want, Bobby Lee?" Cynthia say. "For a innocent person to get punished?"

"I'm just doing my job," he say.

"Why does injustice always got to start with those five words? You say that like it's a game. One of them games where nobody gets hurt. Well, I like games, too, Bobby Lee."

"I'm gon' check these rooms," Ray say, heading down the hall.

"Help yourself," Cynthia say, leaning back. "The girls back there might be busy. Maybe you'll get a show. Then again, there's Albert. Maybe he's heard y'all come in. Maybe he got a bullet waiting for you behind one of them doors. You say black folks off killing white folk. Maybe it's your lucky day."

Ray stops. "Well, when Henry gets back in here, we gon' search every room."

"Look, Cynthia," Bobby Lee say. "We can go room by room, upsetting whatever you got going on here 'til we find her, or you can just bring her out and we can leave you alone. No bother. It's your choice."

Cynthia throws her legs up on the bar. "How 'bout we play a game, instead. Ray, you like games? Bernadette tells me you do."

Cynthia picks up her pistol and points it at Ray's head. Bobby Lee raises his pistol to Cynthia, say, "I won't let you shoot."

Slowly, she opens her pistol's barrel and dumps out all the bullets on the bar top. "I said I was gon' play a game. Didn't say nothing about shooting him," she say and puts a single bullet back in the chamber and closes it. "Unless he wants me to."

⊹⊹

SISSY ROCKS IN her chair, not talking to nobody, the children play coin roll on the floor and Jackson's holding the bread above Josey's head making her leap for it, laughing.

I circle the room, don't know what to do. I can stay here and do my best to protect mine, or go out and face that pack and maybe stop one of 'em. I cain't be everywhere at once.

Rachel gets up and asks Josey if she can scrape the skin off a potato for the stew. Josey rolls one to Rachel and says, "Let me show you how to slice it off without losing too much."

Squiggy swats an onion off the table to the floor and chases it while Jackson puts salt and pepper in a pot of water on the stove. He tastes the broth, adds a last bit of chopped garlic. Tastes it. "That's what it needs more of," he say, wiping his hands down his shirt.

"So you're a regular cook now?" Josey laugh.

"You just watch my pot," he say, smiling. He kisses her on the way to the door. "You'll see what a fresh clove'll do."

Jackson opens the front door, stops when he sees the soldiers emerge from the tree line three hundred yards away. They're on top of their horses, swaying toward us. Colonel's up front.

Jackson slams the door closed, locks it.

"What's wrong?" Josey say.

"We gotta get outta here," Jackson say, frantic. "Right now. All us. We got to go."

Sissy sits up.

He pushes Josey and the babies to the back of the house. "Come on, Momma," he say. "Open this pantry."

Hearing the tone in his voice, Sissy takes the key and its chain from around her neck and gives it to Jackson. He unlocks the door, throws it open, and they all crowd inside. All but Sissy. He lifts the toilet seat cover and the smell of the rotten food they've been pitching down the hole wafts up. He moves the whole seat over.

"Go on!" Jackson say to Josey.

Josey sits on the floor and lowers herself down the hole, standing on rot. She reaches up for her children.

Jackson lifts Squiggy first and fumbles him down the hole to Josey's waiting arms. He grabs for Rachel.

"Daddy, I don't want to go down there," she say. "It's dark."

"There ain't nothin to be afraid of, baby." He puts his hands around her waist.

"And it stank," she say. "Daddy, I don't want to go."

He lifts her. "Nothin to be afraid of. Your momma's right there. And Squiggy." He eases her down.

"No, I don't want to go!" she cries. Kicking now.

"Just help her down," Josey say.

But Rachel climbs over his shoulder, digging her feet in his stomach, stepping up him, falling over him, screaming, her face red and sweaty now. He yanks her away from his shoulder like a kitten caught on a blouse, but she keeps screaming, scratching, her teeth clinched, her face shaking. Jackson stuffs her down the hole with her legs in splits. Josey pulls Rachel through the rest of the way, holds her arms, puts her hand over Rachel's mouth.

"Go!" Jackson say. "Back to the old slave quarters."

Josey hesitates.

"I know . . . I know," he say as calm as he can, apologizing. "I know it's hard for you to go through them woods but you got to. For our children. For me."

Josey takes Squiggy's hand and carries Rachel, running with 'em toward the unfinished trail.

Jackson turns to Sissy who stands at the cupboard opening. "All right. Come on, Momma. I'm gon' lower you down and we gon' go together. I'll carry you if I have to."

Sissy backs away.

"Momma, we gotta hurry."

"Why? For what, Jackson?"

"There's soldiers coming."

"None of us did nothing wrong."

"Men like them only mean to harm."

"To you? You a deserter, Jackson?"

"You got to trust me, Momma. These cavalry men."

"Nobody makes me leave my house," Sissy say, and takes another step back.

"Momma, I promised you I wouldn't leave you again. And I won't leave you here."

"Cain't you?" she say. "You got a new family now. Don't need me. You just gon' throw me out like I've always been thrown out. I shoulda taught you better, Jackson . . ."

"Momma, please." He reaches out for her arm, pulls at her.

Knocks burst at the front door. Jackson's eyes widen. "Momma! We got to get outta here."

Sissy takes a step toward Jackson, pushes him hard into the cupboard. He stumbles all the way back to the hole in the floor, one of his legs fall through.

Sissy shuts the door as he fights his way back up. She locks it from the outside before he can get to it. It's too late for him to turn it open now. He hunches down inside the door, looking through the key hole. "Momma?" She turns her back to him and shuffles to the front door.

✛✛

CYNTHIA SPINS HER pistol's barrel; the single bullet inside is lost now. The other bullets that were on the bar top roll across the counter and one falls on the wood floor, thuds when it hits—my signal to get across this room and out the door. When the chamber stops, Cynthia lays her head on the side of the pistol like it's a pillow. A hush falls over the room.

"Put the gun down, Cynthia," Bobby Lee say.

"Or what?" she say. "You gon' shoot me, Bobby Lee?"

"I can't let you hurt nobody," Bobby Lee say.

"What is this game?" Ray say.

"I call it, 'Who's The Asshole?'" Cynthia say.

Ray laughs. His noisemaking gives me the cover I need to take my first step.

I stick my foot out toward the plank closest to me and hold my belly for balance, touch my big toe to it, slowly lean forward, and ease my weight on it. Slow . . . slow . . . the squeak is loud. Only twelve, thirteen, fourteen steps to the side door.

The front door in the saloon swings open and Henry comes barging back in. "What the hell's goin on in here?"

"She gon' shoot her brains out!" Ray say.

Henry rushes over, happy to see.

The board squeaks under me and the men look down. I hold still and Cynthia croons. "Just in time, Henry. You love games, too."

Bobby Lee say, "Just put the gun down, Cynthia."

"It's just a game, right, Bobby Lee? Just a job?" she say. "Surely, you of all people have nothing against it."

"Come on, Cynthia," Bobby Lee say. "You ain't faster than a bullet."

"Yours or mine?" she say. "I ain't got to be faster than your bullet, just faster than your trigger finger."

I reach out my next foot. Run one, two, three quiet steps and suddenly, my whole body burns. Stabbing pain is shooting up my body and around my belly.

I cringe, hoping it's false labor pain. Cynthia told me these false ones ain't nothin compared to the real ones coming in three or four weeks. But this pain is winding up worser and worser. I hunch over, grunting, look up through the floor boards in tears.

Ray say to Bobby Lee, "Let her do it."

"Yeah," Henry say. "Don't ruin the fun, Bobby Lee. I want to see."

Cynthia smiles. Spins the barrel again.

⊹⊹

THE FOUR SOLDIERS — FATTY, Skinny, Snooper, and Colonel—line the porch in front of Sissy's opened door with their hats in their hands, like they polite and friendly. Fatty stands on the last step, watching their backs. Colonel say with a smile, "How do you do, ma'am?"

"How do, suh," Sissy say.

"We was told we could find Jackson and Josephine here."

Sissy don't answer.

Skinny looks over Sissy's shoulder trying to see in the house. Colonel say, "They haven't done anything wrong, ma'am. We just need to check on 'em. Are they here?"

"Check 'em for what?" Sissy say.

"Well . . ."

"Did—did Jackson run from his service?"

The soldiers look at each other, confused.

"To the contrary, ma'am," Colonel say. "We want to reward him for his honorable service."

"My son? Honorable?"

"Yes, ma'am," he say. "A medal with his name on it. Good conduct and bravery . . ."

"Ain't no ceremony you coulda summoned us to? So everybody could see?" Sissy say.

"We thought we'd deliver it personal," Colonel say. "A hero's service just for your son."

"Then why y'all want to see Josey?"

"We don't have time for this!" Colonel say. "Where is he? We saw your son with that white whore."

"White? Josephine ain't . . ."

"Ma'am," Colonel say. "There's no point in protecting 'em. How much is a woman like you willing to give up for somebody else's mistake?"

Sissy shakes her head, "But . . ."

"People like your son don't care who they hurt, what the law is," Colonel say. "What about the children that come from it? It's selfish, that's what it is. Those like your son take whatever they want, just like these damn Yanks."

Sissy say, "But . . ." A gun shot. Sissy's body jerks.

Colonel has his pistol back at his side before she hit the ground. Blood spreads around the new hole in her heart and through her dress.

"I told her we didn't have time for this," Colonel say.

╅╆

I HOLD STILL as best as I can under the floor of Cynthia's cellar. The weight of my belly is tipping me forward, but I fight it. My nose is running 'cause mildew and dust got in it, making it drip on my yellow dress. I quit breathing through it so I don't sneeze.

"Cynthia, don't play at this," Bobby Lee say.

Click. That's her first pulled trigger.

Outside, a noise like a birdcall comes through the gaps around the door.

And again.

It's one bird, no . . . two. A hoot of an owl, a screech of a falcon. But they don't sound natural—two birds of prey, close enough to be on the same branch?

"We only here to do a job," Bobby Lee say to Henry. "You and Ray search the rooms." But they don't go.

She pulls her trigger again.

Click.

⁘

COLONEL STEPS OVER Sissy's body saying, "Come on out, Jackson. We just want to talk to you."

Fatty searches the room. He draws his pistol, opens the cupboard door. No Jackson. He sees the opening in the floor, kneels down to it, yells back to the front door, "He's a runner!"

Colonel and Skinny run out to the front door. Far off to the left of the porch, Jackson leaps into the woods, his head is bobbing up and down like one of them white-tailed deer, going in the direction of the Grahams' house away from Josey and the children.

"There he is!" Snooper say.

Skinny runs down the porch. Colonel pulls out his rifle, prepares to fire at Jackson. His rifle jams. "Dammit!" he say.

He and the men race to their horses.

⁘

EVEN THOUGH IT'S quiet, I take a chance at another step.

It starts the dogs barking out front.

I shut my eyes. Hold still again. Gon' pee myself. I put my hands between my legs, stop my bladder.

Henry rushes to the front window to see what the dogs is getting after.

"Henry," Cynthia say. "You wouldn't believe how many lives I have." She holds the gun to her head and pulls the trigger twice. Click. Click.

"Goddamn!" Henry say.

"Fine, I'll go look for her myself," Bobby Lee say. "Can't believe y'all want to watch this."

Over the loud barking, I take two, three running steps across the floor. Almost there.

The unnatural birdcalls start again. This time, flashes of light come through the door's gap, too. Quick-like. Flickers in the dark. One flicker. Stop. Then a second and third flicker. A whistle. The Railroad north to freedom.

There must be a dozen of 'em out there, black men and women, children, risking their lives waiting for other negroes to join 'em.

‡‡

I RUSH OVER small trees and skim tall grasses, up and down the lane of Jackson's cut-down trees searching for Josey. For Rachel. Nothin. This is the only path here.

A quarter mile to the old slaves' quarters from Sissy's and Jackson's path is blocked by trees that have grown back and made a wall. There's no way forward, only back. They cain't go back. There's killers there.

I wait here at the wall, confused. There's no way around it and Josey wouldn't have gone through it. Even with Jackson and a blanket over her head.

A small figure walks out of the brush. Squiggy.

He's alone.

I trace his steps back to where he came from and find Josey there covered in the tall grasses, frozen from the touches of shadows. Her knees are pressed against her chest. But Rachel is missing.

Squiggy squats beside her now, "Ma-ma," he say, calling her name for the first time. She shutters. But only her eyes shift toward him. Her gray lips tremble.

‡‡

BOBBY LEE HEADS for the hallway, annoyed and yelling, "This is a sideshow!" and stops short. "You comin, Ray?"

"We're just getting started," Cynthia say, and Ray's attention is fixed on her trigger finger.

Bobby Lee cocks his pistol and turns into the hall. I freeze where I am. Cain't think what to do. And now I cain't remember if I shut that trap door that leads down here. God, let him pass by this bathroom for someplace else.

I count Bobby Lee's steps and hear him walk past the first door—the linen closet. He takes enough new steps to pass the second door, third, and me in the fourth, I think. I don't know what's taking him so long.

He opens the door. "Get out!" Bernadette screams. "Get out! And tell Cynthia I'm not leaving. I just finished decorating this room and I'll be damned if I can't have this one, either."

Please, God, make my door like the linen closet so he pass me by.

An urging rises up from inside me—not the baby—an instinct, maybe. A voice. It tells me, "Go!" and I tiptoe around the edge of this cellar, blocking out the noise from my head that might stop me.

By the grace of God, I make it to the under-porch door and pull.

╋╋

RACHEL WASN'T AT the house.

Only Sissy was there, unmoved.

The soldiers left too fast to have met Rachel when they gave chase to Jackson and I didn't see her along the path to the Graham house. Jackson must have circled back and got her. And now I've beat him here.

I'll wait for a minute.

This house looks different since the war. Weary. The perfectly rounded rosebushes that once lined the drive like watercolor moons are bushy now. A chunk of wood plank is missing from the painted porch—a tan patch in all the white. But the acres of green field out front still roll and dip as they always have 'cause God's still tending to it.

Heavy footsteps run up behind me. Jackson racing to the house. He don't have Rachel.

He runs around to the back, peeking through windows. He could have had enough time to bring Rachel here and hide her. Not wishful thinking. I follow him around and go ahead of him, find one window unlocked before he do. I sail through it, coast inside the room—Annie's new library.

Nobody's here.

Books are on shelves around me and the broken oak table from the kitchen that slaves used to chop and sort on is here, too. But no Rachel. Pamphlets are spread across the tabletop.

I pass through the only door in this room and it leads to a connected room, a study, where Missus Graham is sitting at a desk in a plain blue dress, her hair pinned into a bun. She tilts her teacup to her lips, sips, and sets it down before writing in her notebook.

The scribbles of her pen start and stop and point. Start and stop and point, and start again. I look over her shoulder . . . a letter to her cousin.

I whisper, "You should go upstairs." But she keeps writing.

A thud in the library calls her attention. "George?" she say.

She gets up and I rush back to the library ahead of her, find Jackson inside searching the room. Ain't no way out except straight to where Missus Graham is or back out the way he came. She walks in the room, already talking, "I thought you wouldn't be back until this evening."

Jackson holds his breath from under the chopping table.

She looks around the room, surprised she don't see George. Only the window gapping open. She goes to it and looks out of it, pulls it closed. It sticks before it finally shuts. Jackson's already slipped behind her, through her study and out into the house.

Jackson stops in the hallway in front of Annie's wood and glass cabinet where her rifle is. He reaches inside the cabinet, grabs the rifle, closes the door with a soft click.

He stops.

In the glass's reflection, standing behind him, is Annie. Terror rises on her expression.

+╂+

THE WARP OF a floorboard under this door has swelled. I step on it. Put all my weight on top of it. Pull again.

No use.

Try harder. It squeaks but don't open.

Air whooshes in the bathroom above, rattling the trap door. Bobby Lee walks in.

I stand still.

Bobby Lee's boot heels click slowly across the bathroom floor. I promise you, God, if you save me this time, I'll let go this place.

Cynthia say from above, "Ray, what you think my chances are?"

"None of none," he laughs.

"Cynthia!" a woman's voice calls from outside, just beyond the porch. Bobby Lee stops at the sound of Soledad. He turns to the door. The shadow of his wait eclipses the liquor cabinet down here.

"Cynthia!" she say again, hurrying up the porch steps and into the parlor. "My husband . . . Mr. Shepard—" Soledad goes quiet when she see Henry and Ray. She straightens her clothes and say, flat, "You catch my husband's killer?"

"Sol," Cynthia say. "We was just talking about you. I was just about to tell the boys a story. About how long I've known you and how much you hated the thought of being married to an old man."

"Aw, is the game over?" Henry say.

Cynthia flattens the mouth of the pistol to her head again. Henry smiles.

"Oh no, not this game, Cynthia," Soledad say. "Not this one."

"But isn't that what you want, Sol? For somebody to pay once and for all for all the bad shit that ever happened in your life? You blame me. Your father. Your mother. No doubt Mr. Shepard . . . enough to hurt him?"

"I wouldn't . . . I didn't." Soledad seems lost.

Pain starts in my belly, moves up my back, got me on my tiptoes writhing, gritting my teeth.

I blow quick breaths in and out. Feel dizzy.

"Ray?" Cynthia say. "Did I ever tell you how I betrayed my best friend, turned her into a monster? Wasn't it Frankenstein who needed to put his monster down?"

I cain't open this door.

"My momma," Cynthia say. "She was a good woman. A praying woman. 'Eternal God, help us walk with good companions, to live with hope in our hearts and eternity in our thoughts.'" She goes over to Soledad and holds her hand. A hopeful expression fills both of 'em. "'That we may lie down in peace and rise up to find our hearts waiting to do Your will.'"

Cynthia puts the pistol to her head. Fires.

Soledad screams.

"Shit!" Bobby Lee yells and dashes out the bathroom.

Blood pours through the floorboard.

I cain't move.

I cain't breathe.

Hazel's voice inside me says, "Run!"

I heave open the door and fly through it. The dogs are barking mad beside me.

They cain't have me.

I hold my belly, feel it light as ever, like it's helping me. Saving me. I run toward the woods, ain't gon' stop 'til the Railroad. I see their light through these tears. I know Cynthia's dead and I cain't look back.

One of the men's voices yell behind me, "Is that her?"

"I don't know what that is," another say.

I cain't let them find me. Cain't join that Railroad, either, and put all them in danger.

So I turn from their flickering lights and change my course.

✝✝

JACKSON BEGS ANNIE'S reflection, "Please, Missus Graham," and steps away from the glass cabinet. Annie steps away from him, her face pale.

"I'm not here to hurt you. See?" he says, setting the back end of the rifle down on the floor. He props it against the side of the cabinet, raises his hands, surrendering, and slowly turns around toward her. "I'm Jackson," he say. "Sissy's son."

"Son?" she say.

"Yes, ma'am. She told me y'all ain't been friends a long time but maybe you could be a friend to me now. I need this here rifle, Missus Graham."

Annie dashes up the hall toward her study. Jackson grabs the rifle and runs after her, the door slamming just ahead of him. Annie wiggles the latch to lock the door but Jackson pushes it open before she can. He grabs her arms, quickly lets her go.

She whimpers, "Don't hurt me!"

"Please, Missus Graham. Men are coming to kill me and I've committed no crime."

"I can't help you," she say, trembling.

"Please, ma'am. A dying man's last wish, Missus Graham."

She closes her eyes, shaking.

He backs away from her and takes a deep breath. Another. He says, "If I don't make it home today . . . will you give a message to my wife and children. Tell Josey . . ."

"Josephine?"

He nods. "My wife. She's the love of my life."

A flash of recognition crosses Annie's face. The soldiers' horses neigh just outside the door.

He say, "Please make sure no harm comes to her or my children."

The pack of soldiers stomps up the porch steps and across to the front door. Fatty and Skinny sneak along the side of the house in opposite directions. Fatty moves cautious toward the library window and Skinny goes the other way.

Colonel knocks on the door while Snooper stands at attention next to him.

Annie says to Jackson, "I'll need to answer the door. I'm expecting my brother."

"Yes'm," he says, with tears sliding down his cheeks.

Annie walks to the door, timid, looking over her shoulder at Jackson as he follows with the rifle in his hand. She opens the door and he waits behind it.

Colonel takes off his hat. His hair is drenched and red lines are on his forehead where his hat was. His uniform is sweaty around the neck. "Good afternoon, Ma'am," he say. "I'm sorry to bother you on this fine day. I'm Colonel Barling and this is Sergeant Lowe. Are you George's sister?"

"I haven't seen George," she says and starts closing the door.

Colonel holds the door open one-handed, steps into the doorway. "We're looking for a negro criminal named Jackson."

"I don't know any Jackson," she says. "If you wouldn't mind, Colonel."

"Ah, yes," Colonel smiles, stepping out of the doorway but staying close enough to slyly keep his foot propped at the bottom.

He yanks his gloves off. "You know, ma'am. You can tell me if something's got you spooked. Ain't but one or two men stronger than I am. None quicker."

"You woke me from a nap, is all," Annie say. "If I appear spooked, what you've mistaken is exhaustion. I've been cleaning all day. There's still dinner to begin. So if you don't mind, sir."

"You're not lying to me, are you, Missus Graham?"

"This is *my* house, sir! You are on *my* property, Colonel. And what reason would I have to lie about knowing a negro? A criminal?"

"Of course. Of course. Forgive me, ma'am." He takes his foot from the door and Annie straightens her dress, scowling and huffing. "It's just that your brother seemed to know Jackson quite well."

"George knows a lot of people. So if you don't mind, sir, good evening."

He nods and backs away from the door. He and Snooper put their hats back on. "Thing is," Colonel say. "We saw the boy, Jackson, come this way. Right to this very house."

"If so, Colonel, he didn't stop here. You're welcome to keep across my property to pursue your criminal and we'll all be sure to arm ourselves here," she say. "Again . . . if you don't mind, Colonel, I have a meal to prepare." She begins to close the door.

"Don't you want to know what he's accused of?" Colonel say through the gap of the door.

Annie stops.

"Rape. Raping a white woman like yourself. A Josephine."

Annie swings the door open, "I assure you, sir. Josephine is no white. She was one of my slaves. She's fair but she has black blood in her."

"Is that right?" Colonel say, smiling.

Snooper shakes his head, no, 'cause he's sure of what he saw.

"George also said that you wouldn't let your property go easily. Now, Missus Graham . . . I'm getting different stories here. When something doesn't make sense to me, I'm uncomfortable."

"Are you accusing me, Colonel?"

Colonel leans against the doorway, crosses his legs as he does, staring at her like he's reading her. Finally, he tips his hat and smiles, "No, no I don't believe I am."

He backs away from the door. "Just be careful, ma'am. Until we find him."

"I'll be diligent," she say.

Colonel nods to Snooper and Snooper charges the door, bursts it open, knocking Annie to the ground. She screams. Jackson's gone but his rifle remains. Snooper runs up her staircase, clearing five steps at a time, opens the first door.

Jackson leaps out of the library window and almost falls on top of Fatty. Jackson plows his fist into Fatty's jaw and his body slams straight to the ground.

Skinny turns the corner from the back of the house and when Jackson sees him, he takes off running to the field out front, crashing through the rosebushes. Skinny chases but he's far too slow. Colonel rushes out from inside Annie's house just as Skinny makes it to the base of the porch.

Skinny pulls out his pistol and gets down on one knee. He fumbles with it before aiming it in Jackson's direction—four hundred yards out.

Colonel yells, "No!" from the porch and comes running down the steps to his horse. He unlatches his rifle from it, raises it, tracks Jackson—five hundred yards.

But faster than I can get to him, Colonel fires.

Jackson falls.

He drags himself along the ground, holding his leg.

"Damn!" Colonel say, and drops his rifle. He snatches Skinny's pistol and starts out to the field.

Annie jams her rifle in the back of Colonel's head. "Put it down!" she say.

Colonel don't move.

He drops his weapon and turns around as Annie takes two steps back when she see Snooper is in her doorway. She corrals Snooper and Skinny and Colonel, pointing her rifle between the men. She say, "Nobody'll get broken up today for the color of their skin."

Colonel holds up his hands like he surrenders. "Easy. Easy now, Annie."

"You move, I swear I'll kill you!"

Annie's rifle fires into the air as it's yanked back. Fatty is behind her with his hand under the muzzle. He rips it from her grip and puts her hands behind her back.

"Um hm," Colonel say, smug. And picks up his pistol again. He walks out to Jackson, stands over him and aims.

He lowers his pistol.

A man on horseback, a stranger, is no further than fifty feet from us. His weapon is pointed at Colonel.

He trots his horse toward him. When the man gets close, Colonel's harsh expression cools. He arches his back straight and salutes. Fatty let go of Annie and salutes the man, too. Then, Snooper. All this for a man with no uniform. The brass medallion pinned to his knapsack reads, "Robert L. Smith."

"General Smith," Colonel say, hurriedly and proud.

"At ease," General say.

At once, I know him. Know his voice. He's been here before.

"You saved my life," Colonel say to General Bobby Lee Smith. "Sixty men or more still thank you for what you did. These men were there, too. All of us owe you our lives."

"All of us were ready to die for this great nation," Bobby Lee say. "Lives marked with courage and bravery. We're all owed respect."

"I'll never forget a hero," Colonel say. "Or his story . . . how we were all in retreat. But not you. You charged over enemy rifle pits and through the lines of a whole regiment under heavy fire."

"A long time ago," Bobby Lee say.

"Killed as many bluebellies as you wounded. God was with you."

Bobby Lee nods a little. Weary, he say, "There's a small army a day's journey behind me. My cousin, Ray, and his men are even closer. There's a good sum offered for you and your men on account of the marauding y'all did in Virginia. The peaceful end is to turn yourselves in now. Give folks who still believe in you a chance to call you heroes, too."

"And this man?" Skinny say, flicking his pistol at Jackson.

"Way I see it," Bobby Lee say. "Y'all need to make yourselves square in Virginia. Let the rest be damned."

"He was laying up with a white woman!" Skinny yell but Colonel hold up his hand and Skinny stops talking.

"We're done here," Colonel say. He nods to Fatty to step away from Annie. She rushes out to the field where the men and Jackson are, kneels beside him, tending to him.

"Whatever y'all decide," Bobby Lee say. "You can go or be the heroes you're meant to be."

"We'll consider the offer," Colonel say, and he and his men take to their horses. Bobby Lee stays where he is, watching 'em go. Then he turns to Annie.

"Don't I know you, soldier?" she ask him.

48 / THE RIGOR

JOSEY IS DEATH as she walks. Rigamortis has set into her expression—eyes sunken, mouth seized open, skin frozen to cooled wax, sooted gray. "Rachel!" she screams from the top of the hill. She's heard the gunshots coming from Annie's house and the fear of it has quickened all around her.

She's carrying Squiggy on her hip and managed her way back to the path. But she ain't all right. She's breathing now like she's winded, staggering back and forth across the width of the path. She stops at the tree lines on both sides as if it were a wall of stone and bats at their branches but won't go in. Tears slide down her face. "Rachel!" Her voice is ragged and empty.

She takes another step up the path where a hollowed log is side-lying making a barrier between her and trees—protection—but to the side of it, hidden, the ground seems changed from never walked on to recently worn. The drag marks there capture Josey's attention because above them, in the bushes, there's a near-perfect straight line of color—the yellow-green insides of freshly torn leaves.

When Josey gets closer, she sees a whole splotch of bright color where the bushes have splayed open and re-closed. The broken limbs are man-sized. Josey reaches a shaky hand out to the space and pushes. A path from here to as far as we can see is lined with deep drag marks.

A torn blue corner of Rachel's dress is caught on a branch like a grass-hopper's flag. Josey falls to her knees and Squiggy tumbles out her arms. Her shallow breaths spread the color from her face. A whistle sound shocks her exhales. Her breath is so weak, almost missing. But still, she calls, "Rachel . . ." I ain't never seen her like this before. Not this bad, this afraid.

From her knees, she slouches to the ground, laid on her side now, her breaths screeching.

She's giving up.

I know she is.

I call her name, *Josey!* Who knows better than me the fear that comes with losing a child? She thinks that Jackson is gone, or worse. Rachel, too.

Her face stops me cold. Her doll eyes are back. Flat and unblinking.

I can help her.

I choose to ignite myself. If I only go inside her part way, maybe I can touch her quickly, help her, then move on out. Won't be as bad as Bessie said. I can be quick.

I throw my hand inside her. I'm swallowed up to my arm, a burning coal—heated black, hotter . . . red-orange. A searing pain chars my left side like graying ash and that layer of me crumbles away. Gone forever. Josey's eyes start to blink again. Her breathing becomes more clear as air finds her lungs. And in that moment, Squiggy ambles over and holds her hand gentle.

My God! My tears come directly. His hand on hers is mine. His skin on mine. My own tears, one's I ain't had since dead, sizzle against my burning coal face. I touch his cheek and his skin is smooth and cool like laying a flat palm on the surface of still water.

I breathe.

Take him in.

His hair is the softness of rabbit's fur. The deep arc of his curls, halos. I follow their curve with my fingertips like tracing smiles. He stays handholding me this way like we're waiting in line for something. But I have been. Been waiting for a moment like this all my life and after.

Josey breathes. Inhale. Exhale. Inhale. I pull away from her feeling like I'm in pieces. Not whole. Never be whole again. She sits up on her knees. She reaches her arms out for Squiggy without me and stands but she cain't lift him. Her breathing is clear except for a rattle of phlegm. But she's still winded. She say to Squiggy, "Remember the hide game with Daddy?"

Squiggy squats down and crawls into the log there.

"That's it," she say. He pulls his knees into his chest, smiles up at his momma.

"You don't come out for nothin, all right? For nobody, except me and Daddy. We the only ones who can find you, you understand?"

He shimmies back into the log, waiting to be found. Josey stands and turns into the mouth of the opening. With new tears pouring down her face, she stares down the trees, into the bushes, the dirt, and into the dimming light of dusk—it closes around her in the orange-pink promises for tomorrow. She screams into its shade.

The woods wisp by her as she lumbers forward up the path, my body on fire as I follow. The path ends sudden, dumping her into a small damp clearing, one I ain't never seen here before.

A manmade gate of twisted leafy limbs and young trees form fence posts meant to guard this entrance but Josey keeps going through it.

I drift around the muddied space, slow and careful and hurting all over, and over plugs of sprouted grass. Empty liquor bottles lay alongside a graveyard of half-buried toys—painted and ceramic. A doll's head is cracked in the middle and buried, a broken rolling hoop, and a soldier figure. Their erected parts are sticking out of the ground, sun-dulled and dusted over. May have been a playground. One with no laughter. Maybe never.

An old tree house is grounded at the back of the clearing, broken and torn down by a storm or a person. The outside of it is covered in leaves and weeds and got a new tree snaking through it, partly covering a "Keep Out" sign. Its words are mostly rain-sanded away.

I circle the space and pass a clothesline where a young girl's bloomers hang hand-washed and turned inside out, yellowed in the crotch. Abandoned and dusty cobwebs have made a home on the bloomers, too—a scroll of gray where caught leafs are stuck.

Nobody's here.

A rustling turns me around to the gate again.

There's crying.

Rachel's crying.

The bushes across from Josey give way to George. He got Rachel under his armpit shoving her in the doorway of that house. She pins both feet on each side of the doorway, squats when he tries to push her through. She screams and bites his side. He throws her to the ground and Rachel's head chips a rock, puts her to sleep. She looks like one of his broken dolls.

"Get away from her!" Josey say, coughing and wheezing. She grabs a big jagged rock from the ground beside her. I fall to the ground next to that rock-emptied space, weakened.

George's eyes widen and his whole manner change. "Annie?" he say, not seeing Josey. His voice is childlike now. He say, "I was just taking the girl for a walk. She followed me. We were just playing, is all."

Josey limps further into the clearing, between me and George, wheezing now. Her lips are pale gray.

"Get away from her or I swear I'll kill you." She's hardly holding herself up to stand.

"Did Annie come with you? You gon' tell on me?" George say.

Josey gasps for air. Again. And again.

"I was just going to talk to her. No harm in just talking . . ."

Josey collapses. Her eyes are focused on nothin and shallow sips of air stammer from her lips. The vapors have taken all of her strength.

George seems confused. He steps closer to Josey, cautious at first, then sure. "No Annie. No husband. No daddy. No nobody. Been a long time since we've been in these woods together like this, eh?" He kicks Josey in the side as if he's scattering a pile of leaves. A little louder, "Those were the good ol' days, weren't they?"

He rests back on one hip, wipes the sweat from his forehead with a handkerchief, takes out his flask. Pulls a long drink.

George finds his pistol, fiddles with it, drops bullets in one at a time as he takes his time moseying back to Rachel. He stops just above her, studying her, twisting himself around to get a better look. "Shame," he say. "We didn't even get to play." He cocks the pistol.

With a rage inside me, my body is set to flight. Too weak to reach George. I thrust myself inside Josey—the closest—and I'm coal again. I don't have much time. I fill her lungs, make her breathe, make her grab the stone. Red to silver gray, my forms slough away in fistfuls. My body turning to ash and yet. Stand. We stand. Together we stand. I can feel her strength then. Feel all the years I've had to watch her. Only watch.

Not this time.

I can feel my hand turning into nothing as she takes the heavy stone into hers. Raises her arm as I feel my own taken by the wind. All my strength leaves me as she finds her own and slams its jagged edge into the back of George's head. The thud of rock caving in bone sends his body to the ground. We fall. Together we fall. The rest of me ebbs away to cinder. I feel heavy. Lifted now. Light as the air.

I watch her straddle him, take the rock to his red-wet hair, 'til his whole face is gone.

I cain't see no more.

I cain't hear.

I cai

49

I AM DEAD.

I died a long time ago. Before you born, before your mother was born, 'fore your grandmother.

I was a mother, too. And I've lost her.

No more flashes.

No more watching.

No distance. No waiting on miracles. This ending is mine.

There's only darkness here now.

An arc of light just crossed the sky. A star.

A star.

Around it comes many strands of other light. A shower of 'em like a million shooting stars racing down at once. I want to touch 'em.

White spreads around me, gathering together to form a single tunnel of bright.

I know this tunnel.

I know it's for me.

My vision blurs with tears and I see Momma waiting at the end of it for me, her hand held out to me.

"Naomi," she say, her voice like a song.

"Momma!" I say.

I want to run to her but I'm frozen here. A small window is behind
me, framed in black. And through it I see Josey. This time, walking
away from me with Rachel and Squiggy. Her clothes are bloodstained
but she's safe. My grandchildren are clean. They're so distant now
and almost unreal, like looking at a perfect painted picture you cain't
step in.

But I can, if I go back now.

I hesitate. And I'm not sorry for it. Not sorry for my unsure. I'm too
old to apologize for the ways I feel. So I'm not sorry for my sadnesses
right now, or this love I cain't contain.

It's beginning to burst from me. Toward Josey and my grandchildren
and Jackson. Toward Momma. Everything around me. I'm consumed.

For the first time, there's a new feeling resting on me.

Through me.

It's leading me forward. To Momma.

The flashes are peeling away from me like an undressing. The final
piece a blouse over my head.

I'm naked.

Fearing nothing.

Loved.

ACKNOWLEDGEMENTS

W HERE DO YOU start when thanking people for a dream realized? With the person who was there to help you take your last step, or the person who first believed in you? Or gave birth to you? Or gave birth to one of the people who helped along the way, or the person herself or himself, or the person who organized the event or taught the class that led you to the person or the people? Or the person who made you feel at home? Or the cab driver who got you there on time, or didn't and because of it, there was a chance meeting? Or...

Maybe there are no real beginnings anymore. Maybe the world is too old for that. Maybe there are just continuations of works laid out before we were even born. And what's been said is true: we are all products of ancient loves, and of long relay races orchestrated by the universe. God. And for me, I'm walking with Jesus.

I thank God for choosing me to carry this story and for the privilege to be the one to take it across the finish line. This is a new continuation for someone else. And for me.

To my courageous and loving mother who has had as many names as she's had lifetimes, Mildred Millie "Shirley," my Dad, John, Jr. To the most beautiful person I've ever known, my husband, Lee; and to God's princess and prince, Ava and Ash. To my adorable and wonderful sister, Katrina; my charming and wonderful brother John III; and to these stars, my brothers and sister: Tony, Michael, Fuschia and Parker.

To my family in Alabama and to those who are still living in East Tallassee, Alabama: Uncle "Dolf" Warren and Aunt Della; to the pillars of my childhood: Grandma Lurlean, Granny Harris, Katrina Brasher, and Hazel Ford. To the hope and beacon that has been Oprah Winfrey, to poet Romus Simpson, to Tod Goldberg, to my incredible agent Rachel Sussman and exceptional editor Dan Smetanka, and my publisher Counterpoint Press.

To Michelle Franke, Adam Somers, Jamie Wolfe, David Thomas, Jeff Eyres, Casey Curry, Heather Simons, Danny Corey, to David, Dee and Jason Saunders, to Manjit Sohal: my first friend while living in England. To Neena Bixby, Marytza Rubio, Cynthia, and Robert Eversz. To my pastors and to Nancy Hardin, A.M. Dellamonica, and Marcela Landres.

To the PEN Center USA Emerging Voices Fellowship Program, Breadloaf Writers' Conference, Megan Fishmann, Willie Davis, Kaitlyn Greenidge, Katherine Deblassie, Heidi Durrow, Libby Flores, Jamie Schaffner, Tiffany Hawk, Joshua Mensch, Zoe Ruiz, and all of those artists especially women and writers of color who came before me and those I have the pleasure of working with now; to the publishers who've published my work, and those unnamed friends who have offered words of encouragement, a sofa to sleep on, a cup of coffee, a meal, a dollar, a ride, a discount, a recommendation, a prayer, a good opinion, volunteer time, or have just listened.

To the powerhouse that is the Los Angeles Literary Community.

And finally, to the Beverly Hills Film Festival which honored me with my first award for this novel when it was first born as a screenplay, to the Charleston Film Festival, HistoryPlace.com, the books *The Jews of South Carolina* and *The History of Tallassee*. To Wikipedia, Dickinson House in Belgium, and to my church family including HV Hot Topic who have encouraged me to follow my calling.

I'm so thankful for all of you.